To the Devil His Due

Paul Bernardi

ISBN: 1495455467
ISBN 13: 9781495455469
Library of Congress Control Number: 2014902766
CreateSpace Independent Publishing Platform
North Charleston, South Carolina

ONE

After what seemed like an eternity cooped up inside the narrow confines of the loading bay of the Halifax bomber, Sergeant Peter Bogarde hardly noticed the incessant throbbing of its four engines anymore. He had become immune to all extraneous noise, so focussed was he on the mission ahead. In fact, the constant din was actually having something of a metronomic effect on him—the beat of the propellers counting out the minutes to zero hour. Before much longer, he and his three companions would be hurling themselves out into the darkness over occupied Poland. The goal: to link up with members of the Polish Resistance to undertake a…What had Colonel Blake called it? A spectacular.

If you asked him, however, Bogarde thought it was nothing more than a glorified public relations stunt, designed to show the brave, beleaguered Poles that the Western Allies had not forgotten them nor deserted them in their heroic struggle against their oppressors. Back in September '39, they had put up a brave but ultimately futile fight against the German invader. Defeat had always been inevitable, given how isolated and unprepared they were. Then, to add insult to injury, shortly after they had been overrun by the Nazis, the Russkies had seized the opportunity to drive in from the east to share with Germany in a complete carve-up of the country. Now that really was taking the piss, Bogarde thought to himself, smiling.

To be fair, Bogarde had nothing personally against Poland; as an exile from his own beloved Netherlands, he actually had every sympathy for them. He'd just rather it wasn't his life at risk in what felt, to him at least, like a fairly worthless exercise. To his mind, it would be much better to use his skills and experience in something more beneficial, something that would bring about a significant reduction in the number of German soldiers in the world, for example.

The mission had its origins with Colonel William Blake, a senior officer in the Special Operations Executive, to which Bogarde had been attached, from his commando unit, for the duration. In the weeks running up to the outbreak of the war, Blake had been based in Warsaw as a military intelligence officer advising the Polish government on the rapidly deteriorating situation in Europe. He and the rest of his team had only just managed to escape into Romania, shortly after hearing the news, on September 3rd, that Germany had invaded, but he had departed only reluctantly. As it was, he had been an uncomfortably close witness to the terrifying and devastating German Blitzkrieg. Even now, some two years later, it was clear that Blake still carried a strong and burning sense of guilt at having left Poland and his many friends there to their fate.

This operation was a chance to assuage some of that guilt, and this fact alone was enough, Bogarde believed, to override common sense and the feeling of futility that surrounded the whole undertaking. What the hell was the point of having four highly trained Allied soldiers fannying about in the middle of bloody Poland, trying to link up with what would doubtless prove to be an ill-equipped, ill-disciplined partisan rabble? Chances were that everything would go tits-up and they would find themselves up to their necks in the shit, or worse, in no time at all.

Bogarde shook his head to try to clear his mind of such negative feelings. There was no point dwelling on it any further; there was no turning back now anyway. Instead he forced his thoughts back onto the matter in hand. Looking around the dimly-lit interior of the on-loan RAF Halifax, he could just make out the grim, blacked-up faces of the rest of his team. Like him, they were dressed in the uniform of the Polish army. To be caught wearing anything other than military uniform meant certain death at the hands of a firing squad. This way, the boffins had determined, they might stand a chance if compromised. In reality, though, Peter knew that their chances if caught were slightly worse than those of a snowflake in hell, a thought which he had chosen not to share out loud during the briefing.

To his left on the bench seat that stretched along the side of the fuselage, and also borrowed from the commandos, was Charlie Butler, a demolitions expert and, incidentally, a pure killer. What Charlie didn't know about explosives wasn't worth knowing. His particular forte was the use of time pencils, a means of detonating plastic explosive at any one of a number of predetermined time intervals. Butler was also deadly with a knife at close quarters. In fact, he was so skilled that he ran many of the hand-to-hand combat courses in the commandos and had the scars to prove it. If Bogarde was honest, Charlie scared him shitless. The risks he took with the explosives were unnatural. Evidently, he had more lives than the proverbial cat. Yet he was one of those men that you'd much rather have on your side than against you any day of the week.

Opposite Peter and Charlie were two Polish soldiers that had managed to escape to London in the aftermath of the invasion, along with many of their compatriots. These two, Tomasz and Jerzy (Peter had no idea of their surnames and doubted he could have spelt them anyway, let alone pronounce them), had proved exceptionally proficient in the art of killing and clandestine operations. Whilst this gave Bogarde considerable comfort, the main reason for their presence, aside from their martial skills, was to act as interpreters for when they managed to link up with the Resistance.

All three of them were staring grimly ahead, seemingly focussed on nothing in particular. Peter was sure, however, that they were running over the details of the final briefing that had been chaired by Blake, in the draughty hangar at Duxford airbase in Cambridgeshire, just hours before take-off.

As leader of the four-man team, Bogarde had been aware for some days of the objectives of this mission, but for the rest of the team, the briefing was the first they knew of what they had let themselves in for. Of course, there had been speculation during their intensive training over the previous three weeks, and, to be honest, it could not have come as a huge surprise given the evidence before them. Their training had included parachute jumps, explosives, and close-quarter combat, both armed and unarmed. This, coupled with the fact that two of their number were Polish, suggested to Bogarde that no self-respecting bookie would have offered odds on anything other than a jump behind enemy lines into Poland. Looking at the faces of his men in the brightly-lit hangar as Blake had revealed the map pinned to the blackboard, Bogarde could see that they too had reached the same conclusion. All three faces had been devoid of expression as the objective was uncovered; instead they were intent on the words coming from the tall, immaculately-attired man standing on the raised dais.

"Your drop zone is located two miles west of the town of Skórcz," Blake's crisp, clipped voice informed them. "I'm afraid I haven't the faintest idea about the proper pronunciation, but hopefully that was not too wide of the mark. No doubt the two of you could make a far better job of it than me." He smiled. Tomasz and Jerzy gave the merest hint of a nod, tacitly approving Blake's efforts.

Blake went on to fill them in on the specifics of the mission, all the time tapping his map pointer against the board as if bringing an imaginary orchestra to order. "You will be met at the DZ, here, by members of the Polish Resistance whose job it will be to lead you to the target and to meet up with the rest of your twelve-man attack team.

"The target itself is the railway line where it crosses the river Wda, or Schwarzwasser, as I believe the Germans call it." Blake located the point where the railway crossed the river on the map with the end of the pointer. "Your mission is to destroy the railway line, causing the maximum damage in order to put it out of action for as long as possible. If you manage to take a train with it as well, then so much the better." Blake's eyes betrayed their familiar mischievous look, as if the thought had just occurred to him at that point.

"On reaching the target, you will split into two teams of six. Team A, led by Sergeant Butler, will be responsible for laying and detonating the charges, while team B, led by Sergeant Bogarde, will provide the necessary cover. We believe that the latter will hopefully be just a precaution, as our intelligence indicates that there is very little in the way of German military presence in the area, other than the odd railway policeman guarding the bridge itself.

"On completing the mission, it will be up to the Polish Resistance to get you over the short distance to the coast in the north, onto a boat bound for Sweden and thence home to Blighty. Right," Blake summed up, "you've heard enough from me; any questions from you lot?"

This was Bogarde's cue. "Just a couple, sir. What's so important about this bridge? What difference will it actually make? How can we be so sure that there is minimal opposition at the target? How far is it to the coast? How are we supposed to get there undetected, and how on earth do we find a suitable boat when we get there?" Bogarde had never fancied himself as much of an ideas man, but he was always pretty damned good at knocking holes in other people's. One of his many annoying traits, he thought to himself.

Blake fixed Bogarde with one of his trademark, steely-eyed stares. Peter could also see the bristles on his expertly trimmed moustache almost standing to attention. "Yes, quite a number of questions, thank you, Sergeant Bogarde. I will attempt to answer your points in an orderly fashion, but no doubt you will let me know if I miss anything pertinent?"

The irony was far from lost on Bogarde. He felt himself redden involuntarily but, otherwise managed to maintain his composure.

"Firstly the point, or rather points, which I would have thought were fairly obvious. This railway line is one of the main arteries from the German industrial heartland to the Eastern Front. Therefore, there is an almost constant stream of trains carrying arms, tanks, support vehicles, artillery, munitions, not to mention troops, all bound for the mincing machine that is the Eastern Front. Put this artery out of action for even a short time, and we put a dent in the German war effort and relieve the pressure—to a small degree I grant you—on our Russian allies.

"Secondly the operation is a chance to maintain what are already excellent relations with the Polish government in exile. Their people have been suffering untold hardships since the very start of the war, and the chance to provide a welcome boost to their morale should not be missed. Thirdly, and finally for now, the skills and knowledge that you four can pass on to the Polish Resistance will, hopefully, help them to continue the struggle more effectively after you have gone."

Blake was getting into his stride now. Despite his misgivings, Bogarde could not help but be impressed at the way in which the colonel carried you with him, making this potentially deadly mission sound for all the world like a Sunday morning stroll in the park.

Blake was off again. "As far as the expected opposition is concerned, we are in touch with members of the Resistance by way of radios that we have previously dropped to them. The information we have is accurate at the time of going to press. In the main, the Germans believe the Polish people to be a beaten force, capable of little other than the most token acts of sabotage. As such, they tend not to bother wasting too much in the way of resources guarding things, even things as important as railway bridges on key routes. Clearly they feel those resources are best deployed further east. Obviously I cannot one hundred per cent guarantee the information or whether the situation will have changed when you get there, but then, if that does prove to be the case, perhaps you would be good enough to take that up with our Polish friends on your arrival?

"Now, it's up to you men to punish that arrogance and show the Germans that nowhere is safe. Make a success of this mission, and they will have to review their policy and consider diverting much-needed men and materiel from the front line to guarding these so-called soft targets deep to their rear. Also, think of the impact this will have in terms of the morale of the German soldier when the letters from his wife or girlfriend fail to arrive, not to mention the monthly ration of cigarettes. On top of that, they will find themselves even more stretched in keeping the red hordes at bay given that troops will have been withdrawn to guard their supply lines.

"Last, and by no means least," Blake continued, "we cannot ignore the fact that this organisation, the Special Operatives Executive, has some pretty influential critics within the British government. Men from the old-school way of thinking who do not like to see funding diverted away from frontline troops in favour of what they would call "dirty-tricks warfare." To put a stop to this talk, or at least dampen it down to more manageable levels, we need a major success by which to demonstrate exactly what we can do here. In short, you could say that you men are being entrusted with the very future existence of the SOE!"

Bogarde had heard enough. The build-up to the mission was not the real problem as far as he was concerned. "OK, sir, you have convinced me as to why we are going. What about some of the more trivial details like how we get back home safe and sound? When all hell breaks loose, how on God's earth do we get out of Poland with every Nazi within fifty miles intent on kicking our collective arse?"

Blake smiled, though not, as far as Bogarde could tell, reassuringly. "Are you one of life's natural worriers, Sergeant?"

"No, sir, I have to practise every day in front of a mirror. But so far I have found it has helped to keep me alive just that little bit longer."

"OK, settle down, men." Blake calmly sought to restore order in the midst of the laughter that had greeted Bogarde's riposte. He was fully aware of the tension in the room and appreciated that a little comedy could help to relieve things, as long as it was kept in moderation.

"Do you think we'd really leave such things to chance, young man? This is where our loyal Polish cousins come to our rescue. In return for the arms and expertise that you and Butler bring with you, they have agreed to spirit you across Poland to the Baltic coast and thence on a boat to Sweden. We have it on good authority that there is a complex and widespread network of Poles working underground in the country. Since 1939, they have been instrumental in providing safe passage out of the country for several of their fellow country-men, people the Germans would rather have been able to get their hands on. But let's not take my word for it when we can go straight to the horse's mouth, as it were."

7

Tomasz may not have understood the metaphor, but the fact that Blake was staring expectantly at him gave him the cue he needed. "It is just so, Colonel," he said in his slow, halting English. "Jerzy and I are in this room today as proof of it. Once the Nazi bastards had taken our homeland, many of us, we decided to leave to fight on from the outside. Our countrymen who stayed behind, they were happy to help us escape. For many, the best way, it was to go north to the sea and from there to find a boat, either to hide on it or to pay the captain."

Jerzy took over. "It will be a simple matter for us to do the same again. Every village from the river to the sea will have friends who will help us. We will have plenty food, shelter, and somewhere to hide in the day. We only travel at night."

Bogarde could see from their earnest manner that there was no need to question the Poles further on this point; he was confident that it would be as they said. The main issue would, therefore, be to evade capture immediately after the strike until they could get out of sight.

"We calculate"—Blake was continuing—"that it is fifty miles, or near as damn it, from the target to the coast. Allowing for any evasive or diversionary tactics that you might need to employ, then three, or possibly four, nights should be sufficient for you to reach the coast. On this basis, we have been working with our colleagues in the Polish government in exile in order to come up with a suggested route. This route shows towns and villages along the way where, as Jerzy says, people will be on hand to help you out: food, clothes, places you can hole up for the day, that sort of thing. How much use you make of it is entirely up to you; you may, for example, decide to go it alone and manage things accordingly. Either way, Sergeant, you'll find all the relevant bumf in the mission pack on the desk in front of you. I need hardly remind you that this information is highly sensitive, and so I suggest that you commit it to memory before the drop. I cannot overemphasise the consequences of such information falling into enemy hands. Is that clear?"

As no comments were forthcoming, Blake moved on. "All being well, you should reach the coast on or around the fourth day. Once there, you will need to make contact with the Polish underground, details of which you will find in the pack. There will be a boat waiting to take you across the Baltic Sea to Gothenburg. Once there on neutral soil, you will be met at the docks and escorted to the British Embassy and thence home to base. This should, in theory, be the least traumatic part of the journey.

"Right, if there are no further questions, I will hand over to Wing Commander Bailey, who is going to be your pilot tonight. He will fill you in on what you can expect in the way of weather and conditions both on the flight and in Poland."

———

A sudden lurch accompanied by a dull thump jerked Bogarde back to reality. Down at his feet, Butler was exercising his extensive and colourful vocabulary to register dissatisfaction at not only having been woken up but also dumped unceremoniously onto the floor by the sudden movement of the plane.

"Bastard part-time fly-boys should learn to bastard fly the bastard plane properly. Hasn't anyone told them that we're precious goods? They should be treating us like bloody royalty instead of bastard pigs in a bastard sty! We should be reclining on soft cushions with dusky maidens attending to our every need, instead of lying on rock-hard metal benches with no bastard room to even bastard fart."

Just at that moment, the pilot popped his head round the door from the cockpit. "Sorry, chaps, we've just crossed the coast. Those slight bumps were the result of a bit of ack-ack from Jerry welcoming us to occupied Europe. Awfully nice of them, but there was really no need to go to that sort trouble on our behalf. Hope it didn't upset your flying experience too much."

"What? You mean that this sort of thing is normal?" Butler complained.

"Oh yes, rather! SOP."

Butler looked blank, none the wiser.

"Standard operating procedure, old boy. As we fly so low across the water, Jerry can't pick us up on the old radar. Therefore, they only hear us very late on as we approach the coast and so only have time to loose off a couple of shells in our general direction. With so little time to aim, it's rare that they ever land one on the nose, as it were."

"Jesus Christ, you guys are so laid-back you're horizontal." Butler shook his head, clearly unimpressed with the thought of being shot at, and unable to get his head round the nonchalant approach of the airman.

The pilot was one of those cheery types who refused to be upset by anything or anyone. Damned annoying, Peter reflected.

"No use worrying about it, chum. If your number's up, there's not a lot you can do, so you may as well hold on tight and enjoy the ride. Anyway, just popped through to say we're two hours from the drop. Cheerio!" And with that, he retreated back into the cockpit.

"OK, men." Bogarde started to pull himself carefully up into a standing position. "You heard him. T-minus one-twenty. Time for a final check of the equipment. No mistakes, right? This needs to go as smoothly as possible. We don't need any dropped bollocks tripping us up; we'll have enough to worry about without any of those as well."

Working in pairs, the four men started on the pre-drop routine. It was mundane work but could make the difference between life and death. When dropping behind enemy lines at night, it was essential that you didn't give yourself away to any passing patrols, either by sight or sound. For the former, you had to make sure there were no bright objects that could glint in the moonlight; jewellery, watches, and the like, were all either removed or carefully concealed. It was also necessary to ensure that there were no loose items that could bang against each other in the wind or on landing. It was a fact that sound travelled further at night, and so this was a key precaution. Straps had to be removed from weapons, as they tended to knock against the barrel, making loud metallic clunks. Anyway, it was far better to hold the weapon at the ready, as this had the added bonus of the weapon being closer to hand should you need it in a hurry on the way down.

Having satisfied themselves that they would not give themselves away, they next checked, for the umpteenth time in the last twenty-four hours, their weapons. Each man was equipped with a Sten gun, a Browning pistol, and a commando knife for close-quarter work. The Sten gun was the weapon of choice for this sort of action, as it was light, small, and easily concealable. That said, it was also prone to jamming, especially if you held it the wrong way. Bogarde was aware that the tendency, especially in the heat of the moment, was to hold the magazine, which jutted out horizontally on the left-hand side of the gun. This, however, could lead to problems; the magazine could easily become unseated and so stop feeding bullets into the firing chamber. It might look good as a pose on the recruitment posters, but it was certainly not recommended. The last thing you needed was to confront an enemy soldier whilst struggling with a jammed weapon.

You could not spend too much time looking after your weapons. It was never wasted effort, as you were helpless without them. Many soldiers used much of the vast amount of time that they spent waiting around for things to happen to ritually clean and oil their firearms; Peter considered this to be a pretty sensible habit. It was especially true for parachute drops, as you could never be sure what you were dropping into. Knowing that you had a fully functioning weapon at your side was a definite boost to the confidence in such situations.

Butler, meanwhile, had opened his rucksack and was checking over the explosives contained therein. Peter didn't understand much about explosives— that was Butler's department for sure—and this was probably the reason why he was always slightly nervous when in their presence. Butler caught the look on Peter's face out of the corner of his eye and, as usual, could not resist the opportunity to wind up his superior.

"Relax, boss, this stuff"—he indicated the lump of plastic explosive that he was casually tossing from one hand to the other—"is as safe as—oops—houses." This last word was delivered with his best sheepish look and in time with the thud made by the plastic hitting the floor.

"Still," he continued, "it just goes to prove my point. You can do pretty much what you like with this stuff. Chuck it in a fire; hit it with a hammer. Won't make any difference. It will still end up looking like a lump of dough that smells slightly of almonds."

At this point, Butler reached into another pocket within the rucksack. "But if it comes into contact with one of these babies"—he held up a slim metal tube—"well, that's the time to start saying your prayers. A thing of beauty is the time pencil." Butler was getting into his stride now on one of his favourite subjects. "It's actually ironic, don't you know, that here we are heading for Poland and that's where these little beauties were first developed. It's like they're going home."

Peter had paid scant attention to the explosives training sessions and had no idea whether that particular gem had been mentioned. He had tended to focus on what he considered to be the important bits, like what made them go bang.

Butler, meanwhile, was still in full flow, and Peter knew better than to interrupt. *Smile and nod, smile and nod,* he told himself.

"This pencil"—Butler held up the thin, six-inch-long metal tube—"acts as a detonator which, when inserted into the plastic explosive, creates a chemical reaction that triggers the explosion. You need to ease it in gently, like it's your first go with a new girlfriend. No point ramming it in willy-nilly, as you really do not want to damage it; that could get you a one-way express ticket to see St Peter.

"Before you slip it in, of course, you need to decide how long you want the time delay to be: anywhere from a month, if you have time to go on your holidays before it goes bang, all the way down to ten minutes, though you need to have your running shoes handy if you go for that one. Look." He pointed to coloured lines on the pencil. "They have even made it colour-coded for the hard of understanding. All you have to do is press a ridge on the pencil at the appropriate point as shown by the relevant colour. I reckon even you could manage that, boss!

"Pressing down on the ridge releases the acid, which then eats through a wire of a thickness that matches the time chosen: the thicker it is, the longer it takes to eat through it, in theory. Once the acid has done its job, a spring is released, which enables the detonator to explode, causing the plastic to go up. Apart, they are as harmless as kids' toys; together, they can tear you, and everyone within a fifty-yard radius, a new arsehole if you're not very careful."

Peter had to admit it was a simple concept and, doubtless, very safe in the hands of an expert, but that didn't stop the whole thing from scaring the living crap out of him. "OK, Butler. Stop pissing about with that stuff, now, will you? If you've finished checking it, shove it back in the bag…but gently!"

"Alright, alright, keep your hair on. I know what I'm doing. You'd soon have words to say if this stuff didn't work when it comes to the crunch. I just have to be sure that everything is fully functioning so we don't have any cock-ups." All the same, Butler complied with the order and replaced everything, taking, at least to the outward observer, inordinate care over the task.

Satisfied that all the necessary checks had been completed, Bogarde resumed his seat and tipped his cap down over his eyes. "Right, we've got ninety minutes before the drop. I suggest we all get some sleep. You don't know when you'll next get the chance."

TWO

Peter leaned back against the curved metal wall of the loading bay. It was impossible to get properly comfortable. Pretty much however you positioned yourself, there was some metal strut or other that would dig into your ribs, back, or shoulder. The best you could achieve was to try to wriggle around until your parachute was providing some sort of protective padding, but it would only ever be a temporary reprieve, as the vibration of the plane and buffeting of the wind soon ensured you slipped from whatever comfortable position you had managed to find.

On top of this, and in spite of his own advice, he found he was too wound up to sleep. It was always the same for him in the last few hours preceding any action. He guessed it was down to the adrenalin coursing through his veins, his body pumping itself up, ready to deal with whatever dangers lay ahead. He had heard it called "the fight-or-flight syndrome," but in this line of business, there always seemed to be a hell of a lot more fighting than flighting. Nonetheless, he had to get some rest before the drop. Events had a habit of buggering up the best laid of plans, so it always made sense to take whatever opportunities presented themselves. He shifted again to something approaching comfort and made a conscious effort to shut his eyes tightly, hoping that sleep would soon take him.

The juddering of the four massive engines pervaded throughout the whole plane. Despite the noise, it was almost soporific. He could almost feel it making his mind drift away, helping him to relax. He could certainly see how you might become accustomed to it over time, and, boy, time was never in short supply in this job, especially for the flight crew. They spent hours travelling to a destination where they spent no more than five to ten minutes dropping whatever load they were carrying, before spending hours going all the way home again, hoping to avoid being shot down in the process. It wasn't a lot different for him; hours spent waiting for a short burst of activity was the norm.

Some soldiers he had met hated the waiting with a passion; it gave them too much time to think about what lay in store for them. To Peter's mind, that could not be healthy. You couldn't change the future, so why worry about what might happen tomorrow or the day after? Surely it was better to forget about the uncertainties of tomorrow and concentrate on dealing with the knowns of today. For him, the waiting was actually a welcome relief from the tension, from the constant vigilance that was needed to keep one step ahead of the enemy and so stay alive that little bit longer. There was a limit to the length of time that a human being could cope, physically and mentally, with stress levels such as these. It was important to be able to unwind or even shut down totally as a kind of self-preservation technique. Peter had seen plenty of men crack under this sort of constant, intense pressure; he knew how dangerous it could be and was determined not to let it happen to him.

———

Peter had learnt this the hard way back in his native Holland shortly after the war broke out. Still, all this time later, not a day went by when he didn't think about it. He could vividly remember the day when, not long after the Netherlands had surrendered to the Germans, walking home from college, he had turned the corner into his street and noticed, about halfway down, two large grey trucks parked on his street. The black-and-white cross on the doors clearly marked them out as belonging to the Wehrmacht. As he got closer, his first fears were realised, as he could see that they were stationed outside his house. He had started to run forward, panic gripping at his heart. He could see, beyond the soldier standing guard outside, that their front door was hanging off its hinges, still swinging weakly under its own momentum. Even as he ran, he sensed that everything was moving in slow motion: the faces of onlookers turning to watch him, the late-afternoon traffic filing homewards, the heads of drivers and passengers alike turning to look at the house as they went past. In the days before the invasion, their thoughts would have been around what the occupants might have done to attract the interest of the authorities. These days the thoughts were, more often than not, about which poor souls were being taken this time.

He had no idea what he was going to do when he got to the house, but fortunately it never came to that. Shortly before he reached the sentry, an arm reached out from an alleyway and grabbed him by the shoulder. Before he could react, he was being dragged off the pavement and into the passage, finding as he was that his assailant's other hand was now clamped firmly over his mouth. His initial reaction had been to thrash out wildly, fearing himself caught as well, but there was something familiar about the smell and feel of the person gripping him. Peter actually found that the muscles in his body were starting to relax; he felt his shoulders slumping under the steely grip and the fight going out of him. The arms holding him were slowly turning him round and bringing him face to face with his uncle Stefan. Peter could see his elder sister, Anna, peering out from behind Stefan's considerable form, still in her nurse's uniform, her expression a picture of fear and distress.

"Steady now, Peter." Stefan's calm and slowly spoken words were starting to penetrate the haze of emotions swirling around Peter's head. His uncle was still holding him tight, though, preventing him from any sudden or rash movements.

"There is nothing we can do," Stefan continued. "I have heard that this is happening all over the country. They seem to have some kind of list and are rounding up everyone on it. On top of that, anyone caught obstructing their work is being rounded up as well. The best we can do for now is to get you and your sister off the street and into safety. Then we can try and find out where Erik and Maria are being held and on what charge."

Stefan was the exact opposite of his brother. Whereas Peter's father had been tall, slim, and well-groomed, Stefan was a more stocky type with broad

16

shoulders, which always seemed to be threatening to burst the seams on his shirt. His physique had a lot to do with his profession as a butcher. Years spent lugging huge meat carcasses around had resulted in exceptionally well-developed muscles. His personality matched his physique; he was given to speaking in short but powerful sentences that mirrored the chopping action of the butcher's meat cleaver. Every word, like every cut, was well considered and delivered succinctly.

"But they have no right; we can't just stand by and do nothing." Despite the force of the words, the tone of Peter's voice betrayed both the doubt and the helplessness that was eating away at him. His eyes searched his uncle's face, desperate to find a solution to the nightmare. Stefan had always been such a dependable rock that Peter could not imagine that he would not be able to solve the problem right there and then.

"They have every right, lad. Theirs is the right of the conqueror. I am afraid that there is absolutely nothing we can do at this moment. Let me assure you, I like it even less than you, but it won't help my brother if I were to charge in like a bull only to get myself arrested too. What kind of uncle would I be if I did that and then left you and Anna unprotected?

"Right now the most important thing is to get you two to safety. Then I can try and make some enquiries through official and unofficial channels to find out what the hell's going on."

As soon as Peter and Anna had been settled into the family rooms above their uncle's shop, Stefan was straight out the door to begin his enquiries. He was unable to find out much, but word was that the list contained a large number of prominent members of Dutch society, many of whom were also Jews. They were being rounded up as quickly as possible; clearly the Germans were concerned that they may spark some kind of resistance movement or cause them too much trouble, administratively. Either way they were taking no chances and were intent on stamping their authority over the country as quickly as possible. Peter's parents were on the list because his father, Erik, was a well-known and much-respected lawyer in Rotterdam, while his mother, Maria, had been a schoolteacher in the local high school. They were both members of the local council in the town in which they lived. They ticked all the boxes.

Stefan's search for information was repeated for the next three days with still nothing official being forthcoming. All he had been able to ascertain was that Erik and Maria were assisting with enquiries and that their release was probable over the next few days. Lulled by this information and frustrated by the slow turning of the bureaucratic cogs, Stefan felt that nothing else useful could be done for now. He had spent so much time standing in queues, waiting to be seen, that his legs ached beyond belief.

And so it remained for a further week, until the next Tuesday morning. Stefan burst through the back door into the kitchen, his face as black as thunder. He slammed the door shut, yelled, "Bastards!" and threw a copy of the morning paper on the kitchen table. The headline on the front page staring up at the room was clearly visible: Local Subversives Executed.

Peter glanced at his uncle, who had slumped in a chair in the corner. He picked up the paper and read the article. It was short and to the point. It simply listed the names of all those who had been shot the previous day, thirty-seven of them in total. Peter scanned the list, hoping against hope, but sure enough, just over halfway down, numbers twenty and twenty-one were Erik and Maria Bogarde. In his dazed state, Peter wondered whether there was any particular order to the names. It didn't seem to be alphabetical; did it mean that the first nineteen had been even more subversive than his parents, or was it completely random? Next to each name was a note detailing the crime of which they had been convicted. In the case of his parents, and indeed the vast majority of the list, there was just one small word: "Sedition." Below that was an account of how all of the prisoners had been shot by firing squad in the courtyard of the local prison, the previous day at dawn.

Through the mist clouding his brain, Peter could hear Anna was sobbing. She was sitting at the table, her face pressed into her hands while her elbows rested on the table. Her whole body was shaking uncontrollably in time with each sob. Peter was acutely aware of his own lack of reaction. Why had he not collapsed in tears as well? Instead, he just felt numb. Perhaps it hadn't sunk in; despite the facts in black and white in his hands, he still expected that his parents would be released, would walk back through the door, and life would carry on as before. He was not capable of relating the simple words in the newspaper to the fact that they were dead. He simply stood, his arms limp by his sides, staring dumbly at the newspaper that he had now placed carefully back down on the table.

Looking back later, Peter could see that this was just his way of coping with the pain and shock of the news. It had prevented him from ever really grieving for his parents properly. Instead he had subconsciously chosen to close his mind to the whole affair, blocked it out. He didn't let it get to him anymore and never let it be a sign of weakness. The one thing it had done was ignite a spark of rage in the pit of his stomach. He now used that feeling as a focus for his hatred of the Germans; it had become the one driving force that pushed him onwards. It was a force which burned ever more fiercely over time, a force that had begun to consume him, a force that now filled him with the determination to kill as many Nazis as he could before they could kill him.

These thoughts had shaped the next few weeks in the aftermath of his parents' execution. He had sought out the local branch of the Dutch Resistance and become involved in a number of acts of minor sabotage. He did so with a reckless abandon that, to the outside observer, marked him out as a fearless fighter. To those that knew him, however, Peter's apparent lack of concern for his own personal safety became a significant worry. Stefan became so concerned that he decided that the best thing for Peter and Anna was to escape to England before he found himself in any serious trouble. Many of their countrymen had already taken this option prior to or shortly after the invasion, and so there were plenty of contacts who were only too willing to help take them in. Their family home and most of their possessions had already become forfeit to the occupier as a result of their parents' conviction, so all they had was what they had been able to rescue in the few days after the arrest. With what little they had to their names, they made their way to Rotterdam, where it proved to be a relatively simple matter to secure passage on a Swedish merchant ship on its way to London.

On arrival, they were welcomed with open arms by the existing Dutch exile network. After a couple of days spent in temporary accommodation, which was provided for the constant flow of refugees from occupied Europe, they were set up in an empty apartment within a block that already housed a number of other Dutch families. It didn't take long for Anna to settle in; in fact, she seemed to flourish away from the horror of their homeland. She was helped by the fact that there was huge demand for nurses, what with the almost nightly bombing raids, and was quickly able to find work in Charing Cross Hospital. Here she was in her element, doing what she loved and making good friends with a number of her colleagues. Peter, though, was too restless to settle. He couldn't stomach the thought of getting a job in an office; he wanted to be out there doing something. So, despite Anna's pleas for him to stay away from the war, he took the first opportunity he could to join the army. He loved his sister dearly and hated to go against her wishes, but he felt that this was the only real choice for him, the only way he could channel his rage into something constructive and, at the same time, seek recompense for the death of his mother and father. If he could get out there and fight Germans, then this might start to assuage some of the guilt he retained for having failed to do anything to help them in their hour of need.

Following a brief period of basic training, Peter had been posted to North Africa, where he had not wanted for opportunities to kill Germans. Rather than satisfying his bloodlust, though, it had only encouraged him. He had quickly found that he was well suited to life as a soldier; he loved the routine, the discipline, and, above all, the adrenalin rush he felt every time he went into combat. He could handle himself in most situations but found that his particular forte was as a marksman and in hand-to-hand combat situations. In addition, he had the ability to maintain complete calm when in combat. Despite the chaos, noise, and the general panic that seemed to grip many of his comrades, Peter found that he was able to remain focussed on the objective and see things almost in slow motion, giving him much-needed breathing space to take account of events and react accordingly.

It was not long before his talents were recognised, and he was promoted through the ranks to become a sergeant at the end of his first year in the field, for which he felt immense pride. It was as if he were happy again; he had found a purpose for his life, albeit not one that he could have ever imagined following two years previously.

Every time he went on leave, Peter would ship back to London to be with his sister. Anna was the only thing that mattered to him now that his parents were gone. His main worry in life these days was that he wasn't around to protect her all the time. She constantly tried to convince him that she didn't need protecting, but he couldn't shake off the feeling that he had failed his parents and so must not let anything happen to Anna. What with the regular air raids over London, Peter was often anxious about her safety. He was always on at her to move away from London, but she refused, saying that this was where her skills were needed and where she could do most good. And besides, she would remind him, she was only doing the same as him, her best to support the war against the Germans. If he chose to put himself in the firing line, then he couldn't complain if she wanted to get stuck in as well.

The last time he had come home on leave, though, his world had been turned upside down once again. He had met Anna at the door of the apartment just in time to see her rush out. One of her colleagues had fallen ill, and she, ever willing to do more than her share, had agreed to take her shift at the hospital. This proved to be a cruel twist of fate, as that turned out to be the very night that the hospital took a direct hit from a thousand-pound bomb dropped by the Luftwaffe. When Peter got there in the morning, after Anna had failed to return home from her shift, there was little left of the wing in which she had worked but for a smoking pile of rubble and twisted metal. There was no way anyone could have survived the carnage.

This time Peter did not cope well with the loss. He hit the bottle in a serious way. Without Anna's calming, rational influence, there was no one there to rein him in. He was granted a period of compassionate leave and spent the whole time in a drunken haze, hitting the pub when the doors opened in the morning and leaving only when they closed again at night. The landlord was aware of his situation and sympathetically took care to look after him as best he could, but there was little anyone could do except watch him drink himself into a stupor every day. All the time, however, his anger continued to burn inside him unchecked. It was the one thing that stopped him from slipping completely into oblivion. All the feelings of failure that he felt after the death of his parents came flooding back. For the second time he had not been around to prevent it from happening. The fact that there was little, if anything, that he could have done was irrelevant. All that mattered was that he was not there for her, just as he had not been there for his parents. All he could focus on now was revenge; it was all that was left to him. The Germans had destroyed everyone and everything he had held dear. There was nothing left but to dedicate what was left of his life to balancing the scales as best he could.

Some days later, at the bottom of yet another bottle of whisky, he finally came to a decision. He was not prepared to sit back amongst the rank and file and just do his bit any longer. He desperately wanted to do something that would make a real difference, something where he felt he could have more of an impact. The easiest and most accessible way for him to do this, as far as he could see, was to volunteer for the commandos. They were always on the lookout for new blood.

Peter's theory proved to be correct. With his obvious abilities as a soldier, and his internal determination and drive, he was an ideal candidate. In addition, his knowledge of mainland Europe and fluency in both Dutch and German made him a very rare commodity indeed. He sailed through the training, specialising in marksmanship, and was soon involved in active operations. In no time he had built a reputation for daring and risk-taking that, on the one hand, singled him out as a highly effective operative, but on the other hand did leave some unanswered questions as to his temperament in the minds of his superiors. While he kept delivering results, however, they were prepared to overlook it.

Peter was aware, indeed it had been mentioned to him often enough, that the brass hats were concerned that he was going to get himself killed through some sort of reckless behaviour or, worse still, get other members of the team killed. As far as Peter was concerned, though, he was getting the job done and done well. He was still alive and, to his mind, had not suffered any avoidable casualties on the team. There would always be deaths in this line of business; it was just a case of ensuring that the cost was justified by the benefit and that whatever lives were lost were never given away cheaply. If the mission's objective was achieved along with plenty of dead Germans along the way, then the cost was invariably worth it in Peter's mind.

This brought him back to this mission in Poland. To him this was a virtual backwater in terms of where he could do most good. The benefit part of the equation was not stacking up for him. Whilst he could understand all the points made by Colonel Blake about Polish morale and political links with allies in occupied Europe, the truth was this was nothing more than a small-time operation. Peter suspected that Blake had singled him out to lead the four-man team to show the Poles how seriously they viewed their support, a sort of "We'll put one of our best men on to it" promise. The fact remained, though, that he was committed to it now, and once he had committed to something, nothing would stop him from making a success of it.

THREE

"Green light in ten minutes."

Peter shot bolt upright in his seat and turned to see the wireless operator moving through from the cockpit on his way to the hatch through which they would be jumping. What the hell was his name? As he struggled to shake off his post-sleep haziness, Peter realised that he didn't actually know; he had never been told. Standard procedure: it was best not to get too closely acquainted with the crew in case the plane was shot down on its return journey. The whole operation could be blown apart from airmen cracking under interrogation. It wouldn't be their fault; it was just that the Nazis knew some pretty grotesque techniques for squeezing information from defenceless captives. For their own safety, the crew knew nothing more than the co-ordinates of the drop zone and the number of passengers.

"OK, chaps, time to run through final preps." Peter stood up, stretched his aching limbs, and turned to Charlie to check his harness and parachute, making sure that they were securely and tightly strapped to him before turning to allow Charlie to do the same for him. Jerzy and Tomasz mirrored their movements further down the fuselage. Happy that everything was in order, Peter pulled the group together for a final briefing.

"Remember, lads, as soon as we hit the ground, get the chutes off and hidden away. Then rendezvous on me as quick as you can. Top priority is to secure our position before we do anything else. Usual drill applies: form up on me in a star shape facing out, feet overlapping. Total silence is essential, so the signal for any bother is to kick the foot to your right. Once, and only once, mind, we are sure that we have not been detected, we gather in the kit and move out to link up with the Resistance. I know they are expecting us, but there's no point in taking any silly risks. There's always a very real possibility that our welcoming committee has been compromised and replaced with one that may be a little less pleased to see us. If we go into this expecting the worst, then we can't be disappointed, so stay alert the whole time. We're not going to charge in blindly; we take our time, make ourselves happy, and then, and only then, we look to make contact with our friends. OK?"

Nods all round.

"In which case, good luck, and see you on the ground." Peter shook hands with each man in turn; it had become something of a good-luck ritual for him to do this before every mission.

They clicked their parachute lines onto the overhead bar and lined up—Peter at the front, Charlie at the rear, and the two Poles in the middle—and waited for the signal to go. The airman's eyes were alternating between the light panel and the luminous dial of his watch. He would have to work fast to get all four men and the supplies out within as short a time as possible. The longer it took, the wider the spread of men and kit at the other end, not to mention the longer they had to keep the plane steady, thus not being able to take evasive action should they be surprised by a night fighter patrol. The better aircrews prided themselves on the speed and efficiency with which they could complete the task, and this guy was clearly in that group. Peter took comfort from this fact, thankful that they wouldn't have to scrabble around too much on the ground to gather in their supplies.

"Ten seconds to green light, make ready," shouted the airman above the noise roaring in through the open hatch. "Seven, six, five, four, three, two, one, go, go, go."

As soon as the first "go" sounded, Peter noticed the light changing from red to green, but it was no more than a fleeting glance as, at exactly the same time, he threw himself out of the hatch into the vast expanse of darkness.

———

Straight away, Peter was struck by two things: total silence and biting cold, the latter hitting him like a slap in the face. It hadn't been exactly warm in the plane, but this was on a different level. The wind at this altitude was fearsome and burrowed its way through his clothing right to his very bones. Also, after the constant roar of the four huge Merlin engines, the contrast in sound could not have been greater; he almost felt as if he had suddenly gone deaf. He soon forgot about such discomforts as his discipline and training kicked in. Looking up, he could see that his chute had opened perfectly; no problems there, thank God. He then twisted around, attempting to scan the night sky for the rest of the team. They had deliberately jumped on a moonless night for extra security, so this was no easy task. However, he could just make out another chute roughly fifty to a hundred yards behind him. Any more than that was not visible, so he just had to pray that the other two guys and their kit were also descending safely.

Next, Peter looked down to check for any signs of activity on the ground. The second-biggest fear for anyone dropping in by parachute (after the chute failing to open, of course) was a hail of bullets rising to meet them while they were helpless in mid-air. All seemed to be OK. He could not see lights nor hear any obvious signs of activity, but he continued to hold his Sten gun at the ready just in case. A few moments later, Peter was aware of the ground rising up to meet him, followed by the actual impact, accompanied by the usual involuntary "Oooofhh" that resulted from your legs being pushed back up into your body, almost up to your armpits. He allowed his knees, already flexed for impact, to buckle, enabling him to fall sideways, hoping there were no sharp rocks waiting for him.

As soon as he was down, Peter went onto autopilot. He was back in his element now, back in control. Kneeling up, he banged the catch to release the harness and shrugged it off his shoulders. He then gathered up the parachute, arm over arm, until it was a size that could easily be carried. Then, as agreed, he sat tight waiting for the rest of the team to rally on his position. It wasn't long before the two Poles, followed closely by Charlie, were jogging in, crouched low to minimise the chance of being spotted.

After five minutes of lying silently in their prearranged star shape, Peter was confident that they were undetected. "OK, everyone fit and ready to go?" he whispered.

Various grunts and comments gave him the confirmation he needed.

"Right, let's grab the gear, bury the crap, and move out. We need to rendezvous with the Resistance guys before dawn so we can get out of sight of any prying eyes."

Five minutes of hard graft dragging the supply canisters over to the holes they had dug for them soon had them sweating despite the cold. The canisters were six foot long and needed to be buried quite deep to avoid being found too easily. With the job done, they were able to move out. As he hailed from the local area, Jerzy assumed responsibility for leading them to their next destination. Despite the near-pitch-black conditions, the Pole seemed totally confident in his whereabouts. This allowed Peter, bringing up the rear, to concentrate on watching and listening at every step for any signs of their being compromised. He needn't have worried, however, as the journey passed without incident. Before long, he was being introduced to the head of the local Resistance unit, a great bear of a man who went by the name of Josef. A bear was an appropriate description not only from the point of view of his size but also from the amount of facial hair he was sporting. His face was almost covered by a great, shaggy moustache-and-beard combination. Still, Peter thought to himself, it must keep him warm in the winter. Added to that he wore a huge sheepskin coat with much of the fleece showing, which helped to complete the image. Nevertheless, Josef proved to be a very useful asset in the days ahead, not least because he was the only one of the group with at least a smattering of English.

Back in England, Peter had been cynical about the worth of this mission, but now he was here, he felt many of his misgivings melting away as he was confronted by the sincere warmth and generosity with which his team was being treated. It was clear from their unkempt and drawn appearance that the Poles had been suffering greatly under Nazi occupation. They had been under the cosh from day one, beset from one side by the Germans and on the other by the Russians. Then, in mid-'41, things had got even worse as the Germans took the rest of Poland as a prelude to their invasion of Russia. Peter imagined that they must feel like the forgotten country. His own country had had it bad, of course, but not on the same scale as these poor sods.

The sight of these four men dropping in from England carrying supplies of weapons and ammunition really was a huge boost to their morale; news of which would no doubt spread across the underground network, giving a much-needed lift to all who heard it. This mood continued over the next few days, as their hosts went out of their way to ensure that, as far as their meagre resources allowed, the four of them were well looked after. They were also immensely eager to learn all that they could from these professional soldiers who spent most of each day running training sessions on marksmanship, unarmed combat, skirmishing manoeuvres, and setting explosives. It was clear to Peter that what these men lacked in terms of experience and ability, they more than made up for in enthusiasm and determination. Fighting to free your own country from a hated invader was certainly worth a couple of extra percentage points on the morale scale.

As well as being a great public relations exercise, these training sessions had a practical value, as Peter intended to select the best eight men from the Resistance group to form a team to carry out the mission. From speaking to Josef, Peter now had a much better grasp of the real strategic value of this railway line. Apparently, not an hour went by without at least one lengthy train crossing the bridge: in one direction carrying troops and supplies to the front, in the other direction, wounded and exhausted soldiers heading to the rear for hospital beds or on leave. Not only would this be excellent practical experience for the Poles but it would also cause major disruption to the main German supply line to the Russian Front. Peter knew these supply lines to be stretched to breaking point already as the Germans strove to maintain the momentum of their push eastwards. Putting the bridge out of action, therefore, should have a huge impact. OK, so it wouldn't finish the war in itself, but every little bit helped.

The information about the frequency of trains had convinced Peter and Charlie to elaborate on the original plan. The plan now was to time the demolition so as to coincide with a train crossing the bridge, preferably a train heading east full of fresh troops. Sending that train to the bottom of the valley along with destroying the bridge could really give the Poles something to shout about and, at the same time, put a small dent in the German war machine.

At the end of the third day, Peter and Charlie sat down with Josef and a couple of bottles of the local tipple. Together they went through the group one by one until they had agreed on the best men to form the attack party. Josef was instrumental in the process, knowing the men as well as he did. He kept things mercifully simple by saying, "Is good man," for the ones he recommended and sucking his teeth on the ones he didn't want. Once decided, Peter gathered them together and proceeded to brief them, with Jerzy acting as interpreter, on the intended mission.

Peter and Charlie had spent much of the rest of that third day with Josef on a reconnaissance trip to the bridge, so they had a reasonable feel for the layout of the area, the weak spots on the bridge where the charges should be placed, and the composition of the German defences. For once his faith in British intelligence services had been rewarded. All he had been able to find by way of enemy soldiers was a couple of bored-looking sentries who spent most of the time drinking coffee and smoking in a small wooden hut at one end of the bridge. The only times that they had emerged were when trains had rumbled over the bridge, which, although not absolutely regular, did seem to be roughly once an hour. Obviously they felt that they had to look efficient at these times just in case anyone important was on the train. The last thing they wanted was for their relatively cushy existence to be replaced with a one-way ticket to the Russian Front.

To Peter, the surrounding area was damn near perfect for this sort of mission. The approach to the bridge was heavily wooded, providing plenty of cover along their intended approach route. The densely packed trees practically backed right onto the railway line at some points, so much so that he was confident that the team would be able to close right in on the sentries without being discovered. In addition, the lack of any patrols in the woods told Peter that the Germans were not taking the threat of attack too seriously.

That said, Peter had spotted a village about a mile from the bridge where he surmised that further troops would be garrisoned, probably not that many but enough to give his team a run for their money if they hung around too long to admire their handiwork. Josef confirmed his suspicions, stating that around twenty to thirty troops, pretty much a platoon's worth, were stationed in the village with a couple of half-tracks for transport. Maybe not crack troops but probably with combat experience and so not to be taken lightly. Whilst Peter was pleased with the progress that the Poles were making under their tutelage, he was nevertheless wary of exposing them to a full-on firefight with seasoned troops. That would be a quick way to undo all the good work they had done to build up their morale.

Back at the camp, Peter gathered the team together to run through the key points. Best to keep the information to a minimum, Peter reckoned, to avoid any unnecessary confusion, especially in view of the language barrier. "We will split into two teams of six. Charlie, here, our resident explosives expert, will lead the Red Team, who will be responsible for laying the charges on the bridge supports, wiring them up, and ultimately blowing the thing to hell. Red Team won't be able to go in, however, until the Blue Team, led by me, has taken care of the sentries.

"I can't stress too much how important it is that absolute silence is maintained. If the sentries hear us approaching, they will radio down to the village to raise the alarm. We are not going to give them that chance. Given the proximity of the village, we can't afford to use our guns either. The sound will carry for miles at night and in these hills. So it's knives only unless someone fires at us first. Understood?"

He waited for Jerzy to translate this and for everyone to nod in confirmation. It was essential that they grasped this point, as the success of the mission hinged on the element of surprise.

"Right, Blue Team will go in five minutes after a train passes. This should give us at least forty-five minutes to clear the area, lay the charges, and get under cover. As soon as we have dealt with the sentries, the Blue Team will form a defensive screen fifty yards from the end of the bridge, facing the village, just in case anyone gets curious. At this point, Red Team can move in to set the charges. You will have to work fast to be finished well before the next train. We expect them to be every hour, but it's not guaranteed. Either way, I want the charges laid within fifteen minutes, max. We will be using time pencils to detonate the bridge, so we are going to have to be a bit clever with the timing. When we were checking out the bridge earlier today, we counted just over two minutes from when we first heard a train approaching to when it finally arrived on the bridge. There's a long incline up to the bridge, so it takes them a while to get up there, especially when fully laden. So Charlie here"—Peter nodded in his direction—"will signal for everyone to set the pencils for two minutes. So Red Team, you need to keep your eyes on Charlie and wait for the signal.

"As soon as you get the nod, set the pencil and leg it as fast as you can back to our position. Then we all retire to the cover of the trees and sit back and wait for the bridge to blow, taking the train and its occupants to hell. After that, we take a short break to congratulate ourselves on a job well done and then get the hell out of there as quick as we can before the rest of the Germans show up. This will also be the point where we say farewell to our new-found friends, as we will head north to the coast and our route back home. Any questions?"

Silence greeted him, just grim faces intent on getting the job done.

"OK, I have rattled on for long enough. If there are no questions, I suggest we move out in one hour from now. We can use the darkness to get into position and hopefully find the sentries fast asleep! So black up, and get your kit sorted straight away."

FOUR

Precisely one hour later, the group of twelve men was ready to move out. Each man was kitted out in dark clothing and had streaked his face, neck, and hands with mud from the nearby riverbank so as to better blend into the darkness of the night. Peter was well aware that capture could lead to execution. They might be in uniform and, as such, subject to the Geneva Convention's rules on the treatment of prisoners of war, but the Germans had a reputation on the Eastern Front of shooting first and asking questions later. And they didn't always bother asking questions either. Anything that might help them to avoid detection, therefore, was to be warmly embraced.

The team moved out in two columns of six, each led by one of the local men. They had grown up in these woods and could navigate through them blindfolded, which was just as well given the almost impenetrable darkness that enveloped them as soon as they moved into the trees. Walking halfway down the left-hand column, Peter had to force himself to concentrate on being ultra-vigilant in order to keep his feelings in check. Despite his being out in the open in the middle of a vast wood, he still felt a huge, oppressive sense of claustro-phobia, caused by the inability to see much more than a few feet in front of him. Peter was surprised at just how stressed this was making him; he had never really thought that he would suffer from this sort of thing. Nevertheless, he was painfully aware of an intense throbbing behind his eyes, not to mention a heart rate that threatened to burst out from the confines of his ribcage. *Focus, Peter, focus*, he chided himself.

Suddenly, Peter was aware that the man in front had gone to ground. What the hell? There had been no inkling of any night patrols in this area during their reconnaissance patrols. Perhaps the Germans had somehow got wind of their approach?

Josef was now at his side, with Charlie, and was whispering in his ear, "The track is just one hundred yards in front of us now, boss."

Peter heaved an inward sigh of relief. He had been so introspective that he had not marked the passage of time or distance. He scanned the immediate surroundings as far as was possible and gathered the men around in a tight circle. "OK, this will do fine as the lay-up point," he whispered. "If everything goes to shit, get your arses back here, into a defensive formation. In the meantime, we will wait here for the next train to go past. Then five minutes after that, Red Team will stay put here while Blue moves forward to deal with the sentries. As soon as we're clear, I'll send two men back here to bring you up to the bridge, while the rest of us take up position protecting the approach to the bridge from the west." He waited for this information to be translated and then finished by asking, "Any questions?"

"Roger that, chief." Charlie grinned. "Clear as day."

"Good man. Remember also, total silence from this point, OK?" Plenty of nods confirmed they had understood. "Right, let's do this." Peter went round the group, shaking each man's hand or clapping him on the shoulder or back. They all looked pretty grim but also seemed determined despite that. Even though they lacked formal training or experience, Peter had confidence in their ability. He was sure they had no wish to let him down; they knew how important it was for a good report to get back to London. Only that way would they guarantee further support against the Nazis.

While Charlie and Josef were busy supervising the positioning of their men, Peter and Jerzy crawled slowly and carefully up to the railway line, taking care not to make the slightest noise, as sound always seemed to travel further at night. They stopped at the point where the line and bridge came into vision. As far as they could see, though, there were no sentries or patrols out in the open. The small wooden hut by the bridge was clearly occupied, though, as light was visible around the edges of the shutters and door frame. From the size of it, Peter reckoned there could be no more than two men inside, three at the absolute maximum. Any more than that just would not fit in.

It was a chilly night with a biting wind, Peter reflected, so no doubt the guards had decided that coffee and a burning stove were preferable to strict adherence to duty. From the look of the hut, he wasn't even sure that it was all that effective at keeping the wind out; there appeared to be numerous gaps through which the light was escaping. Peter was pretty sure, however, that they would make an appearance every now and then for form's sake and certainly every time a train passed by, so he couldn't afford to ignore them completely.

After a couple of minutes watching, they continued their slow crawl up to the line itself. Once they reached it, Jerzy lay flat on the ground and pressed his ear to the rail. After a few seconds, he raised his head. "All quiet, boss. Nothing coming for miles in either direction."

"OK, thanks. Let's hope we don't have to hang around too long. It's freezing just lying here. Come on, let's slip back to our previous vantage point."

As they set off, Jerzy grinned. "Don't worry. Josef say trains run all night. Keeps him awake."

"Yeah." Peter smiled. "I guess he'll be looking forward to a few weeks of peaceful rest once we've blown the bridge. Still, let's hope he's right."

Sure enough, ten minutes later they heard a faint whistle followed by the appearance of a faint light in the distance, which grew in intensity in line with the sound of the engine. A couple of minutes later, the noise had become a roar as the train thundered past them. As expected, two guards had come out of the hut, kitted out in the standard-issue grey-green greatcoats and helmets, and were standing stiffly to attention. As soon as the train was out of sight, however, they lost no time in scurrying back into the warmth without a backward glance.

Peter then sent Jerzy back to bring the rest of the squad up to the forward position. While he was waiting, he kept an eye on the luminous hands of his watch. It was always surprising exactly how long it took for time to pass when you actually watched the hands crawling round the dial. The wait was interrupted after four minutes by the arrival of the rest of the team. Peter was pretty impressed; he had only heard them in the last few seconds.

After another minute, during which time there had been no movement from the hut, Peter roused himself from his position, stretching his limbs as a cat would following a nap on a sunny window ledge.

"OK," he whispered. "It's time to start the party—let's go deal with the guards."

Straight away the Red Team bedded in to provide cover in case of disaster, while the Blue Team began crawling forward towards the hut. With rapid, rehearsed hand movements, Peter indicated where he wanted the rest of his team positioned—fanned out around the hut to cover off any possible escape routes. They all had strict instructions to use knives only. Guns could be used only as a last resort, as the noise would effectively mean the end of the mission. Meanwhile, Peter pressed himself against the wall of the hut, next to the door, while Jerzy moved round the back to the window. It was essential that they prevented the guards from either using the radio or escaping to raise the alarm down at the village. Stealth and surprise were paramount.

With everyone hidden in position, Peter gave the signal. The man nearest to him threw a stone at the railway track. It missed the actual rails and clattered uselessly off the stones, into the grass on the other side. Peter cursed under his breath and signalled, impatiently, for him to try again. This time the throw was more accurate; the stone hit the nearest rail full on, where it made what seemed to Peter to be a deafening metallic clang. Peter made ready, hefting the heavy commando knife in his hand, taking comfort from its weight and the snug fit of its handle in his palm. At the same time, he tensed his body for action. As ever in these situations, he could feel the adrenalin literally pumping through his body, and every one of his senses was in a heightened state of awareness. The veins in his temples were throbbing in anticipation, the butterflies were knotting in the base of his gut, and he could feel the familiar unpleasant stickiness starting to form in the palm of his hands.

He didn't have long to wait. He could hear voices from inside raised in reaction to the noise. One guard, clearly the more conscientious one, suggested they should investigate, while the other said they should stay in the warm, as it was probably some kind of animal. As might be expected, long periods of inactivity and boredom spent in the middle of nowhere where nothing ever happened had dulled their senses. This was good news to Peter, not least because neither of them appeared to be reaching for the radio to alert anyone. The next thing Peter heard was a chair scraping against the wooden floor as it was pushed back to allow the soldier to stand. This was followed by footsteps heading towards the door. Clearly the more conscientious of the two had won the debate, as he had hoped.

Peter pressed himself even more tightly against the wall and prayed that Jerzy was listening in and was fully primed as well. At that moment, the door opened inwards, and the barrel of a German rifle appeared, followed closely by the man holding it. As soon as he had fully emerged from the doorway, Peter grabbed him from behind, placing one arm across his mouth to prevent any shout or scream and, with his other hand, slipping his knife up through the ribcage and deep into the heart. As Peter had hoped, the soldier had immediately dropped his rifle, freeing both hands to claw desperately at the arm around his face. This struggle was short-lived, however, as the heart ceased to function as soon as the long-bladed knife tore into it. Peter lowered the body gently to the ground, pleased that he had kept the noise to a minimum.

At the same time as Peter had grabbed the first soldier, Jerzy had launched himself through the window, relying upon speed and surprise to overpower the second man before he could raise the alarm. He was helped by the fact that the soldier had turned away from the window, towards the door, distracted by the sound of the rifle crashing to the ground. He never saw Jerzy coming, and he never stood a chance. Having dealt with the first guard, Peter rushed through the door to cut off any escape via that route. Inside, he found Jerzy lying on top of the German with his knife buried in his throat. There was blood everywhere from where it had been pumping from the severed artery. The force of Jerzy's attack had almost hacked the head clean off its shoulders. Little could shock Peter these days, but he was still somewhat taken aback at the brutality on display.

"One less pig for the slaughter," Jerzy said, grinning as he crouched to wipe his knife on the dead man's trousers.

Peter recovered his composure enough to offer, with a forced grin, "All I can say, Jerzy, is I'm glad you're on my side."

Nonetheless, Peter could relate to the rage that clearly burned within the Pole; being exiled from your country fuelled a man's passion to inflict pain on his oppressor. Although an exile himself, Peter had long since learned to control and channel his aggression. Better to focus on the efficient dispatch of your opponent than an all-out frenzied attack—less risk of things going wrong.

"OK, good job, Jerzy." Peter nodded. "Now, take a man back to Charlie and get his team going with the explosives as quick as you can. I will take the rest of our lot and set up the defensive screen to the west of the bridge. Join us there as soon as you can."

"Sir." Jerzy scurried out of the hut.

"Oh, and stick a rocket up their arse," Peter called after him. "There's no telling how long we have before the next train comes." On reflection, Peter scolded himself for using idioms and hoped Jerzy would appreciate that his instructions were not to be followed literally. They had little enough plastic explosive to waste any in this way.

Twenty minutes later, Charlie led the Red Team into Peter's position. The noise their boots made crunching across the gravel that surrounded the wooden sleepers seemed deafening to Peter. He fully expected a burst of gunfire from an inquisitive patrol to rip them apart at any moment.

"All charges in place, boss. We have positioned four separate charges on each of the main supports. We've been extra careful with the stuff, so we even have some left over for the journey home."

"As long as you have placed enough to bring the sodding thing down, Charlie?" Peter queried.

"Don't you worry about that, sir. She'll blow; you mark my words."

"Excellent! Now we just have to be patient and wait for the one forty to Moscow. Get your men into position, and make sure they know exactly what they need to do."

Charlie nodded and rushed off again, taking four men from the Red Team with him: Tomasz from their own squad, plus the three locals who had responded best to Charlie's training on the time pencils and explosives. Charlie positioned each of the three men by one of the explosive charges and gave them all very specific instructions to break the pencil only on his signal and to be very sure that they each did it on the two-minute marker. Tomasz's job was to serve as the runner between the team and Peter's command post.

Just over ten freezing minutes later, Peter felt Tomasz dig him in the ribs. "Charlie tell me to say the train is coming, boss."

"Well, I'll say one thing for Hitler," Peter quipped, looking at his watch. "He runs an efficient train service."

Peter hoped Charlie was right; the cold was seeping through his clothes and deep into his bones as he lay there. He strained his ears but could hear nothing over the chattering of his teeth. It was something of a surprise, he reflected, that Charlie's hearing was so good after a career spent working with explosives.

"OK," he said. "I'll take his word for it. Go back and tell him to go ahead when ready." Then he turned to the rest of the men. "Right, this is it. Stay sharp and get everything ready for a quick exit. As soon as she blows, we're out of here, OK?"

As soon as he finished speaking, he noted that he too could now make out the sound of an approaching train. He shook hands again with Josef and the rest of the local men, as they were to go their separate ways as soon as the bridge went up. Then he settled down to wait for Charlie and his men to do their thing. The tension of those last few moments waiting for the train to reach the bridge were unbearable. They had to get the timing right; they didn't want to give the train any chance to stop, nor did they want to leave it so late that the train would be able to get over the bridge before the charges went off.

A minute or so later, with the train almost upon them, Charlie and the four other men came scurrying into their position, breathless with exertion. "All set, sir. All four charges primed to go on a two-minute fuse, which, I reckon, is any second now."

Peter offered up a final prayer to whatever deity might be listening that the men had done their job right and that luck would be on their side tonight. He needn't have worried. As usual, Charlie had done the job perfectly. About one hundred yards before the train reached the start of the bridge, there was a blinding flash of light and the almost simultaneous, dull crump of four separate explosions. Looking at the bridge, the track appeared to lift straight up into the air in one piece before crashing down into the valley below in a tangled mess of steel and rubble. There was no time for the train to stop; it was fully committed to its fate. He could hear the despairing screech of the brakes as the crew fought desperately to stop the train, but there could be no escape. The engine continued its inexorable progress until its weight tipped it over into the void, taking carriage after carriage with them into the valley below, folding one on top of the other as they hit the bottom, in a giant concertina effect.

The noise seemed to go on interminably, but in reality, it could have been no more than twenty seconds at the most. At the end, however, there was an almost deathly silence, interrupted only by the groaning of twisted metal on what remained of the bridge, and the occasional crash from the valley floor as the wreckage came to settle. Looking round him, Peter could see the impact on the faces of the Poles. Open-mouthed awe, to say the least, except for Charlie, for whom this sort of thing was business as usual. He was already busy packing the remaining charges away in his backpack, ready to use another day.

Peter took his cue from Charlie; he was keen to be off before the Germans got men up to the bridge. He turned to Josef. "Well, I guess that about concludes our business here. I think we ought to be making tracks, don't you?"

Josef nodded dumbly, still in shock from what he had just witnessed.

Peter continued, "So this is where we say goodbye. It's been an experience working with you and your men, and hopefully our paths may cross again one day. We'll be sure to let your countrymen back in London know that the fight goes on."

Once Jerzy had completed translating this farewell message to the rest of the group, there followed much shaking of hands and slapping of backs. The Poles had by now snapped out of their trance and were chattering and gesticulating wildly as they relived the sight of the bridge disintegrating before their eyes. Whilst Peter was pleased to see how animated they were, he was also eager to bring things to a close, as they had to put as much distance between them and the bridge as possible. It would not be long now before the place would be crawling with soldiers everywhere looking for them.

———

With the goodbyes finally over, the four men set off at pace with Jerzy taking point. Looking back, Peter couldn't see the rest of the Poles anymore. They had already melted away into the hills. For his little group, Peter hoped to put at least a couple of miles in before the Germans reached the scene; not a great head start but it would have to be enough. In addition, he remembered Charlie saying that they had some plastic left, so they would be able to use that to leave a few surprises on the way, which would help slow them down. The immediate threat would come from the garrison in the village. If they could deal with them, then it would be some time before further reinforcements could be brought up. By then, hopefully, they would be long gone.

Their escape route was taking them along a narrow road through a wood, with trees lining each side close to the edge of the road. At best, it was wide enough for one vehicle. It was not ideal, Peter reflected, as it would be easy for pursuers to hunt them down quickly, but on the plus side, it was easy going for them, and they could make good progress as they mixed jogging and brisk walking, the commandos' favourite style of route marching. Peter assessed their surroundings as they jogged along, and glanced sideways at Charlie, who met his gaze at the same time.

"I agree, sir," Charlie puffed. "This road seems to present an ideal opportunity to prepare a small reception for anyone coming along behind."

Peter called the group to a halt. "OK, Charlie, get to work. Rig up a few of your specials along here to slow them down a bit."

"Will do, boss. I was getting pissed off lumping this stuff around anyway. May as well put it to good use."

———

Almost half an hour later, a column of three half-tracks, packed with German infantry, nosed its way along the road, coming to a halt in front of two trees, which had been blown across the road, blocking their progress. Well drilled, the first troops were soon out of the vehicles and into a defensive formation, weapons at the ready for the first sign of trouble. When no resistance materialised, the officers were soon barking orders to get the trees moved. It was while a dozen or so men were fully absorbed in attaching ropes to the fallen trunks that the night air was ripped apart by a twin burst of automatic sub-machine gunfire, emanating from either side of the road. Six men were immediately sent spinning to the ground, almost ripped in half by the ferocious hail of bullets. The rest frantically raced each other to seek cover back behind the vehicles, before returning fire as best they could. In the midst of this mayhem, there was ample opportunity for the gunmen to make good their escape.

It was some minutes before confidence was sufficiently restored. More cautiously now, the Germans sent out patrols to sweep the area on either side of the road for any further signs of attack. Finally, having found nothing, work could resume on shifting the obstacles. Almost an hour later, the remaining men were back in their half-tracks and snaking past the tree trunks, which had been pulled far enough apart to allow a vehicle through.

Less than half a mile further down the road, the column came to a halt at the next barrier, an apparent repeat of the first with two more trees blocking the road. On this occasion, a far more measured approach prevailed in that a good thirty minutes was spent sweeping both sides of the road for the enemy. Once satisfied, the lead half-track manoeuvred up to the first tree to get into position for ropes to be attached as before. Matters, again, did not proceed quite as planned, however, as the vehicle and remaining occupants were suddenly engulfed in a ball of flame, which erupted as the front wheel came into contact with the carefully concealed anti-tank mine.

A further thirty minutes were then required to clear the debris, check for additional mines, of which none was found, and finally to clear the trees. Only then could the remaining two vehicles continue their slow progress to the almost inevitable third barrier. This time, one group of soldiers disappeared into the trees to check for the enemy whilst a further group carefully prodded the ground in front of the trees. Both searches proved fruitless, whereupon half a dozen men rushed forward to begin attaching the ropes. What they hadn't spotted, though, was the presence of a handful of grenades carefully poised amongst the branches and rigged to go off once disturbed. Once again, the night air was filled with the screams of maimed and dying soldiers as the six hapless infantry were hit by a combination of shrapnel from the grenades or long, deadly splinters torn from the tree trunks.

———

"Well, that should keep them busy for a while." Charlie grinned as he and Jerzy jogged back into Peter's position.

After a brief rest to take on water, the four men set off walking again. Charlie was still filling Peter in on his handiwork as any proud craftsman might. "Those grenades on the third block will slow them down yet again, as they'll need to search the area again before clearing the trees. After that they'll come to the fourth and final pair of trees."

"I didn't think we had enough explosives or mines for four sets of obstacles?" Peter asked, confused.

"We don't, boss. And that's the beauty of it." Charlie was obviously pleased with his night's work. "They'll be so wound up by the other nasty little surprises we left them that they'll take forever going over that last one with a fine-toothed comb only to find absolutely nothing. The final block is totally clean!"

"Have I ever told you what a crafty little bastard you are, Charlie?" Peter laughed. "OK, I guess we have put enough space between us and the enemy now, so let's take this opportunity, so lovingly prepared, and piss off out of it."

FIVE

Eighteen months later.

Peter stood on the pavement outside the imposing white stone façade of the Baker Street office building. The only clue that he was in the right place was the number sixty-four staring boldly at him from the gleaming brass plaque by the door. For the fourth time that morning, he took the telegram that he had received at his barracks the previous week from his pocket to check the details. The intriguing communication had instructed him to present himself at SOE Headquarters (at 64 Baker Street, London) on the sixteenth of the month at 12:00 p.m. prompt. There were no other details, no indication of whom he had been summoned to meet or why. All that "Careless talk costs lives" stuff was clearly taken seriously here, as it had ensured that the Special Operations Executive did not announce its presence to the casual observer. Nonetheless, Peter was at a loss to understand why he had been summoned and could only hope that the answer would be forthcoming on the other side of the door.

Another glance at his watch confirmed that he was bang on time: it wouldn't do to be anything other than punctual, after all. He pushed against the right-hand side of the revolving door, noting as he did so that the brass rails and fittings were as exceptionally well-polished as the plaque outside. Spit and polish, the one thing that the British military always excelled at. Peter smiled to himself. Emerging into the spacious reception area, Peter approached the desk manned by a uniformed sergeant. He had the air of someone who took an immense pride in his appearance and probably had a healthy respect for his own self-importance too. Peter had little doubt the gleaming metal was all his doing. His uniform was neatly pressed with not a crease out of place, the buttons were all polished to a high sheen, and his neatly trimmed hair carried an abundance of some kind of hair product clearly designed to ensure that not a single strand dared step out of line.

"Good morning, my name is Lieutenant Bogarde. I have an appointment to see—"

"Yes, sir." The sergeant cut him off before he could go any further. "We've been expecting you. If you would like to take the lift to the second floor, someone will meet you there."

Now that's even more efficiency for you. Peter smiled inwardly as he nodded his thanks. He crossed the reception area in the direction indicated by the desk sergeant, to a hallway in which he found a row of three lifts, each with gleaming brass plaques, from which stood out two black buttons to call the lift for the required direction. Peter pressed the up button, and the door of the middle lift opened immediately. As the doors closed in front of him, Peter selected the number two button as instructed and stood back to check his reflection visible in the, inevitably, highly polished metal surface of the doors. It was always as well to create a good impression, as you never knew what was in store around the corner. His tie needed a fractional adjustment to the left, but otherwise, everything was in order; even his cap was, for once, suitably straight.

The lift doors opened onto another open-plan reception area, though this one had more of the feel of a doctor's waiting room about it. Around the walls were a number of padded wooden chairs, all of which were unoccupied, whereas at the centre of the room was a low table covered with a selection of the day's papers. Interspersed between the chairs were a number of wood-panelled doors with numbers printed on raised blocks of wood.

Hardly had he settled into the nearest chair and laid hold of a copy of that day's *Times*, which trumpeted the latest advances and reverses on its front page, when one of the panelled doors behind him opened, and a voice boomed, "Would you mind stepping inside now, please, Lieutenant Bogarde?"

The voice was familiar, but it wasn't until Peter had closed the door behind him and turned to face the desk that he was sure. Seated behind the fastidiously tidy desk was none other than Colonel Blake. Never one to use two words when ten would suffice, Blake kicked things straight off.

"I expect you are wondering why you have been asked here today. I know I would be!"

Before he could affirm or deny this allegation, Blake had already moved on.

"Last time we met, I was shaking your hand and wishing you 'Bon voyage' as you boarded a plane, bound for Poland. Your mission to link up with the local Resistance and launch a joint assault on a vital rail bridge was a resounding success. So much so, if I recall correctly"—Blake made a show of shuffling his notes as if looking for the relevant piece of information, though Peter suspected that he knew the content off by heart—"that your team were mentioned in dispatches, and both you and Sergeant Butler received written commendations for your part in the matter."

"That's correct, sir," Peter replied, "though I still maintain, as I did at the time, that it was a team effort. The Polish lads were superb."

"Yes, yes. Quite so," Blake continued with just a faint hint of irritation at the interjection. "Anyway, no doubt you thought that would be the end of the matter and the last you either saw or heard of me, and, if I am honest, so did I.

"However, in the course of following up on the ramifications of your attack on the bridge, we turned up a rather startling snippet of information. Aside from the fact that you put the bridge out of action for two months, and sent a troop train carrying upwards of four hundred German soldiers to hell into the bargain, it was what you failed to do that intrigued us more."

Peter visibly stiffened in his seat. If he hadn't been before, he was certainly now wholly focussed on Blake's words. He couldn't for the life of him think where they had failed. It had been a textbook mission as far as he was concerned. All objectives met, not a single man lost or injured. What more could he have done? And why wait for eighteen months before hauling him up to London to account for the mistake? He could feel his hackles rising as he mentally prepared his defence.

In the meantime, Blake had continued with his speech. "Our network of intelligence sources inside Poland—a rather grand title for a rough-and-ready group of fanatical Resistance fighters, don't you think?—told us a few weeks later that the train that you managed to blow up should not have been there at that time. It was, as I understand it, not actually due to be the next train that came your way. As such, it was rather bad luck for the chaps on board that things turned out as they did. You see, apparently, the train which was scheduled to reach the bridge in time for your little show made an unscheduled stop at the final station before the bridge, thereby having the good fortune to avoid the carnage that was waiting for it."

By now, Peter was thoroughly confused. "I'm sorry, sir, but I don't have the faintest idea of what you are talking about, nor what it has to do with me. If there is a problem with the way I carried out the mission, I'd really rather you came out with it, as I fail to see where this is leading."

"All in good time, my lad, all in good time." Blake smiled reassuringly. "As I was saying, this earlier train stopped where it wasn't supposed to and where no one was expecting it. Normally you'd think there would be nothing remarkable in this story, and you'd be right. On this occasion, however, our sources tell us that the fact that this particular train made this unscheduled stop sent everyone at that station into a mad panic. Our immediate question, and no doubt yours too, was why should a train making an unscheduled stop at a small provincial station cause such a frantic burst of activity, eh?

"Well, our contact spoke to some of the station staff after the event. This man told him that there were dozens of crack troops swarming off the train and all over the platform, securing the exits, checking the buildings, and generally keeping the great unwashed, although there were not that many of them at that time of night, at a safe distance. Very suspicious, I'm sure you would agree.

"Anyway, when we eventually got to the bottom of the mystery, guess what we found?"

Peter shook his head, unable to offer a guess, which presumably suited Blake fine, as his thunder had in no way been stolen. He cleared his throat in readiness for the big denouement.

"The train that stopped, and in the process allowed your troop train to overtake it, thereby sealing its fate, was none other than the Führerzug." Blake paused for effect and then continued in a quieter voice. "I am sure that with your linguistic ability, Lieutenant, I have no need to tell you the Führerzug is Hitler's personal train!"

Blake left another short pause, long enough for this revelation to sink in. "Can you imagine? We came within a hair's breadth of killing Hitler and potentially ending this war much earlier than would otherwise be possible. And it would have been a complete and utter fluke!"

Peter's brain was still frantically racing ahead to try to see exactly where all this stuff about this undoubtedly remarkable coincidence was going and how it involved him, but could not piece it together. Meanwhile, Blake was now standing, leaning forward over his desk with his two hands pressed flat against the surface, his posture mirroring the animation that was painted on his face.

"I'm sorry, sir, I am going to have to ask you to put me out of my misery. Whilst I can fully appreciate the irony of the near miss, I still don't see what this has to do with me, other than being an amusing anecdote I can tell the grandkids—assuming I survive this war, of course."

Blake smiled indulgently as if having to coax a young child to answer a particularly tough mathematical question. "You, my dear boy, are an integral part of the whole thing. You see, ever since we found out about the Führerzug, a few of us here at SOE have been kicking around the idea of going one better and actually removing Hitler from the equation, doing the job properly this time, if you will. We came that close by chance, so why not try and go one better, eh? You wouldn't believe, or actually, perhaps you would, the amount of toing and froing there has been on this over the last few months, right up to Churchill himself on a number of occasions, I can tell you.

"But now I am happy to say that we have been given the green light to formally investigate the options for a mission to assassinate Hitler, which, if approved, then gives us the mandate to undertake that mission. Where you fit in, Lieutenant, is hopefully becoming more apparent by the minute. We would like to offer you the opportunity to lead the mission; we want you to pull the trigger, as it were. That's not to say, of course, that a rifle is necessarily the best option; that is still to be decided, along with the best location and a whole host of other things. But the fact remains that with your knowledge of the German language and customs, combined with your obvious military skills, you are a prime candidate to give the mission every chance of success."

"Jesus Christ! Are you mad? That is an utterly ridiculous idea," Peter exploded. "He must be the most heavily guarded individual in the whole of the Third Reich, if not the world. What makes you think that anyone, let alone me, could get close enough to him to get a chance? Let's not forget; that train episode in Poland was pure luck and nothing more. You boffins in your ivory tower have let that go to your head. It's a complete suicide mission, and no one in their right mind would want any part in it, and that includes me."

Blake held his hands up as if in surrender in the face of the verbal onslaught. "No one thinks this will be a stroll in the park, Lieutenant. I fully accept your point about luck, but, if nothing else, it illustrates the potential. However, having spent a significant number of man hours on this project, we firmly believe that with the right intelligence and the right training, the mission has got a chance, albeit a small one. And to be honest, even the slightest chance of success on a mission such as this demands that we give it very serious consideration indeed."

"That's as maybe, but I still say it can't be done. There is so much that we would need to know before we could go anywhere near it. Where is he at any given time? And how would we know when he was going to be there? What is the terrain and environment like in that location? What is his daily routine? How well guarded is he, in terms of the number and quality of troops? And how the hell do we get there to do the job in the first place?

"I could go on and on. The list must be almost endless. Where the hell are we going to get information that we can rely on to any extent? Information that is good enough to make me risk my life on the back of it?"

Blake smiled and his voice took on a more soothing and placatory tone. "We have asked all the same questions, my lad, believe me. We have a team of highly skilled intelligence offices working round the clock on the answers to all those and more questions. We are not approaching this lightly, whatever you may think of us here in our—what was it you called this place? An ivory tower? Nonetheless, I can tell you that we hope very soon to have cracked the vast majority of these issues."

Peter was unable to keep the sceptical look off his face, but Blake ploughed on regardless. "Like you, we felt that the issues around trying to find out about Hitler's whereabouts on any given day, and his immediate entourage, etc., were pretty much insurmountable. A couple of months back, though, we had an extraordinary piece of luck. As part of their latest offensive in Italy, our American allies recently captured practically a whole German battalion. Amongst them, it turns out that there was an ex-member of the First SS Leibstandarte Adolf Hitler Division. He wasn't spotted straight away and so escaped our notice for a while. Anyway, to cut a long story short, it was during his registration at a POW camp that they spotted the tell-tale tattoo on the underside of his upper arm which indicates membership of the elite SS divisions. On interrogation, it turns out that he was booted out for some misdemeanour or other. Lost his sergeant rank and everything. Ended up sent to the front line in a bog-standard footslogger outfit. He was pretty cheesed off about it, I can tell you, and who wouldn't be, losing one's privileged position like that and ending up as cannon fodder?

"Anyway, the real break came in that one of the First SS Division's duties is to provide the ceremonial guard of honour for Hitler, a glorified bodyguard if you will. Some of them are assigned to accompany him wherever he goes outside of the capital, and presumably, the soldiers who spewed forth from the train when it made that unscheduled stop were part of this detail. Another detachment is on permanent guard at Hitler's favourite residence, a place called the Berghof, which is located up in the Austrian Alps, near Salzburg, very close to the border of what is Germany proper.

"Our man, a Private Ernst Bachmann, was part of this latter group for a three-month period back in 1942. Given that experience, what he doesn't know about the Berghof and Hitler's routine when he stays there isn't worth knowing. He also spent a shorter stint on the Führerzug as part of the mobile guard, though not at the time of our Polish escapade, I understand. On top of that, he seems pretty disillusioned about the whole Nazi ideal and how the war is going in general, no doubt from his first-hand experience. Anyway, he's pretty damned keen to spill the beans as a result, if only as he thinks it the best way to save his skin."

"OK," Peter conceded. "So we've got a man with inside knowledge. But tell me this. Why come to me? Why not send this Bachmann guy if he is so anti-Nazi all of a sudden?"

"A good question, and one that deserves an answer. Firstly, Bachmann. Granted that he would have no problem moving around Germany, assuming that we provide him with the relevant papers and cover story, but it's not as simple as that. You must appreciate that it would not be appropriate to entrust a mission of such huge importance to someone that we do not know intimately, nor over whom we have no real control. As soon as he was back in Germany, he would most likely simply disappear rather than risk his own life. This totally rules him out.

"In terms of why we have come to you, there are a number of reasons." Blake spread the fingers of his left hand to prepare to tick them off one by one as he listed them.

"Firstly, you speak German with little or no accent, a huge advantage given that the location of any strike will almost certainly have to take place in Germany, or at least Austria.

"Second, you spent a good deal of time in Germany in your youth, hiking in the Bavarian Alps during your family holidays, if my intelligence is correct. This puts experience of mountainous regions and familiarity of the terrain around the Berghof firmly in your favour.

"Third, and certainly not least, you are an excellent soldier with a distinguished service record. You have that cold, ruthless streak that gives you the edge over an opponent, though you are not simply a bloodthirsty killer. On top of which you are an expert marksman and have proved adept at operating behind enemy lines. All of which demonstrates to us that you would be more than able to cope with the demands and stresses of a mission such as this.

"Fourth and finally…" Blake paused, with what looked like a triumphant smile on his face as if about to play the winning card in a game of poker. "Revenge! We know what happened to your parents back in Holland. We also know what happened to your sister after you came to this country. What better opportunity could you have to hit back at the heart of the monstrous regime that has caused you so much pain?"

Peter's reply was cold and emotionless. "That's quite a speech, Colonel. Your people have clearly done their homework." Though he felt a degree of bitterness at the way in which this had all been thought out without reference to him, Peter had to admit that this last point had struck home. As Blake had said, this was the perfect chance to make a difference. This was the opportunity he had been looking for since Anna had been killed. Could he in all good conscience refuse? It sounded like a suicide mission, for sure, but did he really care about that? What did he truly have to live for? There was no one left to mourn him anyway.

Blake could see that Bogarde was weighing up all the angles in his mind. Whilst all that he had said was true, he had not revealed the whole story. It wasn't so much that this young lieutenant was the best choice, more that he was the only choice. There had already been an extensive search across the armed forces of many of the Allied nations but with no success. There had been any number of candidates put forward, but there had always been something that ruled them out. The specific qualities required for this job were in immensely short supply. Even Bogarde, who had a lot of positive qualities to recommend him, carried undoubted question marks as well, the most obvious and worrying of which was temperament. There were signs in his records of a potential for psychosis; it had been kept under control, but the experts felt it was bubbling under the surface and could be triggered under extreme stress. This mission needed someone with clarity of mind, an unerring focus on the end goal, and was this man really 100 per cent capable? The fact was, however, that the credibility of the SOE was on the line here. They had put so much effort into this, spent so many hours influencing the great and the good in military and political circles to get it off the ground, that if they failed to deliver now, the embarrassment could be fatal. They simply had to get a man signed up now, and Bogarde was the best they had seen, despite the possible shortcomings. They did not have the luxury of time to keep looking.

He had thought long and hard about playing the revenge card, but decided it was the one thing that would swing it if it was in the balance, and thus was a justified means to an end. If he was honest with himself, though, it was a double-edged sword. Yes, it would appeal to his psyche, but would it also come to dominate his thinking, leading him to take unreasonable risks? It was a chance they had to take, though; there was no one else. Blake snapped out of his reverie as he realised that Bogarde was speaking again.

"Assuming I go for it, and I am not saying I will or won't, mind you, where do we go from here?"

"Well, firstly, we would need to get you through the standard SOE training programme for agents who need to operate behind enemy lines. This normally takes three months, but given your experience and ability, coupled with the fact that we need to move quickly, we should be able to get this down to one month if we focus on the essentials.

"While you are doing that, we will be beavering away behind the scenes to squeeze every last drop out of Bachmann, not that we have to press too hard, mind you. This will allow us to define the options for a successful assassination attempt and settle upon the best one. Once we have done that, we bring you back in for briefing with the plan and any final training that is required as a result. Then we actually drop you into Germany to do the job. I know it all sounds very simple, but rest assured, we will be packing a hell of a lot of detail into this time; we have many of our best chaps on this project. We won't let you loose without ensuring that you are as fully prepared as we can possibly make you. If at any time we collectively feel that it's a no-go, then we pull the plug. No questions asked. Send you back to your unit with a firm handshake and our grateful thanks for your involvement up to that point."

"OK. I have heard enough. Let's do it!"

"Excellent." Blake positively beamed. "I'd like to say that you won't regret it, but you'll understand that I cannot formally guarantee that."

SIX

The following morning, Peter presented himself once again at 64 Baker Street. This time, however, he was there to start the formal process of induction into the ranks of the Special Operations Executive. Whilst he was the preferred man for the job, he had been left in no doubt by Colonel Blake that this fact alone did not entitle him to any special privileges. He would still be required to undergo the standard recruitment and training procedures to ensure that he was up to the job. Or as Blake had so eloquently put it: "We can't simply drop you in the middle of the Hun tomorrow. We have got to make sure that (a) you are at least basically equipped to avoid getting yourself killed in the first five minutes, and (b) you have the mental wherewithal not to go totally bananas under the pressure."

Soon after his arrival, he was ushered into a small, featureless room which contained nothing more than two chairs positioned either side of a small wooden desk, the kind you might find at any school in any country. The room was unlit save for a single bulb dangling from the ceiling directly above the table. It gave the room an even more stark feeling than it already had, leaving the edges very much in shadow. One chair was vacant and obviously intended for him; the other chair was already occupied. The door that Peter had come through was positioned directly behind the occupant, which made it difficult to discern any obvious facets of his appearance other than it was a man, seemingly rather on the elderly side if the bald pate glinting in the available light was anything to go by. Peter also surmised that, despite the fact that his clothes had a greeny-brown hue, he was wearing a civilian suit rather than military uniform, judging by the cut of the cloth. He guessed that this was not unusual in SOE with it being more of a cloak-and-dagger, rather than an overtly military, organisation.

Peter's thoughts were interrupted, however, as the man had begun to speak, but more especially so because he was speaking German without the slightest trace of an accent as far as Peter could tell.

"Good morning, Lieutenant Bogarde. Come in and please take a seat. The purpose of this interview is twofold. Firstly, we must ensure that you are able to communicate effectively in German, for which purpose this interview will be conducted wholly in that language. Secondly, it is an opportunity for us to start building an overview of you, so we can understand what makes you tick, if you will.

"It should be a relatively painless process, though I would urge you to answer as truthfully as possible, as it will be to everyone's advantage in the long run. Right, if there are no questions, shall we begin?"

"No, you fire away, er…sir?" Being from a military background, Peter felt bound to acknowledge in some way the perceived authority of the man in front of him.

"There's no need for that sort of thing in here, young man!" He smiled. "We don't all stand on ceremony in the SOE. Now then, question one: Tell me, how does a Dutch national come to be fighting in the British army?"

Peter hesitated a moment before replying. Surely they must know all this already? He assumed it must be a form of psychological testing designed to help build a profile of him. "Well, it's a long story," Peter replied, "but without boring you with all the messy details, the arrival of the Germans in the Netherlands and my arrival in England are not entirely unconnected."

"I understand why you left your homeland, Lieutenant, but I asked you why you joined the British army. What makes this your fight?"

"The occupation of my country is not enough?" Instantly Peter regretted the outburst. He had told himself to remain calm and had lasted about two minutes. He chided himself to maintain better control of his emotions for the rest of the session. He wondered, however, whether it was already too late, as he could see the man scribbling notes in response to his overreaction.

"Yes, I see, but that is true of many men your age, and not all of them come to Britain and join up. What is it that makes you different?"

Peter could see that his inquisitor was going to continue prodding and poking for a reaction. He was clearly being put under the microscope in order to assess his temperament, and thus his suitability, for the mission. He had no real idea what answers they were looking for and so decided to follow the advice he had been given and be as honest as possible.

"Well, as I am sure you know, the Germans have been directly responsible for the death of my parents and my sister. I cannot sit by and do nothing, simply wait for the war to be over. I have a duty to their memory and my honour to do something to help stop them, to seek some sort of retribution for their actions."

More scribbling followed this. "I understand. But what can one man do against a whole nation, a whole ideology, if you will?"

"Not a lot, I grant you, if you put it like that. But if everyone felt that way, where would we be? Lots of individuals like me working to a common purpose is the only way to defeat them. Therefore, whenever the opportunity presents itself, I kill Germans wherever I find them! And if enough people do the same thing, then maybe it will help end the war." This reply seemed to go down a bit better, as it was accompanied by more feverish scribbling of notes, nodding, and understanding noises.

"Would you say then that killing Germans is the most important thing in your life right now?"

"Well, perhaps not right at this moment." Peter smirked. "But I must confess it does play a significant part. There's not a lot else for me to do now, you see. I have no trade to offer and no particular skills to speak of. The only thing that I have found that I am good at is being a soldier. The Nazis killed my parents and my sister; they've invaded my homeland, confiscated my belongings. I think I owe them, don't you? And if I have the ability to do something practical about that, I am going to grab it with both hands."

"Yes," mused the older man. "I do rather see your point. Moving on, how do you prefer to operate: alone or as part of a team?"

The interview continued for a whole hour in the same vein, gentle but incisive probing around Peter's past life and how various events had shaped his feelings and decisions at the time and ever since. It was obvious to Peter that they had their doubts about his temperament and were going to great lengths to try to build a picture as to how he might react under pressure. He had been on missions behind enemy lines before but always as part of a squad. He guessed they were thinking that sending a possible loose cannon in on his own to do this kind of job might not be "good form," as Blake might have put it.

At the end of the hour, Peter was instructed to report to the first floor, where he would be briefed about his immediate future.

———

"So, Simpson, will he do, do you think?"

Major Simpson, fresh from interviewing Bogarde, sat in the armchair opposite Colonel Blake's desk, his elbows resting on the arms and his fingers pressed together to form a kind of steeple. He was drumming his fingertips together thoughtfully.

"If I am absolutely honest, Colonel, I'm not sure. On the plus side, it is clear that he meets many of the criteria for which we are looking. He is brave, resourceful, resilient in battle conditions, and a highly effective killer. That much is beyond doubt. He doesn't appear to be overly rash, more of the cold, calculating type, if you ask me, and I have no doubts around his commitment to the cause. What that lad's been through has guaranteed a lifelong hatred of Nazi Germany."

"Excellent." Blake clapped his hands. "He sounds eminently qualified to do the job." Then, seeing the look on Simpson's face, he added, "Ah, I see. What is it that you are not telling me?"

Simpson took a moment before replying, as if carefully weighing up the words he wanted to use to get his point across. "Well, Colonel, I would say there is a small risk that Bogarde could lose control. There is a danger that this hatred of all things German has the potential to become pathological. In hindsight, it may prove to be nothing at all, but I wouldn't be doing my job if I didn't flag it as an issue. I think there is a chance that under certain stressful conditions, we might lose the ability to control his behaviour in the field."

"Hmmm, I see." Blake himself was thoughtful now. He rested both elbows on the table top and twisted his pen round his fingers. He thought for a couple of minutes before speaking, Simpson maintaining a respectful silence. His job was not to decide or veto, simply to advise and counsel.

Blake eventually broke the silence. "I understand your concerns and agree it is a worry. On the other hand, I can't see that we have any alternative. If we are to get this mission off the ground now, we have to use Lieutenant Bogarde. It took a lot of time and effort to get the green light for this mission; it also took a not inconsiderable investment to select this candidate. To find another with the same mix of skills and experience may take us months, and by then, who knows what sort of situation we will be in? In your professional opinion, Major, what is the likelihood of this problem manifesting itself?"

"Well," Simpson replied, "I wouldn't stake my career on it, but I'd say it was less than fifty-fifty. In all probability, he will turn out to be just fine, but there are definitely some worrying signs; that is all. If it were down to me and we had a choice, I probably wouldn't send the man, just to be on the safe side."

"I see. Well, in which case, Simpson, I must thank you for your expertise in this matter; it is always much appreciated and greatly valued by this department. On this occasion, however, I think we have no option other than to go ahead with what we have. We'll just have to take that risk."

SEVEN

The train out of King's Cross Station was crowded, mostly with soldiers going on leave. Well, that was Peter's assumption based on the general atmosphere; soldiers returning from leave tended to be a lot quieter and more introspective than those on this train. Despite the swarm of bodies in the passageways, Peter did actually manage to find an empty seat in a six-berth compartment on the penultimate carriage. He reached up to stow his kitbag in the overhead rack and sat down, nodding to the other occupants half in greeting and half in apology for disturbing them with his movements.

Moments later, Peter was up again, cursing under his breath. He reached up to the rack, opened the end of his bag, and began to rummage about for the book that he had brought with him to read but had managed to forget to remove before sitting down. Mercifully, he had packed it near the top, which kept the embarrassment factor to a minimum. A further round of nods plus a few "Excuse mes" and he was safely ensconced back in his seat once more. He needed the book, as he knew the journey was going to be a long one, and there was only so much staring out of the window that you could do.

The fact that he was on the train told him that he had passed the initial interview selection process. He was now on his way to the wilds of Scotland to begin the formal SOE training programme. Though London itself was beginning to warm up nicely as spring took a firm grip, he imagined that things would be a little different up in the Scottish Highlands. He'd never travelled that far north and knew nothing other than what he'd heard, a reputation for stunning scenery and the possibility of being hit by four seasons' worth of weather in a single day. He had also never heard of his eventual destination, Arisaig. However, the fact that it was a further four hours by train out of Glasgow, itself an eight-hour journey from London, told him he was in for a long trek into the middle of nowhere. Fortunately, the seats were relatively comfortable, and the book at least seemed to have the potential to be diverting. He smiled to himself as he opened the cover. It felt good to be away from the city again; he was never really comfortable in the middle of so many people and surrounded by buildings. He needed to be able to see the countryside.

He was also looking forward to getting stuck into the training, as he was always keen to learn new skills. On top of this, he was impatient for the actual mission to begin. Ever since Blake had proposed it back in Baker Street, his interest and excitement had been growing. He could never have imagined that a chance like this would have ever come his way. He was literally bursting to shout about it to everyone in the carriage, which was even more frustrating due to the need for absolute secrecy. Even when he reached the training camp, he would not be able to talk about it; no one could be allowed to know what his objective was.

To take his mind off things, Peter took the opportunity to study his fellow travellers while apparently concentrating on the pages of his novel. On the seats opposite him were two women in uniform, though Peter had no idea to which of the many women's auxiliary organisations they belonged. They were engaged in deep conversation, so deep, in fact, that they had not even broken off to look at him when he came in. Peter considered himself pretty useful in English but nevertheless found that he could understand fewer than one in three words, such was the speed of the speech and the obvious familiarity between the two, so much so that they seemed able to finish most of each other's sentences. In the third seat on that side was a soldier in the uniform of an infantry sergeant. He was sitting by the window and staring intently at the rolling countryside, oblivious to anyone or anything else in the compartment. He was apparently lost in his own thoughts, perhaps reliving the horrors of his most recent tour of duty. On Peter's side of the compartment were a vicar and an RAF pilot, the former seemingly engrossed in that day's *Times* crossword, whilst the latter was fast asleep, his legs splayed out in front of him, causing the woman opposite to have to tuck her feet up beneath her seat to keep out of the way.

During the few years since he had first come to Britain, Peter had got used to the traditional British reserve. Back in Holland it would have been unusual for strangers on a train not to strike up a conversation; well, it would certainly have been true before the war, at any rate. But in Britain this seemed to be the norm; everyone kept themselves to themselves. In happier times, Peter might have made an effort to strike up a conversation with those around him, but the events of recent years had taken their toll on his conversational skills, and with his mind fully occupied by what the future might hold in store for him as well, a period of self-imposed solitude suited Peter just fine.

Since that initial meeting with Colonel Blake, Peter had thought of little else but the mission. Looking back on it, he realised that he had perhaps been a little too eager to jump at the chance without any real detailed consideration of the consequences. Far too impulsive, he thought to himself ruefully. Having said that, he also realised that even with the additional contemplation that time had allowed, he would still give the same answer. This was the kind of challenge that, deep down, he had been looking for, and he relished the opportunity. He knew it was a next-to-impossible task, and he was under no illusions as to what the consequences of success or failure might mean. *Let's face it,* he mused, *the odds I get back in one piece must be considerably worse than extremely slim.* Nevertheless, he still couldn't honestly say that he wasn't up for it. Yes, he was scared out of his wits, but at the same time, this was a chance to strike what could be a mortal blow to Nazi Germany. The destiny of the whole war could be in his hands. *Just think, pull this one off, and kids all over the world will forever read about me in history books in years to come.* He hadn't considered himself to be vain, but he had to admit that that kind of immortality definitely had an appeal.

Dragging himself back to the present, though, there was the small matter of the next few weeks to get through. He was confident that general fitness would not be too much of a problem for him. There was one thing to be said for the army; they worked you hard. All that time spent hanging around had to be filled with something, and physical exercise seemed to be the default answer. It stopped you from being bored, made you too tired to make mischief, and had the added benefit of keeping you as fit as a butcher's dog.

Weapons competencies should also be fairly straightforward, he mused. He had won various awards over the years for his sharpshooting abilities, which, as Blake himself had said, had played a significant part in his being selected for this mission. There may be one or two new weapons or combat techniques to get used to, but that didn't concern him unduly. He was also pretty handy with weapons maintenance; one of the things they constantly drilled you on in the commandos was the ability to strip and reassemble all types of guns, your own and the enemy's, in all conditions—night, day, rain, snow, you name it. He could do that sort of thing in his sleep.

Beyond that, though, he was in the dark. He had no idea of what lay ahead of him, just that it wouldn't be easy. Even though he knew that this was a priority mission for the top brass, going as high as Churchill, Blake had said, he still had to prove that their faith in him was not misplaced. He may have passed the initial selection interview, but they could still bin him if they thought he was not physically capable of doing the job. He resolved, therefore, to throw himself 100 per cent into the task, to not allow failure to be even the remotest possibility. *Might as well do the damned thing properly,* he thought to himself.

Looking out the window at the rolling green fields of the English countryside, he could see his reflection staring back at him. It was the face of a man with a purpose, something he hadn't felt for a long time. The jaw was set, the eyes focussed, and the brow furrowed. He broke into a smile. *Lighten up,* he told himself. *You'll scare the other passengers!*

A sudden jolt woke him up with a start as his head banged against the glass of the window. His tongue felt furry, and his mouth was dry, a sure sign that he had been sleeping with his mouth open, always an attractive sight. Luckily this second train from Glasgow had been much less busy, and his particular compartment had been empty right from the start, so no one had been witness to his undignified appearance. Outside, everything was dark apart from a couple of dim light bulbs hanging from fittings under the roof of what Peter could now see was a station building. He rubbed the sleep from his eyes and tried to focus on the board which announced the name of the station. By the dim light of the bulbs, he could just make out the name of the station; it looked like his destination from what he could see. Sure enough, moments later a voice from the platform called out to confirm that this was Arisaig and the final stop for this train.

Peter stood, stretching out his arms and legs as far as he could. He was always surprised at just how tiring it was to sit without moving for so long. He grabbed his bag from the rack, replacing the half-read novel as he did so, and made his way to the door of the compartment. Only now had it occurred to him that he was surprised that someone was working at the station at this time of night. Clearly they were used to receiving travellers at all hours, a necessary evil of having the training centre as a neighbour, he supposed.

Making his way through the ticket office, Peter hoped and prayed that the promised car would be there to meet him. He didn't fancy spending the night on the cold stone floor. He needn't have worried, though; the organisational skills of the SOE were living up to their reputation, as there was a dark sedan waiting for him, lights on and engine running. Seeing him approach, the uniformed driver stepped out of the vehicle, opened the rear door and reached out for his bag at the same time, which was swiftly stowed in the boot.

"Good evening, sir," the driver saluted. "Corporal Winters here to take you up to the Big House. It's an hour's drive, give or take, so my advice to you is to get some shut-eye. You'll be needing it over the next few weeks, that's for sure."

Muttering his thanks in return, Peter could see no good reason to argue and promptly curled up against the rear door and slipped back off to continue his interrupted slumber.

EIGHT

"The first thing you need to do, gentlemen, is to forget everything you have ever learnt in the past about soldiering. We are going rip that shit up and start all over again from the beginning. The second thing to forget is any ranks or lofty titles you may or may not have had before you got here to Arisaig. You're in the middle of nowhere, a large number of miles from civilisation as you know it, so there's no one to complain to even if you wanted to. All you have is me, and you should know that this is one of the few places in Britain where a lowly sergeant major like me gets to push a bunch of fancy toffs like you lot around without fear of reprisal. And believe me, I enjoy my work. Your best bet is to keep your gob shut, do exactly as I say, and get stuck into the training. If you remember these golden rules, we should all get along just fine, and the time will pass much more quickly and pleasantly for us all."

Peter shivered, more from the cold than any sense of apprehension. It was six o'clock, and they were formed up on the lawn in front of what was apparently known as the Big House. The grass was soaking wet with the early morning dew, and the sun was just struggling to rise above the line of imposingly dark hills to the east. Despite the cold, they were all wearing only standard-issue army boots, combat trousers, and white vests; typical PT gear, had been Peter's first thought as he had dressed fifteen minutes earlier. The realisation of what was no doubt awaiting them in the day ahead had dawned on him pretty quickly.

The man doing the talking, well, shouting really, was a pretty fearsome-looking Scot, standing with his hands on his hips, chest out, and chin up, typical regimental sergeant major fashion. Men with a lot of power, whom it was not wise to cross, in Peter's experience, whatever your rank. His Scottishness was reinforced by the fact that he was wearing a kilt, which flapped at his knees in the breeze. Below that he had a pair of well-worn army boots with thick woollen socks, while on his top half he wore a thick Arran jumper. He was clean-shaven apart from a pencil-thin moustache, and his close-cropped hair was mostly hidden under a huge Tam O'Shanter. If anything it was a fairly comical appearance, though Peter knew better than to betray any sign of amusement.

"One fact that you should get into your heads as quickly as possible is that there is no way on God's earth that all of you will complete this course successfully. You might have thought that the life of a secret agent would be pretty cushy, all cloak-and-dagger stuff while staying in nice apartments, but that's not how we look at it here. You're here to get fit, and fit like you've never been before. When we've finished with you, you'll have a better-than-average chance of being able to represent Britain at the Olympics in any sport of your choosing.

"The way to look at this training programme is to imagine a set of sieves, each with progressively smaller holes. At each stage, a number of you will fall through these holes and out of the course, until the wheat is well and truly separated from the chaff. That way we are left with the best and fittest of you. I cannot say how many that will be; it varies from course to course. But from experience, you should know that it is rare that more than half make it to the end." He paused to let those words sink in.

"OK, that's enough of me talking. If there are no questions…"—it was more of a statement than an invitation—"then we will begin with a gentle five-mile run before breakfast. To ease you into things gradually, I am prepared to go easy today and say that there will be no time limit for this run. Rest assured, though, that one will be imposed before too long. Anyone failing to complete the course in the requisite time will be binned, simple as that. Today, your only problem is cold bacon and eggs if you're too slow."

For Peter, the prospect of a five-mile run was not too daunting. He was confident that he would be able to manage the pace, and so it proved. He tucked himself in nicely mid-pack: firstly because he didn't want to expend too much energy too early in the day, as he had no idea what was coming after breakfast, and secondly because experience had always taught him to remain as inconspicuous as possible in situations such as these. It rarely paid to attract too much attention by standing out from the crowd; you always risked being picked on to volunteer for all sorts of extra activities. Instead, he stayed where he was and used the time to check out his new colleagues around him.

Including him, there were a round dozen of them on the run, not counting the instructor, Sergeant Major Campbell. All twelve were men, seemingly in their twenties and thirties like him, and all seemed to be coping relatively well with the early morning exertions. As was always the case, though, there were a couple of extra-keen types out at the front, clearly trying to impress the sergeant major.

"Good morning!" The runner immediately to his left cut into his reverie.

"Huh," Peter grunted in reply.

"My name is Jan Kubcek. Yesterday, I was a lieutenant in the Czech army, but today, according to Mr Campbell, I guess it's plain old Jan again."

"Peter Bogarde, a lieutenant in the British army up until yesterday." Peter entered into the spirit. "And before that, a Dutch citizen. Nice to know I am not the only foreigner in these parts."

"I would be surprised if you were, my friend," said Jan. "The British are forever recruiting us Johnny Foreigners to get involved in their covert operations. I think it's because we have at least half a chance of blending in properly on the mainland. Their stiff upper lips stand out a mile at German checkpoints, and they will insist on always asking for a cup of tea when they go into cafés. And have you heard their accents when they try to talk German? Absolutely shocking!"

Peter chuckled at this and nodded his agreement. He considered a further reply but decided against it for now. Rather than risk censure from Campbell, they lapsed into companionable silence for the rest of the run.

On their return to the training camp, they were packed off to the shower block to get cleaned up before a breakfast of bacon, eggs, mushrooms, and tomatoes, rounded off by toast and coffee. Peter was pleased to note that the food was well cooked and in plentiful supply, though this was probably indicative of the fact that they needed to provide the recruits with plenty of energy to meet the physical demands ahead. Jan had brought his tray to come and sit down next to Peter at one of the long benches in the canteen. Normally, Peter was pretty wary of forming relationships in situations like this. He had learnt the hard way over the years that it helped if things were not too personal when the shit hit the fan. It was a little easier to deal with comrades getting blown to pieces if they weren't your best mates as well. Despite his misgivings, however, he had felt an immediate connection with this guy; he seemed pretty relaxed and easy-going, and they clearly had a similar sense of humour. He also seemed to be physically and mentally fit and suited for the challenges ahead. It was only a training course, after all, and maybe it could be useful to have an ally to help each other get through the coming days.

Over breakfast, it transpired that they had quite a bit in common. Like him, Jan had got out of his country as soon as the Germans came rolling in, though this had been before the actual start of the war, back in '38. There had been a whole bunch of them at the start, and they had slowly been dispersed to various military organisations. Jan had been involved in SOE operations for a couple of years, and so this course was something of a refresher for him, keeping up with the latest best practices for killing people, as he put it. He also had numerous stories to share of his exploits and those of his colleagues. Most interestingly of all, some of his former friends had been involved in the assassination of Reinhard Heydrich in Prague back in '42. Whilst being immensely interesting on the one hand, this also had a sobering effect on Peter in that none of that party had come back from the mission.

"I was actually pencilled in for that one," Jan mused over dinner that evening. "We were just two weeks from the 'go' when I bust my ankle in a training jump. I couldn't believe it! I was devastated not to be going with the rest of the guys. I had prepared for months, down to the last detail, and so it was a complete let-down to have to stay behind."

"So what happened? The mission still went ahead, though."

"Yeah, they had to rush in a replacement at the last minute, and the guy they got was the one that got caught after the attack and cracked under interrogation. Can't really blame him, though, as they do use some pretty horrific techniques to break you. On top of this, the poor guy had not had the time to get the full benefit of the counter-interrogation training to help him endure. I mean, no one can hold out indefinitely, but there are little things you can do to buy time, possibly enough time for your mates to realise you have been caught and get the hell out. Even so, the fact is that I'm still alive and the rest of the guys are all dead because my replacement lost his bottle. Maybe they would never have made it out alive, who knows? But it definitely can't have helped, and I have had to carry that one with me ever since."

———

The four weeks spent at Arisaig soon fell into a pretty standard routine of physical exercise mixed with theoretical and practical lessons about different espionage techniques. A number of these exercises related to various sabotage skills, from how to disable factory machinery to blowing up trains. The latter exercise particularly appealed to Peter, as it brought back memories of his time in Poland. In this case, however, it was a lot more civilised and a lot less dangerous. He had also heard that the local train drivers were in on the whole thing and seemed to enjoy their part in the whole charade as well. Part of the benefit of being a long way from the front line, Peter reflected.

On the day of the train-sabotaging exercise, they were sent off in groups of two at dawn. Their objective was to evade detection for twenty-four hours, during which time they were required to move up to the railway line at the designated point some twelve miles away from their original start point. This in itself wasn't too hard, as their "pursuers" and the "sentries" were recruited from the ranks of the local defence volunteers, who were mostly veterans from the Great War. Once in position, they had to place the charges in such a way as to be concealed from the driver's sight. Finally, they had to use the time pencil detonators correctly to ensure that the charge would have, if it had been live, exploded in line with the scheduled arrival of the train. The train drivers were informed that "attempts" were being made to blow up their train at specific locations along their route and were asked to indicate as they passed whether they could spot the agents or the charge. Peter found it quite surreal to see the driver giving the thumbs up to confirm that he had failed to spot them or the charges at all and that therefore he and his train, and everything on it, had successfully been blown sky-high.

Jan and Peter found that they were regularly paired to work together on operations such as these, and over the weeks, they had formed a highly effective and efficient partnership which had not gone unnoticed by the training staff. They had both demonstrated a commendable aptitude for the work and had been quick to learn and apply the new techniques with aplomb. In addition, they had conducted themselves with professionalism, dedication, and quiet efficiency throughout the course, enabling them to stay out of trouble. Never once had they given Sergeant Major Campbell or any of his cronies reason to bawl them out, or suffered any loss of privileges or rations. Not many, if any, of the other recruits could claim the same.

At the end of the four weeks, the remaining trainees were summoned, after dinner on the final evening, to the main lecture hall in the Big House. Sergeant Major Campbell was waiting for them on the raised platform at the end of the room, wearing his standard uniform of kilt, boots, jumper, and khaki Tam O'Shanter. He waited for a few moments, hands on hips, as they filed in and settled down in the front two rows of seats. There were only eight of them left at the end of the course: two had sustained injuries that brought about an early departure (a broken ankle and fractured skull, if Peter recalled), while the other two had euphemistically been invited to withdraw; in other words, they weren't good enough and were to be returned to unit. Peter had heard from Jan that all four were currently resident in what was known as The Cooler. This was another big estate house in the wilds of Scotland where the inmates, mainly failed special ops trainees, were quarantined for six months before being released back whence they had come. Security for SOE activities was paramount, and thus it was essential that dropouts were kept out of the way until such time as any knowledge they had acquired could no longer pose a risk to live operations. Keeping them in The Cooler, in the absolute middle of nowhere, was an incredibly effective method by which to achieve such an aim.

"Right, gentlemen," Campbell began, bringing Peter's mind back to the here and now. "You've all done pretty well to get this far. If I am honest, I am surprised that so many of you are still with us; four withdrawals out of twelve is unusual to say the least. I also can't say that I agreed with each and every one of you being kept on, but the powers that be have clearly gone soft and allowed some of you a second chance."

Peter tried to see where Campbell's gaze was falling as he said this. He couldn't really tell for sure, but all he could say was that neither he nor Jan seemed to be the focus for these comments.

Campbell continued, "But, you should know this. These four weeks up here in sunny Scotland have been the easy bit, so don't go thinking you've made it and can now rest on your laurels. Tomorrow you will be back on the train south; your destination is Beaulieu House, near London. There you will be instructed in some of the finer arts of the world of the secret agent: what some of us like to call the art of ungentlemanly warfare, or dirty tricks for short. Goodbye, gentlemen, and good luck to you all. You'll need it."

NINE

The journey to Beaulieu House was both long and uneventful. Peter hadn't thought it possible to be this bored. He had long finished his book, and Arisaig had not been the kind of place where you would find a bookshop round every corner, so he'd had no chance to replace it. The only upside was that Jan and the rest of the successful recruits were on the same train. That said, none of them seemed to be a great conversationalist, perhaps because of the line of business they were in. So when he wasn't chatting to Jan about homes and childhood, Peter spent most of his time either sleeping or staring vacantly out of the window at the countryside rolling by.

The last few weeks had been a welcome distraction, but now he had time on his hands to think, he realised that his apprehension about his immediate future was steadily increasing. When he actually stopped to think about it rationally, the enormity of the task seemed overwhelming; the pressure sometimes made his head physically throb. He also found he was often suffering from inexplicable aches in the small of his back and down his thighs. Today was one such day, and the problem was only exacerbated by the cramped conditions in their compartment, occupied as it was by six fully grown men and their kitbags. A number of times, Peter had to clamber across outstretched limbs, offering apologies for squashed toes and bruised shins as he went, in order to reach the corridor outside that ran the length of the carriage. Here at least he could stretch his legs and back to gain some relief. Peter guessed it was caused by the stress getting to him, rather than any actual bodily ailment. In the past he had always felt much better when actually out in the field, and he hoped that the same would prove to be the case on this occasion. In the meantime, he would just have to put up with it. Though a little fear was always good to keep you on your toes, he didn't necessarily think that he was overly scared by the thought of the mission. He had not even begun to consider pulling out as an option. That said, he was pretty realistic as to his chances of coming out the other side in one piece. Getting into Germany would be one thing, but assassinating Hitler and then getting out alive would be a whole different ball game.

His thoughts were interrupted as Jan joined him in the corridor, catching him mid-stretch. "You OK, Peter?"

"Eh? Oh, yes, just a bit cramped in there with you lot, not to mention the stink, you big, sweaty arseholes! I just needed some fresh air and some room to stretch my legs."

Jan laughed, "Perhaps the boiled eggs for breakfast were not such a good idea."

"You could at least let me open a window in there."

They fell into a comfortable silence for a few minutes, both watching the countryside sliding past the window. Jan broke the silence. "So, what do they have in store for you, Peter?"

Peter opened his mouth to reply but caught himself just in time, wary that this might be a test. "I'm sorry, Jan, you know how it is." Nonetheless, Peter felt bad that he could not confide in someone; he had been desperate to shout about it since the day he signed up. To relieve the awkwardness he felt, he attempted to make light of it. "I could tell you, but I would, of course, then have to kill you, my friend."

Jan chuckled and nodded. "I understand, Peter. It was wrong of me to ask anyway. Perhaps our paths will cross in the field one day once we have finished our training."

——

After a change of train in London and another journey in a battered, bone-shaking army truck, they finally arrived at their destination. It was another of Britain's grand stately homes set in vast acres of grounds that had been given over, as many estates had at that time, for military use for the duration of the war. The expansive grounds, surrounded by their high walls and impenetrable hedges, provided suitable space and anonymity for their clandestine activities.

The course briefing that they attended on that first evening introduced them to their new instructors and what they would be covering during their time there. Judging from the items listed, it seemed to be, Peter thought to himself, a finishing school for trained killers. This was apparently where they would be learning the real meaty stuff about staying alive behind enemy lines, together with the relevant skills and techniques they would need to carry out their objectives. By the look of their instructors, they would be in good hands. These guys had clearly been around the block more than once in their time and knew what they were doing and how to handle themselves. A number of them had scars, and quite a few walked with a limp. One even was missing an arm. These were guys who could no longer fight on the front line but still had plenty to offer to help those that were going in next.

From the introductions provided, they would be under the supervision of two main instructors: One of them was a highly decorated former member of the Hong Kong Police Force, an expert in weapons of all descriptions but most especially the knife and its use in unarmed combat situations. The other had been a special agent for many years and knew everything there was to know about field-craft.

The next day, they presented themselves at 07.00 hours as instructed, at one of the many outbuildings on the estate, one which had been converted into a gymnasium. Various pieces of apparatus had been installed around the edges, leaving a sizeable space in the middle which had been covered in mats, no doubt to help break the inevitable falls. Waiting for them, arms akimbo, and dressed in black jogging pants, white vest, and white training shoes, was the ex-policeman, Sergeant Faircross. His outfit did little to hide the fact that he was obviously very fit despite clearly being the wrong side of forty. He was barrel-chested and had upper arms the size of small tree trunks. Around his waist was a belt. Hanging from the belt was a sheath containing a knife, the length of which astonished Peter. As they shuffled forward to the front of the gym, no one really wanting to be at the front, Faircross removed the knife from its sheath and began throwing it up in the air, catching it by the handle on each descent. This was despite the fact that firstly, it was turning end over end in the air, and secondly, he was keeping his eyes on them as they approached. There was no doubt that this man was extremely proficient with this weapon, which looked even more deadly now it was uncovered. Not only was it long but one side had a razor-sharp blade whilst the other had a series of evil-looking jagged teeth all the way along its edge.

"Today," Faircross began as they finally settled into position, "you will be getting to grips with this little baby. This knife was standard issue to all Hong-Kong policemen in the days before the Japs took the place. Nowadays it is issued to all SOE agents operating in enemy-held territory. Let me tell you this right from the start, gentlemen: She will be your best friend; the only thing on which you will be able to rely. You treat her right, and she will see you right every time. Where you lot might end up, you don't ever want to be more than two feet away from her, as when you're caught in a fix, she will be the only one you can turn to, the only one that might get you out alive.

"What we will be covering today is both offensive and defensive manoeuvres with the knife, in other words, how to kill someone as efficiently as possible and how to defend yourself against someone who's trying to kill you with a knife or bayonet. So without further ado, I need a volunteer," he said whilst pointing at Peter. Peter's heart sank, but he stepped forward as directed.

"Good lad! I do like a willing volunteer. Now then"—he turned to face the rest of the group—"when the need to kill someone arises in your line of work, the most important consideration is what…? No? Well, it is, of course, whether you need to do it quietly or not. More often than not, silence will be a key requirement. You can't go shooting your pistols off; that's the last thing you want to do in the middle of a built-up area, populated by Jerry, all of whom are out to get you. But neither can you simply stick a knife in a man's guts willy-nilly. Sure, he will go down and be out of the game in terms of being a physical threat, but he's going to scream the place down until you finish him off, by which time it will be too late! If you're going to use the knife, you need to do it in such a way as they won't make a sound as they leave this earth.

"Using a knife also brings you up close and personal to your target. Shooting someone from a distance is a piece of cake compared to using a knife. All you have to do is pull the trigger and watch them drop. With a knife, he, or even sometimes she, may be the enemy, but they are still another human being. You will be that close to them that you can smell them, feel their breath on you, listen to them whimpering for their mothers as life slowly ebbs from them. To do this job effectively, you must get over any squeamishness you may have. You cannot afford the time to think about it, as that split-second hesitation will be enough time for them to either raise the alarm or to stick you first.

"Right." Faircross positioned himself behind Peter as he spoke. "It's not always possible, of course, but ideally you want to be approaching your target from behind. In this situation, stealth is key, so watch for twigs if you are outside, or creaking floorboards. Your two best options to get the job done quick are to either slip the knife between the ribs and up into the heart, or to slit the throat. Both have their pros and cons: getting the knife between the ribs to reach the heart can be difficult, especially if the clothing is thick, while the throat option makes a whole load of mess, though if done right, it does take out the voice box immediately, stopping any noise. To be honest, you'll have to decide at the time which is the best approach in the circumstances. In both cases, though, I'd strongly recommend that you clamp your free hand hard over the mouth to avoid any sound that might otherwise escape."

On the *p* of "escape," Faircross grabbed Peter's mouth with his left hand, jerking his head back hard, leaving his neck exposed for the knife, which had suddenly appeared there in Faircross's right hand. For a man of his build, the whole move was surprisingly fast. Peter was taken completely by surprise, which was intensely annoying, as he had correctly guessed that Faircross would spring a move on him while everyone was concentrating on what he was saying. In view of that suspicion, Peter had been tensed, ready, and wholly focussed on the instructor, attempting to judge exactly when the move would come. Despite that, he had been completely fooled; no sooner had Faircross grabbed him than he released Peter, who fell in a heap on the mat, choking, and rubbing the back of his neck.

"OK, lad. Up you get and fall back in. Right, any questions? Anyone want to see that again? No? In which case, I want you to pair off and practise the move until you are proficient."

Interspersed with the hand-to-hand and unarmed combat training, they also spent a lot of time on weapons training, under the guidance of the second trainer, whose name was Giles French. Peter was especially keen to learn everything Giles had to tell them, as he had been there and done it before on many missions as an agent in occupied Europe. This guy could give him a lot of information that should go a long way to keeping Peter alive.

The first few days were spent in familiarisation, getting used to the different weapons that they might have to use in the field. This wasn't just limited to the Allied arsenal but also included standard German army weapons as well, on the basis that these would be more readily available behind enemy lines. Your life might therefore depend on knowing how to take the safety catch off a Mauser rifle or how to reload a Luger pistol at the drop of a hat.

They began, though, with the standard-issue items that agents usually took with them, namely the Browning pistol and the Sten sub-machine gun. The Sten, they were told, had a number of key advantages: it was accurate over short distances, could be broken down easily for concealment, was not prone to blockages, and used the same calibre ammunition as the German machine pistol, the Schmeisser.

"Gentlemen, there are two key things to remember when using the Sten gun," French told them as they grouped around him at the firing range. "Firstly, never hold the weapon by the magazine on the side here. It might look good on the recruiting posters or in the newsreels, but it's the one sure-fire way to get a blockage, as the magazine will work loose from its fitting. And I'm sure I have no need to tell you that the seconds it takes you to work the blockage free will be enough to see you six feet under.

"Secondly, it is never a good idea to load all thirty-two bullets into the magazine, despite this being the standard capacity. Again, there is a fair chance that a blockage will occur, as the cartridges are a little too tightly packed. Believe me, it's far better to load thirty and leave a little room for movement."

Both these messages were rammed home throughout the rest of the course by on-the-spot fines of fifty press-ups being dished out to anyone found holding the magazine or experiencing a blockage.

After they had mastered the Sten, including how to disassemble and reassemble it in under a minute, in the dark, they moved on to the Browning pistol.

"The Browning is even more important than the Sten and is second only to your knife." French grinned. "It's actually more important, but Sergeant Faircross gets upset when I say that. Nonetheless, you will rely on this weapon as you would on your wife, girlfriend, or best friend. You will keep it close to you at all times, day or night, awake or asleep. It will get you out of any number of holes and never let you down. It's small enough to be concealed easily about your person and takes a magazine of fifteen bullets, so you are not short of firepower. At close ranges it will stop all but the most determined of opponents.

"As you might expect, there is an art to using it effectively. Time allowing, of course, you should adopt the classic stance as follows." French proceeded to assume the position while describing it to the agents. "Legs about shoulder-width apart, weight evenly distributed on the middle of your feet, right hand firmly clasping the pistol grip, left hand wrapped around underneath the right to form a sort of cradle, and arms extended in front of you. This will give you the most balanced position and steadiest aim.

"The best way to kill someone, however, and make no mistake, that has to be your intention if the enemy is close enough to you to warrant using this baby, is not just to fire blindly and hope for the best. Rather, aim for the essential organs, head or heart in the main, and squeeze off two rounds in quick succession. We call this the double tap; it is best because it gives you two chances of killing someone and allowing you to get away. Aim is important if there is time: There's no point hitting them in the arm because they can still chase you, or in the stomach, as they will scream like a baby for a long time. Two shots in the head or heart is the only sure way to do the job."

They spent the rest of the morning practising with the pistol. Standard range practice was all well and good for honing accuracy levels, but to excel at the double tap, they needed to be able to execute the movement as quickly as possible. This meant bringing the gun up from a relaxed position to aim and releasing two bullets, all in one fluid movement. There was, of course, never going to be a substitute for the real thing, but this was as close as you could get. By the end of the sessions, Peter felt he was as good as he would ever be. To him, more important than the speed and accuracy was the ability to stay calm in a real-life situation. In all likelihood, both parties would be sick with fear; the one who controlled it best and reacted quickest would live. Here, he was sure that his combat experience would come to his rescue. So far, he had never been one to panic in life-and-death situations, and he hoped that being on his own behind enemy lines, with no one to support him, would be no different.

That evening, there was a change to the normal routine for Peter as he was summoned to meet Colonel Blake in one of the offices in the main house. Peter couldn't help but feel honoured that the colonel had travelled down from London especially to check on his progress.

"Come in, come in, Peter, my lad," boomed Blake almost before he had knocked on the door. "Sit down, sit down. There's no need to stand to attention; you're not on the parade ground now, Peter," Blake laughed. "Right, I've been keeping an eye on how things have been going, both down here and up at Arisaig. I am pleased to say I have been hearing good things about you. Seems to me like we've picked the right bod for the job, wouldn't you say?"

"Thank you, sir." Peter couldn't stop himself from grinning at the praise received. "I like to think I have been doing my best."

"Yes, yes, absolutely. Now, the reason for me coming down, apart from the pat on the back, of course, is that I want to be completely sure that you are still one hundred per cent committed to this mission. Things are moving on in the planning stages such that we are getting close to the point of no return. So if you have any thoughts about pulling out, I need to know now, while we still have time to look for a replacement."

Peter took a second to answer, just long enough for the image of his parents and sister to flash through his mind. "No, I'm still on the team, Colonel."

Blake nodded, approvingly. "Good. I don't mind telling you that, ideally, we would like to have a good couple of years to train an agent to the top of their profession. In this game, though, we are lucky to get three or four months, to be honest. With you, however, we are not even getting as much at that! That said, we know you're an exceptionally competent soldier and an expert marksman, which does save us a fair bit of time and allows us to concentrate on the more subtle elements of how to survive behind enemy lines, what we call field-craft. I understand that you will be moving on to this area in the next day or two, so I won't spoil the surprise, eh?"

"Sir? Do you mind if I ask a question?"

Blake nodded his assent.

"Just so I'm clear, what do you think my chances are of making it out the other side in one piece?"

"Ah, been on your mind, that one, has it? Well, I'm not going to lie to you, Peter. I know you wouldn't want me to. If you were being dropped into France, then I'd say you had a one-in-four chance of being killed. France is comparatively easy, you see, as we have a decent-sized network of agents over there; on top of which, in an emergency, you can usually find a friendly native to help.

Germany, however, is a whole different ball game. We have far fewer agents, and the locals tend to be less friendly, or if they are sympathetic to our cause, they are too scared to risk helping. No, if I am honest, it's probably quite a bit less than a one-in-four chance of surviving."

"That's roughly in line with what I was thinking."

"Right, well, if that's it, Lieutenant"—Blake was looking everywhere but at Peter, clearly feeling a little awkward at Peter's direct style—"I'll be on my way. Keep up the good work, lad, and I'll be back in touch in a couple of weeks, at the end of your training."

TEN

Colonel Blake strode purposefully through the door into the wood-panelled meeting room on the top floor of SOE's Baker Street Headquarters. He was slightly out of breath and red-faced, as he was running a bit late, on top of which he had been forced to climb the four flights of stairs. People always seemed to be doing essential maintenance to the lifts in this building.

"Good morning, gentlemen, and indeed lady," he added, smiling, as he noticed the uniformed woman in the corner of the room, equipped with pad and pencil, ready to minute the key decisions arising from the meeting. "I hope you'll excuse my slight tardiness; I was already running late from my previous meeting and had bargained without having to negotiate the stairs. As we have an extremely full agenda, may I suggest we crack on, if that suits everyone?"

To the murmurs of assent and nodding of heads, Blake took the time to survey the room. Aside from the scribe in the corner, there were, as he had expected, four other people present. Immediately to his left was Major Harry Courtney. Harry reported directly to Blake and was the executive planning officer attached to the Austria/Germany country section of SOE. Harry was responsible for the vast majority of the work which had brought them to where they were today; he would play a key part in the meeting by bringing everyone up to speed. He was a dependable, methodical type, typical of officers poached from the army. You could tell him where he needed to get to and when, and then all you had to do was point him in the right direction, and you could rest assured that he would arrive bang on time with the minimum of fuss. This was in no way a criticism, though: as Blake always told him, he actually wished there were many more like him that could be relied on implicitly to get a job done on time.

Next to Harry was Air Vice-Marshal Alan Taylor, SOE's RAF liaison officer. Any operation that would require RAF assistance had to secure their sanction, and it was pretty much a dead certainty that this mission would involve agents being dropped behind enemy lines by air. Taylor was short and slim with slicked-back brown hair complemented by a moustache, which Blake had never seen in anything other than an exceptionally well-groomed state. *He must trim it on a daily basis,* Blake surmised. His piercing blue eyes and pinched nose added to what Blake felt was his overtly weasel-like appearance. Perhaps a little unfair but he did have the reputation of getting people's backs up through an insistence on being niggardly with his resources and with pointing out flaws in other people's ideas.

Next, and opposite Blake, on the other side of the table, was Colonel Brian Stubbs, head of SOE and ultimately Blake's boss. An operation of this profile could not be run independently out of SOE's Germany section, so Stubbs was keeping a close eye on matters. Stubbs was old-school. Born at the end of the last century, he was a career soldier, following in the footsteps of many generations of his family. He had been awarded the Military Cross for his service as an artillery officer in the First World War and had been at the War Office in the twenties and thirties. A small, wiry Scots Highlander, he was tenacious, determined, and exceptionally inspiring as a leader. Under his guidance and influence, SOE had come on leaps and bounds from its early struggles for recognition and acceptance.

Finally, and to Blake's immediate right, was Brigadier William Harris. The brigadier represented the Chiefs of Staff's office and was thus the direct conduit to the very highest echelons of the War Ministry, even to Churchill himself. In effect, he would have the casting vote on the mission as a whole and on any significant issues that needed to be decided. Harris was another career soldier who had joined up as a young man and then served with distinction in the First

World War. That's as far as the stereotype went, though, as he was tall and thin, much as a long-distance runner might look, in fact. Not for Harris was the life of dinner at the club followed by port and cigars. From his previous dealings with Harris, Blake knew that he did not necessarily say a great deal, but when he did speak, it was as well to shut up and listen. This was for two reasons: firstly, he was very softly spoken, so you had to be on your toes to catch what he said; and secondly, when he did speak, he did so with such calm authority that it brooked no argument. Having completed his survey, Blake realised that everyone was looking in his direction, waiting for him to begin.

"Right, as you know, the purpose of this meeting is to bring everyone up to date with progress on our planned mission to assassinate Hitler. As you can see from the agenda in front of you"—Blake picked up the typewritten sheet in front of him—"the items we need to cover off include: number one, the options that we have considered in terms of determining the most effective way to achieve the objective; number two, our recommended solution; number three, the current status regarding that solution; and number four, the next steps we now need to undertake to make this plan become a reality. There will also be an opportunity at the end to raise any other items of business that have not already been covered by that point in the proceedings.

"So, if there are no questions, I will hand you over to Major Courtney, here, to run you through the options and their respective pros and cons."

"There is just one question," this from Taylor, the RAF man. "I would like it to be formally minuted for the record that I am in no way convinced that we should even be considering this mission as a viable plan in the first place. After all, as far as I can see, killing Herr Hitler is by no means guaranteed to achieve the objective of ending the war immediately. Any number of scenarios could then ensue. For example, we may just succeed in transferring command of the armed forces to one of the Wehrmacht generals. It is eminently feasible that they could prove to be a far more skilled military leader than the present incumbent. As we have seen on the Eastern Front in the last couple of years, many of Hitler's decisions have been, at best, questionable and, at worst, have led to significant reverses. On top of this, we may inadvertently provide Dr Goebbels with the perfect opportunity to rally what may be a wavering populace behind the Nazi regime by transforming Hitler into some sort of glorious martyr for the German people. Things are not going well for the Germans, and this might have a transformational effect on their psyche, much like our own King Arthur, who's supposed to be asleep under a mountain somewhere, ready to rise up and defend the nation in her time of need. Though, to be honest, I have my doubts about the truth of such matters, as we certainly could have done with him back in '40, and he was nowhere to be seen."

"Very fair points, Alan, I grant you," said Blake. "I had anticipated this sort of debate and had hoped to cover it off under Any Other Business at the end. However, I am more than happy to take the discussion at this juncture.

"I think it only fair to say that your points regarding possible successors to Hitler have been acknowledged already at the highest level. It is a very real risk and one that cannot effectively be mitigated. Whilst your scenario is undoubtedly a possibility, it is, in the opinion of the War Ministry, just as, if not more, likely that a more moderate figurehead comes to the fore. Perhaps, as you say, one of the senior Wehrmacht generals takes the lead and decides to negotiate a truce. They are getting pushed back every day in the East, and, surely, any moderately intelligent German general can, with a bit of rational objectiveness, see which way the tide is flowing. There is a very good chance, therefore, that they would have to come to the conclusion that calling a halt to proceedings is the best bet.

"Overall, I think the key factor here is that if there is any chance that removing Hitler from the scene could end the war early and thus save the lives of many Allied soldiers, not to mention civilians, then that is a chance we must seize with both hands. I think you would have to agree that we would be remiss if we failed to take this opportunity, and I have no doubt that history would judge us accordingly. Furthermore, the longer the war goes on and the more losses we suffer in the process, the more difficult it will be to keep public opinion onside. We cannot risk losing the hearts and minds of the public."

"That's all well and good," Air Vice-Marshal Taylor retorted, his cheeks reddening as he fought to contain his temper. "But what we are talking about here is nothing short of state-sanctioned murder! I was under the impression that His Majesty's Government was above that sort of thing!"

Silence filled the room.

"In addition," Marshall continued after a pause, "have you considered the consequences here? Do you not recall the aftermath of the Heydrich assassination in '42? The Germans executed hundreds of innocent civilians and totally erased two whole villages in Czechoslovakia from the map! Who's to say that they wouldn't do the same again, only on a ten times greater scale?" His voice might have calmed somewhat, but none of the gravity of his words had diminished.

"I fully appreciate that few of us could have envisaged the necessity to descend to such depths at the outset of this war." Blake was doing his best to be conciliatory, but he was finding this fastidious fly-boy frustrating in the extreme. It was true what they said about the air force, he thought, no real stomach for a dirty fight. Must be something to do with doing their killing from a distance rather than face to face.

"However, in the last four or five years, we have seen that there are no lengths to which the Nazis won't go to win this war. If we are serious about winning this war, we have to be prepared to go to the same unpalatable places and further, and, what's more, before the Nazis get there first."

Taylor still wasn't prepared to let it go. "Even if we did believe the cold-blooded assassination of a foreign head of state to be justified, would you not accept that there is an argument in favour of leaving Hitler in place?"

"Go on." Blake thought he knew where this was heading but needed time to collect his thoughts and marshal a response.

"Well, have we not noted that, as time progresses, Hitler seems to be making more and more rash decisions? I have seen reports in which people state that his errors in judgement are worth many divisions to us. He has, on countless occasions, illustrated his incompetence by issuing orders that border on the criminally insane. It strikes me that if we leave him in place long enough, he will end this war all by himself. There's no doubt in my mind that the man is losing the plot." With that, Taylor sat back, his arms folded, a satisfied, almost smug expression on his face, confident that the argument was won.

Before Blake could respond, however, Brigadier Harris cleared his throat, clearly about to enter the debate. Although Colonel Blake did not directly report to the brigadier, he appreciated that he was technically lower down the pecking order and was prepared, therefore, to defer to the more senior officer.

"I think Air Vice-Marshal Taylor has voiced a number of valid concerns which, on any other day, would merit more detailed analysis and debate."

Blake smiled to himself; it looked like Harris was going to save the day.

"Nevertheless, we have a clear steer right from the very top." As he spoke, Harris lifted his attaché case onto the table and began shuffling through the papers before selecting the required document.

"Two or three days ago," he continued, "and in preparation for this meeting, Colonel Stubbs here submitted a letter to the War Office, copied to the Prime Minister, in which he formally requested official sanction to approve the immediate assassination of Adolf Hitler, should a viable plan be proposed. The recommendation was based on the argument that the opportunity to considerably foreshorten the war outweighed any other risks, such as martyrdom or more-able generals taking over." This last was delivered somewhat pointedly towards Taylor. "This morning"—and at this point he flourished the selected document in front of him—"I have received this reply. Rather than read verbatim, I can summarise by saying that the Chiefs of Staff are unanimous that whilst his military blunders might be cause to stay our hand, in terms of the overall picture, however, the sooner he can be removed from the scene, the better. I will of course ensure copies are made available for later perusal," he said as he replaced the document in his case.

"I am sure you will agree therefore, gentlemen, that this gives us a clear mandate and, indeed, a duty to proceed. Whatever our objections, be they personal, moral, or military, this mission has a green light from the top table at this time. And until such time as anyone on high tells me otherwise, I suggest we all get down to business. So, if there are no further questions on this subject, I suggest we ask Colonel Blake to continue the meeting with the next item on the agenda, which, if I recall"—he made a show of pointing to it on the list—"is to do with the various options open to us to achieve our goal."

Blake avoided direct eye contact with the air vice-marshal but was keenly aware of the body language on display. The folded arms and crossed legs told Blake all he needed to know. Taylor would go along with the plans as ordered, but he didn't have to be cheerful about it, nor would his co-operation be easily forthcoming.

"Right, er...thank you for that very timely update, Brigadier. I suggest therefore that, as you say, we press on with the next item on the agenda. So at this point, I will hand the meeting over to my planning officer, Major Harry Courtney, to take us through the options and their relative advantages and disadvantages. Harry?"

"Thank you, Colonel." Courtney, as efficient as ever, leapt to his feet and began passing round the table folders marked "Top Secret," which contained the relevant briefing papers, filled with closely typed text, together with a few photographs and maps.

"Right, gentlemen. As you can imagine, a great deal of work has already taken place to get us to this point. We have been working closely with the Secret Intelligence Service to gather a mountain of information about our subject, much of which has been absolutely vital in driving our thinking about the most efficient way, or indeed ways, in which to tackle the problem. I think," he said, motioning towards the scribe, "it should be formally recorded in the minutes that we are indebted to SIS for their help in this matter."

"Quite so." Blake nodded.

"The purpose of this next half hour or so," Courtney continued, "is to brief you on the options we have already considered for the assassination of Herr Hitler and to secure your approval for our recommended approach. So, before I begin, may I check whether there are any questions at this point?

"OK, good. Our initial investigations focussed in the main on Hitler's personal train—or the Führerzug, to give it its proper name—our thinking being that this is one area where we could perhaps get close enough to take him out. You may recall, back in '41, a Polish partisan group supported by a few of our agents came very close to killing Hitler when they blew up a troop train. That troop train had overtaken another train at the last station before the bridge, a train which had been due to be the next train over the bridge and thus would have been destroyed. It turned out that, by pure chance, the stopped train did, in fact, have Hitler on board. This chance encounter encouraged us to think that a repeat of this or some other action targeted at the Führerzug would be worthy of further consideration.

"Since then we have gathered an abundance of data about the train from various prisoners of war in Allied hands. We know, for example, that it is made up of three sections: a front, middle, and rear nicknamed Asia, America, and Little Asia. Please don't ask me why; that we haven't managed to establish. We also know the occupancy of each carriage, including general staff members, personal accommodation, bodyguards, and other security personnel. We have detailed plans of the train's defences over and above the soldiers, namely anti-aircraft guns and surface artillery on top of the carriages. More interestingly, we know where the train resides when not in use. One such location is at Salzburg, near Hitler's main residence near Berchtesgaden. Here we have managed to find out that there is a cleaning detail comprising six French women. On top of that, we also know which cafés these ladies frequent when not on duty.

"As you can see, with this much quality data, we had good reason to think that some kind of attack on the train would afford us the best option for the mission. In looking at the train as a target, we considered three alternative methods of attack, each of which I will briefly take you through now.

"The first option that we looked into was using poison, the idea being to somehow introduce some kind of substance into the water-storage system on the train. When we investigated more closely, however, we found a number of problems which suggested that the idea should be dropped. For example, the poison agent selected becomes discernible when added to tea with milk. There is thus a very high chance of detection in these circumstances. Given that we do not know for sure whether Hitler prefers tea or coffee, the chances of success are just too slim. Coupled to that, we would have the headache of how we get the poison into the water. The train is well guarded at its base in Salzburg, and it would by no means be a certainty that we could convince one of the French cleaners to climb onto the roof to access the water inlet.

"Our second thought was that perhaps an agent could shoot Hitler as he boarded the train. We ruled out Salzburg in view of the extreme security arrangements and looked instead at the eighteenth-century palace at Schloss Klessheim, west of the city. Hitler has used this building as an HQ for some time and often boards the Führerzug at the nearby sidings. Closer inspection, however, has again thrown up a number of issues. There are two possible routes by which Hitler's car would approach the train: Turn to the left, and you run past a deciduous wood, which would offer suitable cover but only between spring and autumn. Turn right, and you end up over two hundred seventy metres from the wood, which makes a sniper shot extremely challenging. Given that we don't know for sure which way the car travels, let alone how on earth we would find out when he was going to be there, we have had to scratch this idea.

"The third option was to blow up the train whilst it travelled through a tunnel. Whilst tunnels and junctions, et cetera, had a lot of security earlier in the war, recent setbacks have put pressure on manpower to the extent that security is considerably more lax now. Such guards as there are tend to be pretty slack in their duties, being so far behind the front line. In addition, they are not the best available troops, mostly old men or regular troops that have been invalided out of the front line.

"A couple of agents disguised as railway police could perhaps enter a tunnel via the ventilation shaft, lay the charges, and detonate them as the train passed. Whilst still an option under consideration, there are a lot of imponderables, for example, whether we can ascertain the timetable for the Führerzug. As of this moment, this option seems likely to be scrapped, as it is too uncertain.

"In summary, therefore, whilst at first glance, the train seemed to be a good bet, we are now of the opinion that our best chance of success lies elsewhere."

"Yes, yes," Taylor interjected, clearly in no better temper than before, "it's all very interesting knowing what not to do, but it would be nice if you could get around to telling us what you do want to do!"

"Of course, sir. If you'll bear with me, I am just coming to that very point. As I said, once we had discounted the train option, we began to look elsewhere. Our efforts are now focussed on his HQ in southern Germany, known as the Berghof. High up in the Bavarian Alps, with outstanding views of the surrounding peaks, this is where Hitler feels most at home, most safe. You will probably recall seeing the location in any number of pre-war newsreels, as he often entertained foreign dignitaries there. Indeed, I believe that Chamberlain himself went there when he met Hitler back in '38.

"Security is still tight, of course, but it's a big site for them to cover in any great depth, and we feel there is a reasonable expectation of success here. Specifically, our plan is to infiltrate a sniper into southern Germany and for him to get close enough to take Hitler out at his private estate. On the face of it, this might seem quite a fanciful idea, but we think it has a number of factors in its favour.

"Firstly, Hitler spends a lot of his time here, and, as such, we have a reasonable chance of him being there for a period of time, much easier than trying to track the movements of the Führerzug. Working with a fixed location is one big plus for this plan, I'm sure you'll agree.

"Secondly, we again have plenty of intelligence from a handful of prisoners of war who have previously served a stint as guards at the Berghof. As such, we have been able to mock up a model of the site showing such detail as the location and function of the various key buildings, the siting of the security fences, positioning of sentries, patrol routes, et cetera, et cetera.

"Finally, and most importantly, we have a significant amount of information about Hitler's daily routine whilst in residence at the Berghof. We know when he gets up, what he eats for breakfast, lunch, and dinner, what his work schedule is, and when he goes to bed. Most crucially of all, gentlemen, we know that every morning at around ten a.m., except in the winter months, he takes a short fifteen-minute walk to take breakfast at the teahouse on the Mooslahner Kopf. We're told that this activity is as regular as clockwork. He gets up after nine, is shaved by his personal barber, and then sets off for the teahouse. With this level of regularity, we have a great opportunity to build a viable plan.

"He only ever misses the walk in exceptional circumstances. Nine times out of ten he is unaccompanied; I guess he likes his personal space as a break from being surrounded by flunkies the rest of the time. In fact, we are told that he will dismiss any guard who attempts to follow him. That said, he is never out of sight of an SS sentry or patrol, but they are not close enough to be able to intervene effectively.

"We therefore believe, and recommend, gentlemen, that we insert a sniper to infiltrate the area. The plan would be for them to get as near as they can to the perimeter fence so that they can take a shot from a close enough range to have an excellent chance of it proving fatal. Moreover, with no guards in the immediate vicinity, there is little likelihood of a guard being able to 'take the bullet,' as it were. With such a plan, we also think that there is a reasonable chance that our man will be able to make good his escape after; though if we are being realistic, we would have to acknowledge that the chances of an escape would, at best, be extremely slim. However, with the stakes as high as they are, we believe that this is a risk worth taking."

Blake could see that, while Major Courtney had been talking, the RAF man had been fidgeting more and more, clearly itching to speak but wrestling with himself also, as if keen not to earn a further rebuke for pouring cold water on the plans. But sure enough, he was unable to restrain himself completely.

"Supposing for a minute," Taylor scoffed, "that there was the remotest chance that the plan could be in any way successful; surely the fatal flaw must actually be that you would never find anyone deranged enough to volunteer to do it!"

At this point, Blake felt it was time to intervene. He had heard enough for one day. "An excellent question, Vice-Marshal. Straight to the point as ever. It will, however, no doubt please you to learn that we have just such a chap in training at this very moment. And from what I hear, he's coming along very well indeed."

"Who the hell has been fool enough to sign up for this job? How do we know he's any good? It's no use just sending any old Tom, Dick, or Harry in there, you know!"

"I couldn't agree with you more, sir," Blake replied. "Nevertheless, we're confident that our man is up to the job. He's Dutch in origin and speaks fluent German. He spent a number of childhood holidays in the Bavarian Alps and so is pretty damned familiar with the area. He's an excellent soldier and, indeed, marksman with a number of years' combat experience. We recruited him from the commandos, where he'd been creating something of a stir. To be honest, we don't think that, given the time available to us, we're going to find anyone better. Rest assured, though, that he's under no illusions as to the enormity of the task and his chances of making it out alive. On the other hand, he's mustard keen to have a pop at this one due to the fact that he lost both parents to the Gestapo when Holland was invaded, and, more recently, he lost his sister during an air raid here in London. As you can see, he has one hell of a lot of scores to settle, and nothing left to lose as a result. He appears to be not in the least bit bothered about how high the odds are stacked against him."

"Well," Taylor exhaled. "It seems like every angle has been taken care of." Though he was clearly trying hard to sound supportive, it wasn't quite possible for Taylor to say this with anything approaching sincerity. In fact, it sounded to Blake pretty much like it was coming through gritted teeth.

"Nevertheless, before I put the RAF at your disposal to insert this man into Germany, I do have one further concern."

"Please proceed," said Blake, smiling more warmly now that he perceived that the battle was won.

"I do think it to be bordering on stupidity to rely on just one man to pull this off. If we are going to do this, and it certainly seems to be the case that we are , then it must be done properly. Everything must be done to ensure it has the greatest chance of success. To my mind, sending one man in alone leaves too much to chance."

"You have a point, Vice-Marshal, but I can absolutely assure you that our man is an exceptional soldier, trained to the highest standards, and we have every confidence in his capabilities."

"That's as maybe, Colonel Blake," Taylor continued, "but the fact remains that he is one man, and there's no telling what might happen behind enemy lines. Why, he might even break his ankle on the jump before he can even begin to think about killing Hitler! No, having two men doubles our chances. Not only does it give us a backup in case the initial strike fails, but it also gives us a fall-back solution in case the first man is in some way incapacitated."

"Your argument has merit, sir, but have you considered that it also doubles the risk? Keeping one man undetected deep inside Germany will be hard enough; trying to do it with two is inviting disaster."

At this point, Brigadier Harris rose purposefully to his feet, his chair making a loud scraping noise as he shoved it back across the polished parquet floor.

"Gentlemen, if you will excuse me, I have a further series of meetings to attend, not the least of which is to update the War Office on this session. I will be telling them that the plans are well constructed and significantly advanced to the extent that we have a recommended solution and the means by which to execute it. For the record, I will also be telling them that we will be sending two men to carry out this mission. On which note, gentlemen, I will bid you good day!"

Blake smiled ruefully to himself; that was as good an end to the meeting as he could have expected. Although the wind had been taken out of Taylor's sails, he had achieved a significant face-saving victory in ensuring that two men would be required. Blake leaned back in his chair, his thoughts already turning to who he could possibly send to his death along with Lieutenant Bogarde.

ELEVEN

Exactly one week after the briefing at SOE Headquarters, Peter was summoned to attend a meeting in the main building of the imposing Beaulieu estate. As he marched up the main driveway, his heavy army boots crunching over the gravel, he wondered what the meeting would be about. There had been no clue on the message that he had received that morning. To be fair, he had been expecting a further meeting with Colonel Blake, as it had been some time since he had last seen or heard from the colonel, and he felt it was high time that he was given something more in the way of a formal briefing for the mission. So when the message had been delivered to him at breakfast that morning, it was nothing that he had not expected, so much so that he left it unopened until he had finished his plate of bacon and eggs on toast.

Inside the house, he was ushered into the briefing room by the duty sergeant. The room itself was small, airless, and pretty gloomy, as the window was closed and the curtains drawn, presumably to maintain security guidelines. No room for prying eyes or ears. In the middle of the room was a large table with a thick grey cloth draped over it. The chairs had been moved to the walls so that they could gather closely around the table. On closer inspection, Peter could see it was actually a standard-issue army blanket, and judging from the visible lumps and bumps, there was clearly something of interest under the blanket.

His thoughts were interrupted, however, by the sound of a chair scraping against the floor. In the gloom, Peter had assumed the room was empty, as he was a couple of minutes early; he had totally missed the fact that one of the chairs on the left-hand side of the room was occupied.

"Hello, Peter. Any idea what this is about?" Jan's familiar voice startled him.

His surprise was total. "What the hell are you doing here, Jan?" On seeing the blanket-covered table, Peter's first thought was that this must relate to his mission, but the presence of Jan now suggested otherwise.

"Your guess is as good as mine, Peter. I received a note last evening to come to this room today and to say nothing to anyone."

They were still staring silently at the table when the door opened behind them. "Ah, good morning, gentlemen, I see you have already spotted our little surprise. My name is Major Courtney, and I will be your tour guide for this morning's little trip. If you will please be seated, Lieutenants Bogarde and Kubcek, we shall begin."

"Sir," Peter began.

"All will be made clear in good time, Lieutenant."

"But—"

"Please, Lieutenant, it will be much easier to simply crack on, and then if you still have any questions at the end, then all well and good."

To Peter, Major Courtney, despite his army background, had the air of the classic, archetypal Intelligence Officer—young, classically good-looking, did all his fighting from a distance without ever having to get into a fight, so his looks had never been spoiled. His short brown hair was slicked back from his forehead, held in place by copious amounts of Brylcreem or the like. This served only to accentuate his already prominent cheekbones and jutting jawline. Peter doubted that he had ever seen a stiffer upper lip in all his time in the British army. His uniform was also immaculately presented: not a crease out of place; shoes polished that very morning, by the look of them; buttons all shined to a mirror-like gleam. Peter hoped he was as efficient at mission planning as he was at personal grooming.

"First of all, however," Major Courtney said, turning towards Kubcek, "you, Lieutenant, are no doubt wondering what you are doing here."

Peter snapped back into focus. It looked like he was not going to have to wait long to find out what the hell was going on.

Jan opened his mouth to reply, but before he could utter a sound, Major Courtney ploughed on. "Well, the fact is, the top brass have insisted on there being a change of plan. No doubt you are currently unaware of the nature of Lieutenant Bogarde's mission." Courtney glanced, briefly, in Peter's direction at this point. "However, in summary, the plan originally was for one man to be dropped into Germany. Now the powers that be have decreed that there shall be two."

If Jan was in any way shocked by this revelation, he hid it well. "So, what you're telling me is that Peter needs a big boy to hold his hand, and that big boy is going to be me?"

"That, I suppose, is one way of looking at it." Courtney smiled thinly. "In short, it has been decided that the mission is so critical that it requires two agents, partly so that we have contingency should we lose the first agent, but mainly so that there is support for the main agent should they need it."

"OK, OK," Jan pleaded. "I'm up for it, but the suspense is killing me! Where are we going? What are we doing?"

Before Courtney could reply, Peter interjected, "We're off to the Fatherland to see Hitler and then shoot him, pal."

This time Jan was stopped in his tracks. "This is a joke, Peter, right?"

Peter shook his head slowly, and clapped an arm round Jan's shoulder for reassurance.

"Well, at least I get to go one better than Heydrich, eh?" Jan said without any trace of humour.

Courtney moved on quickly, almost as if he sensed this would be the best thing to do, allow time for the two of them to reflect later. "Yes, well, in a nutshell, I suppose that just about sums it up, Lieutenant. Now that you are both on the same page, I think we should crack on with explaining the precise details. I have no doubt that you are both desperate to know, eh?"

"Putting it mildly, sir!" Peter replied.

"Good, good. Raring to go, I see! Right, I won't waste any more of your time then, gentlemen," he pulled a sheaf of papers from the folder he'd been carrying. "The purpose of this meeting is to brief you on the plans for the assassination of Hitler. We will be looking in some detail at the following items: the location for the kill; the proposed method for the assassination; the climate and topography of the location chosen; what sort of defences or security you might expect to face, and, most importantly, details about Hitler himself, his routine, and how you will get the chance to take him out. What you are about to hear has been painstakingly researched over many months, making use of a number of eyewitness accounts provided by prisoners of war."

"Sir?" Jan interjected. "I hope you don't mind me asking, but how do we know if these guys are reliable? If I am risking my life, I would want a little more than the ramblings of a prisoner of war to back me up."

Courtney's brow furrowed as he considered his response. "It's a fair question, old man. I know I'd feel the same in your shoes. What I can say, though, is that we have interrogated these guys extensively, on several different occasions. We have checked and double-checked for any signs of inconsistencies and have found none. Many of them have proved to be ardent anti-Nazis, eager to do anything to help bring Hitler down. The rest? Well, we had to resort to more traditional methods of extracting information, if you catch my drift. Either way, I'm confident that the information we have is, if not one hundred per cent, then at least ninety-five per cent reliable."

"OK." Jan nodded. "That's good enough for me, sir. Please carry on."

Major Courtney smiled, shuffling his papers. "Now where was I? Ah yes, your briefing. Now then, I'll start with an overview of the location itself, if I may?"

With a somewhat theatrical flourish, Courtney whipped off the blanket to reveal a three-dimensional model beneath. Jan and Peter leaned forward as one to get a better look. Laid out on top of the table was a mountainous diorama, with forests and rivers depicted in some detail. In the valley between the mountains was a cluster of buildings alongside the main river, which seemed to suggest a fairly sizeable town. The only other items of note were a series of miniature white buildings in the foothills of one of the larger mountains, which appeared to be surrounded with tiny fences.

"This, gentlemen"—Courtney pointed to this latter feature—"is Hitler's favourite retreat, high up in the Bavarian Alps. The surrounding area is known as the Obersalzburg, with one of its main towns being Berchtesgaden," Courtney pointed to the cluster of buildings, "which we see depicted here in the valley on the banks of the river Ache. The nearest place to it that you may have heard of is Salzburg, which is about twenty miles or so to the north. This whole area you see before you is in the far south-eastern corner of Germany, very close to the border with Austria.

"The Führer's estate, as depicted by these white buildings and fences, is known as the Berghof. This is where Hitler feels most at home, where he likes to spend most of his time, probably more so than Berlin even. This is where he feels safest; he has even been known to entertain foreign heads of state here."

"Presumably there's a reason for that, sir," Peter chipped in.

"Mmmm? What's that you're saying?" Courtney glanced up, his train of thought temporarily broken.

"I'm saying, no doubt he feels safest there because he is surrounded by vast numbers of crack SS soldiers, every one of them a trained killer."

"Yes, yes, we'll come on to security arrangements all in good time," Courtney replied, so wrapped up in his subject that he had totally missed the sarcasm in Bogarde's voice.

"First of all, however, I want to give you a little more detail on the site itself. If I gave you time to count them all, you would note that the estate comprises over fifty individual buildings, with a variety of functions as you would imagine. I don't propose to go into detail about each one."

Peter noticed that Jan raised an eyebrow at that, presumably in grateful relief for small mercies; fortunately it went unnoticed.

"You will find that they are all fully documented within the paperwork you'll find in the folders beneath your seats."

Jan's eyebrow retreated, to be replaced by a disappointed frown.

"Excuse me, sir, but why do we not simply drop some very big bombs on the whole lot?"

"Because, Lieutenant Bogarde, for one thing, it's far too imprecise to have a guaranteed successful outcome. In addition, there is a huge underground air-raid shelter on-site, and the estate is also protected by an extremely sophisticated early warning system. The first sign of any planes approaching and he'll be off down the tunnels like a rat.

"If I may continue, I would just like to highlight one or two of the more important edifices on the estate. The villa itself"—Courtney pointed to the largest of the buildings—"has been significantly extended since its pre-war origins. This houses, amongst other things: Hitler's private rooms; one of the three telephone exchanges on the estate; and, as I mentioned before, a vast network of underground corridors and rooms to protect him and his entourage from aerial attack."

Major Courtney continued to indicate each relevant building in turn using a pointer stick to indicate each subject. *This guy's done his homework,* Peter was impressed, despite the dry nature of the subject.

"The only other important thing to point out on the estate is this area here." Peter snapped back into focus as Courtney was summing up. "This is a labour camp containing a couple of hundred East European prisoners. May not come to anything, of course, but could potentially be a good place to hide or to find allies. Last, but by no means least, on this model is the Mooslahner Kopf, or tea room, which sits some distance from the estate." At this point, Courtney pointed to a small building surrounded by trees and backed by some of the more imposing mountains.

"What's so important about the tea room, sir?" Jan asked. "Somewhere we can get a nice cup of tea and a slice of cake to celebrate after we complete the mission?"

"Don't worry, Lieutenant, all will become clear." Courtney placed the used papers neatly onto the desk behind him. "Now then, next I want to talk to you about Hitler himself, his appearance and something of his daily routine.

"I think it's fair to say that this is a subject that has been a little less straightforward to investigate. I can tell you that we have had a number of somewhat conflicting reports about Hitler's personal appearance, minor details, admittedly, but real differences nonetheless. The only logical conclusion that we can come up with that makes any sense, is that one or more doubles exist, presumably as a means of providing protection from assassination. Anyway, I am afraid there is little we can do about this; it's out of our control, and therefore, it's a risk that we have to take. On the plus side, if Hitler feels safest at the Berghof, there should be a good chance that it is the big man himself that you have in your sights.

"In terms of clothing, however, we do know that Hitler usually wears a brown or grey double-breasted jacket over black trousers. In colder conditions, you can assume a heavy dark-grey overcoat will form part of the equation as well. The only decoration he wears is the Iron Cross, which was awarded to him during the First World War. But the easiest way to identify him, of course, will be that distinctive moustache.

"Now, moving on to his routine—and this is the really interesting bit, so listen well. Hitler is a late riser: he's never up before oh nine hundred hours. Soon after rising, he is shaved and groomed by his personal barber. After this, he, more often than not, goes for a morning walk before having a breakfast of milk and toast between eleven and eleven thirty. He then spends the afternoon either receiving state visitors or with his personal physician. On occasions, he may have an appointment off-site, in which case he will usually leave by car around noon.

"If he's staying on-site, he will take a late lunch of steamed vegetables around sixteen hundreds hours, after which he is likely to work until twenty-two hundred hours. At this time, we're told that various generals can often be seen arriving for the daily military conference, which Hitler himself usually chairs. This usually lasts for two to three hours, when the day finishes with a light supper around oh one hundred hours before he retires to bed between oh three hundred and oh four hundred hours."

"That's all very thorough and illuminating, sir, but I recall you mentioned that this was supposed to be the interesting bit? I can't see how knowing that he is partial to steamed vegetables for his lunch is going to help us."

"Excellent point, Bogarde. The interesting bit, for your information, relates to the morning walk he takes before breakfast. This ties in with something I mentioned earlier. Because the fact is, gentlemen, that Hitler takes a walk, pretty much every day between ten and ten thirty, from the Berghof to the Mooslahner Kopf tea room. It is here that he sits down for his milk and toast pretty much every day when he is at the Berghof!"

"Actually, sir," Jan interjected, "I've been meaning to ask. How do we even know when Hitler is at this Berghof place? I'd hate to be waiting around in the cold for no good reason."

"I'm glad you asked me that, Lieutenant. Shows you have been paying attention. The answer is, old boy, that, much like our very own Buckingham Palace here, the Nazis fly a flag outside the Berghof whenever Hitler is in residence. Although I should point out that the flag is, thankfully, different to the one outside the palace!

"Anyway, this flag can be seen from far and wide, most particularly for our purposes, from a busy café in the town of Berchtesgaden. Pop in there for lunch every day, sneak a look up the hill to see if the flag is flying, and if it is, then Bob's your uncle. Off you go and get into position for the attack. Right, the next thing on the list to discuss is climate and topography."

"Top what, sir?"

"Sorry, Lieutenant Kubcek. Your English is so fluent I was forgetting it wasn't your first language. Topography is all about the lie of the land, you know, hills, rivers, forests, and whatnot."

Kubcek smiled and nodded his appreciation.

"Anyway, climate-wise, this area of southern Germany is not a lot different from Britain, just a little more extreme. The summers tend to be hotter and the winters colder, if that makes sense," Courtney smiled apologetically. "When it does rain or snow, it tends to do so consistently for a number of days, rather than being on and off as it can be here sometimes. The other main factor to note is that the snow tends to fall somewhat earlier than it does here, due to the altitude. It can start snowing as early as September. We will be kitting you out with German mountain troop reversible uniforms: one side is white and the other is a grey-green camouflage. As such you will be able to blend in according to your surroundings. As mentioned before, this regiment has its HQ in these parts, and, as such, the area is overrun with these troops, as they do much of their training here. Two more should hopefully not make a difference, and you should be able to blend in perfectly as a result. The downside, of course, however, is that the Germans—as indeed do we, I might add—tend to shoot people caught in German uniform as spies, without question."

Peter and Jan exchanged glances, it was always nice to be reminded of the dangers that lay ahead.

"Moving on swiftly, gentlemen." Courtney coughed, apparently embarrassed to have raised the subject. "Just a few brief words on what sort of terrain you can expect over there. In a word, chaps, mountains! I hope that this does not come as a surprise, though, bearing in mind we're talking about the Bavarian Alps and the fact that the German Mountain Corps does all its training there! Nevertheless, the overriding feature of the area is that it's one vast mountain range. In fact, this area of the Alps around Obersalzburg is pretty much one big amphitheatre, the mountains forming the banks of seats around the town, if you will. The mountains themselves are limestone, which are characterised by having bare peaks; the wind and the rain strips away the soil, thus making it impossible for trees or other vegetation to grow. That said, the same cannot be said of the lower slopes of the mountains. These are, in fact, densely wooded, mainly with pine and fir trees so you to be able to find plenty of cover at all times.

"The next item on the agenda, gentlemen, is security; what sort of enemy presence will you find waiting for you? I am sure you would doubtless expect that Hitler's favourite residence is going to be pretty heavily guarded, eh? That is of, course, definitely the case, but we think we may have found a small chink in the defences that two resourceful and well-trained operatives such as yourselves could exploit."

Peter coughed. "I think it will need to be a bit bigger than small, sir."

"Yes, indeed," Courtney chuckled. "Anyway, more of that in a moment. In the meantime, what sort of troops will you find on the Berghof itself?"

Courtney proceeded to hand round a number of sheets on which were pictures of various uniforms. "First of all, there are around twenty RSD, or security, personnel. These are mostly Bavarians and fiercely loyal to the Führer. You can expect no help from this quarter. In the summer months, they mainly wear Waffen SS uniforms, but from September onwards they tend to go for the Gebirgsjäger uniform, the same mountain kit that you'll be wearing. These RSD men patrol the estate and the immediate area around it with dogs. As well as on the Berghof itself, there are some of these boys based down in Berchtesgaden as well. So be on your guard in the town as well; careless talk and all that, you know! Despite their uniforms, these guys are not really bona fide soldiers. That said, you underestimate them at your peril; they will be fanatically loyal."

"Noted," Jan was busy scribbling notes on the sheets.

"In terms of actual soldiers on the estate, there are really four types. First of all, there is the Führerbegleitkommando, or Hitler's personal bodyguard if you like. These are the elite, gentlemen. They are mainly NCOs and officers and spend their whole time guarding Hitler. I guess it's a badge of honour thing awarded to the most highly decorated SS veterans, a spell of duty looking after the big man. Anyway, there is a detachment of them here, probably around twenty men all in all.

"Next is the SS Wachkompanie, literally the Watch Company, which gives you a clue as to their purpose. The unit comprises around one hundred and eighty men, of whom around seventy per cent are based at the Berghof, the rest being at the Reich Chancellery in Berlin. Their main duties are to ensure the security of the estate: they undertake blackout duties on the site, and they even have a firefighting platoon, just in case.

"Third, and probably least important of them all, is the SS Sonderkolonne. They are the motor transport providers. There are between sixty and eighty of them on-site, and they have eight three-axled Mercedes cars to look after. Glorified mechanics, if you will.

"Lastly there is the SS Nebelabteilung. This unit is spread around the Obersalzburg area and is responsible for creating smokescreens in the event of an air raid. There are three separate troops, eighty to a hundred men each, and they are based in small wooden huts all around the estate, normally two to a hut. You may find that these huts afford decent cover overnight, as we are pretty sure that not all of them are occupied all of the time. Like the RSD men, and indeed most troops in the area, these chaps will also be wearing the mountain corps uniform."

"May I ask, sir," Bogarde interjected, "that as well as telling us how many soldiers there are, what they will be wearing, and what their duties are, that you can also tell us how that actually relates to site security? In other words, which ones will actually be looking for us?"

"By God, you are an impatient sod, Lieutenant." Courtney chuckled. "I was just coming to that part! Right, patrols and sentries. There are, in fact, thirteen static guards, or sentries, posted around the site. The precise position where each is stationed is marked with a red circle on the model in front of you, if you'd like to take a closer look."

Peter and Jan as one shuffled closer and leaned in, focussing intently on the model as Courtney continued.

"As you can see, they have been carefully placed around the estate to ensure maximum visibility in spite of the sprawl of the buildings. I dare say that there's little chance of anyone unauthorised moving around the site without being detected. The same applies even at night, as not only are these posts manned twenty-four hours a day, there are also powerful spotlights illuminating the site.

"If that weren't enough, there are also a number of patrols that traverse the estate. These patrols usually comprise one man, armed with a rifle and sometimes accompanied by a dog. Again, these operate all day long and swap over every two hours to remain fresh. Their location and routes are marked on the model with the green circles and dotted lines, gentlemen.

"The final point to make on the subject of security is that the entire estate is surrounded by a wire mesh fence, marked on the model with a continuous black line around the estate. It's some two metres high, supported by steel tubes every three to five metres. Furthermore, the top of the fence bends over inwards and has three or four strands of barbed wire protecting it. I think it's safe to say that there is no way you're going over that particular obstacle! Going through it may be no less risky either, as we have no idea whether the fence is electrified or alarmed in some way so as to detect tampering."

Peter cut in. "If I may say, sir, it sounds like the Germans have the site well and truly wrapped up. How in God's name are we supposed to kill Hitler with that much security?"

"How indeed, Lieutenant, but every suit of armour is only as strong as its weakest link, and we believe we have found it. You will recall I mentioned some time back that Hitler takes a walk every morning from the Berghof to the Mooslahner Kopf tea room?"

The two men nodded.

"Well, that's our chance. We believe that you should be able to get close enough to Hitler, undetected, while he's walking to the tea room. Close enough to be able to take him out with a single shot." With that, Major Courtney took a blue marker pen from his pocket and proceeded to draw, in one bold, continuous line, the route of Hitler's daily walk.

"Right, gentleman, now that I have overlaid Hitler's route, a number of interesting factors come to into play. Firstly, whilst there is a sentry at either end of the walk, they cannot—I repeat, cannot—observe Hitler for the whole length of the walk. The sentry here at the Gutshof building"—Courtney pointed to the main part of the estate—"can only see Hitler for the first one thousand yards. Thereafter there are a few hundred yards before he will come into the view of the sentry at the tea room.

"Furthermore, we have it on good authority that the patrols do not keep close to Hitler. It would seem that Hitler hates being watched or followed. He has even been known to shout at any soldier whom he feels gets too close to him on his morning walk. As you might imagine, none of these soldiers particularly relishes the thought of being bawled out by the Führer, in case they are dispatched swiftly to the Eastern Front. As such, I think this may well work in our favour and give you more room to play with. That said, it won't be all plain sailing: there is a telephone at the tea room, and there are bells dotted around on various trees, so you must still take care not to raise the alarm before you have completed the mission.

"Now in terms of timing, we have already mentioned that Hitler takes his walk between ten and ten -thirty most days. We know it's not absolutely every day, so you will just have to take a chance and come back the next day if you're out of luck. It is, however, very important that you don't get into position much before ten o'clock."

"Why's that, sir?"

"Because, Bogarde, that's the time that a dog patrol passes by on the outside of the estate perimeter, near to the point at which you need to be located. Get there before the patrol has passed, and you can guarantee that Rover will sniff you out, especially if you are wearing that cologne I can smell! We are led to believe that it's two men and a single dog. They do a circuit of the estate every morning, no doubt timed to precede Hitler's morning stroll.

"In terms of the actual plan of attack, you should follow the river Larosbach"—Courtney traced the line of the river on the model with the pointer—"until you reach this bend here. Then you should cut due south up the mountainside, through the trees. When you reach the edge of the forest, here, you should have a clear view of the perimeter fence. That's where you set up position, Bogarde."

"Where will I be, sir?"

"You, Lieutenant Kubcek, will be in position some way away. The way we look at it is this: Bogarde will have one shot at this. If he misses, all hell will break loose, and we can't assume that he'll get a second chance. The planned location of the hit is sufficiently far along the path towards the tea room for us to reasonably surmise that, if he survives Bogarde's attack, Hitler will make his way to the relative safety of that building and the guard stationed there.

"We assume that he will wait there until his armoured convoy arrives from the Berghof to escort him back to the estate. Now, there's no way we're going all that way for nothing; therefore, we need to have a backup plan. That's where you come in, Jan. The road from the teahouse back to the Berghof is heavily wooded, and so we believe that a man could easily conceal himself amongst the trees, yet close enough to the road to have a good view of a car passing. You, Jan, will be in the woods, ready as a backup to take out Hitler's car should Peter miss with the rifle. A combination of grenades and small-arms fire should do the job. Obviously, you will be supplied with appropriate radios so you can stay in touch at this critical time."

"On the subject of kit, sir," Bogarde interjected, "what sort of weapon will I be using?"

"Excellent question. We have selected the standard German army rifle: the Mauser. If you're going in dressed in mountain corps uniforms, you need the appropriate rifle to go with it. No point getting caught out for a silly mistake like giving you a Lee-Enfield, eh? That said, there will be suitable modifications: a top-of-the-range telescopic sniper sight, and special explosive bullets designed to wreak maximum damage."

Peter nodded to Jan in appreciation. "Excellent piece of kit, the Mauser. Far superior to the Lee Enfield if you ask me."

Courtney paused before continuing. "Right, if there are no more questions, gentlemen, I suggest we call it a day. For the next few days, you'll continue with your training, last-minute stuff like local acclimatisation, if you will. I would imagine, however, that within the next week or so, we will be ready to infiltrate you into Germany. We just need to wait for the right weather conditions to fly you in."

The news that they were so close to launching the mission came as something of a shock to Peter. He hadn't really given it that much thought. He knew it would be sometime soon, but he had not actually focussed on it any more than that. As it was, he was all too aware now of a rushing sound in his ears as the blood pumped furiously around his brain, pushed around his head by an ever-increasing heart rate.

"Just what are the right conditions, sir?"

"Well, it's actually a combination of factors: first we need a moonless night so no one can see you coming down on the end of your chute. And secondly we want to coincide with a bombing raid on nearby Salzburg. That way we can get the plane in almost undetected, given that most of the local attention will be on the heroic boys of the RAF in their Lancaster and Wellington bombers. As soon as we manage to tie those two things together, you'll be on your way."

TWELVE

Knowing that he was less than one week away from parachuting deep into the heart of Germany was a surreal feeling for Peter. Perversely, it reminded him of waiting for Christmas when he was a small child. He would tick the days off his calendar one by one, but it would still always seem to take forever. It was the same now; each day just seemed to drag on and on. Every time he had a moment to himself, all he could do was think about the future and what it might hold. He didn't feel particularly scared. Well, at least he didn't think he was. He felt confident in his ability to do the job; on top of which, the training so far had been extremely thorough and stretching. If there was any fear, it was just fear of the unknown, and he was used to that. It went with the job, after all. He wanted nothing more than to get the green light. He felt sure that once the mission was under way, the nerves would fade, and the adrenalin and training would take over.

The instructors weren't stupid either. They knew what must be running through the two men's minds, so they did their very best to fill every waking hour with more and more training routines to distract them as much as possible. The first of these involved a long and tortuous journey in a massively uncomfortable army truck to an airfield just outside Manchester for parachute training. Although Peter had already done one jump back in '41 on the Poland mission, it was felt that a refresher was needed. Part of him had hoped to avoid it, as he recalled he had hated it and been petrified in equal measure, but the more rational part of him accepted it was a necessary evil that he had to go through, whatever he might feel.

They were met on arrival by a captain in the RAF who, from the way he was limping, looked as if he had lost a leg somewhere along the way. Given the purpose of the day, this did not immediately fill Peter with complete confidence. Nonetheless, he pushed such thoughts out of his mind and jumped down from the truck, stretching his back and legs on landing to try to get some sensation back into his stiff muscles.

"Right, come on, chaps, no time to waste! Captain Jackson's the name, and I'm the poor johnny who has to train you soft saps on how to jump out of a plane without killing yourselves!"

Peter realised too late that he had been staring at his leg a fraction too long because Jackson was onto him in a flash.

"Don't worry about the old peg leg, Lieutenant. Used to fly Spitfires until I got shot down by a Jerry Messerschmitt back in '41. I can't fight anymore, but at least they still let me fly, thank God. All I'm good for nowadays is running this training school; but don't worry, boys, you're in good hands. We've not had a single serious accident the whole time I've been here. Well, not unless you count poor Harris last year. But then if I told him once, I told him a thousand times: "Bend your knees on impact!" Never would listen, that one."

Despite everything, Peter felt himself grinning. He had spent quite a bit of time now in various parts of Britain, but he still found himself at times confused by the sense of humour.

"That's the spirit, lads! Now let's crack on."

They spent the next hour in the classroom, learning about how to pack and check each other's parachutes, and then onto a theory session on the impact of environmental conditions on the jump itself. Peter was pleased that he could remember much of the detail of the first session from his previous mission, but the environmental stuff was new to him. He was surprised just how much impact rain, and especially wind, could have in terms of potential drift from the target drop zone. A wind speed of ten miles per hour could add one hundred yards' drift from the target at a height of three thousand feet. Every ten miles an hour on top would equate to a further one hundred yards' drift.

Jackson focussed particularly on jumping at night, which Peter felt to be a fairly clear clue as to when they would be going in. They touched on how to orient oneself by stars and landmarks, and the amount of light to expect depending on the phases of the moon. The training this time round seemed much more thorough; he was sure that last time it was much more a case of "Here's your chute; there's your plane. Now get on with it." All this extra detail was actually helping him to deal with his fears, as it demystified the process and thereby helped to increase his confidence.

After a couple of hours of this, all Peter's preconceptions around jumping out of a plane had been blown away. It clearly was not as simple as stepping out of the hatch and closing your eyes. In fact, there seemed to be so much to remember that landing anywhere within five miles of the drop zone would be a bonus.

Later that morning, their instructor took them to a specially constructed wooden tower where they could practise landing techniques in what the captain referred to as a safe environment. Safer than three thousand feet, maybe, but still a potential leg breaker, Peter thought ruefully.

"Why do I have this feeling," Peter whispered to Jan as they climbed the wooden staircase to the jump-off platform, thirty feet off the ground, "that I'm climbing the scaffold to a hangman's noose?"

Jan coughed to cover his laughter. "Don't worry, my friend. What's the worst that can happen? A broken ankle and you get to sit this one out! What could be better?"

It turned out that Peter needn't have worried so much. Although it was pretty daunting standing thirty feet off the ground, they were fitted into a harness that was rigged in such a way as to emulate the effects of how a parachute would slow their descent to Earth in real life. On top of this, there was some matting of sorts on the ground to reduce the risk of injury. Despite both those factors, the impact on landing was still a little more than he had expected, enough to knock the wind out of him first time around.

"Knees, lad, knees!" Jackson barked. "First rule of parachuting, you must bend your knees on impact or else your legs will hit the ground so hard they'll drive your balls up into your throat, and just think how silly that would look!"

Jan, with the benefit of going second, was able to learn from Peter's mistake and effected a far more convincing landing, bending his knees, crumpling on impact, and rolling over to his left, all in one, relatively, smooth movement.

Jackson, however, still managed to find fault. "Not bad, son, but keep those legs together. Can't have limbs flailing about all over the place. Increases the risk of breakage."

A further half-dozen practice jumps each later and they were getting pretty proficient, if not a little bruised. Fortunately Captain Jackson called a halt to proceedings and sent them off in the direction of the mess to sort themselves out some food.

After a brief lunch of soup and bread, Captain Jackson took them outside to the runway, where a Dakota transport plane was waiting, engines already running. Leaning against it was the pilot, smoking a cigarette and looking thoroughly bored. Next to him were a couple of reasonably sized khaki-coloured canvas packages, which Peter assumed were their parachutes.

"Righto, chaps," Jackson chirped, "may as well put all that learning into practice, eh?"

Peter's stomach lurched. He knew they would have to jump at some point, but there had been no mention of it at all so far that day, and he had kind of lulled himself into thinking that maybe it was on the agenda for tomorrow, allowing plenty of time to deal with the emotional preparations over a beer or three that evening. As such, despite his newfound confidence, the realisation that he would soon be throwing himself out of a plane at three thousand feet left him feeling not a little sick. He hoped he wouldn't let himself down by bringing his lunch up for a second airing.

First of all, they donned thick flying jackets, essentially leather jackets with a woollen fleece lining. This was on account of the fact, as Jackson told them, that it could get pretty bloody chilly flying at three thousand feet with the bloody door open! After the jackets, the men helped each other on with their parachutes and checked each other's fastenings as they had learned that morning.

"Just make sure you check that properly," Peter remarked to Jan. "I'll come back and haunt you for the rest of your life if you cock this up!"

"Don't worry, Peter, I need you to watch my back when we get to Germany, so I'll be checking extra carefully."

Jackson cut across them. "Right, if you two ladies have finished nattering, hop in and get going."

The Dakota was not a particularly graceful aircraft; indeed, it seemed to lumber across the runway to such a degree that Peter doubted it would ever get off the ground. With the fields and treeline fast approaching, the pilot gave a final heave on the controls and managed to coax the plane off the ground, after which it went into a series of wide circling manoeuvres in order to climb to the required jumping height. Some fifteen minutes after take-off, the plane levelled off. Peter's stomach did another somersault, partly as a result of the flying experience and partly as the dreadful moment had finally arrived.

"OK, lads, this is it. Stand up; hook your chute line to the retaining rope above your head." The flight sergeant in charge of their jump had none of the chummy manner of his superior.

"Good, now shuffle forward towards me. Above and to the right of the hatch, you will notice two lights. The red light is currently showing, telling you that we have not yet reached the drop zone. As soon as we are there, the pilot flicks a switch, and the red light goes out to be replaced by the green light below. At this point, it's over to you. Move into the doorway; jump out. Make sure you do jump out so you don't get tangled in the tail fin. Then shout whatever helps to make you feel brave, whether that be 'Geronimo' or 'Bollocks' or whatever. While you're doing that, of course, don't forget to look up and check that your chute has opened fully. If for any reason it has not deployed, then quickly yank the cord on your reserve chute and start praying."

Just as the sergeant finished speaking, Peter noticed the light change to green. *Here we go,* he thought. *No turning back now.* He shuffled towards the hatch, conscious that with Jan behind him, he didn't dare show weakness or fear, as he knew he would never hear the end of it if he did. The feeling he experienced as he stood in the open doorway was like that when, as a child, he stood at the edge of the water at the seaside. He knew it was going to be cold and a shock to the system, but he had to do it before all his friends started to point and mock him. It was the same now, only more pronounced. It didn't last for long, though, as he was acutely aware of Jan pressing from behind, eager to not delay the moment any longer than necessary. Taking a deep breath and closing his eyes, he launched himself as far as he could out into the emptiness. His eyes didn't stay closed for long, as he wanted to be sure that his chute had opened properly. A sudden jolt that snapped him back so that he felt like he was on a piece of elastic attached to the plane told him that it had deployed. Nevertheless, he needed to be sure that it was fully open and not in danger of folding in on itself, leaving him to hurtle helplessly to the ground.

Seeing all was OK, Peter relaxed a fraction. Next he started to scan the sky behind him, looking for Jan. Craning his neck at an unnatural angle, he could see his partner behind him at about two o'clock. He looked to be enjoying himself as he gave Peter a big thumbs up while grinning like a maniac. That was all there was time for, though, as Peter could now see the ground rushing up to meet them. Their landing zone was a farmer's field a half mile from the airport, and from what he could tell, they seemed to be pretty much on target. Peter smiled. At least it would be a short walk back.

For the last couple of hundred feet of the descent, Peter desperately tried to remember the landing instructions and had just reached the conclusion that he needed to bend his knees, when he hit the ground. Despite the parachute, it still seemed to be a huge impact that drove all the air out of his lungs. He lay on the ground, on his back, the chute flapping in the breeze. He felt a good two feet shorter, as if his legs had been driven up into his chest.

"Bloody hell, Bogarde! You hit the ground with all the grace of a sack of spuds!" Captain Jackson barked as he limped over to where Peter lay, still winded. "Come on, up you get. Time to get back in the plane and try again."

"But, I…" Peter began.

"But nothing, lad. You didn't think we'd let you go after one attempt, did you? You're going to keep practising till you get it right."

Sure enough, over the rest of that day and the next, Peter and Jan made five further jumps. And to be fair, Peter did make significant progress such that he was pretty competent by the end. Jan, however, seemed to have cracked it at the first attempt and spent the rest of the time messing about like a kid at the funfair.

After their parachute training, Peter had expected to be returned to the country estate where they had been for the last few weeks. Instead the army truck pulled up outside a small cottage which seemed pretty much in the middle of nowhere. Once again, he was mightily relieved to be leaving the truck; they weren't renowned for their comfort at the best of times, but the problem was significantly exacerbated by the sheer accumulation of bumps and bruises picked up over the last few days. Stretching out and relaxing aching muscles was not something that could be contemplated in the back of one those bone-shakers. On top of this, he felt chilled to the bone; a mean wind had whipped up during the journey south, and the open-ended tarpaulin on the back of the truck provided very little in the way of protection. All that he had been able to do had been to turn up the collar of his greatcoat and huddle down against the metal side wall.

He was in a pretty foul mood, therefore, as he jumped down from the tailgate onto the gravel driveway, his army-issue boots with their thirty-three hobnails in the sole making a satisfying scrunch as he landed. Moving towards the cottage in the hope of finding that some kind soul had lit a fire and run a bath for them, Peter was momentarily taken aback to see Colonel Blake opening the door to greet them. They hadn't seen the colonel for a good few weeks and had been that busy they had pretty much forgotten all about him.

"Good evening, gentlemen! I trust you are keeping well?"

"Yessir," they saluted dutifully.

"Excellent, excellent," Blake continued, unperturbed by their blatant lack of enthusiasm. "Thought I'd pop down to see how you were and to tell you why we're moving you here. I'm sorry to say, it's not for a holiday, even though it is a lovely little cottage, isn't it? Indeed it's quite the opposite.

"We're now into the final stages of planning for the mission. I fully expect you to be on your way anytime in the next week or so. In essence, we are now simply waiting for the right conditions—in other words, a night when there will be little or no moonlight to help you avoid detection when we drop you into Germany. A few days from now, it will be the new moon and therefore the ideal time to go. This cottage may look pretty darned isolated, but it's actually just a couple of miles from an airstrip. Keeping you close by is essential so that we can react at a moment's notice to the perfect meteorological conditions to get you on your way.

"Between then and now, however, we have laid on what we call our finishing school for you, so I'll leave you in the capable hands of Major Courtney to get that under way. Good luck, chaps. Until next week, eh?"

THIRTEEN

Before he had even finished speaking, Colonel Blake was moving towards his staff car, parked on the gravel drive outside the house, to the side of the army truck in which the two men had arrived. A uniformed member of the Women's Auxiliary Air Force sat patiently behind the wheel, waiting to whisk the colonel to his next appointment. As he approached, she jumped out of the driver's seat to hold the rear door open for the colonel.

Peter turned back towards the house, where he could see Major Courtney looking at them from one of the downstairs windows. "Come on, Jan, we may as well make ourselves comfortable. You never know, there may even be some hot water for a bath, and I'm going first if there is!"

Jan grunted more in hope than expectation as he shouldered the weight of his kitbag and trudged towards the door, behind Peter. They didn't get very far. As soon as Peter pushed past the thick oak front door, closely followed by Jan, strong arms grabbed them from each side, pinning their arms to their sides, effectively rendering them immobile. Before they could react or even cry out, rough canvas sacks were forced over their heads, plunging them into darkness. This awareness was short-lived, however, as a sharp blow to the back of the head left them in an unconscious heap on the floor.

When Peter came to, he had no idea of his whereabouts, for how long he had been out, or even what time of day or night it was. His head was still shrouded by the canvas sack, which, whilst keeping out almost all light, did at least allow him to breathe relatively easily. He also had no idea whether he was alone or, more importantly, what the hell was going on. He was acutely aware of an immense throbbing sensation where he had been struck; the pain seemed to pervade his whole skull and felt especially as if it were trying to force his eyeballs forward out of their socket. At the very least, he was sure he must have a huge egg on the back of his head.

All sorts of wild thoughts careered through his brain: Had the mission been infiltrated by Nazi spies who had come to England to eliminate the agents? What about if the British somehow suspected him or Jan of being double agents? What if Jan was a double agent and they suspected him of turning Peter as well?

As he tried to rationalise his situation, he attempted some gentle manoeuvring and quickly established that his ankles and wrists had been tightly bound, allowing very little movement. His boots and socks had been removed, allowing the ropes to be wound tightly against the skin. His exertions were enough to alert whomever else was in the room, as a voice spoke in perfect German.

"Ah, I see our guest is awake at last! So glad you could join us. Perhaps now you can illuminate us as to your name and the purpose of your mission, before we shoot you for being a spy?"

Peter was even more bewildered. However, he resolved to say nothing until the situation and his head became a little clearer. "You'll get nothing out of me, so I wouldn't waste your breath, my friend!" It sounded brave in his head, but Peter wondered to what extent his voice had betrayed the anxiety he actually felt. As he was clueless as to what the hell was going on, he had no alternative but to fall back on his training and hang in there long enough to try to work things out. The only thing that made any sense for the time being was that saying nothing had to be the safest course of action; give nothing away, and no trouble could come from it. He just hoped he could hold up against whatever was thrown at him.

It occurred to him as well that Jan was presumably in the same boat as him. For all he knew, he could be in the same room, though he very much doubted it. If Peter had been in charge, he would definitely have split the two of them up and worked them over separately, looking for inconsistencies in their stories. Peter was fairly sure that his companion was in a similar situation, lying in a foetal position on the floor with a bag over his head, no doubt feeling distinctly pissed off. Despite his predicament, Peter chuckled to himself at the thought, remembering too late to suppress it.

"I'm not sure what you find so amusing." His captor picked up where he had left off. "Clearly the full gravity of your situation has not yet hit home. Perhaps a little persuasion is called for."

Almost before he had finished speaking, Peter was being dragged to his feet, his arms raised above his head, and his bonds were looped over what felt like a metal hook which must have been suspended from the ceiling in some way, the kind that butchers use to hang carcasses once they have been slaughtered. The analogy did not appeal to Peter's current mind-set. The hook had been arranged at just the right height to ensure that Peter had to stand pretty much on tiptoes to keep the weight off his arms and shoulders. Either way he had to constantly shift his position to maintain his balance, a fact which made matters extremely uncomfortable.

Next Peter heard the unmistakable sound of a knife being removed from its sheath. Immediately he stiffened, mentally preparing for an onslaught of pain. He felt the knife against his skin just below the back of his neck, but instead of sinking into his flesh, he felt it pull downwards in one rapid movement as it ripped the clothes from his body. After two slashes of the knife, he stood naked in front of his captors. Peter forced himself to focus on anything other than his current predicament. It was clear that his captors were attempting to use a combination of physical stress and mental humiliation to crack his resolve. He had no idea how many people were in the room, but he had to banish the shame he felt at being paraded naked before them. His head was still shrouded in the sack, which helped, ironically, as it shielded him from the gaze of his tormentors. He just wished it wasn't quite so cold in the room.

Just then, the same snarling voice cut in to his consciousness. "Right, now that we have your undivided attention, we'll begin again, shall we? What is your name, and why are you here?"

Peter concentrated on providing just the minimum information he could. "My name is Peter Bogarde. I am a lieutenant in the British army. I am currently on attachment to a training unit."

"That is not good enough, Lieutenant. Surely you cannot suppose that we are stupid. We know you are engaged on a secret mission, so the sooner you divulge the purpose of that mission, the sooner we can end your discomfort."

"My name is Peter Bogarde. I am a lieutenant in the British army. I am currently on attachment to a training unit."

"I see," mused his captor. "You have clearly resolved to be obstinate due to some misplaced sense of duty. I am afraid you leave me no choice; we shall just have to resort to more medieval methods until such time as you see fit to change your mind."

Peter lost track of how long he was there. His shoulders ached mercilessly, and his calf muscles were regularly succumbing to agonising bouts of cramp, which were almost impossible to alleviate due to the lack of movement available to him. Every now and then, the monotony was broken by a powerful jet of freezing cold water being sprayed over his still-naked body. The pressure of the water felt strong enough to cause bruises, and was especially unpleasant when trained on the more vulnerable areas of his body. He could do nothing but hang there, shivering uncontrollably, waiting for it to be over. Eventually he was lifted down from the hook and forced into a position where he was squatting down on his haunches with his arms held out in front of him. At first the change in position was a blessed relief, as his muscles could at least relax from the stress position they had been in for so long.

Pretty soon, however, the pain in his calf muscles from holding his whole body weight, and his shoulders from keeping his arms extended, had completely taken over. Every time his arms began to droop, a sharp whack with a stick was applied to his forearms to refocus his efforts. Similarly, if he allowed himself to rock back onto his heels, the same punishment was meted out across the buttocks.

Every few minutes the same question was barked at him: "What is the purpose of your mission?"

To which Peter continued to give the same stock answer, as if operating on autopilot: "My name is Peter Bogarde. I am a lieutenant in the British army. I am currently on attachment to a training unit."

After what seemed like an age but was probably only a few more minutes, Peter's body could take no more. He was past caring what happened and so simply allowed his body to collapse to the floor, retaining just enough presence of mind to lie on his side and tuck his knees into his body in anticipation of the beating that must surely come.

He wasn't disappointed. From the flurry of kicks to his back and stomach, he surmised that there must be at least two of them involved. He had no choice, however, other than to lie there and take the punishment, hoping that the damage inflicted was not too serious. He couldn't feel that any bones were broken, but he couldn't be sure; his ribs certainly seemed to be bearing the brunt of the impact. On the plus side, he reflected, they did at least seem to be avoiding his head, focussing on the more fleshy parts of his body instead. He had no idea how long he was there for; he just knew that he must hold out for as long as he could.

Eventually, he must have drifted into unconsciousness, as when he next opened his eyes, he was lying on what appeared to be a hospital bed, comfortably wrapped in clean, starched sheets whose whiteness, combined with the bright sunlight streaming through the huge windows, was almost blinding. Peter tried to sit up but quickly collapsed back onto the pillows as the pain in his ribs and back gave him a sharp reminder of his recent past. Instead he turned his head to one side to see Jan lying in the bed next to him, eyes closed, sleeping but clearly in a similar state. Looking further around, Peter concluded they were the only two in the room. A rustling of sheets next to him indicated that Jan was coming round.

"How are you feeling, mate?"

Jan cleared his throat before replying, "I have had, how you say, better days, I think! Still, nothing seems to be broken, so maybe it is not all bad, eh?"

"Hmmm." Peter admired his companion's positive outlook. He couldn't say that he was feeling the same way for sure. "Any idea where we are or what's going on?"

"I was awake earlier, and a nurse came in to check on us. I think she must have been under orders to say nothing, though, as she would not respond to any of my questions; either that or I am losing my ability to charm the ladies! I tried in German, Czech, and English but without luck."

Before Peter could reply, the door opened, and a familiar face walked in; Peter's jaw dropped in surprise. Major Courtney smiled as he approached the two men, but despite that, he appeared less assured than normal. If anything, the smile seemed to Peter to have a rather nervous look about it.

"Ah." Courtney coughed to clear his throat. "I see you gentlemen are back in the land of the living."

"And in serious need of some explanation if it's all the same to you," Peter retorted. The appearance of the major had set his mind whirling, trying to rationalise what had happened to them over the last few hours. Not one plausible solution was coming to him.

"Yes, quite! Well, there's no sense in beating about the bush, if you'll pardon the expression? The last twenty-four hours has all been part and parcel of your training, gentlemen."

"What the hell-?"

Courtney held up his hand to stifle Peter's protest. "Now look here, chaps, you must understand that we can take no chances at all with this mission. You are going to be dropped deep into the heart of Nazi Germany. And, despite our very best efforts at training you and equipping you to survive unscathed, there remains a very real chance that you will be discovered and captured. As soon as that happens, all bets are off. You will be interrogated, beaten, tortured, you name it. Ultimately you will be shot as spies. Just as we train you how to parachute at night, so we also have to give you training on what to expect from a German interrogation."

"I can't believe what I'm hearing!" Peter shouted. He could contain himself no longer: despite his injuries, he was out of the bed and grabbing the lapels of the major's jacket, pushing him back up against the wall. "You mean to say that you deliberately had us beaten up, physically and mentally abused just as a training exercise? You are supposed to be on our side, you bastard!"

The major was too shocked to react initially, but it didn't take long for him to recover his poise. "Lieutenant, just because you are not in uniform, do not forget for one minute that you are an officer of His Majesty's Army and bound, therefore, by certain standards of conduct. I am sure that I need not remind you that striking a senior officer is an offence punishable by court martial, so think carefully before your next move. You'll be busted to private before you know what's hit you, mission or no mission!" Despite the tense nature of the situation, the major maintained a calm but firm demeanour, whilst holding Peter's gaze. Bogarde, however, was panting heavily, partly with the exertion but more from the adrenaline. He sensed he was out of control but was powerless to stop himself.

Fortunately for Peter, Jan seized that moment to intervene. "Peter, take it easy, my friend. What is done is done and cannot be changed. Do not make it worse by throwing away all that has brought you this far. It would not be worth it."

Peter did not move for a few seconds, his mind in turmoil. He remained standing with his face just a couple of inches from Courtney's, unable to back down. Then suddenly, his shoulders slumped. Releasing his hold of Courtney's jacket, he sank back onto the bed and put his head in his hands in defeat. The pain in his body had kicked back in with a vengeance now that the adrenaline rush was subsiding.

As the fight had gone out of Peter, Courtney's tone eased somewhat. "Look, you're obviously and understandably upset, so I'm going to pretend that never happened. But do be clear on one thing: don't push too hard, Lieutenant! There's a lot more at stake here than you appear to understand."

"That's as maybe, sir, but given that the success of this whole mission is dependent on us, I think you owe us something more of an explanation." Peter may have backed down physically, but his anger had anything but subsided.

"OK, you're putting your lives at risk, so I guess it's only fair that you're fully in the picture. As you know, we will be inserting you into Germany with the intention of assassinating Hitler. Nobody is pretending that this is going to be easy; there is a very real chance that you will be captured before, during, or after your mission. In fact, I would dare to suggest that the odds are significantly less than evens.

"If we run with the assumption that you will be captured, then it goes without saying that you will be tortured, although I imagine that they would refer to it as interrogation in line with the terms of the Geneva Convention! Either way, we have to know how you will react in this situation and under the level of duress to which you will be subjected."

"But why?" Jan asked. "What can we possibly tell them that they couldn't already guess for themselves?"

"Two things really," Courtney continued. "First and foremost, don't for one minute think you are alone out there. Even though this is the heart of the enemy's country, we still have a pretty well-developed network of agents, sympathisers, foreign nationals, and the like. These assets will be available to you while you are in Germany, and to be honest, their safety and continued anonymity is worth much more to us on an ongoing basis than your welfare. At the end of the day, this is a one-off mission which, if it comes off, could have a huge benefit in the overall scheme of things. But if it all goes tits-up, then I don't think we will lose a huge amount of sleep. Sorry to be so frank, boys, but you have to know where we stand on this. The security of these agents in Germany is paramount for us and needs to be protected in the event of your capture. Hence, we had to test you under similar circumstances to know if you could hold out or whether you would blab everything you know in the first five minutes."

"Nice to know somebody cares, isn't it?" Jan said to no one in particular.

"But you could have jeopardised or even ruined the whole mission, beating the crap out of us like you did!"

"Lieutenant Bogarde." Courtney spoke wearily, as if talking to a particularly dense child. "Do not presume that we are complete idiots. You are not the first and certainly will not be the last chaps to undergo such an exercise. Let me assure you that we are well practised at making sure we break no bones or cause any lasting damage. We actively target the fleshy areas for just that reason. I think I can state with a pretty high degree of confidence that your diagnosis is simply severe bruising and not a lot else. Given your high levels of fitness and associated prompt recovery abilities, I would predict a couple of days' rest in here and you'll be as right as rain."

"You mentioned that there were two reasons for wanting to test us in this way."

"Ah yes. Thank you for reminding me, Kubcek. The other key consideration in all of this is to ensure that this mission can in no way be traced back to SOE, or the Allied forces in general. Imagine the propaganda victory we would be handing to Dr Goebbels if they managed to prove that this mission originates in and is funded by London. That is why you will be going in wearing

German army uniforms and carrying nothing that can possibly identify you as SOE agents. In the event of your capture, you need to be able to convince the enemy that you are operating independently. The area around the Berghof has many foreign labour camps full of Czechs, French, Dutch, and the like. The ideal outcome in the event of your capture would be that you are passed off as escaped workers who saw an opportunity to do away with the evil tyrant of Germany and, in the process, knocked off a couple of German soldiers to steal their uniforms as part of that plan. That, my friends, is your cover story. I suggest you work together over the next few days to flesh out the details and commit it to memory so, should the time come when you need to rely on it, you can make it as convincing as possible."

"And just how confident are you that we can pull that off, sir?" Peter wanted to know.

"A good question, Lieutenant. From what we have seen, you both stood up pretty well to the exercise. You both stuck to the party line of name, rank, and serial number and never wavered from it. That's to be commended for sure, but we have to be realistic and recognise that our test, whilst fairly robust, will not bear a huge resemblance to the real thing. They've got some pretty nasty characters over there who have forgotten more than you'll ever know about interrogation techniques.

"Whilst you coped admirably with what we threw at you, we cannot guarantee that you could manage as well in that environment. It is for that reason, my friends"—at this point, the major reached into his trouser pocket and pulled out a metal container, much like the sort of box that would contain pipe tobacco—"that we are going to give you one of these each."

Courtney snapped open the lid to reveal two small translucent capsules, containing, from what they could see as the box moved in the major's hand, some form of liquid.

"These, gentlemen, are cyanide pills. Standard-issue for all SOE agents and to be used as a last resort only. To avoid detection, it fits into a hollow cavity in the heel of the boots we will be giving you. Should you end up being captured and all hope has been lost, then this gives you a way out. Just pop it in your mouth, bite hard to break the shell, and let the contents do the rest. It's fast-acting stuff; five to six seconds and you'll no longer have anything to worry about, other than whether you're wearing clean underwear to meet St Peter!

"I am also informed, though I can't verify this for obvious reasons, that it is pretty painless too. When push comes to shove, chaps, if this is the only way we can protect the identity of the local assets and prevent the Germans from establishing the origin for your mission, then you're going to have to bite the bullet, as it were!"

Peter and Jan looked from the pills to the major's smiling face and then at each other. There was nothing more to be said.

FOURTEEN

The line connected on the third ring: the familiar gruff tones of Colonel Blake barked out a greeting that sounded more like a demand than anything else. Unperturbed, Major Courtney introduced himself and steeled himself for the task ahead.

"Ah, Courtney, my boy. How's everything going down there? Chaps up to scratch, I trust? I bet they can't wait for the off, eh?"

"Yes, sir, I imagine that's exactly how they are feeling," Courtney deadpanned.

"Good, good. That's the ticket."

Courtney couldn't tell whether the colonel had ignored the sarcasm or just hadn't noticed. He suspected the latter as he had a mental picture of Blake seated behind his desk, sifting through piles and piles of reports and paying little attention to the conversation. His suspicions were confirmed as soon as Colonel Blake completed his next question.

"So, chop, chop, Major. Spit it out, man. What can I do for you?"

Courtney decided that there was no point beating around the bush. "It's Bogarde, sir. I have my doubts as to whether he's the right man for the job."

Blake was brusque in his reply. "What on earth makes you say that, man? I've seen the progress reports; looks to me that he is eminently suitable."

"I agree the reports tell a good story, sir," Courtney conceded. "However, I think there's more to it than just scores out of ten on a shooting range."

"Go on…"

"Well, it's the whole temperament thing that has got me worried, sir. My worry is that when it comes to being out in the field, I'm not convinced that he will stand up under the pressure."

"Is this a personal opinion, or do you have some evidence to support that view?" The emphasis on the word "personal" betrayed the dangers of the political waters into which he was now wading.

"I have always had my doubts regarding his profile, to be honest, Colonel. I'm worried that what happened to his parents and sister has had a deep-seated effect on his psyche. Far deeper than we ever thought, if I am honest. I think it is enough to give cause for concern as to his suitability for a mission of this nature and of this criticality."

Blake was clearly not taking this well. "His background is well documented and well known, Major: it is a matter of record. We've been through it several times, and let our top boffins loose on him too. They were happy to give the go-ahead, so what is it in particular that leads you to raise this concern now? On what basis, at this stage of proceedings, are you suggesting that we should pull the mission? You of all people must realise how much time and effort has gone into this over the months. On top of that, this mission goes all the way to the top. Churchill himself has stamped his approval on it. You really want me to pick up the phone to Winnie to say it's all off, less than a week before kick-off?"

Courtney almost wilted under the pressure being applied, but he was not prepared to give up just yet. He had to be true to his principles so he could have a clear conscience if things did go awry. "I am aware of all that, Colonel, believe me. But I do feel I have a duty to raise with you any concerns about the potential success of the mission, irrespective of when they occur to me. I have indeed seen the risk-assessment reports, and it clearly states therein that there is a potential weakness in Bogarde's personality to the extent that he might suffer an emotional disturbance if the wrong combination of events and stimuli should occur."

"By 'emotional disturbance,' I am presuming that you mean he could go bananas?" Blake didn't wait for an answer and ploughed straight on. "I repeat: we have had him observed and assessed by the best trick cyclists available to us at every step of the way, right from the initial interview in Baker Street all those months ago until two weeks ago, if I am not mistaken. And not one of them has raised a red flag. So just what is the problem, man?"

Courtney braced himself for the next step. "The specific issue to which I am referring, sir, occurred in the medical room during the debrief from the last exercise."

"Which was…?"

"The interrogation simulation, sir. Once it became clear that it was an exercise, Bogarde's reaction was concerning to say the least."

"Look, Major! Kindly piss or get off the pot. I am a busy man with many more irons in the fire to manage, so I would be grateful if you would get to the point sometime before the end of the day."

"Well, to be blunt then, he grabbed me by the neck and threatened to strangle me there and then. If Lieutenant Kubcek hadn't been there to calm him down, I don't know what might have happened. In short, sir, I don't believe we can risk using him on this mission. Once he's behind enemy lines, we will have no way of controlling him and no way of knowing how the pressures of the mission will affect him. We cannot afford for this mission to crash and burn; we have too much riding on it. Even its failure must be carefully planned for and managed so we do not end up handing the Germans a major propaganda coup by being found to be directly involved in planning and executing a mission to kill Hitler. Think of the damage that would do to our war effort; think of the potential upsurge in popular support for the Führer, and just at a time when that support could be about to waver as the second front in France gets established. In my professional view, Bogarde cannot be wholly relied upon; he is just too volatile."

There was a brief pause before Colonel Blake replied, "I see. You have clearly given this a lot of thought, haven't you?"

"Yes, sir," Courtney replied. "I'm not trying to be awkward at all. I am just thinking of the mission, the risks associated with it and how we best mitigate them to maximise our chances of success."

"I understand that, Major," Blake continued in more conciliatory tones, "but if we withdraw Bogarde, then we effectively close down the whole mission. Remember how hard it was to find a suitable candidate in the first place? How likely is it that we could find a second one, let alone get them trained and ready? That could take months, and who knows where we'll be by then?"

"Well, sir, could we not send Lieutenant Kubcek on his own? He's had all the same training and knows the mission inside out."

"It's a thought, but it's one that we discounted some months back, if you recall. There is simply too much at stake to risk pinning everything on one man's shoulders. No, we either go with a team of two or not at all."

"In that case, sir, I am not sure I see any other alternative."

"The other alternative that you seem to be overlooking, Major," Blake continued, "is that we carry on as we were. What if I put it to you that what you experienced the other day was nothing more than a well-honed aggressive streak that went a little too far. Indeed it sounds to me like he is displaying exactly the kind of characteristics that we are looking for in an agent being deployed on a mission of this magnitude and peril. Last thing we want is a shrinking violet, what? We need someone who can react at pace and has the balls to make that reaction a reality. So what if you got a little shock to the system as a result, Major?"

"I'm not so sure—"

Blake cut in. "Listen, Major, I don't want to have to spell this out in words of one syllable, but the fact of the matter is, this mission is too far down the tracks to stop now. This has been committed to at the very highest levels in the War Office, and the government is fully on board. You don't get that level of support every day, and we can't put the brakes on now. Too many reputations are riding on this one. The best I can offer you is to say that your comments and concerns have been duly noted, but I am afraid that I must overrule you, and therefore I am ordering you to continue according to plan."

"Is that your final word on the matter, sir?" Courtney asked.

"It is, Major."

"In which case, Colonel, I will carry on as ordered, but I would like it formally recorded that I requested the removal of Lieutenant Bogarde from this mission."

"As you wish, Major. If it will make you happy," Blake sighed.

"Thank you, sir. It will make me happy, as it will mean that I will be able to sleep more easily when this all goes to shit."

FIFTEEN

Two days later, Major Courtney walked into the training room to find Bogarde and Kubcek waiting for him. From their demeanour, they looked to be fully recovered from their recent ordeal. Nor could he detect any signs from their expressions as to whether they still held any residual enmity for him as a result of the exercise. For his part, Courtney had resolved to put the matter behind him: He had escalated his concerns up his line and been overruled. As far as he was concerned, there was nothing more he could do about it, and his position was now clear. His duty now lay in completing his work to train the two agents for their mission, whatever his personal misgivings. He had decided, therefore, to continue as if nothing had happened.

"Right," he began. "We're into the home stretch now. You've come a long way, and there's not a lot more we can teach you now, to be honest. We've taught you how to jump out of a plane without killing yourself, and how to stay alive from the point of view of combat skills, both armed and unarmed. All we have left to focus on now is how to keep you alive once you are behind enemy lines, and the best way to do this is by ensuring that you merge into the background as much as possible."

Bogarde cut in. "If I remember correctly, sir, we'll be dressed as German mountain troops—Gebirgsjäger, I think they're called. Presumably that will be a key part of the 'merging into the background' strategy?"

137

Courtney could not fail to pick up on the sarcasm; he surmised it had been intended purely to goad him into a reaction, one that he was determined not to give. Nonetheless, it required a monumental effort to fight back his immediate reaction to tear him off a strip for his impudence.

"It's good to know you have been paying attention, Lieutenant. However, a uniform is only half the disguise. Of course it will help you pass a casual glance, but not much more than that. There is more to fitting in behind enemy lines than just wearing the right clothes. If we dropped you in there right now, any even half-alert sentry would have you at the end of a gun barrel within minutes. We might as well stick a sign around your neck, saying, 'Shoot me! I'm a spy!'

"So what we need to do is to teach you the little tips and tricks that all agents need to help them be able to blend into the background. The key, gentlemen, is to be able to avoid arousing suspicion. You want to make sure that no one gives you a second glance; no one takes an ounce more interest in you than necessary. Think it through. How many people did you notice last time you walked down the street? Chances are you couldn't describe any one of them to me in any particular detail. People only stand out if they appear unsure of themselves, look out of place, or if they do something out of the ordinary."

"OK, sir," Kubcek chipped in. "You've sold it to us. What do we need to know?"

"Thank you, Lieutenant. I'm glad to see someone values my input." Even though he smiled as he said this, Courtney wasn't sure he had managed to remove all the edge from his voice.

To cover his awkwardness, he cleared his throat and moved on quickly. "Right, let's begin with papers inspection. As you might expect, Germany has a soldier on pretty much every street corner, every train and bus station, and so on and so forth. Being asked for your papers will be a daily occurrence, so you had best get used to it. Naturally, we are giving you the relevant papers, and I can assure you that, from a quality perspective, we are confident that they will stand up to all but the most intense scrutiny. However, if you don't play your part properly, then you risk people getting too interested in you, which may just make them subject your papers to that extra scrutiny.

"The key, as I have said before, is to ensure you do nothing to excite interest. They ask for your papers? Just hand them over with no fuss; there's no need to say anything else at all. Remember, this is a daily occurrence in Germany; you must treat it as such. You should act as if you are bored by the whole thing; it happens all the time, so why react to it in any other way? If you do anything else, then you run a huge risk that something you do or say will stick in their minds or make you stand out in some way. Once that happens, you're for the high jump. Just hand them over; chances are they will take a quick look and hand them straight back. If they do ask you a question, then by all means answer it but do so politely and using as few words as possible. Again, the emphasis is on doing nothing out of the ordinary."

"What kind of things might they ask us, sir?" Kubcek enquired.

"Given that you will be dressed as soldiers from the German mountain corps, the main questions you will be asked will probably be along the lines of: What are your orders? Where have you come from? Where are you going? What unit do you belong to? Who is your commanding officer? And so on. Make sure you have an answer ready for these questions: a delay in answering will only serve to arouse suspicion.

"Beyond this, there's a whole lot more you need to grasp in terms of how to behave normally in Germany. For example, it may sound obvious, but I can guarantee that you won't have considered this. In Germany, they drive on the wrong side of the road."

"Major, you know that we both grew up in mainland Europe, right?"

"I am indeed aware of that fact, Mr Bogarde, but I'll wager that while you have been in Britain, you will have no doubt got used to our cars driving on the left, as God intended, I might add." Courtney added a cheeky grin to let them know he was joking: it was never easy to know whether his sense of humour translated to other cultures.

"When you get into Germany, you very quickly need to get back into the habit of looking left rather than right when you cross the road. It's a small thing, admittedly, but should not be overlooked. I can tell you we have already lost couple of agents for just this reason; one bloody fool stepped out in front of a truck as he was looking the wrong way! The other was spotted by a particularly alert French policeman who noticed him looking right as he stepped up to cross the road. Led to a detailed inspection of his papers, by which time he was so flustered that he confessed everything there and then. That was the end of the road for that particular chap. Lying in an unmarked grave behind the prison-camp kitchen now, I shouldn't wonder. Anyway, if you don't want to be the next one to go this way, you'd better get this sorted in your heads, gentlemen."

This news had a sobering effect on the two men, and so they proceeded to buckle down for the rest of the day, concentrating hard on taking in each and every morsel of information that might help keep them alive when the time came.

"I don't know about you," Peter said as made their way back to their room, "but my head is spinning with all this information."

"Same for me, Peter. I have no idea how I am going to remember all this."

"Yeah, the combat stuff is all fine; that's all second nature and will come back to me soon enough when the time comes. It's all this additional stuff: how to talk to a policeman, what to order in a bar, how to cross a road! I'm bound to make a complete balls-up of it all and get myself arrested and shot in no time."

Kubcek laughed, "I'm sure it won't be as bad as that, my friend. We just need to keep our wits about us and avoid making stupid mistakes. I am sure if we look out for each other and back each other up, we'll be fine. On the plus side, at least we are not British; must be hell for those guys to try and blend in with their stiff upper lips and everything."

"True enough," Peter replied. "All the same, it is good to know that you'll be there with me; doing this on my own is not an appealing thought."

The next morning, straight after breakfast, the two agents were relaxing in the lounge, lingering over a post-breakfast coffee and cigarette, as they had no classes scheduled for that morning. Looking out of the window, Kubcek spotted a car, driven by an attractive young woman in uniform, crunching to a halt on the gravel drive in front of the main building. Almost instantaneously, Major Courtney came into the room where the two men were sitting.

"OK, chaps. Your time with us has come to an end. You have thirty minutes to pack up your kit and be in the back of that car."

Bogarde placed his cup back on its saucer on the table in front of him; it rattled as it came to rest, betraying the fact that his hand was shaking. "What's the story, sir?" He fought to keep his voice even so as not to further advertise his growing anxiety.

"Well, the powers that be have decreed that it's time to step up and be ready to go. There is little more of value that we can teach you here, and so you are basically ready to go over the top, as it were. You are therefore being transferred to what we call a holding house, situated a short distance from Tempsford airfield, which, as I am sure you will recall, is the main one we use for launching agents into occupied Europe."

"Does that mean we're going in today, Major?" Kubcek asked, his eyes as wide as the coffee cup that he continued to grip, his knuckles whitening visibly.

"Not necessarily, lad," Courtney said reassuringly. "There is an outside chance, of course, but equally it could be anything up to one to two weeks before you actually go, mainly to do with the weather. Cloud cover and the amount of moonlight need to be spot on: The last thing you want is to be floating gently down to Earth on the end of a parachute in the middle of a sky that is lit up as bright as day by a huge moon. They'll get the Met boys to check the weather over the landing zone every few hours to see whether you're good to go. And because the weather can change so quickly, they'll want you nearby so you can go at short notice, hence the holding house which will be no more than a five-minute drive from the airfield. I'm told that it's very nice, all the creature comforts that you have become used to here, so I am sure you will be very happy there. I believe that Colonel Blake will even look in on you at some point to see how you're settling in."

———

Less than half an hour later, Bogarde was squeezing into the back seat next to Kubcek with a kitbag between them for company, the boot only being big enough to carry one. It was a tight fit with just the two of them, not least because both Kubcek and he were six foot tall or thereabouts, but the presence of the kitbag made things even more uncomfortable. The woman driving had made it more than apparent that there was no way that they were going to be allowed to put their smelly, dirty kitbag on the spare seat in the front. This had clearly been reserved for her handbag and attaché case! They were going to have to make do.

"Is it far to the house?" Peter tried to get an angle on how long they were going to be cooped up for.

"Please can I ask you to refrain from talking to the driver? I am not at liberty to divulge any information."

"My sincere apologies, miss." Peter glanced at Jan, and in unison they rolled their eyes towards the roof in a knowing gesture. Unfortunately, it was a little too knowing and much too transparent because when Peter looked back to the front, he just caught her eyes as they darted away from where they had been staring at his face in the rearview mirror.

That's torn it, he thought. *No chance of her thawing out for the rest of the trip now.* They lapsed into an awkward silence, Peter and Jan feeling a lot like naughty schoolboys caught making rude faces behind the teacher's back. Peter spent the rest of the journey largely looking at the back of the girl's head, trying to stare through the tightly curled blond locks, into her mind. They had been starved of female company—well, at least the young attractive sort anyway—for a good number of weeks, and he felt like it was an opportunity going begging to not be able to engage in at least a little small talk.

It was to no avail, though. She remained unswervingly focussed on the road ahead, seemingly oblivious to their presence. All that Peter was left with, apart from the back of her head, was the pleasant and distinctive scent of her perfume. Certainly a nice change from the stale body odour that had become all too pervasive in their sleeping quarters over the weeks.

As it was, Peter's worst fears were confirmed, as the journey took all morning, and it was not until early in the afternoon that they arrived in what looked like a small hamlet comprising five charming brick cottages with thatched roofs, positioned around a decent-sized pond: the kind with a little island in the middle where the ducks had made their homes in the reeds and long grass. A quintessentially British scene, Peter thought to himself, and a million miles away from the turmoil and destruction of the war zones across Europe. But at the same time, it was a fitting reminder of why it was worth continuing the struggle to defeat the Nazis, so they didn't get the chance to destroy this way of life.

The car pulled up outside one of the cottages, and Peter noticed that the picture was made complete by the presence of a wooden slatted fence, painted white, which marked the limits of the immaculately maintained garden.

They were met at the door by an RAF officer carrying a clipboard under one arm, his other arm held stiffly behind his back. As they retrieved their bags from the car and made their way towards the gate in the garden fence, the officer stepped forward, looking at the clipboard as he did so, clearly checking for their names on his list.

"Right, you chaps must be Lieutenants Bogarde and Kubcek?" He carried straight on without waiting for a response. "Welcome to our humble abode, here in the village of Shepton Magna, gentlemen. I trust your journey was not too arduous?"

The two agents mumbled appropriate pleasantries and assurances whilst stretching and taking in their surroundings.

"Good, good. Right then, my name is Captain Bowles, and I will be your liaison officer during your stay here. Anything you need or want, you just let me know. If I'm not around, there's a telephone in the hallway. Dial zero, and you'll be patched straight through to the airfield, where someone will be able to get hold of me any time of day or night."

"Er…whereabouts is this airfield, sir?" Kubcek enquired.

"Gosh! How silly of me. Of course you won't have come past it on your way in, would you? Right, it's just around the corner, no more than five minutes' drive. That's our itinerary for the rest of the day sorted, I think. As soon as we have you settled into your rooms, I'll take you over to the base to have a good look round. Show you the ropes, as it were. Charming little place it is, especially now that Jerry seems less inclined to try and bomb us to pieces every night!"

Tempsford turned out to be a compact little airfield hidden away behind the trees that lined the narrow country road along which they travelled to reach it. Even the sign indicating the entrance was so small that you had to really know it was there to be able to find it. Inside the perimeter, there was little sign of activity other than a uniformed guard standing inside a wooden shelter that seemed to pass as a sentry box.

On seeing the car pull up at the barrier, the guard, who was displaying the rank of sergeant on his sleeve, left his shelter and walked up to the driver's window, where he inspected Captain Bowles's security pass closely, even though, Peter assumed, the captain must go through this checkpoint on at least a daily basis. Satisfying himself that all was in order, the sergeant pushed down on the counterweight to raise the red-and-white striped barrier pole to allow the car to pass. In all that time, not one glance was made in the direction of the two men in the back of the car.

"Good to see security is taken seriously here, sir," Peter began, "but I am curious to know why he made no attempt to verify our identity?"

"Good question, Peter. We have a rule round these parts that none of the ground staff at the base takes the slightest notice of any of the agents that pass through. Only the likes of me and the aircrew themselves have any prior knowledge of you; it's easier and safer for everyone that way. The way we look at it, most of us don't need to know who the agents are, where they are going, or what they will be doing when they get there. So we don't ask. We're just here to facilitate the process of delivering the agent to their destination. We know how to do that, and we like to think we're rather good at it too. If we can do it with the minimum amount of fuss and bother for the agents, then so much the better. Allows you chaps to focus on your mission and not worry about all this trivial nonsense, eh?"

"But we could have been anyone!"

"Yes, Lieutenant Kubcek, you could have been. But then, we have developed a series of signals to cater for just such an eventuality. It's all to do with the number of hands I have on the steering wheel when the guard comes to the window. Wrong number, and a signal gets sent through to the guardroom for the vehicle to be intercepted, you see? Not had to use it yet, old boy, and long may that continue."

Inside the airfield, there were even fewer signs of life than before. Peter and Jan glanced at each other, feeling sceptical about the whole place.

Captain Bowles, ever alert, caught the look. "I can see you have some doubts concerning the set-up we have here, gentlemen."

"Well, it does seem to be a bit quiet, sir," Jan replied.

"Don't let that fool you, Lieutenant. We keep things deliberately low-key here, you see. Less likely to get Nazi spies sniffing around if it all looks a bit sleepy. We launch the vast majority of our agents into occupied Europe from here, so the less interest there is in this place, the better. That said, to be honest, there is actually not a lot to see. Despite being the hub of all SOE activity for Western Europe, that doesn't mean we're anything like as busy as Biggin Hill and the like. We only really run one or two flights a week out of here."

Other than the control tower, an air-raid shelter, and a couple of hangars—housing a number of small Lysanders and a larger Halifax bomber, which was being worked on by a couple of ground crew—there was indeed little to see. No more than thirty minutes after they got out of the car, they were walking back towards it in order to return to the house.

"OK, so that's the grand tour just about done. I hope you found it useful and informative." Bowles smiled to show he was joking. "It may look like a tinpot operation, but I can assure you that we run an exceedingly professional outfit here. All our pilots, for instance, have many hours' experience flying over occupied Europe: Most of them have come to us from Bomber Command once they have completed their tours of duty. Those that want to keep flying rather than go into the classroom are grateful for the chance to keep doing their bit, and we're glad to have them, as they are cool under pressure, can find their way round Europe in the dark, and know all the tricks of the trade."

"The fact that they have survived at least thirty bombing missions, being shot at by anti-aircraft guns and Messerschmitt fighters, is quite comforting too," Peter added, echoing the captain's smile.

"Quite! Now then, I should tell you that you will be going in that big Halifax bomber on the night."

"Why's that, sir?" asked Kubcek. "Surely the smaller plane would be less conspicuous?"

"Well, yes, there is that, Lieutenant, but the simple fact is that the Lysander can only really be used for landings. We can't really land you in the middle of Germany, far too risky, you see. On top of which, where you are going is rather mountainous, so finding a nice flat bit to land and take off will be a challenge. No, parachute it is, I'm afraid, and that means the Halifax. On top of that, the other advantages are that the Halifax has a crew, rather than just a pilot. This is a big help in that the pilot can concentrate on flying the big crate while his navigator does the hard bit finding his way. In a Lysander, the pilot has to do the lot, and as this is the first time we have done a drop this deep into Germany, we need all the navigational skills we can get. Also, in the Halifax, you get a dispatcher as well."

"A what, sir?"

"Someone to help you out of the plane safely, Bogarde! Can't have your parachute not opening, or worse still, you banging your nose on the way out!"

Back in the car, Peter enquired, "You don't seem to have much in the way of defences against air attack here, sir. Is that wise?"

"All part of the subterfuge, Bogarde. We like to make it look as if there really is nothing of value here. Having no anti-aircraft guns is part of that. Gives the impression that there's nothing worth defending and hopefully fools the enemy into thinking there's little point wasting any bombs on us. It's worked so far, I'm happy to say, though whether that is by luck or judgement is any-body's guess."

Back at the house, Bowles showed them to their room. Small, sparsely furnished with just two single beds, a wardrobe, and a basin, but comfortable enough for what was presumably going to be a fairly short stay. On the bed already were their operations kits, the centrepiece of which were the uniforms that they would be wearing on the mission, that of a couple of sergeants from the German Mountain Corps, the Gebirgsjäger. Seeing the uniform of the enemy up close had a sobering effect on the two men: the reality of what they had to do was getting all too real now.

Next to the uniforms was a mixture of other items divided between what a German soldier might be expected to be carrying—weapons, identification papers, eating equipment, gas mask, and so on—and the kit that was directly associated with the mission. Captain Bowles spent some time going over the latter.

"Peter, as the sniper, you will be carrying this telescopic sight which fits easily onto your Mauser rifle there." Bowles tapped the rifle's stock. "To avoid detection, we have created an inner sleeve within the inside trouser leg of your uniform, where it can be kept concealed until you reach the objective. In addition, you both have maps stencilled onto these silk handkerchiefs. There's not a huge amount of detail on them, if I am honest, but you have the key local features that might help you on your way in and out. If in doubt, head southwest to Switzerland, eh, lads? Try not to use them to blow your noses, as the ink might run.

"Finally, in case of difficulties, we have a sewn a few gold sovereigns into your belts. Might come in useful should you need to buy yourself out of trouble. Right, that's about your lot. I suggest you take some time to familiarise yourself with everything, try it all on, make sure it's comfortable, get anything adjusted that needs it. After that, get some dinner and then get your heads down. For all you know, you might be off tomorrow."

"How will we know if we are, sir?" asked Jan.

"Oh yes, good point, I'd clean forgotten about that. When you come down for breakfast, you'll see the operations board up on the wall in the hallway. If the weather and everything else is in order, you'll see an entry on the board stating the departure time. You're the only chaps with us at the moment, so it will be for you if it's there. Best of luck now, chaps. I'll leave you to get settled in."

The next morning, the two men came down at seven o'clock as instructed, ready for breakfast. As they made their way down the hallway to the dining room at the rear of the house, something caught Peter's attention from the corner of his eye.

"Jan, look!" Peter exclaimed, grabbing his partner by the shoulder and spinning him round.

There on the operations board on the wall at the bottom of the stairs by the front door were the words: "Today's scheduled flights." Below that was listed a single flight, commencing at 2200 hours.

"Think that's for us, Peter?" Jan asked.

"Well, you heard the man. There's no one else staying here, Jan." Peter's voice sounded level and calm, but inside, his stomach was churning. This was it; the day had arrived. All the waiting, all the training, all the lectures were for this moment.

Just then, Captain Bowles strode purposefully through the front door. "Ah! Glad I caught you chaps. I see you've noticed the ops board. Looks like a green light for tonight, eh, lads?"

"Yes, sir," Peter answered. "Nothing can stop us now, I guess," he said, doing his best to sound a lot more confident than he felt.

"Not strictly true, but I admire your enthusiasm, Bogarde."

"What do you mean, sir?"

"Well, we're happy with the moon this week; not too bright, which is good news. The variable factor today is really the weather. At the moment, all looks good, but there is a chance that a fog bank may hit us later on. If it holds off, we'll be all set to go; otherwise we'll be postponing. I understand that currently we have an eighty per cent chance of going.

"On top of that, there's the last-minute checks on the old girl herself. We service the Halifax regularly, of course, but we always do a full pre-flight check on the day of an operation too. That said, I wouldn't concern yourself with that one; we've never had a failure yet, old boy!"

"So what do we do now, then?" Jan asked.

"Not a lot, if I am honest." Bowles shrugged. "Just a case of waiting, I'm afraid. With a flight time of twenty-two hundred hours, we should be making the final decision as to whether we go by seventeen hundred. So until then, don't wander off! You're best spending your time checking your kit, making sure you have everything with you, and getting some rest, as you don't know when you might next get to have an uninterrupted sleep. Oh, and don't forget to check your kit for anything that can be traced back to either you or England. I'm sure they told you that in your training, but I can't overstate the importance of that check. If you are picked up, your cover story goes up in smoke in two minutes flat if you have a Marks and Spencer's label in your underpants!"

After a breakfast of bacon, eggs, tea, and toast, which Bogarde tried hard not to imagine being the last meal of a condemned man, the two lieutenants went back to their room to begin the methodical kit check. They were glad to have something to do, as it helped to keep their minds off their imminent departure. Despite that, Kubcek found that he couldn't stay off the subject for long.

"So, Peter," he began, "do you think we will come out the other side of this in one piece?"

Peter sighed. "Jan, I think we have to face up to the fact that the chances of that are minimal at best, mate. Even if we manage to get past all the soldiers and get into a position where I can take a shot, you can bet that all hell will break loose if we actually manage to pull this off."

"Perhaps all the confusion will give us a chance to escape?" Jan mused.

Peter had to admire his friend's optimism, but for him, he had long ago reconciled himself to the fact that this was nothing other than a black-and-white suicide mission. They would get one shot to take Hitler down, and after that, it would just be a matter of time before they were caught. He was under no illusions that this would be the outcome, but he didn't want to be quite that blunt with Jan just yet. He needed to believe they stood a chance, to keep his motivation levels high.

The one thing that Peter did know was that capture was not an option, especially if they had successfully achieved their objective. There would be no telling what horrors the Gestapo would practise on them, and it was not something Peter would allow to happen. The last bullet in the revolver would be for him; he was not going to be taken alive.

Instead he replied, "Indeed, there has to be a chance, Jan, but we must also be realistic. Everyone will be out to get us. The first few hours will be key; if we can avoid capture during that time, then maybe there is some small hope that we can escape. But you can be sure they will set up a watertight cordon around the whole area, involving hundreds of guards, vehicles, dogs, the works. Our best chance will be to use the terrain to our advantage; if we can lose ourselves in the mountains and the forests, then maybe we can avoid capture long enough for the focus to move elsewhere."

Having completed their kit checks, the two men went down to the back garden to relax in the sun. It was a beautifully kept garden, in keeping with the whole tenor of the village; the lawn was neatly trimmed and was edged by neat flower beds that were bursting with colour. Towards the rear of the lawn, someone had thoughtfully placed a couple of deckchairs, the kind you see on any beach, in the shade of an apple tree. Peter and Jan stretched out in these and closed their eyes.

They were awoken a few hours later by Captain Bowles striding through the house, calling their names. "Stand down, lads, stand down. The op's off for tonight."

Peter felt a strange sensation of almost tangible relief mixed with an impending dread, like a dentist trip being cancelled when he was a child, but knowing that he would have to go the next week instead. "So what's the problem, sir?"

"It's the weather, you see? Yes, I know it's nice and sunny here"—Bowles had noticed both men looking up at the sky with mock incredulity—"but there is a new frontal system coming in from the east that will mean that cloud cover over Central Europe will be greater than ninety per cent tonight. Simply too damned cloudy to be able to see where we're going amongst those mountains, which in turn means it's too risky for you. We can't be dropping you way off target into the middle of a hotbed of Nazi fanatics. That just wouldn't do, wouldn't do at all, eh?"

For the next couple of days, there were no further updates on the operations blackboard, which was something of an anti-climax after all the excitement of that first day. Bogarde and Kubcek had little to do but wait for the weather conditions to be deemed acceptable. To pass the time, they fell into an uneasy routine involving a five-mile run before breakfast, followed by a full kit check and a review of the plan. The afternoon and evening were made up of further fitness training to stay as sharp as possible, combined with relaxation time.

Given the secrecy which shrouded their mission, they were not allowed off-site, which was a shame given that Peter recalled driving past a delightful-looking country pub no more than a mile away from their cottage. The house was well stocked with books, and the daily papers were always available to stay in touch with developments, but there was no doubt that boredom was becoming a significant factor with the lack of a change of scenery.

It wasn't until the third day after their first abortive attempt that the operations board was updated once more to show details of a planned flight, again for 2200 hours that night.

"Looks like we're on again, Peter." Jan frowned.

Sure enough, Captain Bowles appeared while they were having breakfast to confirm their suspicions. "We have a green light again for tonight, chaps." He beamed. "We'll wait for the seventeen hundred hours confirmation, of course, but every indication shows the weather to be pretty stable and unlikely to change. This is it, I would say!"

SIXTEEN

In keeping with the airfield's operational instructions, Bogarde and Kubcek were dressed in their uniforms and fully kitted up, ready to go by 20.00 hours, some two hours before take-off. They were now sitting in the lounge of the cottage, waiting for the car to come and take them to the airfield in time for their pre-flight briefing. Even though they sat opposite each other in the small living room, neither man spoke, each preferring to be alone with his own thoughts. For Peter, staring out of the window over the back garden, which was still bathed in early evening sunshine, this meant running over the details of the oft-rehearsed plan in his head over and over again, trying to reassure himself that nothing had been forgotten. He noticed that his right leg was drumming up and down, keeping time with the speed of his thought processes. He had to make a conscious effort to will his leg to stop, in the end resorting to slapping his right hand down on his thigh to bring the incessant movement to a stop. Successful, he glanced over at Jan to find his comrade grinning at him, no doubt recognising the same feelings of stress in himself.

At that moment, a knock on the front door was followed by the sound of footsteps down the hallway towards their room. The door of the lounge opened, and Captain Bowles poked his head round the corner. "Right, lads, the car's here. Chop, chop."

Peter and Jan grabbed their backpacks and Mauser rifles and followed Bowles into the hall. As they reached the front door, Bowles shook each of them firmly by the hand. "Well, good luck, chaps. Happy landings and all that. And I hope to see you back here again sometime soon for your next mission."

"Thank you, Captain, and thank you for looking after us so well here," Jan replied awkwardly before climbing into the back of the car. Peter could only nod his thanks and smile wanly.

As they pulled the doors closed, the driver turned round and said, "Hello, chaps, so the big day has arrived, eh?"

It took a moment with the sun low down in the sky, causing him to squint, but Peter suddenly realised that the driver was none other than Colonel Blake.

"Thought I'd drop by to see you off and wish you all the best for a successful outcome."

"Thank you, sir. That is very much appreciated."

"Not at all, Bogarde, not at all! This mission has been a long time in the planning, and it would be remiss of me not to be there at the launch, eh? So, all sorted, raring to go and all that, I presume?"

"We're about as ready as we'll ever be, sir," Jan replied. "Everything has been planned down to the last detail, as I am sure you are aware. It's now down to us to do the job and hope that Lady Luck smiles favourably on us."

"True enough, Lieutenant Kubcek. All the planning in the world can't legislate for the unforeseen. All you can do is try and pre-empt it and build contingency plans for how you would react, if that doesn't sound too crazy?"

"No, we're used to crazy here, sir," Peter replied. "Wouldn't be taking this on if we weren't."

"Ah, indeed so! I quite see your point." Blake tailed off, as if sensing the tension of the situation. All of them were acutely aware that the likelihood of their survival was minimal at best. The chances of a successful outcome were even more remote.

The remainder of the journey was completed in silence. Having passed the security check at the sentry gate, Blake pulled the car to a halt at the rear entrance of the two-storey control tower. Releasing his seat belt, he turned round to face the two men in the back.

"Now then, chaps. I have no need to emphasise the importance of this mission and what's at stake here. Pull this off and you may single-handedly shorten this war and save thousands, if not millions, of lives in the process. We've been fighting for the best part of five years, and who knows how much longer it will go on and how many more will die before it ends? But by removing Hitler, much like amputating a diseased limb, we believe we can bring this whole damnable war to a close. It's a long shot, of course, but I can tell you that all the way up to the Prime Minister himself, we believe that it's a chance worth taking."

As they got out of the car, Blake continued. "And let me tell you two boys in no uncertain terms that I am immeasurably proud to have been involved in some small way in this mission and to have known you chaps into the bargain. With men like you fighting for us, I have every confidence that we shall prevail in the final reckoning. Gentlemen, I salute you!" And with that, Blake straightened to his full height, brought his heels together, and brought his hand up to his peaked cap in as smart a salute as he could muster.

Bogarde and Kubcek glanced at each other briefly, making sure that the other was treating the moment with the appropriate gravitas, before returning the salute as crisply as possible. Later on, Peter would reveal to Kubcek that he had felt a strong temptation to stay in character by giving a Nazi salute, which he had managed to overcome only by sheer force of will. It had been a sincerely meant gesture from Colonel Blake and deserved to be treated as such.

"Right!" Blake cleared his throat and recovered his normal composure. "Time we got the ball rolling, eh?" He strode towards the back door of the control tower, but as he placed his hand on the handle, he stopped as if another thought had occurred to him.

"Oh yes, before I forget, I have a couple of things here for you that may or may not come in handy." Blake returned to the car in order to place his briefcase down flat on the bonnet. He then undid the catch, reached inside, before turning to the two men, holding two small cardboard boxes and a couple of belts.

"In these boxes, gentlemen, you'll find some pills—Benzedrine. There may well be times out there when you cannot afford to take time out to sleep no matter how tired you are. These chaps will keep you going that bit longer until you reach somewhere safe to rest.

"These belts are the latest thing. They have been made in the exact design used by the German army and with a buckle specific to the Gebergsjäger regiment so they won't be out of place. Where they differ is that sewn into the lining are a number of gold coins. Might come in handy should you need to bribe your way out of a tricky situation, eh?"

Blake coughed to cover his embarrassment. "Right." He turned back to the car to close his case, avoiding eye contact with the men. "I think that about covers it. I suggest we get inside and crack on!"

They were met inside by an RAF officer carrying a clipboard. "Ah, there you are, gentlemen. We were just about to send out the search parties. Never mind, you're here now, eh?

"My name is Captain Briggs, and my job is to look after you from this moment until you step onto the aircraft in a couple of hours' time. First thing we need to cover, gents, is the fact that we don't need or want to know your names during your time with us. It's better that the flow of information is kept one-way: from us to you. As such, we will henceforth be referring to you"—he nodded at Peter—"as Joe, and you"—he nodded at Jan—"as Joe."

"I'm sorry? Is that not going to be a little confusing?" Kubcek asked.

"Oh no, we find it works well. We call all the agents who come through here, Joe. Keeps things nice and simple. The chances are that whatever we need to say needs to be said to the pair of you, so it saves time if we just say, 'Joe,' and you both pay attention at the same time!"

Peter and Jan exchanged bemused glances but decided against saying anything more about it.

"Right. In terms of what's going to happen between now and take-off, we'll start shortly with a quick briefing of tonight's flight plan, before passing you on to your handlers for final kit checks. Then finally we'll pack you off to the flight crew to get you acquainted with the aircraft we're going to be using today. As you already know, you'll be going in on a Halifax. She's a lovely old bird who's served her time faithfully with Bomber Command and has now been put out to grass with us for general light duties such as dropping agents behind enemy lines and whatnot. Worry not, though. She's sturdy in all the right places and will easily do the job required of her.

"If there are no immediate questions, gentlemen, I'll take you through to the briefing room, where I will run you through the plans for tonight."

They followed Briggs through a door on which a sign said Operations Room. They had not been allowed in here on their tour, and they expected to find a vast crowd of people inside, poring over maps, monitoring radar screens, and such like, but whilst the room had all the equipment, there was only a couple of female RAF auxiliary staff seated in one corner, drinking cups of tea.

Seeing the look of surprise on Peter's face, Briggs smiled and said, "Things are a little quieter here than your normal Fighter or Bomber Command ops room. We only do the odd mission now and then, so we can afford to be a little more low-key in our approach."

In the centre of the room was a table, about twelve foot square, on which was marked out a detailed map of Western Europe. Around the walls were numerous chalkboards, clocks, and posters, the latter being the kind of stuff you saw everywhere these days: "Careless talk costs lives," "The walls have ears," "Mum's the word," and so on.

Briggs led them over to the map table on which a number of pins, joined by string, were laid out. "Right, chaps, gather round. As you can see, we've mapped out the route that you'll be taking tonight. We'll be running the standard procedure for this kind of sortie, taking a series of dog-legs from here to the drop zone. First leg goes from here pretty much due east to the coast. From there you drop south-east until you hit the coast of mainland Europe, somewhere just north of Antwerp, as we need to avoid built-up areas as much as possible to minimise the chances of a bit of unwanted flak from alert anti-aircraft gunners.

"From there you head south across Belgium and France to just north of Reims, where you turn south-east again, which takes you all the way down to the border of Switzerland. That then is the last leg, where you turn east and keep going all the way to the drop zone, which is situated just to the south-east of Berchtesgaden. I think that about covers it, gentlemen. Any questions so far?"

"How long will we be in the air, roughly?" Bogarde enquired.

"Well, it's hard to be precise about such things, Joe, but we're talking about over nine hundred miles at a cruising speed of roughly two hundred and fifteen miles per hour. That works out somewhere around four and a half hours flying time. What's more important, however, is making sure we time the arrival at the drop zone correctly. We need to be dropping you off in that half-hour period in the run-up to dawn, where you have enough light to see where you're landing, but there's enough darkness to keep you out of sight of the casual observer, should there happen to be any about at that ungodly hour! In order to do that, the dog-legs help as checkpoints. Every time they reach a turn and change the heading onto the new course, the navigator will calculate the location, time, and speed to work out if you are ahead or behind schedule and ask the pilot to adjust accordingly. Things that can't be planned, like wind speed at different altitudes, can make a mess of flight schedules, and they need to be tracked closely."

"Four and a half hours?" Kubcek sounded put out. "Wouldn't it be quicker if we just went in a straight line?"

"That is true, of course, Joe. However, it also would help the German radar operators to track your route, make an educated guess as to where you're heading, and have a reception party waiting for you in the shape of a couple of Messerschmitt night fighters. No, we need to make this as difficult as possible for the enemy to prevent you from getting to the objective."

"Er…this Messerschmitt thing…does that happen very often, by any chance?" Peter enquired, a nervous smile spreading across his mouth.

"Oh God, no! Not when we take these sensible precautions. Don't worry, lads, you'll be fine. You'll be glad to know also that Bomber Command run pretty much nightly raids over occupied Europe, and tonight is no exception. Directing their fighter squadrons to intercept in excess of three or four hundred of our bombers can be pretty much guaranteed to keep the Hun busy, allowing the odd single aircraft to slip through unnoticed, by and large.

"Right, if you're ready to move on, I suggest we take you to get kitted out in your flight gear and parachutes and then off to meet the aircrew, what?"

Thirty minutes later, Peter and Jan were ushered into the crew room, moving slightly less freely than before as they were now wearing full flying suits and parachutes. The suits themselves were heavy and thick, designed as they were to withstand sub-zero temperatures up at thirty thousand feet or more, and made walking difficult, not to mention squeezing through the door into the room.

Once inside, Briggs introduced them to the seven men gathered there—all similarly equipped in flying suits and parachutes. The names were a blur to

Peter and Jan, though they did manage to latch on to the pilot—Captain Bill Hawkins—who was introduced as the veteran of two full tours of duty in Bomber Command. There was no telling how old he was. Peter assumed he could only be in his mid to late twenties, but he had the look of someone significantly older. He was aware that most aircrew served only one tour, thirty operational missions over enemy territory, if they even survived that long. After that they were "retired" to non-operational duties like training new recruits or troop transportation. To have served and, indeed, survived two tours was exceptionally rare and could well account for his worn-looking demeanour and prematurely greying hair. Nevertheless he stood tall and straight and spoke with a calm authority which immediately filled the agents with the confidence that they were in good hands.

"Good evening, gentlemen, good to have you here with us. I will be your pilot for tonight's mission, and these"—he gestured to the men gathered around him—"are the rest of the crew." This statement was followed by assorted nods and greetings from the assembled airmen.

"Why seven, sir?" Kubcek enquired.

"Well, beyond the pilot, co-pilot, and radio operator, the rest of the chaps operate the machine guns. Something we have learned the hard way is that the last thing you want to do is fly a slow, cumbersome bomber a few hundred miles over enemy-held territory with no protection! Of course," Hawkins went on, "as we are flying solo tonight, I don't expect we'll need them much, if at all. They tend to come into their own when we're flying as part of a huge bomber formation. In that scenario, they need their wits about them to defend against the German fighters buzzing around all over the place.

"Anyway, I understand you have been briefed as to our flight plan tonight, which just leaves me to talk you through the drop zone procedure. Now the drop zone itself should be plain sailing." Hawkins moved towards a table on which were laid out a number of photographs, indicating that the two agents should follow. There were eight of them, organised in two rows of four so as to cover a wide expanse of the area around the Berghof. "We've had some

161

aerial reconnaissance photos of the surrounding area sent over from the RAF Photographic Reconnaissance Unit, and we believe we've identified just the spot."

Hawkins pointed at the centre of the photograph that was second from the left of the bottom row. "Just here, you see there is a significantly sized piece of open ground? Looks like your typical Alpine meadow in the foothills of the mountains. So whilst it won't be flat, I don't envisage it causing you too many problems in terms of executing a safe landing."

"It looks a little exposed, if I am honest," Peter remarked.

"True, but you'll also note this forest here"—Hawkins pointed further up the photograph—"just on the edge of the meadow, giving you quick access to cover. Also, we're dropping you before dawn, so it should be pretty dark, but I agree, the sooner you get into cover and stow your chutes, the better, eh? Pine forests tend to be fairly dense, so this should be ideal for your needs.

"OK, so as I say, I understand that Briggs has been through the flight plan in terms of the route we are taking?"

Peter and Jan nodded.

"Excellent, no need to go over that again then. I will just add a little more information to help put things in context. For much of the trip, we'll be flying fairly low, at around six to eight hundred feet above sea level. As we approach key radar zones, like the French coast and the German border, for example, we'll drop down really low, trimming the treetops, if you will. That way, we should stay below radar and hopefully avoid detection as much as possible. Once we are past the danger areas, we'll climb up to about fifteen hundred feet while we get a bearing on the new course. Once we get onto the last bearing, we'll stay at eight hundred feet all the way to the drop zone, all being well, where we'll climb to three thousand feet for your drop.

"To be honest, you don't really need to know all this: just lie back, enjoy the ride, and leave the flying to us, eh? But if you were in any way concerned by the changes in altitude, at least you now understand what's going on. What's more important to you fellows is the drop zone procedure. When we get close, I'll radio one of the gunners here to get you up and ready. Do a final check of your chute and kit; make sure it's all secure, that sort of thing. We don't want bits dropping off you all over the place on the way down. Then he'll hook you up to the static line and open the trapdoor in readiness for the big drop."

"Trapdoor, sir?" Kubcek ventured.

"Yes, Joe, it's what we call the special modification that has been made to the Halifax. We've cut a nice little hole, about three feet square, through which we'll be dropping you chaps. It's much safer than using the door, as it keeps you away from the propellers and the tail fins, which has to be a good thing, right? That said, though, it's not quite as simple as all that; there is an art to getting it right. Basically, the right way to do it is to sit on the edge with your legs dangling out into space. Then when you get the nod, you push yourself off the edge and through the hole. You need to be careful, though: push too hard and you get a bloody nose when you smack into the far side of the hole; not hard enough and you risk catching your chute on the near side of the hole. Experience shows it's best to aim bang for the middle.

"So, you're in the hole and ready to go. Above your head and to your right, you will notice two lights. One is red, the other green. When we get within five miles of the drop zone, I will switch on the red light. This is your signal to be ready to go; first man gets into position. When we hit the DZ, the red light goes out, and the green light goes on. This is your cue to go, and go quickly. We need to get both of you out within thirty seconds, or you'll risk being spread over a large number of miles when you get down. Even though you are jumping from only three thousand feet, the wind can still play havoc with you, so it's best to be as close as possible when you jump. Don't worry too much, though. As I say, one of my lads will be on hand to give you a boot up the arse if you appear to be dilly-dallying unnecessarily!

"While you are floating gently down to the ground, we'll circle round in a loop and come back down on the DZ on the same bearing as before to drop the container carrying your kit. Do not forget about that, lads; I would hate you to get a bump on the head for forgetting to look up!

"As soon as you are down, get out of your chutes as quickly as possible and recover the container. Then get into cover in the forest. First thing you've got to do when you get there is bury your gear, the chutes and the container, as you won't be taking them with you. Don't spend hours over it, but make sure you do a good enough job so it can't be seen or stumbled across too easily. OK. I think that about covers it. Any questions? No? In which case, let's go meet Betty."

"Who's Betty, Sir?" Peter asked.

"She's the other member of the team, Joe. Been with me throughout the whole of my last tour. Thirty missions through thick and thin. She's been patched up a few times along the way, but she's still fighting fit and raring to go. She'll get you there; don't you worry about that."

Peter and Jan gathered up their kits and followed the aircrew out of the room and into the night air. It was cool but otherwise calm and cloudless, with a bright moon illuminating the way to the hangar.

Hawkins saw Peter looking up at the sky and reassured him. "Don't worry, Joe, the Met guys assure me that there is light cloud cover over Central Europe, so you won't be too brightly lit up as you float down to Earth. And tell me, when have you ever known a weather forecaster to be wrong?"

SEVENTEEN

Colonel Blake stood at the window of the operations room, watching the two agents walking behind the aircrew towards the truck that would take them all to the aircraft. The Halifax was waiting at the end of the runway in the distance, visible in the darkness only due to its flashing recognition lights. Finally, after months of planning, innumerable meetings, and much soul-searching, they were under way. The point of no return as it were. If his mind was racked with doubt, he could only imagine what Kubcek and Bogarde were feeling right now. That said, he could see no outward indication of any issue, as both men appeared to be striding purposefully and briskly over the tarmac, well, as briskly as they could in their bulky flying suits.

As they climbed into the truck, Blake turned back away from the window to face the room. Other than Captain Briggs, there were just two others in the room: the two female telephone and radio operators waiting patiently, ready for the mission to begin. The door opened, and a third woman in uniform entered carrying a tray loaded with steaming mugs of tea.

Briggs took one, thanked the woman, and turned to the colonel. "Best make yourself comfortable, sir. It's going to be a long night."

"Indeed, indeed," Blake mused absent-mindedly, his mind still wrapped up in his own thoughts. He took a mug and spread his hands around it to help take

165

away the chill of the night. "I'll stay here to see them safely delivered to the drop zone and then make a move."

"Right you are, sir. We'll be getting regular reports from the radio operator on board, but there may be long periods when nothing seems to be happening, but, in a sense, that's a good thing, as it means there are no issues to worry about."

The two men lapsed into silence, each alone with his own thoughts. The only noise was the gentle hum of the machinery and the quiet conversation of the two women, who had now been joined by the tea-bearer.

After a few minutes, the silence was broken by the sudden crackle of the radio coming to life, after which the voice of Captain Hawkins boomed out across the loudspeaker. "Control, this is Whisky Tango Five confirming we are all loaded up and ready to go. The kangaroos are safely strapped in and looking forward to their trip. Requesting permission to take off. Over."

One of the women leant forward to the microphone in front of her and pressed the transmit button. "Whisky Tango Five, this is Control. Report understood. You are cleared for take-off." Then, almost as an afterthought, she added, "Put them safely back into the wild, won't you?"

"Roger, Control. Over and out."

Blake turned to Briggs, his eyebrows raised quizzically. "Kangaroos? Wild? What the hell is that all about?"

"Just a little play on words, sir. You will recall that we call the agents 'Joe' rather than use or even know their real names? Well, it is a short hop, if you'll pardon the pun, from there to Joey, which I am reliably informed is what you would call a young kangaroo. It's part of standard radio procedure to use codes just in case anyone unsavoury is listening in, and this is our way of keeping track of the agents and their progress to the drop zone, or back into the wild, if you will."

Blake smiled, appreciating the fact that even amongst all the tension, there was still room for a bit of levity to keep everyone grounded.

"OK," Briggs continued, "should be all quiet now for an hour or so. Next scheduled report, barring incident, should be as they cross the coast due east of here, at which point they'll change course to head south-east towards Antwerp."

"Righto. In which case, I think I'll finish my tea and go for a wander round the base. Stretch my legs a bit."

———

Bogarde glanced across the loading bay to where Kubcek sat and smiled. The noise coming from the four massive Rolls-Royce Merlin engines was intense, making any attempt at meaningful conversation pretty futile. A few shouted questions or comments were about all that could be managed.

For Peter, his thoughts went back a couple of years to the first time he had been sat inside a Halifax bomber, waiting to jump into occupied Europe. Then, as now, his feelings were a mixture of apprehension and excitement. Fear of jumping into the unknown, straight into the enemy's backyard, was offset by the buzz of the mission itself: finally being let loose after all those months of training, finally having the chance to strike a lasting blow for freedom, and finally delivering on his promise to avenge his parents and sister.

He didn't know whether it was the same for Jan, but he had been plagued for a long time by this gnawing feeling that the war was going on around him while he sat idly by. Hundreds of thousands of men and women were risking, or even sacrificing, their lives every day while he had been sat in relative comfort and safety back in England. At last he felt that he was back in the game, and there was no bigger game than this! If this came off, the chance to bring the war to a close was almost unimaginable. Sure, he had read the papers and seen the newsreel reports, all suggesting that the tide was turning against the Nazis, but who knew how long it might go on for? Who knew what new, appalling weapons might be developed? What happened if Russia made a separate peace, allowing the Germans to focus on the West? So many unknowns, all of which made pulling up the weed by its very roots a very sound idea in his book.

The sensation of the Halifax banking fairly sharply to the right brought him back to the present. He reached out his right hand to steady himself on the bench and smiled again across to Jan. Sometime after the plane had steadied itself again on its new course, he stood up to stretch his legs. He decided to make his way forward to the cockpit to check in with the pilot. He reached as far as the navigator, who held out an arm to stop him going further.

"Sorry, Joe. Rule number one: no one talks to the pilot unless he wants you to."

"Fair enough," Peter replied. "I was just interested to know how we were doing."

"All good, all good. Wind speed is moderate, and we're on schedule to hit the drop zone on time. You probably felt us turn a while back? That was us reaching the English coast and heading on our new course south-east to pick up the coast again in Belgium, a few miles to the north of Antwerp."

Peter nodded and then looked ahead at the blackness outside the cockpit window. He never ceased to be amazed how these guys could plot where the hell they were at any one time. "How on earth do you know that we will hit the coast with that degree of accuracy?"

"Years of practice, Joe." The navigator smiled. "But just to be sure, we will climb to about fifteen hundred feet as we approach the coast to double-check our bearings. We should see the bright lights of Antwerp just off to our right. If we don't, we'll know we've gone wrong!"

Sure enough, not long after the crewman had finished speaking, Peter felt the nose of the Halifax starting to point upwards as the pilot pulled back on the controls. It was a gentle shift, so gentle that Peter didn't even need to reach out to steady himself. Five minutes later, the plane levelled off again at its new height, at which point the navigator reached out and nudged Peter on the arm and pointed out the window to his right.

Following the direction he was pointing, Peter could see in the middle distance hundreds, if not thousands, of lights, which gave away the presence of a significant town or city. Some of the closest lights appeared to be shimmering and moving from side to side almost imperceptibly. Peter surmised that what he was seeing was the reflection of the harbour lights on the waves as they lapped against the sea wall. From in the cockpit up ahead, Peter could just make out the sound of the pilot's voice as he radioed back to base to confirm they had reached the next checkpoint and were setting a new course. At the same time, the plane banked further to the right, as it started to head due south, combined with a shallow dive back down to eight hundred feet.

"I suggest you head back to your seat, sir. We've a few hours to go yet, so you may as well try and get some sleep while you still can. God knows when you'll next get the chance."

Peter nodded in agreement and made his way back to where Jan was already dozing peacefully. He made himself as comfortable as he could against the struts which held the fuselage together, and closed his eyes.

EIGHTEEN

Peter jolted upright, brought back to sudden consciousness by a sharp pain in his lower leg. Blinking the sleep from his eyes so he could focus on his surroundings, he saw one of the crewmen stomping down the fuselage, with the purpose of rousing him and Jan from their slumbers. Rather than waste time to bend down and gently shake them by the shoulder, he had clearly reckoned that the best way to achieve this task with the minimum of fuss was to deliver a swift kick to the shin on the way past to the hatch, which he now proceeded to open. The sudden rush of cold air and noise from the open hatch meant that he had to shout to be heard clearly.

"Wakey, wakey, gentlemen! This is your early morning wake-up call. We are now just twenty minutes from the drop zone. Please complete final kit checks, attach your static line to the bar you see above your head, and then make your way down here towards the hatch. Hurry now, gentlemen. There's no prizes for being late!"

Peter and Jan scrambled to their feet as best they could, hampered as they were by the constant lurching of the aircraft and their bulky kit. Following the oft-practised procedure, they checked each other's kit methodically, taking it in turns and taking their time to ensure nothing was loose and nothing was going to rattle noisily, or worse, become detached, on the way down. First they faced each other for Peter to check Jan's front before Jan then turned round so Peter could check his back. The procedure was then repeated in reverse, enabling

Jan to confirm that Peter was ready. The whole thing took no more than ten minutes but was vital to ensure a safe descent.

Next, both men reached up and connected the clasps on the end of their static lines to the bar as directed. The crewman checked both were secure before helping them move down the body of the plane towards the trapdoor, through which they would shortly be launching themselves.

"Right, in a couple of minutes, chaps, this light here"—he pointed to the uppermost of a pair of lights on the wall above the hatch—"will go red. At that point, the first man needs to get into position, ready to go. Sit on the edge with your legs dangling out. Then, when the light goes green, don't think twice; just go! I will, of course, hit you on the shoulder just for good-natured encouragement.

"As soon as the first man has gone, I need the next man to already be in position, as quickly as that, please. I will then bang you on the shoulder as your signal to go as well. We need to keep the gap between you as short as possible to ensure that you don't get too spread out down on the deck. It's not that windy tonight, thank God, but the longer you leave it, the further you'll have to walk to find each other.

"While you are drifting gently down to Earth, no doubt admiring the lovely mountainous scenery, we'll circle round back onto the same course to drop your container. We'll drop it as close as possible to the same point that the first guy jumped, so that should give you a rough guide in terms of where to expect it. Remember to keep an eye out for it, or you'll risk a nasty bump on the bonce! Right, any questions?"

Bogarde and Kubcek both shook their head, focussed 100 per cent on the hatch in front of them. Peter realised his heart was pounding, and he was swallowing repeatedly. He could feel the sweat breaking out on his forehead despite the chill. He hated parachute jumps, hated the thought of not being in control, hated being reliant on an inanimate object. *Calm the fuck down, man!* he willed himself. He had to focus on the job and not let his fears run away with him.

Just then the first light went on, casting an eerie red glow over the interior of the fuselage. Peter was grateful, as it meant he could push his anxiety out of his mind and get on with it at last. Without hesitation, Peter edged forward to the hatch, sat down as best he could with the parachute and rifle that he was carrying, and swung his legs out into the void. His adrenalin levels were maxing out and helping to shield his mind from the biting wind that was tearing at his flight suit.

Peter sat in position, breathing deeply in an attempt to control his apprehension. After what seemed an age but was, in reality, less than a minute, the light went green, and he simultaneously felt a thump on the shoulder as a reminder, as if he needed one. Without taking a glance back, he placed his hands either side of his thighs on the edge of the hatch and pushed off.

He was immediately struck by the silence that surrounded him. He could still hear the engines of the Halifax, of course, but they were fading fast. Instead there was no other sound than the wind swirling around him as he dropped towards the ground. Remembering his drills, he looked up to check the chute had deployed correctly. Satisfied that all was in order, he then glanced round to try to catch a glimpse of Jan. There he was, not too far behind him at least.

He had forgotten to check his watch before he jumped out, but he figured that dawn was fast approaching. Surrounded as they were by the high mountains of the Alps, the sun was going to take a little longer to rise than normal, but he could see, over towards what must be the east, that the sky was starting to glow a little as the sun slowly began its climb to start the new day.

Snapping back to the moment, he turned his attention to what was beneath him. First priority was to make sure he was not going to land amongst the trees. Sure enough, recalling the photographs he had been studying just a few short hours previously, he could make them out about a quarter of a mile to the north of his position, as expected. He couldn't yet distinguish the individual trees in the gloom, but they stood out as a dark smudge against the lighter colour of the grass-covered slope for which he was heading. From a risk-assessment perspective, Peter surmised that the slope looked fairly even. Other than the possibility of a few outcrops of rock, he reckoned he should be fine.

By now the ground seemed to be rushing up fast to meet him. Recalling his training, he prepared himself for impact. Pulling his legs together and bending his knees slightly, he prepared to land, hoping that the ground was spongy enough to absorb some of the shock. Sure enough, the impact was not as bad as he had feared, as the soil was still soft from the snows that had melted earlier in the year. At the same instant as his feet touched the ground, he collapsed to the left in what he felt was a textbook parachute landing. He was only sorry that his instructor was not there to finally see him manage it.

Almost immediately he was on his knees, pulling armfuls of parachute cord towards him as he attempted to gather the bundle together so he could get it hidden. The rigorous exercise had the additional benefit of helping to get his blood pumping; warming him again after the freezing cold pre-dawn air had chilled him to the bone.

Hitting the clasp on his chest to release the straps of the parachute, he stood up and looked round to where he thought Jan would be. Sure enough, Jan was also safely down and was just starting to gather his chute in. Picking up his chute, Peter jogged over towards his partner, conscious of the fact that the container would be coming down soon, roughly where he had himself landed. He could already hear the engine noise increasing as the Halifax circled round to begin its second run over the drop zone.

"Come on, Jan, let's get these chutes and flight suits buried quickly and then get the canister sorted. The earth round here seems to be pretty soft and should be deep enough to keep them hidden. All being well, we won't be around long enough to worry about them being found anyway."

Jan grinned. "I'm not sure whether you mean we'll be safely on our way to Switzerland, having successfully completed the mission, or lying in a ditch somewhere with a bullet in the back of the head!"

All the same, he released his chute and started cutting away the turf with his knife before scooping at the ground with his helmet, soon shifting enough soil to be able to hide the two chutes with no fear of discovery. Not long after, there was a thud behind them as the canister landed not far from where Peter had himself touched down. The two men finished piling the earth over the top of the chutes and replacing the turf before scrambling back over the ground to where the long metal tube was lying.

Working as quickly as their cold fingers would allow, they got the canister open. From within its confines they retrieved their backpacks, the radio, and the camouflage suits that went with their Gebirgsjäger uniforms, having been too bulky to fit under their flight suits. In their place they quickly stuffed the canister's parachute and their discarded suits before closing it. Digging a hole to hide the canister took that much longer given that it was almost five feet long, and they were sweating with the exertion, despite the cold, by the time they had shifted enough earth to do the job. By this time the sun had pretty much risen over the top of the mountains to the east, lending additional urgency to their task.

"Hurry, Jan, let's get this bloody thing hidden and get out of sight as quick as we can."

Jan didn't need telling twice and was already shovelling the soil back on top of the canister as fast as if bailing water from a sinking boat, while Peter flattened it down as much as possible to avoid it being obvious that something was hidden there. Less than two minutes later, the two men were trudging down the slope towards the dense forest of fir trees just over a hundred yards away. It was hard going, weighed down as they were with their kit, as the ground was uneven, with stones hidden within tufts of heather that threatened to turn an ankle. As they got closer to the treeline, so the ground evened out, and they were able to increase their pace to cover the remaining ground in no time at all.

In amongst the trees themselves, the trunks were closely packed together, which meant that the branches above their heads formed an effective barrier to prevent much of the light from reaching the ground. Despite that, it was, nevertheless, a degree or two warmer, being nicely sheltered from the breeze. They stopped to knock the cloying clumps of earth from their boots against a couple of tree trunks and then walked on for a minute or two to ensure they were fully out of sight from where they had landed. Peter then stopped, slipped off his backpack, and sat down.

"Let's take a few minutes to take stock and get our bearings, Jan."

NINETEEN

Opening one of the pockets on the outside of his backpack, Peter pulled out a silk handkerchief and, resisting the temptation to mop his brow with it, instead spread it out on top of the pack. On it was inscribed a rough sketch map of the surrounding area. As he studied it, Peter repositioned it so that it matched their current orientation.

"Right, if my bearings are correct, we are somewhere in this area here." Peter pointed to a section of the map shaded to indicate the presence of woodland. The area he pointed to was on the slopes of Mount Untersberg, to the south-east of its summit. Jan moved in close and squatted down on his haunches to get a better view.

"To our south-east, a couple of miles away down in the valley, is Berchtesgaden. About a mile and a half to the east of that, across the river Larosbach, which runs through the town, is the Berghof estate itself, probably three to four miles away, then, from where we are now. May not sound like far, but the terrain is clearly pretty mountainous, and it's not as if we can simply walk from A to B as it were.

"If you ask me, our priorities for now are to find some kind of shelter so we can get properly out of sight, get some rest, and run through some more detailed plans for our next steps. What do you think, Jan?"

Jan nodded his assent. "Agreed. If I recall from the briefings, there are loads of little wooden huts dotted around these slopes, either for shepherds to use in the summer when they move their livestock up into the mountain pastures, or for the smoke units stationed around the estate. I think it best if we head in the general direction of Berchtesgaden and find a suitable hut on the way. Make sense?"

"OK," said Peter. "Let's get moving. Probably best to limit our movements as much as possible to dusk and dawn so we can pass unnoticed more easily. There's no sense in leaving ourselves open to being challenged by all and sundry every five minutes."

Peter folded the map away carefully and stowed it back into his backpack. Then, slipping his arms through the straps, he shrugged the pack onto his shoulders, grunting as it thudded into place. Slinging their rifles over their shoulders, they made their way slowly but steadily through the woods in an easterly direction, heading towards the town but aiming to skirt it on the northern side.

Sure enough, after a few hundred yards, Peter felt Jan grip his upper arm, pulling him firmly but carefully to a stop. "Over there," he whispered as they dropped to one knee in unison. "About fifty yards away."

Peter followed the direction in which Jan was pointing and could just make out, between the thickly clustered pine tree trunks, a small log cabin.

"Jesus!" he exclaimed. "I'm glad one of us was paying attention. Let's stake it out for a while rather than rush in. We need to make sure it's not occupied."

Using hand signals, they moved to points on either side of the hut, remaining at roughly the same distance, where they could keep the door under surveillance. Peter could see there was only the one entrance, which made life a little easier. Working himself into a position amongst some low-level undergrowth, Peter settled in to watch and wait. From what he could tell so far, the hut was unoccupied, but far better to wait awhile and be sure of that rather than risk a contact at this early stage.

After an hour lying in the undergrowth, Peter felt it was safe to move. He was pretty certain there was no one within the hut. He could see that there were no signs of disturbance around the door, suggesting that no one had been near for quite some time. Hopefully this was one of those shepherds' huts and it was either abandoned or not currently in use.

Attracting Jan's attention, Peter indicated for them to approach the hut from either side, from where they carefully peered into the windows. There were no signs of life. Jan remained in position, gun at the ready, while Peter moved round to the door, knife in hand, and carefully and quietly pushed it open. It wasn't locked; there was no point; looking inside, he could see that there was nothing of value within that needed protecting. He called to Jan that it was safe to join him and then stepped inside to complete his survey of the interior. It was a one-room hut with a window at either end. In the centre stood a wood-burning stove, positioned effectively so that it heated the whole building equally. To the left of the door was a table with a couple of chairs around it. On the right were a couple of rudimentary wood-framed beds with straw-filled mattresses. Between them was a cupboard which contained a few blankets. Beyond that, there was not much else. It was also clear from the layers of dust and cobwebs that it hadn't seen any usage for quite some time, not that year at least.

"I don't think we'll be disturbed in here for a while at least," said Jan as he walked over to one of the beds and dumped his backpack on the floor by its side.

"Yes, this will do us nicely," agreed Peter. "Let's settle in here for the rest of the day."

Jan offered to take the first watch while Peter stretched out on the bed and went to sleep. It seemed like only minutes later that Jan was shaking him awake.

In reality, though, it was clearly much later, as Peter could see that the shadows had moved around the hut and had lengthened considerably.

"What time is it?"

"About four thirty," Jan replied.

"Any issues?"

"No, all quiet, Peter."

"Good. OK, I suggest you get some sleep now. I will wake you at about midnight. In the morning, I suggest we head down into Berchtesgaden and take a look around. Get our bearings and see what we can find out. In the meantime, I'll slip out and send a message back to base to let them know we're down safe."

Jan was soon dozing peacefully, despite the cooler air seeping into the hut as the sun went down and evening drew on. They didn't dare make a fire for fear of attracting unwanted attention, but fortunately the winter camouflage uniforms they had been equipped with were beautifully warm. Peter certainly hoped so as he prepared to venture out to use the radio set. He would need to head back up the slope to where the treeline ended: the combination of both these factors would help to ensure a stronger signal back to England. With a stifled grunt, he hefted the radio onto his back and pulled the door open, the cool night air stinging his exposed face as he did so.

Outside it was perfectly still and silent, the only sound being the crunch of his boots on the carpet of twigs and pine needles. Every hundred yards or so, he stopped by a tree trunk and listened for a couple of minutes to make sure there were no sounds of movement. After about twenty minutes of hard uphill slog, he reached the point where the trees thinned and finally ended. From this point he needed to be quick. It was unlikely that anyone would be monitoring for a signal, but the field-craft he had learned over the preceding months was deeply embedded in his mind. Spend as little time transmitting as possible. Don't let the bastards get a fix on you. Get on, get the message done, and get out as quick as you can. He was also conscious that up here, beyond the treeline, his form was silhouetted against the mountain slope, should anyone happen to be looking in his direction.

He had planned the message while he was walking, so it was just a case of setting up the radio and getting it done. After slipping the radio off his back, he settled it onto a flattish piece of ground, unclipped the canvas flap that protected the control panel, and tuned it in to the pre-agreed frequency. Straight away he began trying to raise a response from base.

"Red Kite calling Hawk's Nest. Red Kite calling Hawk's Nest. Are you receiving? Over."

Immediately after he had finished transmitting, the response came through. "This is Hawk's Nest. What is your status? Over."

"Red Kite down safe. No problems. Popping into town tomorrow to look round. Over."

"Understood, Red Kite. Have fun. Over and out."

Peter flicked the off switch, closed the protective flap, and lifted the set back onto his back. He was pleased that they had been alert, waiting for his contact, as it meant that the time spent transmitting had been kept to an absolute minimum. Fifteen minutes later, he was back in the hut; the going downhill was much easier on his tired legs.

It looked as if Jan hadn't stirred at all. He was still lying in the exact same position as when he had left him, though now he was snoring gently. Smiling to himself, Peter eased himself into one of the chairs facing the door and settled down to wait until it was time to swap shifts.

TWENTY

The next morning, over a quick breakfast of biscuits and cheese from their ration packs, they discussed their plans. They made do with water from a nearby stream to drink, as they dared not risk lighting a fire for a brew in case the smoke attracted unwanted attention. The cold of the water coming down from the snow line higher up the mountain made them suck in their cheeks and wince as it came into contact with their overly sensitive teeth, but it was beautifully refreshing all the same.

Peter knew that they would need to come face to face with the locals sooner or later, but he would much rather make sure they were properly prepared for that encounter rather than simply blunder in unwittingly. Whilst he was confident that their German was good enough to see them through most scenarios, he was all too conscious that unplanned events could lead to mistakes being made in the stress of the moment. All in all, it was best to stay as alert as possible.

"So," Jan mused, "what shall we do this fine day? Go for a walk? Fly a kite, perhaps?"

"I like the kite idea, only I think I forgot to pack it." Peter smiled. "Let's make our way down into Berchtesgaden to see if we can buy one there, and, while we are about it, we can have a look round. Might be a good opportunity to find out if the man himself is actually here at the moment."

"And if he's not? What then?"

"Well, I'm hoping we will find some of the Berghof guards down in one of the bars in town. With luck we might pick up some gossip about when they expect him to arrive next. It'll be good to have an idea as to how long we'll be hanging around. It would be just our luck to find that he's just left and not expected back for a couple of months! The longer we are here, the greater the risk of discovery, so if we can get in and out in a couple of days, then so much the better!

"I also suggest we look for alternative lodgings as well. As lovely as it is here, I'm not sure it's all that sensible to stay too long in one place. There's more chance of being found, for one thing, and we risk getting complacent if we get too comfortable here."

"It's a shame, as I was just starting to get cosy here, but I suppose you are right, Peter," Jan agreed. "OK, so we head into town to see how the land lies. In case we run into any patrols on the way, I suggest we make sure we are clear on our backstory."

"Absolutely. We should have no trouble blending in, as there should be plenty of Mountain Corps chaps around. There's going to be a constant flow of soldiers going to and from the front lines, so in theory, two more new faces won't make any difference to anyone."

Jan picked up. "So how about we say that we are returning from fighting partisans in the mountains of Yugoslavia? It is an area I know well from my childhood, so I should be able to cover any nasty little questions if need be. There's almost constant fighting with Tito's boys up in those hills, so we'll have no problems from that perspective. We should say that we picked up some minor injuries during the fighting, which were treated at the front-line field hospital, but we have been sent back here for recuperation and light duties for a few weeks."

"That works for me," Peter agreed. "Should be enough to help us get by in any casual conversation. Right, let's pack up our gear and head down the hill to town."

182

It was fewer than two miles to Berchtesgaden, and all of it downhill. They took it steady all the way, though, not so much because of the terrain, as this levelled out the further they went, and ceased to be any form of hindrance, but rather due to the fact that people in a hurry tend to attract more attention from curious observers. Their journey took them east initially, along a well-worn path which they followed until they reached the edge of the forest, where it joined a road which skirted the edge of the trees and headed down in the direction of the town. They hefted their packs into place, shouldered their rifles into the correct position, and turned to the right, onto the road, their standard-issue hobnailed boots crunching their way along the tarmacked surface.

Now that they were out in the open, it was essential that they played the part of two German mountain soldiers to perfection. They consciously assumed a more military bearing, not to the extent of formally marching but avoiding any unnecessary slovenliness that might land them in trouble with any over-offi-cious superior that they might bump into. They felt a little exposed on the road compared to what they had been used to in the forest. To their left were wide-open pastures stretching along the valley floor, and to the front, they could see the roofs of the town less than a mile away now. Beyond Berchtesgaden they could see the mountains rising up in majestic stature to surround the town as an impenetrable barrier, the bare limestone peaks, coated in snow, rising up proudly above the collar of pine forests that wrapped around their shoulders. Peter knew, however, that amongst this gloriously picturesque scenery, some-where up there, between the town and the mountain peaks, lay Hitler's lair.

The trees on their right eventually thinned and then ended as they hit the outskirts of the town. It was only as they came to this point that they actually saw anyone close up. If it weren't for the presence of a few soldiers, walk-ing along the pavements in twos and threes mostly, it would be difficult to tell that the country was at war. Life looked pretty normal here in the deep south of Germany. There were no ruined buildings, no bombed-out houses, no civilians pushing their belongings in front of them in old wooden handcarts. Instead, a few old men cycled sedately along the streets, one or two carrying dogs in their front baskets. Women pushed prams, some with toddlers hanging on to the handlebar, between the numerous shops, gathering their groceries.

As far as Peter could tell, there was little if any rationing happening here. The shops seemed to be fully stocked, and there was no evidence of any queuing or shortages. Clearly, living in the shadow of the Führer's favourite home had its advantages. There was a world of difference between this idyllic Alpine scene and the relative devastation they had left behind in London. If anything, with the exception of the troops, it reminded Peter of the family holidays he had spent in Bavaria in his youth. He couldn't remember ever having been to Berchtesgaden as a boy, but the scene was reminiscent of many a town in this region. The houses were all brightly painted in either white or pastel shades of pink, blue, yellow, and green. Many of them sported wooden balconies with iron railings, festooned with brightly coloured floral arrangements, on their second or third floors. All of them had gently sloping v-shaped wooden roofs which overhung the walls by a good three or four feet. It was nothing short of a picture-postcard scene, for sure.

Nevertheless, one thing did seem odd: the people here might not have wanted for anything, but they didn't seem to be particularly happy about it. People were going about their business, apparently as normal, but they did so with a lack of joy. Sure, there were people having conversations, but they were generally doing so in rushed, quiet tones, as if afraid to be overheard. Otherwise, people were just going quietly about their business and keeping themselves to themselves. On one corner, two women had stopped to chat. They didn't even give the two men a second glance as they walked past, a fact that pleased Peter initially, as it gave him confidence that they were blending in just fine. What was interesting, however, were the snatches of the conversation that they overheard as they passed by.

"Have you heard from Claus recently?" enquired the first.

"I had a letter this morning, actually. I think he wrote it about a week ago."

"Oh, that's good. Any news?"

"Well, they're not allowed to say much, and if they do, it gets censored before it reaches me. Big black pen marks all over the page. What I could make out, though, was that they seem to be continually retreating away from the advancing Russians. Between you and me, Heidi, things seem pretty desperate out there."

"I know. I heard a soldier in a bar telling his mates the other day that he thought that if they keep advancing at the rate they are, the Russians would reach our borders in fewer than six months."

"Shh, Heidi." The first woman had noticed the two soldiers walking past them. "We must trust in our Führer and the final victory he has promised us. I am sure these new superweapons we hear so much talk about will be our saviour."

Whatever Heidi said in response was lost to them as they moved further along the road. Once he was sure they were out of earshot, Peter remarked, "All is clearly not well in the heart of the Third Reich."

"So it seems," Jan responded. "Fear of the marauding Russkies is clearly taking its toll."

"They have probably heard tales from the front about atrocities supposedly exacted upon retreating soldiers. Looks like their cosy little existence may not last much longer at this rate. I'm sure it explains why everyone looks so pissed off round here."

"Interesting that comment about the Führer, though. Do you think they still believe in him and his promises, or was that little show for our benefit only?"

"Hard to know," Peter mused. "I am sure there are diehards out there who still believe victory to be inevitable, but I bet there are an equal number of sceptics, especially those with husbands, sons, or boyfriends at the front, who have their doubts, even in a place as steeped in Nazi ideology as this."

They continued following the road in what they assumed must be the direction of the centre of the town. They were heading for the Café Rottenhofer, which they remembered from their briefings held especial importance, it being one of the few places from which you could see the Führer's residence perched up in the foothills. Peter recalled they had been told that the flagpole in front of the Berghof was clearly visible from the café's rear windows, and if the Nazi flag was flying from that flagpole, it would mean that Hitler was in residence.

Rounding another corner, the two men found themselves in the main square, the centre of which was dominated by a grand stone fountain. From the centre of the fountain rose a column about ten to twelve feet high, on top of which sat a statue of a lion resting on its haunches. On the far side of the square, they could make out the sign for the café: large black letters in the classic Gothic style set on a painted yellow background, stretching almost the whole width of the façade.

"There it is. Come on, I'm gasping," Jan said as he stepped out to cross the road that ran round the edge of the square.

"For God's sake, Jan, be careful," Peter hissed as he caught up alongside his friend, grabbing his sleeve.

"What's wrong?"

"When you started to cross the road then, you looked to the right. We're not in England, you stupid bastard. For one, you could have been killed, but worse than that, you could have given us away."

"Jesus, you're right," Jan said sheepishly. "That was what the English would call a schoolboy error."

"Alright. No harm done as far as I can tell." Peter had been furtively glancing around the square as he spoke, but no one seemed to be taking any particular notice of them. "Just start to bloody focus, will you, and let's forget it happened. We're about to go into this café, so you need to be one hundred per cent switched on, OK?"

Jan nodded thoughtfully, as if the gravity of their situation was finally dawning on him. He cleared this throat. "Right, I'm ready. Let's go and sample the local beer."

Pushing open the door, the two men were immediately struck by the heavy, oppressive atmosphere. Despite the relatively early time, the room they entered was thick with the fumes of spilled beer and cigarettes. As far as they could see, the occupants, with the exception of a couple of barmaids, were exclusively male, and most of them were in uniform, many of which were the same as theirs. They were gathered in groups of two, three, or four around the various tables, chatting away noisily, supping on huge steins filled with lager, most of which appeared to have a good two or three inches of foam on top. Another, slightly larger, group was gathered around a piano in the corner where one of their number was crashing out popular army tunes accompanied by their raucous singing. Most of them completely ignored the new arrivals, whilst those that did look up at the door gave no more than a cursory glance before returning to their conversations. Another hurdle successfully passed, for which Peter offered up a silent prayer.

Peter and Jan made their way to the bar, behind which the landlord stood drying glasses with a stained beer towel before placing them on the shelf above his head. He was what Peter took for a typical Bavarian: a large, round-bellied man with a huge, bushy moustache that seemed intent on engulfing half of his face. His cheeks were ruddy as if he had just completed some major exertion.

As they approached, the barman threw the towel over the edge of the sink behind him, wiped his hands on his equally beer-stained apron, before turning to greet them with a broad smile. "What will it be, gentlemen?"

"Two beers, please," Jan answered.

"Of course, of course." The landlord beamed as he began to pull the first glass of beer. "So, I don't think I have seen you two before. Are you new in town, or have you just been kicked out of one of the other bars?"

"No, we're new here. We've been sent back from the front to complete our recovery with a few weeks' rest and recuperation."

"Ah, been in the thick of it, have we? Well, I hope you have a nice stay here, gentlemen."

"Thank you," replied Peter. "It is certainly a most beautiful town."

This made the barman's smile widen yet further, which Peter had not thought possible. "You are too kind. Tell me, your accents are a little strange, certainly not local. Where do you boys come from originally?"

Peter hesitated, trying to summon an appropriate response for something he realised they had not prepared, but luckily Jan stepped in to save the situation. "We're from the Sudetenland, so you could say we are more Czech than German in a way." He grinned. "We've only really been proper Germans since Herr Hitler annexed us in 1938."

"Ah, that would make sense," the barman laughed. "We always think you lot are a bit weird, if you'll excuse me for saying. You know, a bit like country bumpkins, if you will. But you two seem quite normal in all fairness. Seem to have the right number of fingers on each hand and everything!"

Peter and Jan laughed along with the joke at their expense whilst the beers were set on the bar in front of them. They paid, thanked the barman, and then took their glasses to the nearest empty table.

"Well, that seemed to go alright," Jan whispered from the side of his mouth as he sat down.

"Yes, well done on the Sudetenland thing, that was a stroke of genius. But we can't afford to relax. We must stay on our guard, Jan." Peter nodded over Jan's shoulder, towards the rear of the bar, just to the left of the singing group. "Looks like the toilets are over there at the back of the room. I'll go in a few minutes and see if I can manage to get a look up at the Berghof on the way."

"Sounds like a plan," agreed Jan.

After about twenty minutes, during which time they did their best to swap small talk about the weather and the beer, Peter got up, stretched, and began wandering in the direction of the toilets. When he emerged a couple of minutes later, he casually paused by the window as if to admire the view. Berchtesgaden was positioned in a little bowl-like valley, surrounded by imposing, snow-capped Alpine peaks. You could easily forget yourself and just let your mind wander in awe at the majesty of the scenery.

Peter pushed the thoughts to the back of his mind and focussed instead on the job in hand. He didn't want to be seen staring for too long in case he aroused unwanted attention. Unfortunately for him, however, one of the group standing around the piano peeled off and came to stand next to him.

"Magnificent, isn't it?" the newcomer said.

"Most certainly," Peter replied, keeping his voice as even as possible, despite his nerves.

"Is this your first time in Berchtesgaden?"

"Yes, though I used to come to Bavaria and Austria before the war, on walking holidays," Peter answered truthfully.

"Ah, myself also. I never grow tired of looking at these mountains. It is no surprise that our Führer chooses this location for his home."

"Really?" Peter replied. "I did not know that."

"Yes, yes," the solider enthused, grabbing Peter's arm as he spoke. "You see there?" He pointed out the window, slightly to the left of centre. "That mountain peak about two miles from here, the one that rises sharply to a point? Just to the right of that, do you see that big white house? The one with the flagpole just in front?"

Peter followed the directions and soon spotted the house. It was exactly as he recalled from the photographs they had been shown in the briefings. The house was surrounded with trees above and below, apart from a small clearing behind and in front. The centre of the building, the main living accommodation, looked to rise up about three stories to a peaked roof in the classic Alpine style. On each side was a two-storey annex, set at a perpendicular angle to the main building, which also had a similar-style roof. Peter knew that these buildings were separate to the main building and housed servants' quarters on the right and a telephone exchange on the left.

"Ah yes, I see," Peter responded non-committedly. "You say that our Führer lives there?"

"Indeed so. Of course, he is not there all the time, as he has many responsibilities and commitments all over the Reich, but whenever he can, he loves to come back here. I think he is happiest when he is here."

"Is he there now?" Peter asked conversationally, though he had already worked out the answer.

"There is an easy way to find out, let me tell you. Do you see the flagpole just to the left of the main building, yes?"

Peter nodded.

"You can tell whether he is in residence, as they always fly the swastika flag when he is. I see there is no flag flying, so would have to conclude that, today, he is not there."

Peter smiled. "I guess that makes sense. If I recall from my lessons at school, I think the British do the same with their King and Buckingham Palace."

"Indeed, I believe you are right. Anyway, it is nice to have met you, Herr…?"

"Matthaus, Claus Matthaus," Peter offered without a pause whilst extending his hand.

"Hans Ludendorf at your service." The grip was firm and uncompromising.

Peter released the grip and turned to go.

"One more thing, Sergeant Matthaus." Ludendorf smiled. "Will you be with us here in Berchtesgaden for long?"

"Hopefully just a few days," Peter replied. "We have been sent back for light duties to help complete our recovery from wounds we picked up fighting down in the Yugoslav mountains. Why do you ask?"

"I am in charge of the Führer's security detail up at the Berghof. I make it my business to know everyone's business, especially if I have not seen them before."

Peter smiled. "I congratulate you on your dedication to duty."

Peter nodded his farewell and returned to the table, where Jan had almost finished his beer, and sat down with a heavy exhalation of breath.

"Everything OK?" Jan asked.

"I thought it was, until he tells me that he runs the whole security show up at the Berghof."

"You don't think he suspects anything, do you?" Jan whispered over the top of his glass.

"I don't think so. I am just trying to think back over whether there was anything I said or did that could possibly give him any cause to investigate. As far as I can recall, it was a normal conversation that any two soldiers in a bar might have. He told me about the flag and the fact that it indicates whether the Führer is in residence. He's not in, by the way. But then he started asking how long we are here for, which unnerved me, and when I asked him why he wanted to know, he tells me he is head of security up at the Berghof or some such."

"Jesus," Jan exhaled. "You know how to pick your friends, don't you! On the plus side, I guess we know now that the big man is not in town, which is a help. But do we have any idea when he may be putting in an appearance?"

"Not in the slightest." Peter shrugged. "Fingers crossed it is sometime soon, though, eh? I suggest, for the time being, we keep a low profile, whilst establishing something of a routine, so we don't arouse suspicion by not being seen for days on end in town."

"If you mean we have to come back here for another beer tomorrow, I'm OK with that. Got nothing else planned anyway."

Peter laughed, drained his glass, and stood up. "Come on, let's go."

TWENTY-ONE

For the next few days, they stuck to a routine to ensure they remained as inconspicuous as possible. After a couple more visits to the same bar, they had become accepted almost as regulars by the landlord; he had already taken to greeting them by name on entry. Each evening, as far as possible, they tried to move around different mountain huts so as not to stay too long in the same place. They didn't have a lot of kit with them, and, other than the radio, none of it was in any way incriminating: their careful preparations back in England had seen to that. That said, it paid to be careful.

They saw nothing more of the security officer as well, which suited Peter down to the ground, as he was keen to avoid any further awkward questions. But, more frustratingly, they also saw no sign of the arrival or even the potential arrival of their target. The flag remained resolutely missing from its pole outside the Führer's residence. Each day they reported back to SOE Headquarters with the same message: "Bird has flown the nest."

As Peter lay on his cot bed that night, trying to go to sleep, he did not feel too concerned about their current predicament from a practical perspective. They had enough currency for a while yet to ensure that they stayed well fed; they were staying fit by regular walks down into the town and back up into the mountains each evening. On the flip side, though, the longer they stayed, the higher the probability of their being discovered or them making an error that led to them being found out. As far as he could see, however, they had little choice but to sit tight and wait it out, while staying as low-profile as possible.

The next morning, Peter woke with a start. Jan was shaking his shoulder while holding his hand over Peter's mouth to prevent any sudden sound. Peter's eyes, widening with concern, darted towards the door.

"Shh," Jan whispered. "There's an old boy and his dog heading in this direction. Moving slowly with no particular purpose but clearly heading this way. I reckon this is his hut we have holed up in."

It was true, Peter recalled, that this particular hut had seemed to show signs of more recent occupation, but it had been late and already dark when they arrived, and they had felt little inclination to go looking for anywhere else. Peter cursed, with the benefit of hindsight. It was a sign that they were getting lazy. The long days of doing very little had taken the edge off their field-craft skills. Perhaps they were fortunate that it was not a German patrol, but the point was still plain to see. They had to sharpen up, quick, and now they had a situation that needed to be managed one way or another.

"There's no time to make a run for it," Jan continued. "He'll see us for sure. Do you think we'll have to kill him?"

"I'd rather not, as it makes things way too complicated, but we can't rule it out," Peter replied. "But let's just play it by ear and see what happens. Follow my lead."

Moments later, the door creaked open. The man was clearly of farming stock, dressed in an old but well-made tweed suit which he wore over a thick-knit woollen sweater. Jutting out from between his bushy moustache-and-beard combination was a smoking pipe. On seeing the two soldiers inside his hut, he simply stopped in the doorway, removed his pipe, which he proceeded to knock against the door frame, and, with his other hand, rubbed his chin. His dog, meanwhile, trotted into the hut, where it approached each man in turn for a sniff before settling down, with an air of familiarity, in front of the fireplace, even though it was long cold. Seemingly uninterested in the two men, the dog rested its head on its two front paws as it stretched out for a snooze after what must have been a long walk.

"Good morning, boys." The farmer smiled. "What brings you to these parts?"

"Our apologies, sir," Peter replied. "We're new in these parts and got lost last evening while on patrol. We saw this hut and decided to bed down for the night. We were just about to get on our way to report in before they send the search parties." As he spoke, Peter made a show of packing his kitbag, keeping his knife close at hand at the top of the bag in case it was needed in a hurry.

"Ach, it's not a problem. You're not the first lost soldiers I have found in here, and I am sure you won't be the last. Would you take some breakfast before you go?" The farmer unslung his rucksack off his shoulder, set it on the table, and removed some fresh bread and sausage followed by a flask of steaming hot coffee.

Peter caught the pleading look in Jan's eye but replied instead, "That is very kind of you, sir, but we must decline. No doubt we are already in significant trouble for failing to report in last night. We should not make it any worse if it can be avoided."

"I understand. I will not be offended if you go. No doubt everything is mad busy for your lot at the moment anyway."

"Why do you say that?" Jan asked, his interest pricked.

"Ha! How long did you say you have been lost for? You must be the only two soldiers in the whole area who don't know that the Führer himself is due to arrive sometime this week."

"Ah that." Peter feigned indifference. "You get used to it after a while, to be honest. There is always somebody important here or there almost every other week. Though to be fair, we have not met the top man before, so that is a little out of the ordinary."

The farmer, munching on his sausage, grinned. "I guess it's all the same to you boys. Truth be told, it's much the same here. If it's not Hitler up at the big house, then it's Goering, Goebbels, or Bormann or one of the others. Still, it's been a fair few weeks since he was last here. Things must be busy with the war to keep him away from his favourite spot for so long. And there's no way of knowing how long he'll stay this time either. One new crisis and he'll be off back to Berlin, no doubt."

Peter hefted his pack onto his shoulders and picked up his rifle. "Well, it was nice to meet you, sir. And thanks again for the roof over our heads last night. Perhaps we'll meet again."

"Aye, best of luck to you, boys. May you spend a long time away from the front line, eh?"

Although he could barely contain himself, Peter managed to wait until they were well out of earshot before speaking. "Finally, Jan! Finally we have the news we've been waiting for!"

"Yes." Jan grinned. "Ironic that we have been going to town every day for a week and heard nothing when all we had to do was wait for the information to come to us. Still, the beer was nice, I suppose."

Peter was almost bouncing as he spoke. "Come on, let's put in a call to base to let them know the news, and then I think it's time we scouted out our approach to the point where I need to take the shot, not to mention getting an idea of sentry positions and patrol patterns and such like. Given that he will be here any day now, the sooner we do that, the better."

TWENTY-TWO

As soon as they had put the call in to inform HQ about Hitler's imminent arrival, Peter and Jan set about preparing to reconnoitre their planned route to the intended firing position. Using the handkerchief maps, they could see that they would need to strike north from Berchtesgaden, keeping off the roads and paths as far as possible to avoid detection. Eventually they would reach the river Larosbach, which ran in a roughly south-easterly direction.

At this point they would turn to follow the river as it meandered through a densely wooded valley for a couple of miles. Then they would turn south-west through the trees and go up the slope of the mountain until they reached the picket fence around the estate. From here they should have a commanding view over the estate and, more importantly, the supposed route that Hitler liked to take on his morning walk to the Mooslahner Kopf teahouse for breakfast.

Having memorised the planned route, they slipped on their backpacks, shouldered their rifles, and set off. They walked in silence at first, each alone with his own thoughts, and made good progress as the terrain was no more than undulating. Within an hour they had reached the river, having encountered no one. Here they called a halt for five minutes to rest. Despite the cool temperatures, they were nonetheless sweating at the exertion. They munched on a couple of chocolate bars from their German army rations and drank their fill of water, refilling their canteens in the river. The cool mountain water was immensely refreshing.

"I'm always amazed how good ice-cold water tastes when you're thirsty." Jan smiled. "Might even say I prefer it to beer at this precise moment."

"We must be climbing higher," Peter deadpanned. "Your brain is clearly starved of oxygen."

Being careful to leave no evidence of their presence, they set off again, striking south-east to follow the course of the river. The going was that bit tougher now as the water meandered between ancient boulders, its course defined by erosion over the centuries. Rather than sapping their strength by clambering over the boulders, not to mention risking turning or even breaking an ankle on surfaces that were slippery with moss, they walked ten to twenty yards away from the river. They were careful, however, to keep it in sight, or at least in earshot, so as not to lose their bearings.

After another hour or so, they stopped for a lunch of bread and local sausage, which they had bought in town the previous day. The site of their picnic was the point where they needed to turn away from the river to start to head up the mountain.

"From here we must be as stealthy as possible," Peter said between bites. "There's a good chance that there are patrols, probably with dogs, in the forest around the estate. We need to be alert, speak only in German, and make as little noise as possible."

"Understood." Jan nodded.

Although this was only a recce, the danger was nonetheless all too real. They fully expected security to be tight around the estate and needed to be on their guard at all times. All that was in their favour was that, as the Führer was not currently on-site, the Germans may not yet have ramped up the number or extent of the patrols. That was offset in Peter's mind, though, by the thought that if it were him in charge of security, he would be sweeping the area around the estate in the days prior to the arrival. He could only hope that the Germans were less conscientious in their approach and more complacent in this the heartland of the Third Reich.

"I reckon it's about two miles from here to the wire. We'd best take it nice and steady, so we'll be looking to get into position in about an hour to an hour and a half."

"Makes sense," Jan confirmed.

From this point on, they unslung their rifles and carried them at the ready. Peter had no intention of using them; the sound of a gunshot would echo round the mountains and potentially bring every patrol within a five-mile radius down on their heads. That said, it made them feel more secure to have them to hand, and it might buy them a couple of seconds in a confrontation—time, perhaps, that would allow them to get close enough to use their knives, or at least to use the rifle butts as bludgeons.

This final leg of the journey proved to be much tougher. Not only was it pretty much constantly uphill, but it was also densely wooded, meaning they couldn't maintain a straight course, and rather had to pick their way forward in a series of twists and turns. On the plus side, Peter mused, if it was hard going for them, it would most likely deter German patrols as well.

After an hour and a quarter of hard slog, Peter put his hand on Jan's upper arm and went down on one knee, pulling Jan down with him. With his other hand, he placed his index finger to his lips, indicating the need for silence. Peter leaned over to Jan and cupped his hand over his comrade's ear.

"I think the forest ends just up ahead. This must be it."

Jan nodded in reply.

"From here, we crawl forward slowly and carefully to get to a spot where we can get a decent vantage point."

Again, Jan nodded his understanding.

It took them a further ten minutes to cover the remaining hundred yards or so, but much better to be slow than risk detection, in Peter's mind. They stopped a couple of yards from the edge in a clump of ferns, which provided suitable cover but which also allowed them a decent view ahead. Directly in front of them, about 150 yards away, Peter estimated, was the wire fence that surrounded the Berghof estate. They could see it stretching away to either side of them, curving round the estate as it went. It was tightly meshed, having the look of wire you might see on a farm to enclose the chickens. At the top, leaning outwards to deter anyone from trying to climb the fence, were three strands of vicious-looking barbed wire. Rigidity and tension in the fence were provided by a series of equally spaced metal poles which were the same height as the fence. Speaking of height, Peter reckoned the wire fence must be around seven or eight feet high, with the barbed wire adding the best part of another foot: a pretty formidable obstacle to anyone wanting to get over it.

Peter nudged Jan with his elbow and pointed to the left. They could clearly make out the Führer's residence about half a mile away. Peter noted that there was still no flag hoisted on the flagpole at the front of the building. As far as they could see, there were no sentries outside the building, and this seemed to confirm their briefing in which it had been stated that normally there was a sentry posted at the front only overnight or when the Führer was in residence.

In turn, Jan then nudged Peter and pointed in front of them and slightly to the right. Just over a mile away on the edge of some trees, they could make out the shape of a stone building.

"That must be the teahouse," Jan whispered.

Peter nodded. He was on the verge of replying when he froze. An SS solider had appeared from the side of the building and begun walking towards them, following the line of the wire fence. As he came closer, Peter and Jan slowly lowered their heads to maximise the cover of the ferns. Even at this distance, they hardly dared breathe. Peter wished the guard would get a move on, but he was clearly in no hurry, almost sauntering along as if taking a pleasant country stroll, enjoying the scenery. It took him about twenty minutes in total to reach the section of fence in front of their position, but when he did so, he kept walking without even missing a step. Peter exhaled slowly, offering a silent prayer of thanks as he did so. They kept watching him until he reached the big house, which seemed to be the end of his patrol route. It also seemed to be the end of his shift, as he was relieved by a new soldier who then immediately began walking back along the same route, again passing their position without a glance or a pause.

Peter noted the time on his watch at which the changeover had taken place: 14.31.

They stayed in position until darkness fell, building a profile of the pattern of activity. It was clear that the guards changed shifts near enough every two hours, presumably to alleviate the monotony. The patrolling was not continuous, though, as it appeared that, more often than not, when they reached the teahouse, they stopped for a while. Whether to grab a coffee and cigarette or to chat with the staff was unclear. Either way, they were out of sight of the estate up at the teahouse and no doubt felt they could get away with taking a breather for a while.

There were no other patrols around their location, and no further sentries appeared either. It remained to be seen how far security increased once Hitler arrived.

They resolved to stay in position overnight so that they had a more complete picture of a full day's proceedings. Each of them took it in turns to observe for two hours while the other slept. During Peter's turn, he noted that the patrol continued throughout the night, the guard carrying a torch, the main purpose of which seemed to be to help him avoid tripping over tufts of grass rather than to scan the surroundings. The gaps at the teahouse end were shorter too; presumably as the café was closed, there was no reason to hang around any longer than the time it took for a sneaky cigarette break. And even though it was July, the weather up this high was still that bit colder at night, so no doubt this meant that the patrols also preferred to keep moving to stay warm.

The only other difference was the appearance of the expected additional sentry at the front of the Führer's residence. Peter could just make him out standing next to his sentry post, silhouetted in the light cast by the lanterns positioned on the walls of the buildings.

Morning came, and the additional sentry returned to the barracks. Everything seemed back as it had been the previous afternoon. Peter nudged Jan awake. They watched for another hour, during which time the patrol changed shifts again, Peter noting with satisfaction that it was pretty much bang on eight thirty.

"There's nothing like German efficiency. You can set your watch by it."

"I'm getting hungry," Jan complained. "How about we head back down to town? We've seen enough."

Peter nodded and was just about to start shuffling backwards when he heard a bark, followed by voices. They flattened themselves against the earth whilst trying to peer to their left in the direction of the noise to see who or what was coming their way. About two hundred yards away and on their side of the wire fence were two SS guards, one of whom was holding a lead, at the end of which was a huge German shepherd dog. It was clearly keen to be off and rummaging in the undergrowth, as it was straining against the leash. The guard holding the dog had a rifle slung over his shoulder, while the other carried the classic German machine pistol, or Schmeisser, across his chest.

It was too late to move now without being seen. There was nothing they could do but lie completely still and hope that the ferns provided enough cover and that they were upwind from the dog's sensitive nose. Peter calculated that the guards would pass them a good hundred yards away, as even though they were on the same side of the fence, they were staying pretty close to the wire, presumably as the terrain was more even.

At the point where the patrol was almost level with the two agents, the dog became even more agitated and even let out a few barks in the direction of the trees where they hid.

"Shit," Peter whispered, reaching down to ease his knife from his jackboot as gently as possible. "They see us, then we're completely stuffed."

The guard with the sub-machine gun stopped, turned, and started to take a few tentative steps towards them. The guard with the dog, meanwhile, stood his ground and was pulling at the leash, trying to get the dog back under control.

"It's nothing, Klaus," he shouted. "You've seen what she's like today; she's spooked by every little thing. I don't know what's got into her."

"All the same, Hans, we should check it out to be sure," came the reply. He had levelled his machine pistol in the direction of the forest. He had stopped to reply to Hans, but now started walking again, and the other guard reluctantly began to follow, though he had not unslung his rifle.

Peter tensed, ready to spring as soon as the guard got near enough. He was not confident, however, that they could deal with both guards and the dog without the alarm being raised. The Berghof-to-tea room patrol was not in sight, which was something, but there was every chance one of the two guards would get a shot off, or at least a shout, and give the game away. Nevertheless, doing nothing was not an option, and if the guard kept walking, he would be on top of them in another minute or so.

The guard was now only fifty yards away, looking left and right along the treeline. Peter was amazed that they had not been spotted. He could feel his heart pounding in his chest and his blood pumping ferociously in his neck. He could also feel the sweat dripping off his forehead and into his eyes, causing a stinging sensation. He forced himself to slow his breathing as best he could, trying to regain control of his body and focus the adrenalin rush onto the potential need for action.

Just when he thought that detection was inevitable, there was a rustling sound about ten yards to their left; two large hares suddenly broke cover and raced away across the open ground, darting left and right as if to evade pursuit. The soldier called Hans was fighting frantically to keep the dog under control as it tried to give chase, eventually having to resort to bending down to give it a hefty thwack on the snout to calm it down.

"I told you it was nothing, Klaus," Hans moaned, straightening up. "This dog is a complete pain in the arse today. I'm going to ask for a different one tomorrow and have this one sent on mine-detection duty on the Eastern Front! That will teach it a lesson."

Klaus grinned and turned back towards the fence, away from the two relieved agents. "Shh, you'll hurt her feelings."

"I don't care. She's annoying the hell out of me."

Peter waited until they were a couple of hundred yards further on before relaxing. "Jesus! That was a close one. I thought we'd had it then for sure."

"Can you smell anything?" Jan grimaced. "Only I think I may have soiled my pants."

TWENTY-THREE

They lay still for a further ten minutes, just to make absolutely sure that no alarm had been raised. It also gave them time to recover more fully from the whole nerve-racking experience. After a final check to make sure they were not being observed, they crawled back from their position, masking any signs of their having been there as they went. Some twenty metres back from the edge of the trees, they got to their feet and began to retrace their steps back to the river, staying vigilant all the way. Back at the river, they allowed themselves a break to take on food and water.

"How the hell could we be so stupid as to forget the damned dog patrol?" Peter exclaimed. "I remember it quite distinctly being mentioned at the briefings now. Every morning between nine and ten o'clock, two men with one dog walking the perimeter of the estate boundary in an anticlockwise direction." Peter was quoting almost verbatim from the briefing a few weeks ago.

"Now you come to mention it…" Jan nodded sheepishly.

"Well," Peter continued, "I suppose, on the plus side, at least it did help to verify the timings for the actual mission."

"You're right, Peter. We need to time our approach to be in position after the dog patrol and before Hitler takes his walk. If I recall correctly, his daily routine indicates that he usually leaves the Berghof not long after ten and has never been known to leave before ten."

Peter took up the thinking. "So, he should be hitting our section of the fence ten to fifteen minutes later. If the dog patrol keeps to the same schedule as today, it should be past our position by roughly nine fifteen. We need to be in position a good half hour before the target arrives, so we are looking to be in place by nine forty, a good twenty or so minutes after the dog has passed. It's tight but should just about be OK."

"And given it took us about three hours to reach our position," Jan confirmed, "we want to be setting off no later than six thirty. God, I just love an early start."

They sat in silence for a few minutes, each mulling over the plan. After a while, Jan raised what both of them were thinking.

"So, having now observed the target area in some detail and for some time, do you think it can really be done?"

"I don't see why not," Peter replied. "It's a shot of fewer than two hundred yards; back on the range, I can nail the target every time at twice that distance."

"That is true, of course, Peter, but here you have a target that is moving and is a real human being. And not just any human, but the leader of the Fascist regime and the cause of what must be millions of deaths globally. That has got to bring a level of pressure you will never have experienced before, surely?"

"Not thought about it until you brought it up, so thanks for that, mate!" To Jan's mind, Peter was doing his best to make light of it despite what he might be feeling inside. It was only a temporary moment of self-doubt, however. "Don't you worry on that score, Jan. I have been waiting for an opportunity like this since the Nazis killed my parents back home in the Netherlands in 1940 and since my sister was killed in an air raid in London not long after. Ever since I was selected for this mission, I have dreamt every night of pulling that trigger and seeing him go down. This is all that I have left to live for, Jan."

Jan could see the passion burning in Peter's eyes. For a moment he felt a pang of anxiety; Peter seemed to flip from levity to deadly serious within a heartbeat. Was this because he was not fully in control of his mind? Or was it just excessive excitement now that they were so close to their goal? The pressure must be intense, and he could not, hand on heart, say whether his friend was able to deal with it. He decided not to press the matter there and then but to keep an eye on him as discreetly as possible.

"I don't doubt that, Peter."

They made the rest of the journey down the mountain in silence, Peter seemingly lost in his thoughts and Jan unwilling to interrupt them. Down in the foothills, a mile or so outside of Berchtesgaden, they found a suitable refuge in which to lay up for the rest of the day to catch up on sleep. It was another of the typical farmer's wooden huts that were dotted around the countryside. This one, however, seemed to have been taken over by the army as a supply room for one of the many smoke batteries that were positioned in the local area as a defence against air raids. Jan was a little nervous about staying there but was won over by a combination of extreme fatigue from their near-sleepless night and the evidence that there seemed to have been little activity at the hut for some time. There were cobwebs on top of the cobwebs, and thick layers of dust on every surface. For security purposes, they piled four of the heavy crates against the door. Jan was not sure how much protection they would provide in the event that they were disturbed, but they both agreed that it kind of made them feel a little safer.

Soon after this, they settled down on the floor with their packs as makeshift pillows. Despite their tiredness, it was hard to get to sleep with the early afternoon sun still streaming through the one window in the hut, albeit filtered as it was by layers of grime and numerous cobwebs. Jan, having never been keen on the thought, let alone the presence, of spiders tried to take his mind off them by giving voice to his thoughts.

"Peter? What do you think will happen?"

"What do you mean?"

"I mean, if we manage to kill Hitler, what happens then?"

"I wouldn't worry about it, Jan. Let's just focus on getting the job done, eh?"

"No, seriously. I've been thinking about it a lot. Will the war end straight away, do you think?"

"I'm sure that's what the bigwigs are hoping for, my friend."

"But how likely is that, Peter? I mean, we're risking our lives here, and yet we don't seem to have much of a clue as to whether it will work."

"Well, to my mind, leaving aside the impact he has had on my family, the man is pure evil, responsible for more deaths than pretty much any other single person that I can think of in all of history. Whatever the outcome, the world is surely better off without him in it?"

"That's fair, Peter, but do you not also wonder what might happen once he's dead?"

"Not really, Jan, if I am honest with you. I just want the guy in a grave, and I want to be the one to put him there."

Jan was not to be put off, though. "To my mind, there are a number of scenarios which could play out, each as likely as the others."

"Go on?"

"Well, surely a big factor would be who takes over as leader. If it's one of the cronies—you know, Goebbels, Himmler, and the like—then I think the war carries on. Those men are in too deep to back down. I can imagine Goebbels trying to create a massive propaganda boost out of the assassination, you know, to try and rally morale. It must be flagging with all the setbacks recently on the Eastern Front, Africa, and Italy. The Russkies especially are making huge gains, pushing the Germans back all the time. It won't be long, at the rate they are going, before they have kicked them out of Russia altogether, and I bet you they don't stop and all go home when they reach the border."

"Yes, but if someone from the army takes over," Peter reasoned, "then things could be a lot different."

"I agree. You would expect the generals to have a more rational response. They must have a more realistic and objective understanding of the military position and Germany's chances of victory, which look slimmer with each passing month. They might well see Hitler's death as an opportunity to cut their losses and make peace."

"Or even to try and join with the Western Allies against Ivan. Have you thought of that, Jan?"

"I guess it's possible. But again, that might rely on someone like Goebbels stirring up fear about the so-called unwashed Bolshevik hordes sweeping over the Steppes towards the civilised peoples of Western Europe!"

"Another big factor in the equation, Peter, would be who they find to blame for the assassination. If they pin it on the Allies, and find the evidence to support that, then that would help them to make him into a martyr to fire up the population to continue the fight with renewed vigour."

"I certainly wouldn't put it past them, Jan, whether they have the evidence or not, to be frank."

"It's a fair point, my friend. We went to a lot of trouble making sure all our kit is one hundred per cent authentic and that nothing can tie us back to

England, but that may not stop them from saying that the Allies were behind it anyway."

"Especially if we get caught and they go to work on us, Jan. How long do you think we could realistically hold out for under a Gestapo interrogation?"

"I don't know about you, Peter," Jan spoke with a quiet resolve, "but I'm not planning on letting it come to that. The last bullet in my Luger is for me. And if I don't get the chance to do that, then there's always the capsule that Courtney gave us."

Silence fell between them as they both considered the enormity of their situation. "I hear it's over pretty quickly," Peter said eventually. "Just a couple of seconds of pain and then nothing."

Jan smiled. "The bullet to the head would be a little quicker, I think."

Peter smiled in return. "But you need a steady hand, Jan. Imagine if you missed! Especially when you're as crap a shot as you are."

———

They slept until dawn and awoke as refreshed as was possible in the cramped conditions of the hut. After a few minutes, Peter went outside to take a leak, taking the radio with him so he could check in and report the successful reconnaissance mission. On his return, some twenty minutes later, Jan was packed up and ready for the off.

"So what's the plan today, Peter?" he said, handing him a lump of bread and cheese from their provisions.

"Well," Peter replied between bites, "it's a question now of waiting. There's nothing more we can do to prepare, really. We just need to sit tight, lay low, and wait for our moment."

"OK, but presumably we'll need to venture into town to find out if and when he arrives?"

"Yes, we have no choice but to take that risk, and keep taking it until we see the flag go up outside the house. We'll just have to stay alert and at the same time remain as inconspicuous as possible. Do nothing to arouse suspicion in anything that we do or say."

———

They spent the next few days locked in a monotonous routine, spending most of the daylight hours out of sight in a number of abandoned huts in the hills surrounding Berchtesgaden. The only variety to their existence came with a brief excursion into the town, during which they stocked up on supplies and checked out the Berghof via the back window of the bar. They varied the time of their visit and the route by which they approached and walked through the town so that they did nothing that made people stop and take note.

It seemed to Peter that the town was busier than it had been when they arrived. He hoped this was a sign that Hitler's arrival was imminent but at the same time wondered whether he was just desperately looking for clues where there were none. Privately he was even beginning to doubt the truth of what the farmer had said. How the hell would he have known if Hitler was due to stay at the Berghof? It had been madness to pin their hopes on the words of the old man. Eventually Peter realised that it was beyond their control and to waste more time worrying about it was futile. He would arrive when he arrived, and they would just have to sit tight and stay focussed until that point.

TWENTY-FOUR

The news that they had been waiting for came on the fourth day after their reconnaissance mission. They had settled into the bar as usual, with a glass of beer at a table near the back window. Peter was just taking a sip when he felt a sharp dig on his shin where Jan had booted him to get his attention. He looked up at Jan, irritable at having nearly spilt his drink and at the sharp pain in his leg. Jan, ignoring his friend's protest, nodded briefly in the direction of the window. Catching his meaning, Peter, with as much nonchalance as he could muster, placed his glass back down on the table, swallowed, and gazed out of the window as if taking in the scenery.

He could clearly see the Berghof from his position, and there, beyond any doubt, was the swastika flag at the top of the flagpole, flapping wildly in what was a pretty stiff breeze. Turning back to face the room, Peter did a quick assessment to see whether anyone was taking any notice of them. He needn't have worried, though, as there were only a few clients in that lunch time and most of them were engrossed in a highly competitive and noisy game of cards. The landlord was also otherwise engaged: he had his back to them, vigorously polishing the glasses he had just washed, before reaching up to place them in line on the shelf above the bar.

"Well that's very interesting," Peter said in a low monotone.

"I thought it might grab your attention," Jan replied, with the briefest of smiles.

Peter took another sip of beer, noticing as he did so that his heartbeat seemed to have doubled in pace. He also felt noticeably warmer; he was conscious that a few beads of sweat had formed at the edge of his hairline. He mopped his brow with a folded handkerchief, which he extracted from his trouser pocket while trying to force his breathing back under control before speaking again.

"I suggest we finish these and head back to discuss the implications."

Jan nodded, draining his glass.

Once outside, they walked as calmly as they could out of the town and up into the surrounding woods to the north. While they were in danger of being overheard, they kept their conversation casual, waiting until they were out of sight in the woods before changing the subject.

"OK, Jan, this is it. The big man has finally arrived."

Jan grunted. "So what do we do now? Do we go tomorrow?"

"I can't think of a reason not to, mate," Peter confirmed. "All we need to do is radio in as soon as it gets dark to confirm that the target is here. They should hopefully give us final sanction to proceed. Though, to be honest, it should just be a formality. I can't see why they would not give a green light, given we've come this far."

"Yeah, I reckon you're right, Peter. We'd best get some rest now, as it will be an early start to get into position."

"Agreed. I suggest we pop out at around ten o'clock tonight to radio in."

———

Later that evening, they made their way silently up through the trees from the hut in which they'd bedded down for the afternoon. After a brief hike, they

213

reached the edge of the treeline. Here they stayed for a while to make sure nothing seemed out of place. Satisfied that all was well, they crept forward, crouching to keep their profile against the landscape to a minimum, even in the darkness that surrounded them. They reached a point where they felt the signal would be good enough and stopped to set up the radio set.

Having tuned in to the correct frequency, Peter pressed the transmit button. "Red Kite calling Hawk's Nest. Red Kite calling Hawk's Nest. Are you receiving? Over."

Over the static noise, it was hard to make out a response. Peter repeated the call sign while marginally turning the frequency dial either side of the expected position. After the third attempt, they heard the response coming through, faint but understandable.

"Hawk's Nest receiving you. Over."

Peter smiled at Jan. "Excellent! Had me worried for a second." He then leaned into the microphone once more. "Hawk's Nest, this is Red Kite. Sparrow has come home to roost. Requesting permission to proceed tomorrow. I repeat, Sparrow has come home to roost. Over."

"This is Hawk's Nest. Message understood. Please stand by for confirmation. Over."

There was little that they could do now but sit tight and wait. They hoped it would not be too long, as transmitting left them in danger of being located by the Germans if they happened to be monitoring radio traffic nearby.

After a few minutes, Jan asked, "What do you think is causing the delay?"

"Probably the fact that the guy on the radio has no one sufficiently senior with him to make the call. It could take a while to call up the relevant bigwig for a decision. Something as big as this may even require the nod to come from someone really high up. Maybe even Churchill himself."

"Do you think?" Jan asked, open-mouthed.

"Wouldn't be surprised," Peter confirmed. "It doesn't get much bigger than this, mate. There will only be a few that are in the know and still fewer that have the authority to say yes."

While Jan was still pondering this, the radio crackled back into life. It had taken less than five minutes by Peter's reckoning. Someone must have been fairly close to the end of a phone, after all.

"Red Kite, this is Hawk's Nest. Come in. Over."

"Hawk's Nest, this is Red Kite standing by. Over," Peter answered.

"Red Kite, you are cleared to engage. I repeat, you are cleared to engage. Please acknowledge. Over."

"Hawk's Nest, this is Red Kite. Message received and understood. We are cleared to engage. We'll let you know tomorrow how it goes. Over."

"Please do, Red Kite. We await your next report with interest." There was a slight pause before, finally, in a quieter and more measured tone, "Good luck, boys. We wish you well. Over and out."

The two men looked at each other across the now-silent radio set. Jan broke the silence.

"Are you OK?"

"Fine."

Actually, Peter couldn't help but feel that he was anything but fine. It was alright for Jan, it wasn't him that had to pull the trigger—well, not unless something happened to him anyway. Either way, Jan did not seem inclined to probe any further. Instead, he helped Peter pack away the radio, keeping any further thoughts to himself. .

They retraced their steps back to their shelter and settled down to get a few hours' sleep before it was time to set off.

———

When Jan woke the next morning, Peter was already up and ready. Jan wondered whether he had even slept. His eyes certainly had a redness around them which suggested that he hadn't. He seemed alert enough physically; if anything, he had an almost hyper-intensity about him as he fussed around Jan, pushing him to get ready. It was as if he had drunk several cups of coffee already. To counteract Peter's hyperactivity, Jan did his best to stay calm and measured in everything that he did. He needed to keep Peter focussed and had to bring him down a notch or two from the high he was on. The risk of error was much increased when your mind was incapable of processing information rationally. For some time now, Jan had accepted that his role on this mission was like that of a best man for a nervous groom. He had to get Peter to the right place at the right time and in the right frame of mind to go through with it. Though he also knew that if this particular groom failed to show, he would have to step into his shoes. That in itself was a highly motivating factor to make sure he did all he could to help his friend.

Half an hour later, they were off, retracing their steps from a few days previously. Jan was pleased to note that Peter seemed calmer now they were under way. They kept the pace steady but at the same time kept one eye on their watches. It was critical that they timed their arrival to be after the dog patrol had passed but before Hitler took his walk. If necessary, they would have to stop and wait a few hundred yards away from their firing position to avoid being too early. As it was, though, they timed it perfectly, arriving within yards of the edge of the wood at 09.42. As before, they crawled the last few yards as slowly and as quietly as possible, making sure the ferns provided the maximum cover for their movements.

As they eased into position, Jan looked left and right for signs of the dog patrol. Sure enough, he could just make them out about half a mile to their right, walking away from them. They were not walking particularly fast, so it seemed likely that they had passed their current spot at least ten to fifteen minutes previously. *So far so good*, Jan thought to himself.

Meanwhile, Peter had begun to prepare his rifle. It was laid out on the ground in front of him, and he was now reaching down to the secret pocket stitched into the inside leg of his trousers. After a few seconds of rummaging, he withdrew the telescopic sight. Having cleaned the lens of dust and bits of fluff that had accumulated over the days, he clicked it into position along the top of the rifle. Next he adjusted the sight to the appropriate yardage before lying down again. Finally he slipped the magazine out of its holding and checked that each of the five bullets was firmly seated within its housing. The last thing he wanted was a blockage at the critical moment. Having slotted the magazine back into place, he pulled the stock into his shoulder. Squinting down the sight, Peter made a couple of miniscule tweaks to the rangefinder before looking up.

"Wind seems pretty minimal today," Jan whispered.

"Yup," Peter confirmed, "I've got it pegged at no more than five miles an hour, east to west. I think it just needs the smallest of adjustments to the aim to cater for it, if at all."

Jan was keen not to put too much pressure on Peter's shoulders, but was also keen to make sure his partner was thinking clearly. "How many shots do you think?"

"Ideally I'll only need one, but hopefully I can get at least two off if I need to. It depends who he has with him. We know he doesn't like having guards near him, but there's a decent chance that he'll have a couple of cronies with him. As soon as they hear the first shot, they will most likely try and shield him from the second. So I really need to make the first shot count."

Jan nodded his understanding and lapsed into silence. Now was the time to concentrate and empty the mind of all other thoughts. There was nothing to do but wait for their moment to change the course of the war. Jan kept one eye on his watch as the minutes ticked by slowly. It seemed like they had been there ages already, but it was only 9.57, only fifteen minutes since they had arrived. It was dragging interminably, and it was as much as Jan could do to stay still and keep calm. To ease the tension, he pointed his toes as far as he could, stretching his leg muscles as he did so. They might well need to make a rapid exit, so he didn't want to find his legs cramping up at the critical moment.

9.59. Only another two minutes had passed since he last checked. Hitler usually took his walk soon after ten, so any moment now he should be making an appearance. Jan nudged Peter and indicated in the direction of his watch. Peter looked up from the sight, glanced at the watch face, and nodded. He then resumed his position. Jan realised he could hardly hear him breathing. Like all good marksmen, Peter had the ability to make his breathing so shallow that it was almost inaudible. It was part of the relaxation technique that enabled him to slow his heart to around fifty beats per minute, which in turn gave him that little bit of extra steadiness when it came to taking the shot.

10.04. Nothing. Jan told himself to be patient. No point getting wound up about it.

10.06. Movement to his left. Peter had noticed it too and had tightened his grip on the underside of the barrel of his rifle. He was holding it so tight that his knuckles were showing white through his skin. After a few more seconds, though, it became clear that it was just the soldier beginning his patrol to the teahouse.

"Jesus wept," Jan exhaled quietly. "When's the bastard going to show?"

They watched the soldier walk all the way past their position until he was out of sight to their right, all the while scanning left, back to the Berghof, for any further signs of movement that might indicate the start of Hitler's daily walk. Another ten minutes had passed, and it was now 10.16. Jan was beginning to doubt if they would see their quarry today.

By the time the patrol had returned to the Berghof and gone back towards the teahouse again, another hour and a half had passed. Jan was, by now, as stiff as a board from having lain still for so long. Peter, though, seemed to show no signs of flagging. He remained intensely focussed on the target area and had hardly moved at all in all that time, let alone speak. He was so still that Jan had wondered several times whether he was actually asleep, but every now and then, the slightest of movements of arm, head, or leg reassured him that he was still awake.

It was now almost midday, and Jan was convinced that it was going to be a no-show. The longer they stayed put, the more risky it was; they needed to get back under cover to wait until the morning, when they could try again. Jan nudged Peter in the ribs, gently so as not to alarm him unnecessarily. Peter lifted his head and turned to face Jan, who leaned in close to speak quietly in his ear.

"I think that's it for today, Peter."

"What time is it? I've lost track."

"Nearly twelve," Jan replied. "Let's head back down, and have another go tomorrow."

Peter nodded his assent. He unclipped the telescopic sight and returned it to the pocket in his trouser seam. Carefully they both then crawled backwards from their position, covering signs of their presence as they went and trying not to disturb the undergrowth too much with their movements. They didn't want to leave any obvious clues as to their presence for anyone who happened to be patrolling close by.

They arrived back at the river without incident. Shortly after turning to follow the river back towards Berchtesgaden, their luck turned for the worse. Not fifty yards in front of them, a three-man patrol had appeared from behind a group of boulders and was heading unmistakably in their direction.

"Shit," Jan hissed. "No chance of evading them, they have already seen us. Just act as normally as possible. I'll take the lead, OK?"

"Sure," Peter confirmed.

After a few more steps, the patrol leader issued the order to halt. From his uniform, Jan could see he was a lieutenant in the Berghof's security detail, the Wachkompanie. He had left his machine pistol casually slung over his shoulder on its strap, but the two infantrymen with him had unslung their rifles and now had them pointing at the two agents, ready for action. Jan prayed this was a normal patrol rather than a search for them specifically.

"What's the problem, Herr Leutnant?" Jan enquired.

"Papers please, gentlemen." The officer ignored the question.

Jan decided to play things by the book. This guy didn't seem the type to engage in small talk. In unison, the two men reached inside their Gebirgsjäger tunics and produced their identity papers. As he did so, Jan offered a silent prayer that the SOE forgers back in London were as good as their reputation had promised.

Silence reigned as the officer took his time to study the documents. As the moments passed, Jan started to get nervous, as this seemed to be more than just a cursory glance. He got the impression that Peter was feeling the same, as he felt rather than saw that his partner had taken an imperceptible half step backwards, giving him a modicum of cover behind Jan. He was clearly hoping that this would provide an extra second or two to ready his rifle before the patrol could react, if push came to shove. Either way, Jan felt it would nonetheless be a forlorn hope, as the two soldiers had them covered already and would easily be able to drop them before they could even get a shot off. *Full marks for Peter's fighting spirit, though,* he thought ruefully.

Finally the officer finished his inspection and handed back the papers, asking as he did so, "May I ask your business in these parts, gentlemen?"

Jan spoke in clear, precise tones, hoping it would convey appropriate confidence and authority. "We have been ordered to conduct an inventory of the smoke units on this side of the mountain to ensure stock levels are sufficient after the last air raid."

"I see. I do not believe I was informed of this." The officer undid the catch on his document case, withdrew a clipboard, and started to leaf through the sheets of paper, clearly checking the various activities listed.

"We were only given our orders this morning, Herr Leutnant. Perhaps the paperwork has not yet been completed?"

"Who by, Sergeant?"

The question caught Jan for a split second, but he hoped the momentary delay did not register. "Hauptmann Dunzl, Herr Leutnant." It was totally fictitious, of course, but he hoped it would buy them out of the situation safely.

The officer's brow furrowed as he considered this new information. "I am not familiar with this Dunzl, but then I do not claim to know every officer from the Gebirgsjäger regiment. I will make a note and follow up with him when next I have business at their headquarters. They know they are supposed to inform us at the Berghof security department about all activity in the region of the Führer's estate, especially when our Führer is in residence. We cannot tolerate such slipshod attitudes towards our security protocols."

"Of course, sir. I am sure it was a simple oversight on his part. Nothing more."

"That is as maybe," the officer continued, "but I will still have to follow it up to make sure there is no repeat."

"As you wish, Herr Leutnant," Jan replied.

"Carry on about your business, gentlemen."

Peter and Jan both came to attention, clicking their heels as they did so in the standard German army fashion. They also saluted, remembering not to drop the salute until the officer had acknowledged it with a casual flick of his fingers in the general direction of his cap.

The two men moved off without looking back, walking for several hundred metres before they dared even speak. It was Jan who finally broke the silence. "Do you think they were looking for us?"

"I'm not sure, but I don't think so, Jan. I think it's just the extra security they lay on when the big man is in town."

Let's hope you're right, Peter. Nonetheless, we still have a problem."

"What's that, Jan?"

"When he checks up on this Hauptmann Dunzl fellow and finds he doesn't exist!"

"Yes. Tricky one," Peter replied. "You didn't have a lot of choice there, though. We have to hope his rounds keep him busy for a while and he doesn't get time to head over to the regiment's HQ. Either that or he forgets altogether or can't be bothered."

"I'll not hold my breath on that, if you don't mind," Jan sighed. "He seemed a fairly typical German officer, a stickler for attention to detail. You saw how long he was studying our papers."

"I tend to agree, Jan. I think we should assume we now have limited time to complete the mission; perhaps tomorrow will be our last chance. As soon as they discover there is no Herr Dunzl, they'll be crawling around the estate like flies trying to find us. We can but hope there is enough of a delay to give us a chance tomorrow.

"For now, however, there's not a lot more we can do. I suggest we radio in tonight to let them know we had no luck today and about this new threat. Then we can see where we go from there."

TWENTY-FIVE

Colonel Blake took the stairs two at a time. The phone call to his office had made it very clear that the meeting was top priority and required him to drop everything and get over to Whitehall straight away. Getting an urgent summons to the Ministry of Defence was about as rare as rocking horse shit and required an immediate response. He hadn't even stopped to collect his raincoat, but thankfully the persistent drizzle, which had begun the previous evening and carried on throughout the morning, had finally abated. Plenty of puddles remained, though. He had tried to avoid them, but in his haste, the odd one had splashed up over his highly polished brown shoes and onto his sharply pressed trouser legs. Blake hated turning out in anything less than a completely immaculate appearance, and he knew there would be no time to spruce himself up before going in to see the bigwigs. It left him in a state of considerable frustration, which was not helping the anxiety he was already feeling about the purpose of the meeting. It felt not unlike being back at Harrow School having being summoned to the headmaster's office for a caning.

This feeling only grew in intensity when he arrived at the ministry. As he entered the door, held open for him by one of the two uniformed soldiers on sentry duty, he checked his watch. Fifteen minutes since he had received the call. Not bad, he thought. Just over half a mile, and whilst he hadn't run, as such, he had walked at a brisk pace. He presented himself to the reception desk in the marbled foyer, where his name was taken, added slowly and deliberately to a ledger in black ink, along with the date and time. In return he received a visitor's pass with his name handwritten in the same black ink, which he was advised to wear so that it was visible at all times. He had been through this routine on his several visits to the ministry, but he knew better than to complain that he knew the protocols. Bureaucracy had its time and place and nowhere more so than in the offices of His Majesty's Government.

Finally he was invited to take the lift to the second floor, where he would be met and escorted to the appropriate office. Sure enough, as the lift door pulled back, he found himself face to face with a pretty young woman, also in uniform, who requested that he follow her. No pleasantries, no handshake, just a brusque but efficient manner in all that she did. He was still breathing heavily after the walk and had a job to keep up with the lady as she set off smartly down the corridor to the left. As he walked, the memories of Harrow came flooding back even more strongly: the passage was fully panelled in some kind of dark wood, with several doors, made of the same wood, on both sides. Most of the doors had nameplates, which he struggled to read as they strode past at pace. In between the doors, spaced at regular intervals along the panels, were numerous portrait pictures. Here they were clearly pictures of previous ministers who had served in the office over the years, whereas back in Harrow, they had been forbidding portraits of previous headmasters. Nevertheless, the pictures here had a similar look to them: stern-looking men in dark suits with mainly grey or white hair stared out at him as he passed, the only difference being the men in the Harrow pictures had been wearing their formal black masters' gowns over their suits. As they walked, Blake wondered idly whether anyone had been both a headmaster at Harrow and a minister of defence. Unlikely, he mused, but not impossible.

His reverie was cut short by the sudden halt of the lady in front of him. He realised just in time to avoid bumping into her. As she turned, she indicated to a row of chairs outside a set of double doors at the end of the corridor.

"Please take a seat, Colonel. I'll let them know you are here."

"Thank you, miss," he muttered as she retreated whence she came. He was glad to take the weight off his feet. Glancing down he saw his shoes had dried and were not too dirty, all things considered. That said, the bottom two inches of his khaki trouser legs were spotted with darker blotches where the rain had splashed up. He sighed, hoping that no one would notice. Still, he took the time to remove his handkerchief from his trouser pocket and use it to polish the end of his shoes. As he folded it and replaced it in his pocket, he noted that it was now stained with brown polish which had lifted from the shoes. Oh well, another one ruined, but at least he felt more at ease knowing his shoes were up to scratch.

Moments later the left hand of the double doors opened, and another uniformed woman leaned through the gap. "Colonel Blake? If you'd come this way, they are ready for you now."

Blake stood, smoothing out his uniform jacket as he did so. "Thank you." He smiled as he walked as calmly as he could towards her.

The room was similar in style to the corridor: oak panels around all four walls, broken only by two large windows on the external-facing wall and another door in the far wall. The paintings in this room, however, were renderings of various airplanes of the Royal Flying Corps from the Great War, some pictured in dogfights with German counterparts, others stationary at their airfields, with pilots stood next to them. The centre of the room was dominated by a large wooden oval table, the centre of which was covered with green leather. Each of the dozen places around the table was set with its own blotting pad, pens, paper, and pencils. Just three of the places, all at the far end of the table, were occupied. Blake recognised two of them: the man on the left was Colonel Brian Stubbs, head of SOE, who had green-lighted the operation a few months back. Blake had been sending him regular situation reports ever since, keeping him apprised of progress. The other man he recognised was Brigadier William Harris, who had also been involved in the original meeting to approve the mission. Harris was a linchpin within the armed forces' Chiefs of Staff office and a key player in the management of the overall war strategy. The other man was introduced as Sir Percy Harrington, principal private secretary to the Prime Minister himself. Blake did a double take when Harrington was introduced. Churchill's own PPS in this meeting! That immediately told him the gravity of the situation and the depth of the shit in which he could be. Harrington's presence indicated to him that Churchill had wanted to attend but was unable to do so. Harrington had therefore been asked to represent the Prime Minister. Clearly something big was brewing.

Blake took the seat offered to him as calmly as he could. He was at the opposite end of the table to the other three, which made it feel like an interview or even a court martial. He was already agitated and could do without the extra strain on his heart rate. He also noticed that the woman who had ushered him into the room and shown him to his seat had now left. This was going to be a closed meeting with no minutes, Blake realised.

Having completed the introductions, Stubbs then opened the meeting by asking Blake to provide a précis of the mission's current status.

"Well, gentlemen," Blake began, hoping he sounded more confident than he felt, "our two agents were dropped into Germany almost two weeks ago now. During this time, they have conducted a detailed reconnaissance of the area. This has included planning the route into and out of the target area and assessing the best possible shooting position on the ground. Since then they have been waiting for the target to arrive in order to execute the key objective of the mission." Blake felt he didn't need to spell out what that key objective was.

"And do we know if and when the target is due to arrive?" Harris asked.

"Indeed we do, sir. We heard just last night that he had arrived the previous day. As a result, and as per the standing order sanctioned by this committee, I authorised the agents to put the plans into effect at the first available opportunity."

"And by 'first available opportunity,' you mean what exactly?" Stubbs asked.

Blake knew that Stubbs was fully aware of most, if not all, of this information but was simply establishing the facts to allow the two other attendees to get up to speed quickly.

"I mean that they should take out the target as soon as possible, any time from today onwards. As soon as they are able."

Harrington then spoke. "So what you're saying is that it may already have happened?"

"Yes, sir, I am saying exactly that."

Silence descended around the room as the three men considered this news. Eventually, Stubbs spoke. "The fact that we have heard nothing through official or unofficial channels cannot, I think, be relied upon as one hundred per cent proof that he is still alive."

"True," Harrington acknowledged, "but I think we have to assume the worst until we know for certain either way."

Blake became increasingly concerned during this exchange. "Gentlemen, if I may interject, I sense that you have me at a disadvantage. I am clearly missing a key piece of information to which everyone else seems to be privy."

"Ah yes, indeed," Stubbs replied. "Apologies, Blake, very rude of us to keep you in the dark. To summarise as succinctly as I can, we need to abort the mission."

Blake forgot himself for a brief moment. "We need to bloody what?"

"Yes, I imagine this is not the most welcome news," Stubbs continued. "But look, the fact is we have just received intelligence from the most reliable sources that there was a serious attempt on Hitler's life within the last couple of weeks. From what we gather, it happened at his headquarters in East Prussia. At, er...ah yes, a place called Rastenburg. All the indications are that those responsible for the attempt were members of the German military, supposedly a group of officers who have become disillusioned with his leadership and wish to remove him from the scene to pave the way for a settlement with the Western Allies."

"I am presuming that the fact that Hitler has arrived in southern Germany indicates that the attempt was not successful?" Blake enquired.

"Indeed not. We have not got the full details, but we don't believe that he sustained any serious injuries in the attempt. This does, though, appear to be something of a miracle, as the assassins had planted a sizeable bomb within the briefing room, which went off only a few feet away from him. There were some fatalities, those closest to the blast, as you might expect, but Hitler himself survived. His arrival at his Berchtesgaden home is no doubt part of his planned recuperation from the ordeal."

"This is significant news, indeed," Blake agreed, "but how does this affect our mission? Why do we need to abort?"

Harrington took that question. "The fact is, Colonel, that since the attempt, there has been a huge surge in support for the Führer, and for the Nazis in general, amongst the rank-and-file civilian population. Of course Goebbels is stirring things into a frenzy with the full force of his propaganda machine, as you would expect, but the indications are that the people are showing what appears to be genuine support for the regime. As such, we are no longer convinced that the key objective of the mission, that is to force a German surrender, would be achieved. Our intelligence analysts now suggest that the most likely outcome would be that a member of the upper echelons of Hitler's closest supporters would take over and use the assassination as a means of rallying the people to their cause and driving the war effort even harder."

"On top of which," Harris took over, "the last few weeks have seen some significant developments in the European theatre of war which we cannot ignore. The landings in Normandy have gone better than expected, with large gains being made through northern France. We have pushed most of the way up through Italy as well, and the Russians are slowly but surely driving the Germans back towards Poland. It has to be said that a not-inconsiderable factor in these successes has been the fragmented and, at times, frankly, irrational decision making of the German high command. As you are no doubt aware, this high command operates pretty much in name only. The decision making is done almost exclusively by Hitler, and very few dare to challenge him openly. It is now the firm opinion of the War Office here, an opinion shared by our American allies, I might add, that Hitler is best left where he is. In short, he has become more valuable to us alive than dead."

Blake was not yet prepared to give up without a fight. "This mission has been months, if not years, in the planning. We have two extremely brave and resourceful agents on the ground right now, ready to pull the trigger and most likely die in the process. We owe it to them at least to let them see it through to the end."

Harrington became terse, clearly frustrated by the conversation and keen to move to his next appointment. "Look here, Blake. I don't expect you to understand all the vagaries of international politics, but the fact remains that the order, coming from the very top, I might add, has been given to stand your men down. The situation has changed, and we need to react accordingly. I can only hope for your sake that your two trained monkeys have not already done the job!" With that, he pushed back his chair sharply and stood. "Now, if you'll excuse me, gentlemen?" he said, nodding towards Stubbs and Harris; Blake clearly was no longer of interest. "I need to return to Number Ten for a cabinet meeting. Good day."

Stubbs and Harris both rose from their seats to acknowledge the civil serv-ant's departure. Blake was too deflated to even move.

"Right," Stubbs said when Harrington had closed the door behind him. "I'm sorry he was so blunt, old chap, but we have no option but to toe the line on this one, however much it may hurt to do so."

Blake, staring into the middle distance, nodded absently.

"So, from a practical point of view, what do you need to do to abort the mission?" Stubbs was trying to snap Blake out of his stupor by getting him to focus on the here and now.

"Well"—Blake cleared his throat—"they are due to radio in tonight with their next update, an update which may well, of course, confirm that they have completed their objective."

"Well, like the man said, let's just hope that is not the case, eh?" Harris smiled.

"Indeed," Stubbs agreed. "I suggest I accompany you back to the ops room, Blake, so I can help explain the situation to your boys when they do make contact."

"Yes, sir. I'd appreciate that." Blake wasn't sure whether it was a genuine offer of help or whether Stubbs wanted to be sure he actually gave the order. Either way, on balance, he did feel grateful that his superior officer was going to be there. Having been so close to the mission and the two men, he really didn't want to be the one to be the bearer of bad tidings.

TWENTY-SIX

Leutnant Joachim Kraus pushed open the door of the guardroom that was home to the Berghof security detail command centre.

"Hey, Kraus, shut the damned door, will you? You're letting all the warm air out! I know you are from Bavaria, but I didn't really believe you had been born in a barn, until now."

"Christ, Heine. Give me a chance to get through it first!"

Kraus smiled to himself as he pushed the door closed. Leutnant Heinrich Brehme was the clown in the unit; there was always one. You could guarantee that however bad a day you'd had, Heinrich would have you smiling within a few minutes.

Kraus dumped his backpack in the corner, hung his machine pistol over one of the available wall hooks before finally slumping heavily in the battered old armchair in the corner. Placing one foot under the heel of the other, he prised off his leather boots. It felt great to finally get them off, he thought, as he stretched his calf muscles and wriggled his toes to try to coax some life back into them. His legs ached like he had just run a marathon, whereas his feet were throbbing and appeared to be a little swollen having spent too long in tight, uncomfortable boots.

"How was your patrol, Joachim? Non-stop excitement from beginning to end, no doubt?"

"I tell you, Heine, I hate it when the Führer comes to stay. Not only does it mean that all leave gets cancelled, but on top of this, I have to spend most of my waking hours patrolling the whole damned area surrounding the estate. I know that security is really important when Adolf is here; that's not in question; but it would be nice, however, if they could see their way to drafting in some additional troops to cope with the extra burden, don't you think?"

Kraus found the extra patrolling to be particularly frustrating for two reasons: Firstly, he thought it was a waste of time, as surely it was unlikely that they would ever find anything untoward. It was hard to believe that anyone would be sufficiently stupid to try something this deep within Germany and with so much security around. Secondly, because the area surrounding the Berghof was almost totally mountainous, meaning that he was in a permanent state of exhaustion from all the hiking up and down hills.

"Ach, stop moaning, Joachim. Look on the bright side, this is still a cushy number when you think you could be freezing your balls off on the Eastern Front. And anyway, it's never more than a week or two at most before the big man is off on his travels again. We can all relax once more when that happens."

"What do you mean 'we'? When was the last time you were out on patrol?" Kraus laughed.

"You know I would l love to join you, but my leg won't let me. Or rather, my lack of leg, to be precise." Brehme nodded towards his right leg, the bottom half of which he had lost to a grenade burst on the Eastern Front last winter. The flap of his trouser leg was pinned over just below the knee.

"Ha, that old excuse?" Kraus laughed. "No one is fooled, you know. But to answer your question, the patrol was a case of the same old shit, just a different day. And now I have the unbridled joy of having to write up my report, which will confirm that absolutely nothing of any importance happened at all."

This being the German army, everything had to be done just so, or someone would want to know why. It wasn't worth complaining; it was much easier to just follow the rules and have done with it. Much less hassle in the long run. Every patrol had to be rigorously conducted, and each one then required a report to be produced within twenty-four hours with details of the start and end times, the area covered, and any events that occurred during the patrol. When he wasn't spending hours trudging over miles of steep, boulder-strewn slopes or through dense forests, he was spending even more hours writing about it. Kraus sighed.

"There's no point moaning about it, Joachim," Brehme scolded. "Just get on with it. The sooner it's done, the sooner you can get into town with me for a beer."

Kraus retrieved his notebook from within its leather case, which still hung from a leather strap around his neck. The most recent entries, which summarised that day's activities, were near the back. Nothing out of the ordinary, he noted as he flicked through: checked a few unoccupied buildings to ensure they were secure, inspected the fencing around the estate at various points to make sure it was intact (the local wildlife had an annoying habit of trying to burrow under it every now and then), conducted several documentation checks with various individuals they had encountered. Nothing too extraordinary and nothing which would require anything more than a cursory note in the report. *At least this report should be a quick one,* he reflected.

That thought was stopped in its tracks when he noted the entry at the bottom of the last page. The two sergeants from the Gebirgsjäger regiment conducting an inspection of the air defence positions on the mountain slopes south of the Larosbach River. Their papers had been in order, but there had been no record in Kraus's daily worksheet of the inspection taking place. The rules were clear: all formal duties, which included inspections, had to be logged with the Berghof security department when the Führer was in residence.

Oversights did, of course, happen, but protocol stated that they had to be followed up within twenty-four hours.

Kraus toyed with the idea of ignoring the entry. On every previous case he had investigated, it had never turned out to be anything other than the duty officer having forgotten to log it. It was sure to be a total ball ache to waste valuable time investigating what was going to prove to be a total certainty. The problem was that the note was at the bottom of the page. He couldn't very well rip the page out and pretend it had never happened. If he had written it at the top of a new page, he might have been able to get away with it. He cursed his luck; he could not ignore it, or sooner or later, it would come to light, and he would land himself in a whole heap of trouble. There was no option; he would have to follow it up.

"Shit!"

"What is the matter now, Kraus?" Brehme sighed.

"Just remembered there was one minor issue. We bumped into two NCOs from the Gerbirgsjäger. Papers were fine, but they claimed to be under orders to inspect the air defences, only there was no record of it in the log."

"Ach, they were probably just taking the piss, my friend. Spun you the first story they could think of to cover the fact that they had been up to no good with a couple of the local ladies. Forget it: cut them some slack."

"I don't know, Heinrich. The rules are clear. I am supposed to follow up with the duty officer to investigate why the activity had not been logged."

"It was not logged because it does not exist, Joachim. They made it up to cover their tracks. Come on, you're holding up my beer."

Kraus glanced down at his watch: eight fifteen. "Well there's not much point going now; the people I need to see will be off duty. OK, let me get this report done, and I will look into it first thing tomorrow."

"You know it makes sense, mate." Brehme raised an imaginary beer glass in salute.

Kraus pushed himself up out of the armchair and relocated to the desk in the corner, on which stood a lumpen old typewriter. After inserting two pieces of paper, separated by a sheet of carbon paper, he began to type.

TWENTY-SEVEN

The two men waited until it was dark before leaving the hut. The darkness was a big factor in their favour, helping to mask them from unwelcome attention. Now that they knew that extra patrols were in operation while Hitler was in town, avoiding detection was paramount. They had also taken care to ensure that none of their kit was loose, so that they could keep the noise to a minimum as they walked as well. After the previous day's encounter, it was only a matter of time before people came looking for them, so there was no sense in making it any easier for them.

They walked slowly, taking their time, stopping every couple of minutes to listen for sounds of anyone following them. All Peter could think about was that they were so close to their goal that to get caught now would be devastating. Tomorrow they might get the chance to end the war, but the hours since that morning's failed attempt had ticked by so slowly. At least now they were active again; doing something helped to take his mind off things to an extent.

Just then Jan, who was leading, stopped suddenly and held up his hand in silent signal for Peter to stop too. Together they sank slowly down onto one knee, Peter looking from side to side to try to work out what Jan had seen or heard. Soon he could hear it too, a rustling coming from in front of them. Someone or something was heading in their direction. Peter prayed it was not another patrol, as they would have little excuse for being out at that time of night.

They remained absolutely still, rooted to the spot. Jan had eased his rifle into a firing position, whereas Peter, crouched behind him, had slipped his knife out from his boot and was holding it ready to throw at whatever appeared. In the darkness, Peter hoped that they might be mistaken for a couple of boulders or even that they might not even be spotted at all, both outcomes hugely preferable to having to fight. One shot and the game would be up. There would be scores of soldiers out looking for them in no time, and the chances of completing the mission would have gone up in smoke.

Whatever was out there was still moving slowly but surely towards them. Every now and then, the noise ceased for a moment before starting again. Classic night patrol behaviour, Peter thought, as if they too were listening for sounds of movement. A few moments later, Peter sensed a disturbance in the trees away slightly to their left. Peter slowly put his hand on Jan's shoulder and pointed in the direction, about ten o'clock if it had been a watch face. It was too dark to make out any actual form or forms at this range, but they both tensed, ready to react. Again it stopped for a few moments before continuing its progress towards them. It was clear that they had not yet been detected, but it was only a matter of time. If the same course was maintained, it would walk straight into them in another twenty paces or so.

Peter slowed his breathing, as if lining up a shot on the range. He focussed all his concentration on the form coming towards them. Rather than throwing the knife, he decided it would be better to wait until the last second before springing with a knife attack, and shifted his grip on the hilt to allow for that. With luck, the surprise factor would cause his opponent to freeze and therefore fail to get a shot, or even a shout, off. Fifteen paces now: if it was a patrol, it seemed to be only one person, which Peter thought was strange. Moreover, whoever it was seemed to be crouched down, as Peter could tell the form was only just over half the height of a normal adult. Ten paces: Peter readied himself; he would go at five.

He left it to the last possible moment before launching himself forward. As he did so, he suddenly realised what it was. At the same moment, the stag, startled, jerked to the left and kicked away into the trees. Peter managed to twist to one side, out of the way, and landed in a heap, the wind knocked out of him. He rolled onto his back, chest heaving to get air back into his lungs, the sound of his breaths rasping in the night air.

Jan crawled over to where he lay. "You OK, Peter?" Concern was clearly audible in his voice.

"I think so, Jan," Peter said, struggling to control his breathing. "I think it's stress more than anything. I'm not sure how much longer I can keep a lid on this. Tell you what, I'll be bloody glad when we get this over and done with and get the hell out of here."

"That's true for me too," Jan laughed. "But you don't see me trying to take things out on the local wildlife, though!"

Peter wanted to laugh too, but his heart was still racing from the fear and exertion. He was so pumped up it hurt. Deer or no deer, he needed to get the job done before he had some kind of a breakdown.

A few minutes later, they were back under way. Emerging from the treeline eventually, they continued upwards for a few more minutes, crouching to ensure that they minimised their profile, before lying down. As quietly as possible, Jan shrugged the radio pack off his back and unclipped the flap that protected the control panel. In the meantime, Peter removed a folded piece of paper and a small torch from his jacket lining. He then removed his jacket and draped it over his head. Shuffling next to Jan, he spread the jacket over his friend's head as well. When he was sure that they were properly shielded, he switched on the torch, and together they located the appropriate frequency for the day's date. With the details in his head, Jan then shifted the jacket so that it was draped over the radio control panel, preventing any light from being detectable. Turning the tuning dial slowly, he moved towards the required frequency, keeping the volume way down low so that the crackling of the airwaves was barely perceptible.

After a few moments, Jan nodded to Peter to confirm the frequency had been located. Peter picked up the transmitter and pressed the button on the side. "Red Kite calling Hawk's Nest. Red Kite calling Hawk's Nest. Are you receiving? Over."

This time, the response came through immediately. Peter smiled to himself; they were clearly desperate for news back home, and why wouldn't they be? They must be at least half expecting to hear news of success.

"Hawk's Nest receiving you loud and clear. Please provide status update."

"Christ, they're keen." Jan chuckled. "Not even got time for small talk about the weather. I thought the British always discussed the weather over several cups of tea before doing anything else."

"Shh," Peter admonished with a cheeky grin before pressing the transmit button. "This is Red Kite. No sign of cuckoo today. The cuckoo did not leave its nest. Over."

There was a couple of moments' pause before the response came back, more measured this time. "Red Kite, this is Hawk's Nest. Please repeat. Over."

"This is Red Kite. The cuckoo did not leave the nest today. I say again, we have not seen the cuckoo today. Over."

Again there was a delay before the radio crackled back into life. "This is Hawk's Nest. Message received and understood. Over."

Jan looked at Peter. "What do they mean 'Over'? I was kind of expecting a little more than that."

"So was I, Jan," Peter replied. He lifted the transmitter to his mouth once more. "Hawk's Nest, this is Red Kite. We will look again tomorrow. Please confirm. Over."

This time the response was immediate. "Red Kite, this is Hawk's Nest. Please be advised: you are no longer required to locate the cuckoo. Please pack your bags and return to base. I repeat, all attempts to hunt the cuckoo must cease with immediate effect. Please confirm. Over."

For a moment Peter was too stunned to speak. He stared dumbly at Jan, his mouth forming a round O shape of surprise. After a moment or two, he recovered enough to respond, but all attempts to follow transmission protocols had gone out the window.

"What the hell do you mean 'cease'?" he shouted. Jan grabbed his arm, urging him to remain calm and to keep his voice down. They might be alone up here, but there was no point risking detection.

"Exactly what we say, Red Kite. All efforts to hunt the cuckoo must cease with immediate effect. Please confirm. Over."

"But why, for heaven's sake?"

This time a new, more authoritative voice responded, "Red Kite, that is no concern of yours. Please confirm your orders as requested. Over."

Peter looked at Jan. "What do you make of it? What the hell is going on? And who the hell was that talking at the end?"

"I couldn't tell you, Peter. Something has clearly changed, but I am clueless as to what it might be."

"They owe us an explanation at least," Peter said through gritted teeth. "We have risked our lives on a daily basis deep in enemy territory for a number of weeks now. We are that close to achieving the most amazing operation of the whole war. Who knows, we could even bring an end to the war! But now they tell us to stop?"

Again the new voice came back over the airwaves, slightly more insistent than last time. "Red Kite, please confirm your orders. Over."

"You'll have to answer them, Peter," Jan said softly, urging his friend to respond.

"This stinks, Jan. They have no right to pull the plug on us at this stage. What the hell would have happened if I had taken the shot today? What would they have said then?"

"I don't know, Peter. All we know is the here and now. We have orders to abort the operation, and we need to confirm."

Peter stared grimly at the radio, struggling within himself as to what to do. His soldier's head urged obedience, but his heart resisted passionately. In the meantime, the voice came back for a third time. "Red Kite. For the final time, confirm your orders!"

Slowly, and with a steely look in his eyes, shocking in its intensity, Peter picked up the transmitter and pressed the button. "Orders understood. Out."

——

Back at the operations room at the airfield, Stubbs put down the transmitter and turned to face Colonel Blake. "Well, Blake, old chap, I think that went as well as could be expected in the circumstances. First of all, we know Hitler's still alive, and secondly, we've managed to abort the mission. I'd be inclined to put that down as a good end to a bad day, wouldn't you?"

Blake felt unable to return the enthusiasm. He had found the call extremely uncomfortable, so much so that Stubbs had had to ease the transmitter from his white-knuckled grip halfway through. He had invested so much time and personal interest into the mission that he hated not to be able to see it come to fruition. Moreover, he hated himself for having to be the one to tell the boys to come home.

Stubbs sensed his subordinate's unease. "Buck up, old chap," he said, clapping him on the shoulder. "It feels bad now, but it'll work out for the best in the long run, you'll see."

"You're probably right, sir. It's just hard to see it that way at the moment."

"I understand that, Blake. It's never easy to make or deliver these big decisions. We've seen that time and time again throughout this war. Usually with many more lives riding directly on the decision than is the case here, I can tell you. Which reminds me, there is a bright side to be looked upon, you know."

"Bright side? What the hell's that?" Blake couldn't help but snort.

"The chances of your two lads getting out of there alive just increased significantly."

———

Peter said nothing the whole way back down to the hut. Jan had no intention of intruding on his thoughts either; he needed time to come to terms with the change of orders, to get his head round the crushing disappointment. Now was not the right time to go sticking his oar in to make things worse. All the same he resolved to keep a close eye on his partner; he was clearly angry beyond measure, and Jan needed to make sure that he wasn't going to do anything stupid in the immediate aftermath.

It wasn't that Jan himself was not upset about the turn of events. He was hugely frustrated to have to step back from the brink having come so far over such a long period. He found, however, that he could stay calm and objective about it. He understood that things could change with the wind at the top table. He knew that people like him and Peter were but pawns to be moved around the board at the whim of these people. The one thought that really helped him come to terms with this new position, though, was the realisation that he might actually survive this whole debacle now. Inside he was grinning at the prospect; he hadn't dared hope that he might make it home, and now it looked like there was every chance that they would. He wanted to shake Peter to make him realise, but he had the sense to realise that this was not the right time.

He had come to terms with the fact that once they took the shot, their life expectancy was virtually nil. There would be Germans everywhere, swarming across the whole region, desperately searching for the culprits. The chances of getting away without being caught would have been almost non-existent. He was also under no illusions that if they were captured, they would be subjected to the most horrific tortures. Not only to wheedle out of them who was behind the plot and who they were working with but also as recompense for what they had done. He had already resolved to go out fighting and hopefully get himself killed in the process. Failing that, the cyanide capsule would have been his fall-back position. There was no way he was going to allow them to go to work on him. But now that the mission was aborted, he could see a way out, a chance to disappear as cleanly and as quietly as they had arrived. Despite Peter's current mood, Jan did need to talk this through with him as quickly as possible. The sooner they could agree a plan and get started, the more chance they had of making it out of Germany intact. He therefore resolved to broach the subject as soon as they got back to the hut.

TWENTY-EIGHT

As the hut came into view, Peter grabbed Jan's arm and finally broke his silence. "You go ahead, mate. I need a piss."

"Sure," Jan replied, carrying on walking towards the hut. He pushed open the door and stomped inside, his mind full of thoughts about the events of the night.

"Hands up!"

Jan froze, rooted to the spot, with no time to react. He raised his hands and turned slowly to face the direction of the voice. He recognised the officer, whom they had met when coming back down from the Berghof. He was sitting in the one chair in the hut, with his right leg casually crossed over the left. His right boot was swinging back and forth languidly, as if he were bored by the whole thing. His uniform was immaculate, with a razor-sharp crease down the middle of each trouser leg. Round his shoulders was draped his army-issue greatcoat, while his officer's cap was positioned at a slight angle over one eye, giving him a vaguely quizzical look. In his right hand, he held his Luger pistol, which was aimed loosely in his direction. He was flanked on either side, however, by a soldier, both of whom had rifles levelled at his chest. Jan had no idea whether they were the same troops that had been with the officer the other day. Frankly it did not matter. He was powerless to do anything.

"Place your rifle on the floor. Slowly! Please do not try anything stupid. These men have orders to shoot to kill if necessary." The German was smiling and being impeccably polite, but the threat of menace was clear from the tone of voice and the cold stare of his eyes.

Jan began to comply with the order, slowly unslinging his rifle and lowering his right arm, in which he now held it. His mind was racing; he needed to warn Peter somehow. The last thing they needed was for Peter to barge unthinkingly into the hut like he had. As long as one of them was still on the loose, then they stood a chance. When his arm was just below shoulder height, he made a show of appearing to fumble with the unwieldy weapon, resulting in it clattering to the floor. He immediately raised both his hands again, looking as sheepish as possible, trying to convince them that it was an accident. The noise in the confines of the hut was deafening. He just hoped it had travelled far enough to alert Peter.

The officer sighed but appeared to be no more than mildly annoyed by his clumsiness, as if he were not impressed by the calibre of man in front of him. "Please do try to be more careful. My men have itchy trigger fingers.

"Now if you would be so kind, please also remove that knife from your left boot and place that on the floor next to the rifle."

Jan did as he was told without complication this time. He didn't want to push his luck any further at this stage.

"Now, I'd like you to give me your name and tell me what you are doing here."

"Sergeant Dieter Rohme of the Second Platoon, First Company of the Gebirgsjäger Regiment, conducting checks of the air defence supplies in this area, sir."

"And now your real name and purpose?" The German's smile appeared to be chiselled into his face.

Jan repeated the same speech.

Again the officer sighed, twirling his pistol around his finger. "I had hoped that this would prove to be rather easier than this. I can see I was mistaken. Let's try a different question, see if we have any more luck. Where is your comrade?"

"I do not know, sir."

"And why is that, pray tell?"

"There are a lot of places to check spread over a wide area, so we agreed to separate so we could get the job done more quickly. We are due to meet back here before returning to the barracks, sir."

"I see." The officer appeared pensive, as if mulling over the information that Jan had offered. "The problem is, Sergeant…"

"Rohme, sir," Jan offered.

"Ah yes. The problem is, Sergeant Rohme, that I have just come from Gebirgsjäger HQ, where I was informed that there was no officer by the name of Dunzl—it was Dunzl I think you said had signed your orders, wasn't it?" He didn't wait for a response. "And, moreover, there was no record of any orders having been given for two men to go checking the air defence supplies in this sector. Finally, and most worryingly of all, there is no record of any Sergeant Rohme or Sergeant Matthaus in the Gebirgsjäger personnel lists."

Jan stared dumbly at the officer, deciding to wait and see where this was going rather than offer anything to further incriminate himself.

"So, you see, I am at something of a loss to explain your presence in these parts and need your help to fill in the blanks. So, if you don't mind, I will ask again. What is your real name and purpose here?"

Jan elected to stick to the same story. He had little option, in reality. "Perhaps there's been some kind of administrative error with the personnel lists?"

"I have already proven this to be a lie. You surely cannot expect me to believe that you, Matthaus, and Dunzl would all be missing off the lists? Please do not become tiresome; it's been a long day, and you are keeping me from my favourite bar, not to mention my favourite barmaid."

Jan stayed silent.

The officer waited a moment, seemingly weighing up his options. Finally he gave a nod to the man to his right. Jan had expected this development; it had only been a matter of time really. He braced himself for what was coming, but there was no way to ward it off entirely. The soldier advanced towards him, reversing his rifle as he walked. As soon as he was in range, he rammed the butt of the gun into Jan's midriff with as much force as he could muster. Jan doubled over and hit the deck, the impact of the blow forcing all the air out of his lungs. He curled into a ball as quickly as he could but not before the soldier followed up the blow with a kick to his head and another to his stomach. Stars exploded around his head, and he felt a tooth loosen, tasting the blood as it filled his mouth.

"Steady, Hans," the officer cautioned as the soldier prepared further blows. "We still need to question him, and for that we need him to be conscious."

The soldier grunted and seemed disappointed at having been told to stop, but he stepped back all the same and raised his rifle to point at Jan once more.

Jan, still curled in a protective ball, was in agony from the pain in his head and the blows to his gut. He was glad of the respite, though, as he just needed to lie there for a while to recover his senses.

"Perhaps you will be ready to speak more honestly now that you have had a taste of what lies in store for you?"

Jan could only groan in response.

—

Outside, Peter pressed his back against the wall of the hut between the door and the window, straining to listen to the sounds from within. Having finished taking a leak, he had been on the verge of walking through the door when he had heard the sound of Jan's rifle hitting the floor. Even then he had been about to open the door and call Jan a clumsy bastard, but something had nagged at his subconscious and made him stop in his tracks. It was as well that he had.

Fortunately his captors did not seem to be all that well prepared. There was no obvious sign of any sentries outside the hut. If there had been, he was certain that he would have also been taken, or perhaps even dead, by now. Instead, the enemy were clearly all inside. Peter reckoned on at least two Germans but more probably three. He thought he recognised the officer's voice as being the same man who had demanded to see their papers the other day. Clearly the guy had been super-efficient in checking up on their story and had found it to be a steaming pile of bullshit. It was always a risk that this would happen, but Peter had thought they might still have a few days before being tracked down. Peter was surprised, and not a little impressed, that they had been found so quickly.

He racked his brains, trying to work out a plan that might have at least a marginal chance of success. For the moment, though, he had no idea what to do. Bursting into the hut was not likely to work. He might get one of them, but it was highly likely that he would be dropped by one of the others before he could get any further. He might have more luck trying to entice one or more of them outside, but how to do that? He also had no idea where in the hut Jan was and in what sort of state he was in either. Was he in any position to be able to help him? It seemed unlikely. Peter had heard a few indistinct thuds coming from within but could not genuinely discern what they were. Worst case, though, was that Jan was out of action. Peter thought it best to assume as much, and then anything else would be a bonus. Decision made, he started to think about how to coax someone out of the hut. Before he could get any further, however, the situation changed again.

———

Inside the hut, Jan was still curled up on the floor, trying to get his breathing under control and waiting for the mists in his head to clear a little to allow him to focus. Whilst the pain remained unrelenting, he didn't think that any real lasting damage had been done, yet. He knew, though, that he would soon be in for another dose if he didn't tell them what they wanted to know. Nonetheless, he had to steel himself for that eventuality. He could not betray Peter. Sooner or later they would have to give up and take him back to their barracks. At that point he would take the opportunity to end it with his cyanide capsule before they started on the more inhumane methods of interrogation. He clung on to the hope, though, that Peter had realised what had happened and had made good his escape. With the mission aborted, at least one of them could still make it back to England.

The officer pushed himself up out of the chair, stretching his legs and yawning as he did so. He was clearly growing bored of the situation. He clasped his hands behind his back and started pacing up and down in front of the window.

"So, Sergeant Rohme, or whoever you are, have you had time to reconsider your position? Is there anything more you wish to add?"

Jan slowly pulled himself upright and stood to attention as best he could. "I am Sergeant Rohme of the First Company of the Gebirgsjäger regiment, sir. Along with my colleague, Sergeant Matthaus, I have been ordered to conduct an audit of the air defence positions in this locale. I am waiting here for my colleague to return, before reporting back to barracks with the outcome of the audit."

The officer swirled round, slapping Jan hard with the back of his gloved hand. "Enough of this charade!" he shouted. "Why don't you make it easy on yourself and just tell us the truth?"

Before Jan could reply, however, the officer stopped and turned, looking suddenly pensive. "Wait," he said. "Corporal?" He turned again to the man who had dished out the beating before. "Go outside and take up a position in the trees where you can see the hut but are out of sight. Whatever the truth of his story, the fact remains that his partner is not here and could therefore be turning up in the near future. Hell, he may even be out there right now.

"As soon as he shows, arrest him. Shoot him if he tries to run or if he attacks you. If you do have to shoot, try not to kill him, but do not worry too much if that does happen. In the meantime, we will sit tight here and wait. I'll send Wiesmann here out to relieve you in a couple of hours."

"Yes, sir." The man snapped to attention, shouldered his rifle, and made for the door.

———

Outside, Peter had managed to pick up most of this last exchange, an indication, perhaps, that their luck was changing for the better. He just had time to bend down and slip his knife out of his boot. It was the same knife that he had carried throughout the war, from his early days in Poland with the partisans till now. Many hours had been spent cleaning it and honing the edge of the blade so that it was always wickedly sharp. He took a firm grip of the rubber handle and edged towards the door. As luck would have it, he was the right side of the hinges, so that when the door opened outwards, he would be completely hidden behind it. This should give him the element of surprise and, consequently, a vital few seconds to take the guy out. He didn't really know what he would do after that, but at least the odds would be much more in their favour, and he would have bought himself some precious time to decide what to do next.

The door opened. Peter tensed. If it was all going to go wrong, then this was the moment. Incredibly, his luck held. The soldier was oblivious to the possibility of any immediate danger as he kicked the door closed with the heel of his jackboot without even glancing back.

Peter wasted no time. With his knife held tightly in his right hand, he moved quickly but stealthily after the soldier. The ground was pretty mossy, which helped to muffle any sound; plus the soldier was fairly stomping along anyway. Within half a dozen steps, Peter was right up behind him. He reached up with his left hand and grabbed the man's mouth, pulling back as he did so to expose the neck. At the same time, he drew the knife across the neck in one smooth but deep cut. He held the man upright as the life poured from the gaping wound, doing his best to avoid any blood splashing over him. It wasn't long before the man had gone limp, allowing Peter to gently lower him to the ground. He had made no sound, partly because he had been taken entirely by surprise, but mainly because the blood had flooded his throat, making it impossible to speak.

Though the killing had been up close and brutal, Peter felt no emotion or any remorse for his actions. It was a job that had needed doing, nothing more. He could not afford to dwell on it; that way lay insanity. Start thinking about the man, whether he had a wife and kids back home, kids that would grow up without a father now, and you might hesitate the next time you needed to kill. That was all it would take for the other bloke to get the knife in first, and then where would you be? Lying dead on the ground with the other bloke stood over you, that's where.

He wiped the knife clean on the dead man's trouser leg before putting it back in the side of his boot. Next he dragged the body about thirty yards into the undergrowth, out of sight of the hut. The growing darkness would prevent the blood from being seen, but it would be foolish to risk anyone seeing or tripping over the dead body. Peter sat down on the man's back to ponder his next move. He removed his cap and wiped his forehead with the back of his sleeve. It wasn't particularly warm, but the adrenalin and effort of shifting the dead weight of the body had caused beads of sweat to sprout across his hairline, stinging his eyes as they dripped down his face.

He took his time, allowing his breathing to get back to normal. There was no need to rush, after all; he had heard the officer say that he would send the other soldier out to relieve him in a couple of hours. Nonetheless, he really was at a loss regarding what to do next. On the plus side, he had at least reduced the odds; it was two against two now, but could he realistically expect any help from Jan? He was pretty sure he would still be alive, but he had no way of knowing what sort of state he was in. Best to plan without his help, to be on the safe side.

That still left him with the problem of how to take on two armed soldiers without either him or Jan getting killed in the process. For a fleeting moment, he considered whether he should simply start walking to try to get out of Germany. It wasn't far to the Swiss border; he could probably walk there in under a week. What would he want Jan to do if the roles were reversed? Deep down he felt that he would want Jan to escape rather than risk his life trying to save him. At the same time, however, he knew he could not be comfortable with the thought of leaving his comrade. He had known him for only a relatively short while, but they had been through a lot together, and he could not in all conscience just leave him to his fate. They had both come into this with no illusions about their survival chances, but this was different. He was still free and still had the opportunity to do something to help his mate. If he left now and made it out, could he live with the regret of not having even tried? That was a burden he didn't want to carry to his grave. He had to do something.

On top of which, he still could not believe that the mission was truly over. The goal was in touching distance. It was approaching midnight: in eight or nine hours' time, they could be back in position waiting for Hitler to take his morning walk. Waiting to fix the sights of his rifle on the man's chest. Waiting to take the shot that would blow the most hated man in the world away for good. So simple and so close, and yet they had been told to walk away. Madness!

Peter snapped out of his reverie. The longer he left it, the worse it could be for Jan. The only plan he had was to get inside the hut and to take it from there. Getting through the door and having time to assess the situation was critical. How the hell was he going to manage that? As he pondered that problem, he put his hand down without thinking and touched the dead man's shoulder.

"Bingo!" Peter exclaimed. "About time you switched your brain on, Peter."

He rolled the body over, stripping off the man's greatcoat as he did so. He used ferns and clumps of grass from around him to brush off as much of the blood as he could, so it didn't look too bad, enough to get him through the door anyway. He then removed his own mountain trooper's jacket and put on the greatcoat. Next, he replaced his cap with the soldier's steel helmet. Finally he noticed that the solder had a pistol in a holster on his hip. A pistol would be far easier to use and far more effective in the confines of the hut. He should be able to get a couple of shots off in the same time as it took to fire the rifle once.

Peter stood up, buckled the greatcoat around his waist. Next, he adjusted the helmet to ensure it was on straight, fixing it in place with the chinstrap. He pushed it down as low as he could to conceal his features as much as possible. He then shouldered the rifle and placed the pistol in the right-hand pocket of the coat. He practised pulling it out a couple of times to make sure it would come out without getting snagged on the flap of the pocket. He had no mirror in which to check, but he felt he looked good enough to buy himself a few crucial seconds before they realised he was not their man.

He walked back up to the door of the hut, steeling himself for what lay ahead. As he stood there, he remembered something his father had told him when he was a young teenager back in the Netherlands. "Everything you do, do it with confidence like you belong." He wasn't sure the words had been meant for exactly this scenario, but they seemed to apply all the same. He needed to stride into the room as if he owned it. That would support his disguise yet further by distracting the Germans from his real intent. He took one last deep breath and grabbed the door handle.

The next few moments passed in a blur. Peter pushed the door open and stepped boldly into the room. The officer, who had been talking to Jan, looked up at the sound of the door opening before looking back at Jan when he saw the coat and helmet. Too late he realised his mistake. To add to his luck, the other soldier had his back to the door, covering Jan with his rifle. In the first couple of seconds, Peter decided that the guard was the immediate threat, as the officer was not actually holding a weapon. He therefore pulled the pistol from the pocket and, in one continuous motion, brought it up to point at the target. Not waiting to aim, he pulled the trigger, at the same time as shouting, "Jan! Duck!"

The bullet took the German in the small of the back. He collapsed in a heap immediately but was still clinging on to his rifle. He was not dead but was in no fit state to take any further part in proceedings. Seeing this, Peter turned his attention to the officer and saw, to his alarm, that he had moved more quickly than he expected. He clearly was not a desk jockey and more than likely had recent combat experience. He already had his pistol out of its holster and was preparing to fire. There was little Peter could do. The officer would get his shot off before he could even aim at him. Instead, he desperately flung himself to the right, at the same time bracing himself for the impact that was sure to come. The sound of the explosion of the officer's Luger was deafening; Peter felt an intense pain in the side of his head before darkness consumed him. The last thing he heard was what sounded like Jan shouting his name.

———

The sight of the officer pointing his pistol at Peter had galvanised Jan into action from the trance he had been in since his friend burst in. As the officer pulled the trigger, he had shouted Peter's name, it becoming a roar of anger as the gun went off. He charged wildly into the officer, his right shoulder connecting with the German's midriff. The impact, combined with Jan's momentum, drove the pair of them onto the floor, with Jan on top. He wasted no time; he could not afford to lose the momentum, as he knew his strength would not last long after the beating he had endured. He grabbed the dazed officer's right wrist and proceeded to smash it repeatedly against the floor, until the grip on the pistol loosened, and it bounced away across the room, coming to rest by the wall under the window. He then dragged the German up towards a sitting position before driving his forehead down into his face. He connected with the bridge of the nose and felt the bone crunch as he did so. The force of the blow knocked the officer out cold, blood flowing freely from his ruined face.

Jan staggered to his feet and launched a powerful kick at the side of the German's head for good measure. The other soldier was still alive but was fading fast; the bullet must have punctured something critical and he was haemorrhaging internally. He was already unconscious from the shock and blood loss and would be dead within minutes. Jan therefore turned his attention to Peter, fearing the worst. In the melee, he had not had time to check on him, but he was pretty sure he had been hit by the officer's bullet, and he certainly hadn't moved or made a sound since.

Peter was lying face down where he had thrown himself to try to avoid the shot. Jan knelt by his side and gently rolled him onto his back, trying to find where he had been hurt. The first thing that hit Jan was that he was still breathing, something about which he had not been convinced at first. Also on the plus side, there was no massive pool of blood to be seen either. In fact, he was struggling to see any sign of impact as he checked his torso and limbs. Turning Peter's chin to one side, however, revealed the truth. An ugly gash had been cut across the right-hand side of his head, just above the ear, thankfully not too deep. The blood was already congealing nicely, but the force of the blow had clearly been sufficient to knock him out cold.

Jan sat back and laughed with relief. "That's gonna be one hell of a headache when you wake up, mate."

TWENTY-NINE

It took a further thirty minutes for Peter to come round. Jan had been getting more and more anxious because the longer they stayed put, the more risk there was of follow-up patrols catching them. And with three dead or injured Germans on their hands, they would have a lot of explaining to do.

Peter groaned and slowly eased himself into a sitting position, holding his forehead as he did so. As he started to recall events, he gingerly touched the wound on the side of his head with his fingertips.

"Jesus." He winced at the pain.

"You are one lucky sod, my friend." Jan smiled. "That bullet had your name on it for sure."

"Well my head doesn't feel lucky right now, but I guess it could have been worse."

"Are you OK to move? Only we really ought not to stay here any longer. On top of which, we need to be making plans to get the hell out of here."

A strange look came over Peter's face, which Jan noted but put down to the fact that he must still be feeling queasy from the blow.

"You're right, Jan. Let's get away from here and find another shelter. I could really do with some rest, though, to help me get my head sorted out. How about we get started first thing in the morning? Sound like a plan?"

Jan nodded warily. He would rather have got under way there and then, under cover of darkness, but he had to accept the fact that Peter needed rest. It wasn't every day that you got shot in the head, and it must hurt like buggery. The most important thing, however, was that they got away from the hut without further delay.

"OK, Peter, sounds good. What do we do with this fellow?" Jan asked, nodding in the direction of the officer, who was still out for the count.

Without saying a word, Peter bent down by the side of the officer as if to check his condition but instead pulled his knife from his boot and plunged it into the man's heart.

"What the hell?" Jan exclaimed, shocked by the sudden and cold-hearted action.

"Better this way," Peter explained. "We can't risk him going for help."

"We already have two dead bodies, Peter. Did we really need a third? Could we not have just tied him up and left him? By the time he was found, we'd be well on our way."

"We can't afford it, Jan. We have been sloppy too many times on this mission. No more chances. From here on we do everything by the book. If that means we have to be ruthless killers in the process, then that doesn't bother me, and, to be honest, it shouldn't bother you either."

The menace in Peter's voice was palpable. Ever since the mission had been cancelled, Jan had sensed a new side to Peter, and this was the clearest indication yet. He seemed to have flipped a switch in his brain; he had become single-minded and cold-blooded. Sure, he had always been focussed and determined—you needed to be to sign up for this sort of caper—but this new manifestation of his personality was disconcerting to say the least. It was all well and good being focussed on your goal, but Jan could not help but wonder what that goal currently was. Whereas he was feeling a sense of relief at the mission being binned and the resulting boost to their life expectancy, he did not get the same feeling from Peter. If anything, Peter seemed more grim than ever before.

Peter broke into his thoughts. "Right, let's not hang about any further then, mate. Let's find ourselves another shelter, catch a few hours' rest, and then go from there." As he spoke, Peter picked up Jan's pack and rifle and threw them both towards him. After heading outside, they walked over to where Peter had dumped the first body and shifted it back into the hut with the other two, keeping them out of sight from the window. Then, recovering Peter's kit and rifle from where he had left them, they began hiking to find a new hut.

Thirty minutes later they had what they were looking for. They watched for a few minutes, but there were no signs of anyone being in residence and no indication of any recent activity as far as they could see. Seeing no further reason to delay, they went inside and quickly settled down to catch a few hours' rest.

Jan could not settle immediately, too many thoughts in his head about what the coming days held in store. "What's the plan then, Peter?" he asked. "For me, our best bet is to head south-west through the mountains until we reach Switzerland. It can't be that far, perhaps just a few days' walking, and I can't imagine it's all that well defended."

"You're forgetting the small matter of the border, Jan." Peter yawned.

"Well, yes, I suppose that will be a more difficult obstacle to cross. I imagine there will be fences and checkpoints and such like. But can it really be guarded heavily all the way along? Surely they can't spare the men to patrol the whole length. We must be able to find a place in the mountains where we can just slip over unnoticed?"

He paused, but there was no reply. Clearly his enthusiasm was not infectious, for Peter was fast asleep.

THIRTY

The early morning sun was streaming through the window of the hut when Jan awoke. He could tell it was quite breezy outside, as the shadows cast by the branches of the surrounding trees were dancing on the opposite wall. He yawned, stretched, and began to think about the day that lay ahead. It was essential that they made good progress today, as, in all likelihood, it would be not be long before it was discovered that the three soldiers were missing. They needed to be well away before the search patrols started to swarm over the area. It was time to get moving for sure.

"Hey, Peter! Time to shift your lazy arse, mate," he called.

There was no answer. Jan shifted to a sitting position and twisted around to look where Peter had been bedded down. He was not there. *He must have gone out to deal with a call of nature,* Jan surmised. He sat up and began to pull on his boots. He stopped halfway through the second boot and looked again. Then he looked more urgently around the rest of the hut as well. There was no sign of Peter's rifle or his pack. What did this mean? Perhaps he was simply outside, waiting for him to be ready. But surely he would have woken him earlier rather than let him sleep on? Jan was now getting anxious. He finished getting his second boot on, grabbed his jacket, and headed for the door, pulling it on as he went.

Outside there was no sign of Peter. Jan walked round the whole hut to make sure, but he was nowhere to be seen. Jan returned to the front of the hut and sat with his back to the wall to gather his thoughts and to try to work out what had happened.

Clearly Peter was no longer anywhere near the hut; that much was certain. But where had he gone, and why had he left without telling him? He couldn't believe that Peter would have set off without him. He must have had something else in mind other than escape. The more he considered the alternatives, the more he came to realise that there was really only one possible solution. Ever since they had been given the order to stand down, Peter had completely withdrawn into himself. Jan had noted it but had put it down to an exaggerated sense of frustration at the futility of their position and the time and energy they had wasted getting to this point. Now, however, it seemed clear that it went deeper than that. It was clear to him exactly what Peter had in mind. In hindsight it was obvious, Jan chastised himself. How could he have been so stupid so as not to anticipate this? He was so wrapped up in the fact that they might be able to get away alive that he had failed to realise that Peter's mind was elsewhere. He checked his watch; it was seven thirty. He was going to have to move quickly if he was to have any chance of catching him in time.

———

Peter had stayed awake all night, listening to the sound of Jan's rhythmic breathing as he slept. He was tired, for sure, but had to force himself to remain alert. He couldn't risk falling asleep, as that could blow his plans wide open. To occupy his mind, he went over it again and again. It would be that much harder on his own, but it should not be in any way impossible if he stayed focussed. He had considered confiding in Jan to secure his help, but when he weighed up the pros and cons, he felt he could not take the risk, and nor was it fair on his partner. Yes, they had been through a lot together, and he would trust Jan with his life, but this was too much to expect, and he could not put that sort of pressure on him. Nor could he risk Jan trying to stop him. Ever since the abort order came through, it was pretty clear to him that Jan was relieved and was looking forward to getting the hell out. Peter did not think any worse of Jan for that; it was not cowardice: God knows they had been brave enough getting this far, living not just behind enemy lines but in the heart of Nazi Germany for several weeks. No, it was a sense of relief that they no longer had to go through with a job that would more than likely get them killed. But that right there was the difference between them. To Jan, this was just a job. It could be blowing up a bridge, training a local resistance movement, or anything. He would do it professionally, to the best of his ability, but it went no further than that. He had no personal stake in it, no skin in the game, as it were.

For Peter however, this was way more than a job. This was perhaps the most significant action of the whole damned war. This was a massive opportunity to make a life-changing mark on the world. On top of which, he would be killing one of the most evil tyrants the world had ever seen. Who could ever be able to say such a thing? Such moments were few and far between, and when they came along, you couldn't just let them go. If Peter was honest with himself, he felt that his whole life had been building up to this moment. He was still young, in relative terms, but this would complete his sense of purpose; it would be the pinnacle of his life, and for that reason, he was reconciled with the risk, reconciled with the realisation that it would not only be the pinnacle, it would also be the end. But that didn't matter. He had nothing to go home to, after all: no family to mourn him, no girlfriend or wife waiting for him. There was no one else in his life that he cared about or who cared about him, and the main reason for that would be in his sights in a few short hours.

He checked his watch for something like the fifteenth time: five thirty. Whilst he had plenty of time, he was keen to be on his way well before Jan woke up. The longer he left it, the greater the chance that he would be disturbed by the sound of him moving around the hut. He got to his feet, moving catlike to keep the noise to a minimum. He picked up his boots and placed them gently outside the door, followed by his pack and his rifle. Once outside, he pulled the door closed very slowly and softly, keen to ensure that the sound of the door clicking shut was muffled as much as possible. Next he sat down by the door and pulled his boots on. Standing up again, he hoisted his pack onto his back, taking care not to bang it against the wall of the hut. Picking up his rifle, he struck off at a steady pace in the direction of the river Larosbach. He planned to follow the same route that they had mapped out a few days back: find the river and then turn south-east to follow its course until it was time to turn south and start climbing up to the vantage point they had located. Timing was everything; Hitler would be on his walk sometime after ten, and the dog patrol went by somewhere between eight-thirty and nine-thirty. He had set off really early to avoid waking Jan, so he would need to hole up somewhere along the way to ensure that he did not arrive too soon.

———

The nature of the terrain, with its myriad trees, boulders strewn haphazardly, and overall gradient meant that Jan could not run. In retrospect, that was probably a good thing, as he needed to be alert for enemy patrols, just in case. Nonetheless, he needed to move as quickly as he could in spite of the constraints. Within a few minutes, he was blowing with the exertion. The sweat was starting to drip down his forehead. Several times each minute, he had to wipe his head with his sleeve to avoid the sweat dripping into his eyes. He was also distinctly aware that the back of his shirt was drenched with sweat and was sticking to him uncomfortably with the weight of his backpack. He could not afford to slow down, though. He didn't know how far behind Peter he was, but he knew he didn't have very long to find him before it would be too late. Ideally, he would catch up with Peter long before that, but he could not be sure of it. He had to keep the pace up, come what may; he dug in, and shut his mind to the pain in his legs and lungs.

All the way his mind was racing. What if he were too late? What if he couldn't find Peter at all? What on earth would be the ramifications if Peter managed to pull it off? He had never been one to worry about the big picture or strategies or anything of that ilk; he was much more a point-and-shoot kind of guy. Give him an order, and he'll see it through to completion. Even he, though, could see that greater minds than his had decreed that carrying out the mission was no longer the right thing to do in the current circumstances. There had to be good reasons for that decision, and while he did not profess to understand entirely what they were, he just knew that he had to stop Peter to prevent what could turn out to be a disaster.

———

Peter, meanwhile, had now finally arrived at the point in the forest that was not far from the shooting point they had previously selected. He looked at his watch and saw he was early. The dog patrol would not go through for another half an hour. Thinking on, he realised that using the exact same position might not be the most sensible option. If Jan did come looking for him, that was sure to be the first place he would check. That said, he couldn't stray too far, as the field of fire was fairly narrow; plus the cover afforded by the trees and undergrowth did not extend this close to the fence around the estate for very far on either side of this point. He had about fifty yards to play with in either direction before the range, the angle, and the level of cover became too risky or too difficult. It would have to do.

As he had enough time, he tracked both left and right, crouching all the time to avoid detection, in order to locate the optimum point. He found it about forty yards to the left, plenty of ferns to keep him concealed and a lush, mossy carpet to lie on, which was a nice bonus if he was going to be there for some time. All in all, he considered it was probably even better than the previous spot, certainly more comfortable.

He knew that the dog patrol would not be far off now, so he retreated twenty or so yards back from the edge and hunkered down behind a slight ridge to wait for them to pass. He would have to brave it out, as he had no visibility from this location, and nor did he want any. He couldn't risk spooking the dog again; this time he might not be saved by a passing rabbit. He had to stay silent and out of sight. The wind direction was, at least, in his favour; plus he reckoned he must smell pretty rustic by now, as personal hygiene had not been high on their list of priorities in recent days. His last wash was a quick dip in the freezing cold river, which must have been the best part of a week ago now.

He resolved to give it until nine-thirty before moving up into position. That was a good seventy minutes away, so he settled down on the bed of moss and ferns up against the back of the ridge to wait it out. Staying alert was going to be the big problem. He already could feel the tiredness creeping over him as the lack of sleep tried to edge out the adrenaline that was coursing through his system. Lying down on the soft earth was making it worse, as his body was crying out for him to close his eyes even if for just ten minutes. He couldn't risk it; he was so tired that if he did allow himself to drift off, he could be out for hours and miss the opportunity altogether. He forced himself to focus on what he was there to do, visualising the whole thing step by step, over and over again, to keep his mind active.

While he lay there, his mind also strayed to what might happen after. He had purposefully avoided this up to now, as he had no expectation of survival, but he realised he had to do something. He couldn't just simply lie there and wait to be caught. He knew that whatever happened, he would have to try to take a few more with him. He had his rifle and a pistol and was a pretty good shot with both. It occurred to him too that he might be able to help Jan in some small way. If Jan was heading to Switzerland, he could head in the opposite direction to draw the focus away from his partner. That last fact decided it in his mind; he would head down to the river and then strike north. He would then keep going as long as he could to give Jan the best chance of escape.

———

Jan had reached the river in good time, but he knew it was still going to be tight. He stopped long enough to glug down the contents of his canteen before refilling it from the cool waters of the river. He poured half of it over his head to try to cool down a bit and then filled it for a second time. His breathing was slowly returning to normal, but he knew he had to get going again. He still had a good ninety minutes to go to reach the destination, and it was already gone half past eight. At this rate, he would be arriving just as Hitler set off on his walk.

———

Shortly after half past nine, Peter edged forward over the ridge, propelling himself forward slowly and carefully with his elbows, feet, and knees so he could stay as flat to the ground as possible. Every couple of yards, he stopped to listen for any sounds of alarm, or any activity at all for that matter. He kept going until he reached his desired position at the edge of the treeline, in amongst all the ferns. He lay still for a full five minutes to make sure he had not been observed. All was quiet. To his right he could see the dog patrol about half a mile away and moving further round the perimeter fence away from him. That was the first hurdle overcome at least. To his front he could see the sentry walking slowly back towards the Berghof. With luck he would be well onto the outward route towards the teahouse by the time Hitler showed up, though he had no doubt he would be back soon enough after he took the shot. The chances were that he would be the first man on the scene, shortly to be followed by any number of troops streaming out from the Berghof estate itself. That first couple of minutes after the shot would be crucial. Peter had to be up and away immediately, and out of sight, before anyone arrived. He hoped that the confusion arising would cause temporary paralysis amongst the soldiers, at least until someone with suitable authority arrived to take control. With luck, that confusion would also help to ensure that there was no clear understanding of where the shot might have come from. All of which should give him valuable time to get a head start from his pursuers and lead them a merry dance far away from Jan's escape route.

For now, though, everything was going according to plan. Peter wriggled out of his backpack and then pushed it in front of him. It was just the right height on which to rest the barrel of his rifle for that extra little bit of stability. He pulled up a handful of ferns from behind him and draped them over the edge of the pack to ensure that its harsh, unnatural edges did not stand out against the undergrowth. Satisfied that the pack could not be detected, he began to assemble his rifle, retrieving the telescopic sight from its home in the secret compartment in his trousers and clicking it into place. Squinting down the sight, he began to adjust the rangefinder to match the estimated distance. Looking up from the rifle, Peter scanned the treeline, trying to gauge the strength of the wind. It had eased noticeably since he had woken up, for which he was hugely grateful. As far as he could tell, it was minimal; the tops of the trees were barely moving. It looked like it was going to be one less thing to worry about. The wind speed, such as it was, should have no material impact on the trajectory of the bullet; as far as he could tell, therefore, he would not need to make any adjustment to his aim over that short a distance.

Squinting down the sight again, Peter began scoping out the route that the path took, as he had done a few days ago. He was both familiarising himself with the direction Hitler would be walking, and trying to select the optimum point at which to take the shot. There were a few places where the undulation of the ground on this side of the fence obscured the path to a degree. Not completely, admittedly, but it looked like the bottom couple of feet would not be visible. Peter saw no sense in making things any harder than they needed to be, so he mentally discounted these sections from the selection process. Instead he found an area, just to the left of where his position faced, where there was a good thirty to forty yards in which the path was wholly visible to his line of sight. This looked to be the best target area for sure. He resolved to take the shot about half to three-quarters of the way along; that gave him a few seconds to zero in and adjust to the pace of the walk before pulling the trigger.

Peter glanced at his watch again, 09.50, only a few more minutes to wait. He wondered what other variables might occur that he would need to take into account. The biggest risk was that Hitler might not show at all, like the previous day. He was still in residence, as the flag was clearly visible at the front of the Berghof, but there was no guarantee that he would appear. If that was the case, Peter doubted whether he could continue the mission. It was only a matter of time until the bodies were found in the hut, and then all hell would break loose. He might be lucky and evade capture for another day, maybe even two, but it wasn't likely. If he didn't show today, it was, realistically speaking, over and done with.

What if he was not alone? He remembered from the briefings that Hitler liked to take his walks alone, but it was not always the case. The more people that were with him, the greater the risk that his shot would be obscured. That could drastically reduce the time and space in which he could get a shot off. He might have to take the shot whenever the opportunity presented rather than wait for his carefully selected spot.

He couldn't think of any other significant permutations beyond that, and, to be honest, there was little point worrying about them anyway. These things were beyond his control, and stressing about them was a waste of time, especially when he needed stay calm in order to slow his heart rate to help focus on making the shot.

———

Jan was approaching the edge of the treeline at pace. It was almost ten. He prayed he was not too late. Nonetheless, he had to force himself to slow down. Charging forward like a bull in a china shop would only risk giving away their position to the sentries or patrols. He dropped to all fours about twenty yards back from the edge and crawled slowly. He also wanted to keep the noise down so that he gave as little warning as possible of his arrival to Peter. The state of mind he was in, he could not be sure how he would react.

Soon he was just a few paces behind the firing point that they had selected a few days previously. He had not spotted Peter so far, but he hadn't expected it to be easy, as there was a lot of undergrowth, and Peter was bound to be well covered and completely still as he waited for his shot. He crept forward silently, taking care to avoid snapping any twigs.

"Shit," Jan hissed under his breath as he reached the edge of the trees. No sign of him. He slumped down onto his belly to relieve the strain in his arms and legs. Had he misjudged the situation? Had Peter not decided to go ahead with the mission after all? But that made no sense. There was no other logical explanation for the fact that Peter had disappeared that morning. Where else could he have gone? *Think, Jan, think! There's very little time left: Hitler could be coming into range at any moment.*

Suddenly it hit him. What if Peter had found another place to take the shot? Perhaps he had guessed that Jan might come after him and had taken steps to avoid detection by moving elsewhere. That made sense, for sure, but where? Surely he could not be too far from their original spot? That said, it could be left or right from here, and then there was no way of knowing how far. He did not have the time to get it wrong, though; he had to guess right first time.

Jan took a moment to scan the undergrowth in both directions. There was nothing that gave him any clue as to where Peter might be. If he was anywhere nearby, then he was clearly well hidden. He looked once again, to the right and left, a feeling of anxiety growing ever stronger in his chest as time ticked inexorably forward. He didn't bother looking at his watch anymore. He knew he was out of time. As if to confirm the awful truth of this fact, as he looked left, he could see movement around the Berghof, about half a mile away. It was too far away to be clearly discernible, but there were definitely three men coming out of the front of the building. Two of them appeared to be wearing the standard field-grey uniforms and peaked caps favoured by the Nazi generals. The third was wearing dark, probably black, trousers with a lighter brown jacket and no headgear. As they began to walk, a large dog came bounding out from the building and ran up to the man in the brown jacket, who stopped and bent down to tickle the dog behind the ear.

That seals it, thought Jan. *That's the man himself. Ten to fifteen minutes from now, he will be level with me. Last chance time, Jan. Either find Peter now or it's all over.*

Without further delay, he turned and started crawling as fast as he could without risking detection. He prayed to whatever gods might be listening that he had made the right choice.

THIRTY-ONE

Peter had been lying in wait for ten minutes now. His heart rate had slowed, and his breathing was shallow. The butt of his rifle was pulled tight into his shoulder, and he was staring down the sight with his left eye firmly closed. He was in the zone now and oblivious to his surroundings. There was nothing more he could do; he just had to sit tight and pray that Hitler made an appearance this morning. There was no guarantee, after all.

Moments later Peter's attention was caught by the appearance of three figures and a dog outside the front of the Berghof. He slowly moved the barrel of his rifle to the left, careful not to dislodge any of the foliage he had used to mask any light glinting off the lens. The figures soon came into view in his sight. His attention was immediately drawn to the figure in the brown jacket who had stopped to fuss the dog. Not only were the other two in more conventional army uniforms but they also stood at a respectful distance, clearly deferential to the other man while he enjoyed this intimate moment with a beloved pet. If that was not already proof enough, when he focussed on the man with the dog, the appearance was a giveaway. The black hair which he swept back every time it fell forward into his eyes as he was bent down stood out a mile. It was a mannerism he had seen several times on newsreel footage from pre-war rallies. He could also discern the small black postage-stamp moustache above his top lip, if he needed any more confirmation.

This is it, Peter thought to himself with a surge of adrenalin that he had to fight back down. This was the moment. Everything he had been training for, everything he had been risking his life for, everything he had wanted as recompense for the loss of his family was about to culminate in this one moment. He could feel his pulse starting to rise. Damn! He needed to calm the hell down; he needed once more to get his heart rate under control. He calculated he had about ten minutes, at the pace they were moving, until the party reached the section of path that he had designated earlier as the target zone. That should be plenty of time to get himself back under control.

From what he could see so far, he should have a clear shot despite there being three of them walking together. The two soldiers, generals of some kind, Peter surmised, were maintaining their station a couple of paces behind Hitler. Every now and then, Hitler would stop to speak with them before continuing. Hitler was actually paying more attention to the dog than he was to them. Peter supposed that perhaps he hadn't seen the dog for a while, especially if he had been in Berlin or one of his military HQs for some time, and they were becoming reacquainted. Watching him, it was almost strange to consider that this paragon of evil had anything approaching a human side. At one point he even bent down to pick up a stick, which he then threw for the dog to retrieve, its tail wagging frantically as it did so. For a split second, Peter felt a twinge of remorse, as he had a sense of the man behind the monster, but he quickly expelled the thought. He deserved to die for the suffering he had caused across Europe and the world. No amount of him petting his dog would save him from his fate.

He zoned in once more on the target area, ready for the moment when the party came into view. He forced himself to remain calm; he reckoned he had another four of five minutes until they were in his sights. He bent again to squint down the sight. As he did so, however, he felt a hand on his arm, a firm grip but one that felt more reassuring than aggressive. At the same time, a voice spoke, calmly but with authority.

"Peter, don't do this. It's not too late to step away."

Jan had taken him completely by surprise; he had been concentrating so much on the target that he had never even heard him approaching. He jerked his head up from the rifle and turned in the direction of the voice. Jan was lying next to him, smiling calmly as if he were a parent trying to hush a distraught child. It took a moment for Peter to recover his poise.

"You don't understand, Jan. I have to do this."

"We can't, Peter. You heard the top brass on the radio. Things have changed. We need to stand down. We can go home." Jan's voice was calm and reassuring, so much so that Peter almost wavered.

"What the hell do they know? They sit in offices miles away from the real fighting. They don't understand the actual impact on people's lives, what people have had to go through in the last five years as a result of this man's warped sense of reality. They don't see the destruction, the bodies, the desperation."

"I know, Peter, but they do carry the responsibility on their shoulders to make the big decisions that could affect the lives of hundreds of thousands of us all. They have the best information, the best advisers available to them to make those calls; we don't. They have made the decision that it is better overall to leave Hitler alive. I don't pretend to totally understand their thinking, but I am prepared to trust their judgement on this."

"Well I, for one, don't!" Peter was becoming more and more agitated with every moment; he kept glancing back to the front to check where the walkers had got to. "I am here; I have a rifle; I have the opportunity to do what's right. No one would blame me for that."

———

Jan knew they were on a knife edge. Talking him down was going to be no easy matter. "Peter, look at it this way. If you take this shot, you kill one man: a man that absolutely does not deserve to live. That I can't argue with. But what will be the ramifications of that one bullet? What effect will it have on the war?

How can you know whether more or fewer people will die as a direct result of your action? That is what the generals and politicians have analysed, that is what they have debated for many long hours. At the end of the day, they have decided that it is better for everyone to leave him where he is and who are we to disagree with the experts? Think about it: the British and Americans have invaded in France; the Russians are pushing the Germans backwards all the time. There can't be long left until it's all over. You have to see that. You have to respect that. You have to walk away."

"All of that is unknown, Jan. Who can say what will happen in the next few days, let alone weeks or months? The war could go on for years yet. The Germans could well become more resistant and more desperate the closer the enemy gets to their homeland. And what if the rumours of new superweapons are true? Who's to say what destruction could be caused if the Germans start to use them? How many more have to die at the whim of this one man? I have to take him down. There's no other way."

Jan felt like he was losing the argument. He couldn't get through to Peter in this state of mind. It looked clear that he had made his decision, and there was nothing he could do to dissuade him. Nonetheless, he hadn't thrown in the towel just yet. If talking was not going to work, he would have to try more drastic means. He had to be stopped one way or another. Glancing over towards the estate, he could see that Hitler was now about halfway between the house and being level with their position. There was no time to waste. He didn't want to hurt Peter, but he had to stop him taking the shot. There was therefore only one available course of action left open to him.

Avoiding any sudden movement so that he didn't alert Peter to his intentions, Jan edged marginally closer to get into a position where he could grab the rifle. Peter was facing the front again, seemingly intent on the quarry and oblivious again to his colleague. Jan reached slowly forward, all the while watching Peter's head for any signs of movement or awareness. He planned to get as close as he could before making a sudden grab for the barrel and jerking it away, all in one movement. He took a deep breath and lunged.

———

Unfortunately for him, it was exactly the move that Peter had been expecting. As soon as Jan had stopped trying to argue, he knew that his friend would not be able to give up. Peter had therefore mentally prepared himself for the next step whilst staring ahead to lull Jan into a false sense of security. Almost before he even felt the shift as Jan lunged forward, Peter twisted away from him, keeping both hands on the rifle as he did so. As his momentum turned him sideways and away from Jan, he used it to bring his right arm up sharply.

Having dived forward with his right arm to grab the rifle barrel, Jan had left himself dangerously exposed; he therefore had no defence against Peter's counter-attack. He may have seen the move coming towards him, but there was nothing he could do to prevent it or protect himself. As Peter moved his right arm upwards, he brought the stock of the rifle up to connect with the side of Jan's head. The cramped conditions meant that it wasn't the hardest blow he could muster, but it was enough to knock Jan out cold.

"Sorry, my friend," Peter whispered. "You know I couldn't let you stop me. Just let me get the job done, and we'll get out of here. You and me, together."

Peter took one last look at the unconscious form of his friend and turned his mind back to the job. He feverishly scanned the area to his front to locate his prey, praying he had not gone past while he had been distracted. It took a few seconds, during which he became more and more frantic. Finally he found his quarry just to his left, partially hidden behind a slight rise in the ground. Thankfully they had been moving slowly; the presence of the dog had turned out to be a godsend, as there had been frequent stops to fuss the animal and to throw sticks. Without that, he may well have missed his chance completely.

Peter eased himself back into position behind the sight of his rifle. He reckoned he had no more than a minute before his target came into his firing zone—only just enough time to settle, calm his breathing again, and focus on his target. He checked the sight to make sure that it had not been knocked during the melee. Thankfully it proved to be unaffected, one less thing to worry about. With his mind at ease on that score, Peter pulled the stock into his shoulder once more and fixed his right eye to the sight. He eased the rifle to the left, tracking slowly and smoothly until the target came into view. Hitler was still walking in front of the two other men, the dog now trotting dutifully by its master's side. Peter focussed in on Hitler's chest area. He was in two minds where best to place the shot: head would be most likely to be fatal but was a much tougher shot; chest was much easier to hit, but there was a risk that it would not kill. That said, the bullets he was using were designed to cause maximum damage on impact. Either way, he didn't have time to debate any further now, as he was finally entering the kill zone.

Peter trained the sight on the man's face, to get one last look at the man he had come to kill. Age had not been kind to him; his cheeks had turned quite pudgy, and his skin seemed quite pale, with several angry red blotches. Peter found himself wondering if these were the effects of a poor diet mixed with too much stress. No matter, it would all be irrelevant in a few seconds. Peter refocused marginally downwards, fixing the sight on Hitler's chest region, as he had decided this to be the least risky option. He took a moment to adjust for the speed of Hitler's movement, and then he took and held a deep breath. He took a couple more seconds to make sure he was fully focussed and gently squeezed the trigger.

The recoil from the butt of rifle thumped him hard on the shoulder, even though he had been expecting it. As quickly as he could, he redirected the sight back on the target to assess the outcome. To his satisfaction, he could see that Hitler was down on the ground. Unfortunately, it was not possible to tell exactly what sort of condition he was in, as he was only partially visible, and the other two men were already crowded round him, both to check his condition and to shield him from further attack. He could also hear the dog; it was alternating between barking and whining where it lay next to its master. All he could tell from this distance was that the body did not appear to be moving. He was pretty sure that the bullet had caught him slap bang in the chest, right where he had aimed. With luck it would have ripped a hole through his heart, or perhaps the lungs, which would be now filling with blood, enough to drown him in but a few short minutes.

Either way, he couldn't wait around any longer to find out. One of the two men with Hitler was already scanning the treeline to try to identify whence the shot had come. More worrying, though, was that Peter could also see, a couple of hundred yards to his right, the patrolling solder was racing back towards where Hitler lay, gesticulating wildly in his direction as he ran. It seemed pretty clear to Peter that he must have been looking in his general direction as he had taken the shot. He must have seen the muzzle flash or traces of smoke, which, despite the undergrowth, had given away his position.

One of the officers with Hitler had now worked out what the guard was saying and had sprinted off back to the Berghof, where Peter could already see troops coming out of the building. It wouldn't be long before the officer had organised the soldiers and sent them off to begin hunting down the assassins. Peter needed to move, and move fast, but before he could, he had to decide what to do about Jan.

Jan was still out cold. Peter had to assess the options quickly. If he did nothing, Jan would be found. There was no doubt about that. This was clearly a non-starter; he could not allow his friend to be caught without the chance to defend himself. If the end was going to come, Peter wanted Jan to have a say in how he met it. He could attempt to rouse Jan and escape with him. It was a better option, but Peter discounted it swiftly, as he was worried that Jan might be too groggy to move at pace, which would mean that they would soon both be captured. The third and only viable option was to move Jan to a decent hiding place and hope he evaded discovery until he was in a fit state to move.

Resolved to a course of action, Peter wasted no time. He dragged Jan back from the edge of the trees and then lifted him across his shoulder in a fireman's lift. The weight was heavy, but bearable for a short while, hopefully long enough to get Jan to some decent cover. There was no point trying to find a hut or similar; they would be obvious places to search. The best bet was to find an area of thick undergrowth and try to hide Jan within it. After about half a mile, he found what he was looking for, a close-knit group of trees with thick ferns in between. He eased Jan into the middle of the ferns, taking care not to disturb the undergrowth too much. He didn't want to make it too obvious, after all.

Having placed Jan carefully, Peter then tried to arrange the ferns so that he was completely covered. He stepped back to survey the result: excellent, completely invisible. You'd have to literally trip over him to find him. It would have to do, anyway, as he couldn't waste any more time.

The major worry, however, was dogs. If the Germans started patrolling with dogs, and they surely would, then there was a high chance that Jan would be found despite how well hidden he was. This weighed heavily on Peter's mind as he started walking away from Jan's hiding place. He hoped he would come round pretty soon and be able to make his escape. The more he thought about it, though, the more he realised what he had to do. Jan's life was down to him. They could have got out safely, but he had effectively forced Jan to come after him, and now he was deep in the shit. He had to do what he could to give his friend a chance of survival. He didn't care any longer for his own safety, but he might still be able to do something useful to help Jan.

His mind made up, he carried on walking for a short while. Moving as carefully as possible so as not to disturb the undergrowth too much, he carried on moving in what he felt was a roughly northerly direction. He had to try to ensure that he did not signpost a path back to Jan. Once he was about a mile from Jan, he stopped and listened. It was hard to hear much, as the trees prevented the sound travelling too far. Even so, he felt fairly sure he could hear, off to his right, the definite sound of dogs barking. The chase was on. He smiled wryly to himself.

He checked his pistol was fully loaded, readjusted the straps on his pack to prevent it bouncing around too much, and then began to run north, making as much noise and disturbance as possible as he went. He reckoned it wouldn't be long before his pursuers would pick up his tracks, and he could lead them far away from Jan before they caught up with him.

THIRTY-TWO

Three weeks later.

Jan was sitting in a small, square room in the British Embassy in Zurich. The room was below ground, so there was no natural light; the only illumination came from a single light bulb suspended from a wire in the middle of the ceiling. There was no lampshade. The room itself was pretty run down, with paint, or what was left of it, peeling off the otherwise bare walls. In the middle of the room was one dilapidated wooden table flanked by two equally tired-looking wooden chairs, one on either side. On the table was a film projector.

He had been sat here for over thirty minutes since being shown to the room by one of the armed guards. He hadn't bothered trying the door, as he had heard it being locked behind him as he sat down. In all, he had been at the embassy for a week now; he had been treated well enough, but it was clear that he was not free to leave. He was doing his best not to feel like a prisoner, but it was hard not to, in view of his experience over the last few days. No one would talk to him, and the only time he saw anyone was when they brought him his meals. At least, he reflected, he had access to clean clothes and decent washing facilities, which were a godsend after the last few weeks, but that was it. He had no contact with the outside world, nor access to any newspapers, radio, or anything. He was desperate to understand what the hell had happened since Peter had knocked him out, but he could find no one to answer his questions, and neither could he find out for himself.

All he knew was everything had gone pear-shaped and that orders had been disobeyed. God knows he had tried to stop Peter and had been knocked out for his pains. He still had the scar on the side of his head to show for it. There had been nothing more he could do.

He had no idea where Peter was or what had happened to him. He hadn't seen him since their fight. When he had come round, covered in ferns in the middle of a clump of trees, there had been no sign of his friend. He had lain there for a short while waiting for his head to clear whilst considering his options and trying to piece together what had happened. He had to assume that Peter had taken the shot; after all, there was no doubt that it had been his intention ever since the mission had been aborted. The moods, the anger, it all made sense in hindsight. That said, from where he lay, he had no idea if Peter had succeeded. For someone of Peter's skill with a rifle, and at the relatively short distance involved, he must surely have hit the target. Jan rubbed his temples, trying to make sense of everything. The fact that he was some way from the edge of the treeline meant that Peter had found time to drag or carry him to cover, but why was he not there as well? The more Jan thought about it, the more he realised that Peter must have chosen to sacrifice himself to save him. He had chosen to try to lead the Germans away from Jan to give him a better chance of escape. He shook his head in silent contemplation of his friend's courage and selflessness.

Jan knew there was little point trying to find Peter. He had no clue in which direction he had gone, for one thing. He offered up a silent prayer for someone to watch over Peter to help him get away or, as was more likely, at least to give him a quick and painless end.

Jan had known he had to get moving soon; the Germans would surely realise there had been more than one assassin and would be back to scour the area. Nonetheless, the professional in him wouldn't let him leave without trying to verify Hitler's condition. Checking his watch, he could see it was a little after eleven o'clock; he had been out for the best part of an hour. Despite this, he could hear no signs of activity at all from where he lay. Peter's diversion appeared to have worked quite brilliantly. Jan crept forward as slowly and as vigilantly as possible; it took him a few minutes to reach a point where he could see the estate. Immediately he was struck by the fact that it was a hive of activity, like an ants' nest that had been kicked over. There were soldiers everywhere, including a group that were posted in a protective screen around a couple of men who were kneeling around someone lying on the ground. It was too far away to be certain who the someone was and whether he was alive or dead, but from the frantic arm waving and gesticulations, it looked pretty serious.

Jan reckoned he had seen enough; he crawled back from the edge of the trees and had headed south, following their pre-planned escape route through the mountains to the borders of Switzerland. It had taken a few days, but he had thankfully accomplished it without major incident. At the first opportunity, he had stolen some clothes from a washing line and buried his German papers, his rifle, and his uniform, not before removing his forged Czech papers from where they had been sewn into the lining. He had also kept his sidearm for self-defence purposes, keeping it hidden in the inside pocket of the jacket he had acquired. In this way he had been able to travel incognito to the border, where he was able to cross into Switzerland without hindrance. From there it was just a case of finding his way to Zurich, where he made himself known to the British Embassy, who had been warned to look out for the two of them. From that point he had been kept in isolation as per the orders from the Ministry of War. It was clear that they did not want him talking to anyone about the mission and what had happened.

His thoughts were interrupted by the sound of the key being turned in the lock. Looking up, he saw the guard who had brought him to the room holding the door open, through which a familiar face was now walking.

"Colonel Blake!"

"Good morning, Jan. I must say it is good to see you." Blake smiled warmly as he approached the table.

Jan stood to greet him, the feet of his wooden chair protesting loudly as he did so, and found his right hand clasped firmly in both of Blake's and pumped vigorously. He really was pleased to see him, Jan mused.

"I am sorry about all the cloak-and-dagger stuff, Jan, but you understand we could take no chances in the circumstances. We needed to keep you isolated until we could get to see you face to face and start your debriefing."

Jan smiled thinly and mumbled, "No problem, sir."

"Good, good," Blake continued, unperturbed. "Now, I'll come straight to the point if you don't mind. The fact of the matter is that we urgently need to piece together what happened after our last radio contact with you. If I recall correctly"—Blake made a show of consulting his notebook, as if looking for the transcript of the conversation—"you were given a clear order to abort the mission, yes?"

"Yes, sir," Jan replied. He had decided already to keep his responses short and to the point until such time as he had a better idea of where this was heading.

"From that moment, we had no further contact with either you or Lieutenant Bogarde until you turn up at our embassy in Zurich, alone and in a rather dishevelled state. Perhaps you can help us fill in the gaps between then and now, including what the hell has happened to Peter?"

Jan covered his surprise as best he could. He had not expected that question at all. He was completely confused and at a loss as to how best to answer.

Blake seemed to interpret his hesitation as some form of stress or exhaustion. "Don't worry, lad, take your time. I know it's been a rough few weeks for you, but we do need to work out how the two of you became separated and only one came back. Is Peter alive? Do you have any idea where he is?"

An image came to Jan of Peter racing through the woods, soldiers with dogs hot on his heels and straining to be let off the lead. He truly hoped the end had not been too bad. "I honestly don't know, sir, but I must assume that he is dead."

Blake's brow furrowed. "I think you need to explain in full, Jan. We do not like to lose an agent at any time, especially when the mission gets aborted and everyone is expecting a successful exfiltration. Don't get me wrong, I know it happens; casualty rates are higher than we would like, of course. But we must take steps to learn the lessons and try to protect future agents from the same mistakes."

Jan was totally nonplussed. Blake was talking as if nothing more had happened than the loss of an agent. What the hell was going on? Jan wanted to grab him and shake him by the shoulders, shouting, "What is wrong with you? Hitler is dead! The war should be over!"

Instead, he fought to remain calm and professional. "Well, sir, the fact is I don't know what happened entirely, as I was unconscious at the time, and when I came around, Peter had gone."

"What do you mean, unconscious? How on earth did that happen?" Blake was busy scribbling in his little notebook and was not looking at Jan as he spoke.

"Well, the fact is, sir, that Peter knocked me out. It seemed that, despite the order to stand down, he was still intent on fulfilling the mission. He did not take kindly to my trying to stop him."

He had Blake's full attention now. He had put the pen down and was looking directly at Jan, his eyes staring intently as if trying to pierce Jan's mind. "Please elaborate, Lieutenant. Bogarde refused to abort and knocked you out when you tried to intervene. Is that what you are saying?"

"In a nutshell, sir, yes."

"Go on."

"Well, sir," Jan continued, "he had been withdrawn ever since we got the order to stand down, but I had put it down to frustration and no more. But the morning we were due to leave, Peter left the hut while I was still asleep and went back up to the estate, to a position where he could take the shot. I went after him once I realised where he must have gone and managed to find him just as Hitler started his walk. I tried to talk him down, but he was not interested. It was like a personal vendetta that nothing and no one could stop. Time was short, though, so I decided to make a grab for the rifle. In hindsight, perhaps I should have been more aggressive, but I didn't want to hurt him. Either way, I underestimated the strength of his emotions. Peter had guessed I would try something and was waiting for me. That's the last thing I remember until I woke up an hour or so later with a massive bruise and a huge headache."

"Are you sure, though, that Bogarde took the shot? How would you know if you were unconscious?" Blake asked.

"I'm not one hundred per cent sure, sir, no. I mean, I didn't actually see him do it."

"So what makes you think he did?"

"I came a few hundred yards away from where Peter had been lying. He must have dragged me there to try and conceal me from any pursuers that would come after us. That alone suggested to me that he had gone through with it, but to be sure, I crawled back to where he had been. There were soldiers running everywhere. I could also see that someone was on the ground, but it was hard to see detail, as there were soldiers forming a protective cordon around them. From the obvious panic, though, it seemed pretty clear to me that there had been a major disturbance."

"Christ Almighty." Blake ran his hand through his thinning hair. "This makes no sense at all." He was looking down at his pad, shaking his head, almost oblivious to Jan's presence.

Jan decided that silence was his best option for the time being. He was still uncertain as to what was happening; something clearly didn't feel right, but he was not about to force the subject just yet.

After a moment or two, Blake seemed to gather his thoughts. He looked back up at Jan. "Lieutenant Kubcek, this is important. Did you actually see Hitler's body? What degree of certainty do you have that he was actually killed?"

Jan thought for a moment or two before answering, "Well, if I am honest, no, I did not. Someone was on the ground, but I could not tell who it was, but my belief is that it was Hitler."

"Let's be absolutely clear on this point. When you were struck by Bogarde, Hitler was alive, correct?"

Jan nodded to confirm.

"And when, after you recovered consciousness, you went back to the same spot as before, there was a body on the ground?"

Jan nodded again.

"But you cannot be certain who that body belonged to?"

"No, sir. Not one hundred per cent certain."

"And was that body, whomever it belonged to, alive or dead?"

Jan racked his brains to bring up as sharp an image of the memory as he could. "I honestly can't say, sir. There was no movement as far as I can recall, but that does not mean he was dead, I suppose. It is just my feeling that a man with Peter's ability as a marksman, at that short range, would nine times out of ten make the kill. I would therefore assume he is dead, sir."

"Yes, but you cannot say with one hundred per cent certainty that Peter succeeded in killing him. Correct?"

"Well, I suppose not, sir. I couldn't get close enough to see clearly, and I didn't want to hang around long enough to wait for a coffin to arrive."

"Quite," Blake returned, ignoring the sarcasm. "Could it not be the case that all that frenzied activity you saw was simply the reaction to Peter having taken a shot and *missing*? Could they not have been simply surrounding him to protect him against any further shots? Or perhaps, if he didn't miss, maybe he simply grazed him without doing any serious damage?"

"Both are possible, I guess, but I keep coming back to the facts: the distance was relatively short for a sniper, there was no wind, and Peter is an expert marksman. If I were a betting man, I would say that Peter hits the target every time in those conditions."

"True, but he could conceivably have missed, yes? That one-in-a-hundred chance may have happened? He may have been distracted due to the altercation which had just taken place with you? Thrown out of his stride, as it were?"

Jan was completely perplexed now. "Well, it's always possible, sir, but, like I say, I would consider it highly unlikely with someone of his ability."

Jan decided enough was enough. It was time to bring matters to a head. "Look, with all due respect, sir, there is something here that I am just not getting. As far as I am concerned, Peter took the shot. Hitler is, in all likelihood, dead, or seriously injured at the very least. Yet you seem to be avoiding the possibility of that outcome. I have been in here a week, and I have heard not a sniff of what's going on. I expected there to be streamers, parties, everything. Hitler's dead! The war is over! Or at least it should be.

"Yet, when we started this conversation, your main concern seemed to be what had happened to Peter, rather than the death of the most evil and dangerous man alive. What the hell is going on…sir?" The last word was added after a pause and accentuated for effect.

Blake pushed back his chair and got to his feet. "Wait here, Lieutenant," he barked.

Five minutes later, Blake was back in the room, accompanied by an orderly carrying a film canister. The orderly proceeded to load the film onto the projector, while Blake shifted his chair to face the wall where the image would be projected. Before the orderly could flick the switch to turn on the machine, Blake introduced what he was about to see.

"We received this film yesterday from one of our agents in Germany. We know it was filmed three days ago, as it is backed up by newspaper reports from the same day." With that, he signalled to the orderly to begin.

The projector whirred noisily into life, and the reel started to turn. After a few seconds, a grainy image appeared on the screen. It was newsreel footage of some kind of event in Berlin. Flag-waving crowds were gathered on either side of the road, held back behind barriers manned by uniformed guards. Approaching along the road was a motorcade comprising half a dozen or so of the big six-wheeled Mercedes touring cars that Hitler favoured. As the cars came closer, the commentary began.

"Crowds gathered in Berlin today to welcome our glorious Führer back to the capital for the first time since the cowardly bomb plot last month."

And there he was, in the lead car, standing up and raising his right arm in his own inimitable Nazi salute to all sides. The rest of the reel passed in a blur for Jan. He was staring open-mouthed at the screen, unable to grasp or believe what he was seeing. The reel ended with footage of Hitler inspecting a line of troops, to whom he then proceeded to hand out medals, shaking each man's hand as he did so. Sure, he looked old and jowly and was walking with a definite stoop, but it was, without doubt, the man himself.

As the reel ended, Blake cut into his shocked state. "So, given what you have just seen, I think you can see why there's no victory parade, no bunting hanging from every building, no dancing in the streets. The war continues as it has done these past five years."

Jan shook his head, dumbfounded "I don't understand. I know what I saw, sir. I am certain Peter shot him".

"That's as may be, but what you can't deny is the evidence of our own eyes and ears, man."

"I know, sir, but it just does not make any sense at all."

Blake smiled. "That much we are agreed on, for sure. What does seem apparent, however, is that Bogarde threw his life away for nothing."

Jan stopped to consider this, a thought forming in his head. "That may indeed be so, Colonel. But there is a bittersweet irony to the whole thing too."

"How so?"

"One thing I recall from our briefing some weeks ago now, was the possibility that Hitler had a number of doubles."

"Never proven, mind," Blake interjected.

"True, sir, but it is the only logical explanation. Think about it: Peter and I saw a man matching Hitler's appearance. Peter then succeeded in shooting this man dead. A few days later the same man appears in Berlin, waving to the crowds as if nothing had happened. How can that be, unless there were two of them?"

Blake's brow furrowed. "I grant you it's a possibility, but even if that is the case, what on earth is ironic about this whole god-awful mess?"

Jan smiled. "Well, sir, in some ways it could be said to have worked out for the best for all concerned. Peter goes to his death believing he has killed his nemesis, thereby successfully avenging his family. The top brass, meanwhile, get what they wanted; a living, breathing Hitler who can continue to lead his country to defeat."

Blake nodded his head, thoughtfully. "I see your point, Jan. There's only one problem as far as I can see."

"What's that, sir?"

"Which one did he kill, Jan? Which one did he kill?"

Printed in Great Britain
by Amazon.co.uk, Ltd.,
Marston Gate.